JOHN MORTIMER

DUNSTER

VIKING

VIKING

Published by the Penguin Group
Penguin Books Ltd, 27 Wrights Lane, London W8 5TZ, England
Penguin Books USA Inc., 375 Hudson Street, New York, New York 10014, USA
Penguin Books Australia Ltd, Ringwood, Victoria, Australia
Penguin Books Canada Ltd, 10 Alcorn Avenue, Toronto, Canada MV4 3B2
Penguin Books (NZ) Ltd, 182–190 Wairau Road, Auckland 10, New Zealand

Penguin Books Ltd, Registered Offices: Harmondsworth, Middlesex, England

First published by Viking 1992
This edition published 1992
1 3 5 7 9 10 8 6 4 2

Copyright © Advanpress Ltd, 1992

The moral right of the author has been asserted

Set in 12/14 pt Sabon
Printed in England by Clays Ltd, St Ives plc

A CIP catalogue record for this book is available from the British Library

ISBN 0–670–84060–2

I am greatly indebted to Eric Morris, who told me about the SAS activities in the Italian mountains during the last war. He also traced the probable wartime histories of two old soldiers. These characters are, however, entirely fictional, as is the small town of Pomeriggio and the events that are described as having occurred there.

WHO IS THIS FELLOW DUNSTER?

So oft it chances in particular men
That – for some vicious mole of nature in them,
As in their birth, wherein they are not guilty,
Since nature cannot choose his origin –
Carrying, I say, the stamp of one defect,
Being nature's livery, or fortune's star,
His virtues else, be they as pure as grace,
As infinite as man may undergo,
Shall in the general censure take corruption
From that particular fault. The dram of evil
Doth all the noble substance of a doubt,
To his own scandal –

Hamlet
Shakespeare

Chapter One

I worry a good deal. That's my nature. Sometimes I tell myself that I have nothing to worry about, and then I worry about that too. At very rare moments, when I'm not actively worrying about Natasha, my daughter, or the overdraft, or the VAT man, or the next board meeting, or whether I'll get the part of Trigorin in the Mummers' production of *The Seagull*, or whether, if I did get it, I'd make a proper cock-up of it and get a filthy notice in the Muswell Hill *Advertiser*, or the strange, hysterical whining noise, much like an elderly person in pain, that the Volvo is making when I decelerate – on the rare occasions when I'm worrying about none of these things I start to worry about global warming or the future of the Russian economy. Then I take a poor view of myself because global warming and Russia are things I can do absolutely nothing about, so I lose patience with myself for wasting time worrying about them, and that makes me extremely worried.

I started early that morning because I was going to drop Natasha at her tutorial college in Highgate on my way to the Isle of Dogs. I always feel at my best first thing, as though the day is going to pass by without any real cause for alarm. The first cup of tea is drunk in almost complete calm, but by the time I get out to the car I usually manage to think of something more or less appalling with which to become obsessed.

'Put your foot down, Dad,' Tash said. 'I told you. I wanted to be at the Tute really early.'

I didn't tell her I'd been waiting for her for a quarter of an hour, from a now distant moment when the world seemed comparatively untroubled. Instead I turned out, as unobtrusively as possible, into the traffic of Muswell Hill. My daughter has two expressions, a rare smile and the more frequent scowl of a particularly stroppy and put-upon villein about to start the Peasants' Revolt. At that time of the day she wasn't smiling.

'How's college?' I tried asking her brightly.

'All right, I suppose.'

'And how's George?'

'Pretty ghastly.'

'I thought he was meant to be your boyfriend?'

'So he is. But honestly, Dad, he's so servile! He keeps asking what I'd like or what he can do for me. I told him he sounds like an airline hostess. I do really need someone who's going to represent a bit of a challenge.'

I slowed down in Muswell Road to avoid a swarm of killer cyclists, wearing dark glasses and those sort of gas masks which make you think that chemical warfare has broken out. Their bright yellow, walnut-shaped crash helmets were pulled down over their foreheads and, as they crouched low over the handlebars, their bottoms, in black Lycra shorts, rose into the air like gigantic squash balls.

'I really feel I can do without people who represent a challenge,' I told Tash. 'I've had enough challenges to last a lifetime.'

'I know, Dad. You would say that.'

'Why would I?'

'Well, let's face it. You are a bit of a moral coward, aren't you?'

I looked at her sideways. She had the strawberry hair, wide eyes and pale beauty of her mother. I had changed her nappies and fed her with tins of spinach which she blew back at me in a soggy, green cloud from her high chair. I had been the first to tell her about cavemen and Queen Elizabeth and Vikings and Malvolio and *The Merchant of Venice*, and here she was, at the age of seventeen, passing judgement on me. Without mercy.

'That's a little bit unfair.' A kamikaze cyclist, a girl in a chintz blouse and knee-length, green phosphorescent socks to go with her shorts, was bearing down on me, her gas mask lowered. I swerved to avoid her, like a matador in the path of a charging bull.

'Oh, I've got used to you being a moral coward. It's just you, isn't it? Like the side parting, and the Y-fronts, and the Bob Dylan records. Anyway, why does this car squeal when it goes round corners?'

'Tash,' I said to change the subject, 'they may be going to offer me Trigorin. In *The Seagull*.'

'I know what Trigorin's in.' She thought the matter over and said, 'I don't think you'd be right for the part.'

'Why? Don't you think I'm old enough?'

'You're not a writer. Trigorin was a writer.'

'Natasha. I hadn't killed my uncle when I did *Hamlet* all those years ago. I wasn't even suffering from hereditary syphilis when I made what I believe to have been a reasonable shot at *Ghosts* at Oxford. I do have some vague idea of what acting's all about . . .'

'It's not just that you're not a writer. You're nothing like a writer, you're an accountant.'

My daughter has a remarkable talent for hitting you exactly where it hurts most.

The offices of Megapolis Television plc occupy what I believe to be an unnecessarily large area on the Isle of Dogs. We no longer own Megapolis Studios near Slough, that grim area which was once the Hollywood of Britain, as most of our programmes are farmed out to independent producers. However, I regard my work as a branch, even though remote, of show business. Producers and directors often meet in our canteen, having called in to ask for Megapolis's money, and I sometimes catch sight of actresses who are up for a part there. I usually recognize them, remember having seen them, and make some fatuous remark like 'You were absolutely terrific in *Social Workers*.' I'm afraid that's the Muswell Hill Mummer coming out in me. They look mystified and wonder if I'm someone important on the production side. But, as Natasha said, I'm in accounts. A talent for mathematics, a certain adroitness with figures, an ability to read a balance sheet and uncover its hidden meaning, are among the disadvantages I was born with. Without my childhood facility for doing sums I might have been arriving at Megapolis up for the part of some decent and long-suffering father falsely accused of child abuse in *Social Workers*, or even have become a director in an unstructured suit and Raybans, who would sit romancing his PA and drinking decaff in the corner of our canteen.

Well, as I say, I was driving through that huge, messy development which was to be the triumphant creation of the Big Bang of British prosperity in the last decade, and now looked half-built, half-abandoned and prematurely depressed. Many of the office blocks were unused. In the apartments with views of the river, designed for occupation by double income co-mortgagees on a permanent curve of upward mobility, attractive waxwork dummies, young stockbrokers and commodity dealers, had been set in the windows to make passers-by believe that these desirable residences were greatly in demand and should be snapped up while stocks lasted. This device appealed to my sense of theatre. I admired the artificial tenants each morning as I drove past them and respected the estate agents for a rare display of imagination. All the same, the waxworks were a sure sign of the financial desperation which infected England during those uncertain times. Even in the balance sheets, which had much of the charm of works of fiction, Megapolis profits were down around 25 per cent.

I parked the Volvo in the space with my name on it, a privilege I had enjoyed ever since I became the personal accountant working directly to the chairman. Sir Crispin

Bellhanger, KCB, DSO, MC and so on, despite the handles to his name, was the most democratic of bosses. He had his lunch in the canteen every day with his coat off, exposing his bright blue braces and white shirt. He carried his tray and sat wherever there was a space available, beside a flurried typist, a visiting actress or the sullen *oberführer* of the parking lot. No one, in his presence, remained tongue-tied for long. Everyone, for weeks afterwards, started sentences with 'As Cris said to me the other day' or 'Cris was only just telling me up in the canteen.' Everyone called him Cris, not because he had issued any sort of memo on the subject, that wouldn't have been his style at all, but because we knew that was what he wanted and most of us were flattered to oblige him. From all this, you may have gathered that working for Cris was one of the pluses, together with a somewhat remote association with the performing arts, of life at Megapolis Telly.

Our office block, built when the advertising revenue was at its height, had the fashionable look of an X-ray. Its bones, guts and arteries were on display to the outside world. Huge conduit pipes decorated the façade and the lifts, all glass, crawled up the building like glow-worms in the dark. I have no head for heights and as I went up to the top floor I paid careful attention to my feet. Anyway, I didn't have much time to admire the view. Waiting for Tash and taking her to college had made me almost half an hour late and I'd have to hurry to get everything ready for the board meeting.

'If I could waste a minute or two of the Board's valuable time to make an interjection, which I'm sure you will all find laughably inept . . . I mean, I know you, Chairman, will shoot me down in flames immediately. But all the same, one does speak, as an inhabitant of the real, sometimes uncomfortably real, world of men, women and money, with one eye on the balance sheet and one ear to the ground.'

'That must make you a bit of a contortionist, Sydney.' I

was seated next to Cris and his mutter was meant for me
alone.

'I'm sorry, Chairman –' Sydney Pollitter, head of the firm of
City accountants Pollitter, Michaelson & Spratling, was giving
his usual amateurish performance of humility. He was one of
the unhappy few who refused to call Crispin Bellhanger, Cris
and the most endlessly vocal member of the Board. He had
long-lobed ears, which he tugged affectionately as he talked,
and he wore, on the end of his nose, gold half-glasses. With a
thatch of greying brown hair and a tendency to snuffle he
looked at times like some cartoon animal, Mr Anteater,
perhaps, dressed anthropomorphically in a three-piece suit.
Unlike Cris, he never took off his jacket at meetings but kept
it neatly buttoned. Often his lengthy, apologetic protests were
about Megapolis programmes which he had found alarmingly
erotic. '– Not that I mind for myself, of course. After a lifetime
spent on the City's golden mile one becomes used, unhappily,
to hear of the sins of the flesh in all their, to coin a phrase,
Chairman, which you may find inappropriately flippant, . . .'

'Good God. Is he going to make the joke?' Cris would mutter,
his eyes fixed on the huge, operating theatre lights which hung
over the black marble slab that formed our boardroom table.

'. . . In all their 57 varieties!' Sydney Pollitter delivered his
punchline into a silence only broken by the eager laughter of
the managing director, who had heard it all before but who
was at pains to treat Sydney and Cris, who never agreed about
anything, with equal respect. 'It's not I who am distressed,
Chairman. But it's the average housewife in Bexleyheath I'm
concerned about. Does she really want to be treated to a view
of the naked buttocks of some long-haired actor as he dives
into bed with yet *another* promiscuous social worker?'

That day, however, it was not sex that was uppermost in
the Pollitter mind. It was war. After another endless apology
for wasting the time of the Board on a trifling matter, which
we might well, with our superior knowledge of the technicali-

ties of programming and audience research, dismiss as of quite exaggerated importance, he suddenly said, 'Isn't it the duty of all of us not to do anything to undermine the morale of our young men as they go into battle in a distant land? I merely ask the question, Chairman, so that you may shoot me down.'

'I don't want to shoot you down, Sydney. I don't want to shoot anybody down. I've seen quite enough shooting down to last a lifetime.'

'I'm sure you have, Chairman. We all know your war record is impeccable. That goes without saying. And I'm sure everyone here will rebuke me for wasting the Board's precious time by repeating it.'

'I don't really think a war record' – Cris was smiling with more than his usual charm – 'is a thing for anyone to be proud of, exactly.'

'You say that, Chairman, of course. We all hear you say it and we all have the greatest respect for your modesty. But if I may just waste a further moment of your time, and I speak as one who served his country as a national serviceman, albeit in a clerical capacity.'

'Pay Corps' Cris wrote on his doodled-on copy of the minutes and nudged it in my direction.

'I am just anxious, and you will no doubt tell me at once that I am unnecessarily anxious, that an intended programme suggesting that our own record in time of war may not have been, let us say, beyond criticism is not the sort of thing we should allow to creep into the schedules at this particular moment in our island story.'

'No longer an island. Since the Channel tunnel,' Charles Glasscock, partner in a firm of solicitors and the latest addition to the Board, piped up and was immediately ignored.

'I mean, of course, *War Crimes*. Now let others speak. You must all be heartily sick of the sound of my voice. No. I mean that in all sincerity.' At which Sydney Pollitter closed his eyes and appeared to compose himself for sleep.

Gary Penrose, for the management, did his best to explain the situation. '*War Crimes*. We're commissioning it from Streetwise. We see it as a late night show. Around eleven o'clock. Certainly when the kids have been put down for the night. It's going to take the place of something like *Great Hotels of the World*.'

'It's quite far in the future, as I understand it,' Cris said. 'This war, if there is a war, will no doubt be over. Now, if we could move on to the financial report. Philip . . .' He looked hopefully at me, but his smile faded as Sydney Pollitter stirred, opened his eyes and started up his engines with another firm pull at his ear lobe. 'May I, at the risk of being howled down by the rest of you, who no doubt have far more important things to talk about, just say that I think *Great Hotels of the World* an absolutely *super* programme. I mean, all sorts of perfectly ordinary, decent people, who could never hope to go to the Peninsular in Hong Kong, for instance, get a chance to see what a really luxurious hotel looks like.'

'I've been to the Peninsular in Hong Kong —' The newest arrival on the Board was clearly going to be a chatterer. Cris returned to a close study of the ceiling as Sydney Pollitter carried on.

'That seems to me to be exactly the sort of thing we should be doing. Bringing glamour and excitement to the ordinary housewife in, let's say for the sake of argument, Bexleyheath. But when I hear talk of a series apparently designed to show that all sides in a war can behave equally badly, then I wonder, in my probably quite uninformed and extremely naïve way, if that's exactly the sort of thing we should be concentrating on. Particularly in times of National Emergency.'

'I think Philip's going to take us through the financial report, Sydney.'

Pollitter threw up both hands in an exaggerated gesture of surrender. 'I am rebuked, Chairman. I am courteously but fairly rebuked. Of course the financial report is far more important. But can I just leave the thought in your mind. For you to dismiss as utter nonsense, of course. If you decide so to do.'

'Bloody marvellous place, that Peninsular Hotel,' Glasscock told us. 'Soon as you go into your room a little old Chinese chap turns up with a trolley and offers you the choice of about thirty varieties of soap: Guerlain, Roger & Gallet, Chanel. My lady simply couldn't believe it.'

'Please, Philip' – the moment had come for Cris to take over command and he did with authority – 'the financial report. *If you please.*'

I started to go through the figures which I knew by heart and the board members of Megapolis did their best to look as if they understood them.

Up till then the meeting had followed its usual pattern; a boring formality in the work of the company. The hint of troubles to come, the cloud no larger than a man's hand, appeared when Cris asked me to stay behind for a moment.

'Sid Vicious,' he said, 'was especially unbearable this morning.' I was surprised that Cris, well over seventy and only staying on by special dispensation of the Board, whose pop musical experience might have been expected to stop short at Cliff Richard, should have heard of anything like the Sex Pistols. But his knowledge of many matters was unexpected.

'If only he'd stop apologizing,' I agreed, 'the board meetings'd take half the time.'

'Talking about my war record!' Cris was tall and lanky. His braces supported the trousers of a tweed suit of indeterminate age. He had clear features, blue eyes and wings of white hair brushed back over his ears. But he looked suddenly shy, at a loss, like a young man. 'It was bloody embarrassing!'

Stories of Cris in the war circulated in the company. He had been parachuted behind the German lines in Italy with the odes of Horace in his pocket. He had fought in the desert wearing a silk scarf and a pair of old cricket trousers. He had been dropped into Yugoslavia with the 'Balkan Air Force'. None of these were incidents I ever heard him mention.

'My war record! Three quarters of the time I was bored to death and the rest I was scared shitless. We need to do these programmes so people like Sid Vicious can understand what war's all about.'

'I suppose so.' At that time my feelings about *War Crimes* were neutral. I would have been more excited by *Great Acting Moments to Remember*.

'Streetwise've come up with rather a bright treatment. Gary's asked me to have a look at it. It seems to ask all the right questions.' He was looking out of the boardroom windows, down the glittering river towards the suburbs and patches of green that might still be countryside. I was standing by the marble slab of the boardroom table that was as cold and as uninviting as a tomb.

'The writer's called Richard Dunster.'

It was the last name I expected to have thrown at me, in that place, on that morning. When I was silent he asked, 'Who is this fellow Dunster? Do you know anything about him?'

'A little.' Of course I knew a great deal about him. He just wasn't anyone I wanted to think about, let alone discuss with Cris.

'Is he any good as a screenwriter?'

'I don't really know.' I tried to sound as unapprehensive as possible. 'I haven't seen Dunster for years.'

Chapter Two

'And the ungodly shall be cast out into outer darkness when that day comes, my friends. And only those who have given their hearts and their souls to Jesus shall walk into the light.'

'What about the Chinese?'

'Only those who have stepped forward for Our Lord will be received into His company.'

'And the Indians: Hindus, Muslims, Buddhists? Millions of them. Aren't they going to walk into the light?'

'Come on, Dunster,' I said. 'Please. We'll miss the matinée.'

'And how shall we know when the day is at hand? you ask.'

'No,' Dunster said. 'I didn't ask that. I asked about Buddhists.'

'The signs will be a mighty rushing wind. Then shall there be an outbreak of small fires.' The speaker, standing on a little stepladder at Marble Arch, was squat and grey-haired with glasses. He looked like a bank manager or an insurance salesman and uttered his dire warnings in a matter-of-fact voice, as though he were discussing the times of trains from Waterloo. It was Dunster, supposedly my best friend at school, who looked a fanatic: bright-eyed with a lock of dark hair fallen across his forehead, his unbuttoned mac flapping in the wind and a voice which trembled on the verge of indignation or sarcastic laughter – you could never be quite sure which would emerge. My idea of pleasure was to see *Othello* at the Old Vic, his was to heckle the orators at Speakers' Corner. The man on the stepladder should have been grateful as, apart from a few released secretaries and their lovers who paused for a moment on their way to a vacant patch of grass and then walked on, quite uninterested in the end of the world, Dunster and I were his only audience.

'What's troubling you, young man?' The speaker, unwisely, decided to confront Dunster.

'All those Buddhists. Are they going to be cast out into darkness?'

'Unless they have stood up for Jesus.'

'They've probably never even heard of Jesus.'

'That is why, young man, I have taken it upon myself to spread the word.'

'Well, you're not spreading it much here, are you? You're not exactly surrounded by Buddhists waiting to be converted. In fact you would hardly have had anyone here at all if Progmire and I hadn't turned up.'

'Please, Dunster. Let's go. We're going to be late.' I wanted to put an end to this scene. Not only did I find it embarrassing but I was sorry for the man on the stepladder. He seemed to me to have enough on his plate, what with the rushing wind and the small fires and the Day of Judgement, without having an argument with Dunster to contend with.

'Oh, all right. You never want to do anything interesting.' Dunster agreed to leave with a good deal of reluctance. I looked back at the preacher, who stood in silence on his stepladder for a moment, the wind disturbing his neat grey hair, before he drew breath and shouted after us, 'Outer darkness, my young friends. I ask you to beware of the outer darkness. Just you mull it over!'

We went to St George's, a long-surviving London day school in the dark alleyways around the Guildhall and the Mansion House. When it was felt that we needed fresh air, we were bussed out to a set of rented playing-fields in Barnes where we stood and shivered and longed for the warm, dark ride back, the shared crisps and bottles of Coke and the aimless fights and sudden friendships. When we arrived, the headmaster lectured all new boys on the school's history, which stretched back, more or less uneventfully, to the reign of Henry VIII.

'What you will all get here,' he said, as he looked out on an assortment which included a good many Indians, Jews and a smattering of Japanese, 'is a sound Church of England education. St George's has always been a school at the heart of English life, as the name of our patron saint will probably have made clear to you.' 'Absolute balls!' – the boy beside me had a penetrating whisper – 'St George was a Palestinian pirate and a brothel-owner. I thought everyone knew that.' It was my first meeting with Dunster.

I didn't choose to become friends with him. When I look back on it, the number of actual choices I've made in my life seem minimal. As I have said, I didn't choose to be an accountant. It was a disability I was born with. I didn't choose Natasha's mother. She chose me for reasons which I still find hard to explain. Looking back on my schooldays, it doesn't seem to me that I chose my friend, any more than I chose my school, or the uniform of straw hats and red blazers we wore, or even the part of Rosalind into which I was forced with considerable terror at the age of thirteen – and which I now look upon as one of my greatest achievements, more successful, in its way, than my Hamlet at university, which is another story entirely. So the fact of the matter is that I didn't pick out Dunster but he did, deliberately and inexplicably, choose me. He became, as the years went by, inescapable.

He always seemed to be closer to me than I really cared for. I thought, at times, that I was quite alone and then I would turn my head and there he would be, pale-faced and bright-eyed, his hair flopping down from under the ridiculous boater and his blazer buttons hanging by a thread (Mrs Dunster had left home and Dunster's father and his son cared for, or neglected, each other). He was eager to tell me some disgraceful secret he had discovered: that our headmaster, Mr Sheldrake, had got a Fourth in History and was only chosen for his present post because he was a member of the Freemasons, or that the yapping little cocker spaniel of a man who tried to teach us football had been dismissed from a job at Borstal for suspected buggery and even – and this was a story which lasted with considerable embellishments throughout the whole of one long, wet summer term – that the angry stringbean of a man who taught us French had been a close friend of Burgess and Maclean and lived in daily terror of being arrested as an old Cambridge leftie and still-active Soviet spy.

'That fish they give us,' Dunster hissed into my ear as we stood in the cavernous school canteen in the basement under Threadneedle Street, 'condemned throw-outs from Billingsgate. They bulk-buy and make a profit. I heard the bursar on the telephone.' I didn't believe him, but I opted for the vegetarian plate. You never knew, with Dunster, whether his far-fetched allegations might not have some truth in them. Anyway, I had long ago given up arguing with him. If you argued, the story would be repeated endlessly, with more and more uncheckable evidence called in support. In time my nods of assent failed to convince him and he would say, 'It's true, but you don't really want to hear about it, do you?'

'Oh, yes,' I said, to keep Dunster quiet. 'Of course I do.'

'No, you don't. You don't really care about anything very much, do you, old man?'

'I care about acting,' I told him. I, Philip Progmire, who had been Rosalind.

'Rosalind!' Dunster said with contempt. 'You were a boy pretending to be a girl who was pretending to be a boy. I don't call that anything very much to care about.'

All of which will make it clear to you that Dunster and I were chalk and cheese, or creatures from different planets. And yet, at St George's, we were thought of as great friends and inseparable. '"O, Wind,"' the English master, Mr Cheesy Cheshire, who fancied himself as a wit, was fond of saying, 'if Progmire comes, can Dunster be far behind?' Dunster needed me, I suppose, as an audience: no one else would stand and listen so patiently when he started on some long and incredible revelation. He also, perhaps, hoped that some day, with some story, he would be able to shock me into saying, 'Good God, Dunster. But that's appalling! It's a scandal! Can't you get your dad to write about it in the *Guardian*?' He may have been waiting for this satisfactory outcome to his confidences, but I never said anything like that. I could never bring myself to do so. But did I, in all truth and honesty, actually like Dunster?

I suppose I needed him. A boy starting at school, even at St George's from which he goes home in the evenings, needs a friend so that he has the consolation and protection of not standing alone, a target easily picked off, and Dunster offered his friendship almost too eagerly. But did I like him? Sometimes, as when he showed such a total lack of interest in my theatrical triumphs, I disliked him very much. And yet it was hard not to have some affection for Dunster. He was brave. His continual arguments brought him perpetual trouble. Masters would lose their tempers with him, fling books at him and turn him out of the room. Boys would make fun of him, lie in wait for him and attack him. He would put up with all this with a wan and contemptuous smile and he did not, I have to admit with shame, get much support from me.

'I didn't notice you coming to the rescue much when Porker Plumstead and his friends cornered me in the bogs.'

'No.'

'You like to keep out of things, don't you?'

'If I can, I suppose I like to.'

'There's nothing much you want to stand up for, is there, old man?'

'Well, not your idea that Whittington's Bank is financing the slave trade in Madagascar.' Porker's father was on the Board of Whittington's, which was why Dunster had started the argument.

'You mean you don't care about slaves?'

'Well, yes. Of course I do. Everyone does. But I don't see

that being punched by Porker's friends round the bogs is going to help the slaves in Madagascar.'

'You don't care much about slaves, and you don't care at all about friendship.'

'Oh, come off it, Dunster. Now you're making me feel a shit.'

'Good!' He smiled at me with sudden, unexpected charm. 'That is exactly how you ought to feel.'

I suppose the truth was that I recognized in Dunster all that I wasn't. Although I had no desire to be in the least like him, he made me feel timid, compromising, time-serving and, if not envious, in some way inferior. Here was I, waiting for *Plays and Players* each month to discover who was starring in what, dreaming of being an actor and settling for being a maths specialist because I found it easy. And there was Dunster, enormously concerned about the slave trade and the Race Relations Act and the Chinese Cultural Revolution, thriving on a series of head-on collisions with the masters and the boys which would have left me trembling with nervous exhaustion. And yet most of the time, to my amazement and occasional respect, Dunster seemed to achieve, in the centre of his frenzied universe, an absence of anxiety which I had never known. But then, as I have made it clear to you, I worry.

Dunster and his journalist father occupied, in almost unbelievable chaos, the top two floors of a house in Camden Town which had been the Dunster matrimonial home. After Mrs Dunster moved out, the father let half the place to a man on the *Financial Times* who had recently married. The Dunsters despised this couple, mainly because of their habit of taking regular meals and the orderliness of their existence. The Dunster cuisine considered almost entirely of bacon and eggs, eaten with doorsteps of fried bread and cups of strong tea, so that about their home the smell of burning fat indicated that a traditional English breakfast was available at all hours of the day and night.

I went to his house and sometimes I let Dunster visit mine. My parents lived, as I do now, in Muswell Hill, a high and windy part of north London, with pink and white Edwardian villas dominated by the curious fantasy of Alexandra Palace, from which you can see much of the city laid out like a map. When I was at school, it was the old glass palace with minarets, although the roof had been damaged by a flying bomb during the war and, during one hard winter, the organ in the Great Hall was covered with snow. When I was very small, a steam train from Highgate stopped at Muswell Hill on its way to the Palace and until I was twenty there was a racecourse in the suburb. When it closed, life there remained quiet until, in a moment of high drama the old Palace was consumed by fire and has since been rebuilt. Communications with the area are difficult and many Muswell Hill inhabitants, like my parents, seldom left it in the evenings or at weekends, shopping there, seeing friends or regularly visiting the splendours of the local Odeon. One Saturday I warned them, 'There's a friend called Dunster coming this afternoon. As a matter of fact, he's rather a menace.'

'So far as I know,' my father said, 'Dunster's a small town in Somerset that's never been a menace to anyone.'

I dreaded the Saturday afternoon visit. My parents' house was disgracefully tidy; souvenirs of their holidays abroad – bronze statues from Greece, bits of pottery from Morocco – were arranged on shelves and carefully dusted. My father was a civil servant in the Home Office and clearly open to attack from Dunster. My mother was the person from whom I have inherited my talent for anxiety. She brought out our best tea service, the one my grandmother left us in her will, for Dunster, and gave him chocolate biscuits and small cucumber sandwiches, which he ate as though he hadn't seen food for a month.

'So you're in the Home Office, sir,' Dunster said to my father, with his mouth half full of cucumber sandwich. I had never heard Dunster call anyone 'sir' before, not even our masters, and he managed to make the title sound especially contemptuous. 'I suppose you do your best not to notice the corruption in Scotland Yard?'

'I wish to God we could. To be quite honest with you, Dick' – my father's use of his Christian name seemed to startle Dunster – 'it worries the hell out of us. I wish your father'd write a series of his magnificent articles about it. We need all the public support we can get.'

It was the first time I'd seen Dunster deflated. I loved my father then, and he was always my idea of a reasonable, tolerant human being who took life with a large pinch of salt and stood in no particular awe of anyone. Years later, when I came to work for Cris Bellhanger, I suppose I was attracted to him because he was the same sort of character.

'Do your people come from that little town in Somerset? Sleepy sort of place.' My father pressed home his advantage.

'We got that milk jug in Dunster' – my mother, quite without meaning to, turned the knife in the wound – 'the one that's shaped like a cow. We thought it was rather original.'

'Wonderful cream teas in Dunster,' my father remembered.

'Is your dad going to write about Scotland Yard?' I asked my guest when we had gone up to my room to smoke Gauloises Bleues, an activity which I'm sure my parents knew about but never mentioned.

'I shouldn't think so.' And Dunster added mysteriously, 'he's got a much bigger fish than *that* to fry.'

'Sex,' Dunster said more than once, 'I don't know how people do it.'

I had often wondered, but I said nothing.

'Not it. Not the actual thing. That's absolutely vital. For your health. I mean, you can't do without the actual thing. Any more than you can do without breathing.'

I didn't keep a close watch on all of Dunster's movements, but I had never known him to miss school, even for a cold. Was this because of his ardent and regular sex life? Was

Dunster, during the hours we didn't spend together, the Casanova of Camden Town? I found this hard to believe, but then it was unsafe to make any assumptions about Dunster, a boy who was full of surprises.

'It's the lies you have to tell people. Leading up to sex.'

'Lies?'

'All that "you're so beautiful", "you're such a marvellous person", "you're the only one I've ever felt like this about during my whole life". It's all the lies you're expected to tell. I don't know how people manage to do that, all the time.'

I wonder now whether it was not having any lies told to her that caused Mrs Dunster to leave home.

Friendship with Dunster was a full-time occupation, and nobody else seemed anxious to join our group. I was an only child and, in the holidays, if I wanted to go up to the West End it had to be with Dunster. He was prepared to compromise by joining me at the theatre provided I bought the tickets and we did what he wanted for the rest of the day. So that's how we found ourselves at Speakers' Corner on our way to the Old Vic.

Othello came on to the stage in a white robe and dark brown make-up with a rose between his teeth, walking cat-like on the balls of his feet. When he said, 'Keep up your bright swords, for the dew may rust them', my senses swam with the nobility of it all. Dunster said, 'This is ridiculous. He's not even black.'

'Of course not. He's Laurence Olivier.'

'It's all completely false.'

'Will you shut up or else go?' For once I said something decisive to Dunster.

With the maximum of disturbance he went, stumbling over feet, causing muttering customers to half rise in their seats, and failing to apologize. When he had gone, I decided that once and for all I was finished with Dunster. I stared after him angrily, siding with all those whose toes he'd trodden on and whose knees he'd bumped against. Then I sat until Othello drew his hidden sword.

> 'And say besides, that in Aleppo once,
> Where a malignant and a turban'd Turk
> Beat a Venetian and traduc'd the state,
> I took by the throat the circumcised dog,
> And smote him thus.'

So the actor died in a manner Dunster would have said was false, but which seemed utterly truthful to me. So all alone, and thankful to be so, I set off for Muswell Hill. Home was boring, uneventful perhaps, but better than Dunster. I sat in the Tube re-reading the programme and then I heard an awful rustling beside me, eager breathing and a mac flapping like the wings of an ill-omened bird.

'I saw you coming out of the theatre, old man. I ran to catch up with you.'

'You needn't have bothered.'

'Do you want to know where I've been?'

'Not particularly.'

'I went back to see that silly sod at Speakers' Corner.'

'Whatever for?' I made the mistake of showing an interest and knew, with a sinking of the heart, that I would never be rid of him. He smiled triumphantly and moved uncomfortably close.

'I took him out to tea. We had bacon and eggs.'

'That must have made a change for you.'

'I wanted to prove my point about all the Buddhists in the world. I couldn't let him get away with the nonsense he was talking, could I?'

Why not? I wanted to say. However do you imagine you're going to stop all the nonsense being talked in the world, single-handed?

'In the end I think he saw my point.'

Or he gave in, as I had given in, for the sake of peace.

Chapter Three

'Hamlet, let's face it, for God's sake, was a complete drip. I hope we're all going to agree about that?' Nan Thorogood ('My mother wanted to call me Nanette. What sort of a God-awful name is that? Did she expect me to go around in a short black skirt with a feather duster? Ooh la bloody la!') taught English at St Joseph's College. We all agreed she was brilliant, bringing the fresh and revolutionary air of the seventies to blow around the dusty subject of Shakespearian studies. I didn't do Shakespearian studies, of course. I read economics, which was a fact I tried to keep as quiet as possible, but I joined the college dramatic society the moment I arrived, and I'd already done *Ghosts* in my first term, mainly because the boy slated for Oswald suffered a nervous *crise*. Whether or not this was brought on by the gloomy nature of the role it provided my great opportunity; I did an audition at a desperate last moment and got the part.

My Oswald was a modest success and even attracted a perfectly decent notice in the *Cherwell*. But that was before an anonymous hatchet man, who cowered under the name of Paul Pry, took up reviewing and everyone went in fear of his passionate abuse.

But about *Hamlet*. When the college society decided to do it in St Joseph's gardens at the end of the summer term, we asked Nan Thorogood to direct because of her new approach to Shakespeare. Now she stood among us, wearing a trouser suit and a black high-necked jumper, her hair scraped back and tied with some sort of bootlace, her high, pale forehead wrinkled with distaste for the wimpish Dane. I had wanted to hug her and vow eternal devotion when she selected me for the lead. Now my confidence ebbed away like tepid bath-water as she explained the reasons for her choice. It had nothing whatever to do with my modest success as Oswald.

'Do you think Shakespeare thought of Hamlet as a hero? What's heroic about him? He can't cope with his relationship with Ophelia. He can't face up to the basically erotic nature of his feelings for his mother. What the hell is this guy? Is he just the failed central figure of Shakespeare's least successful play? Or is he a repressed homosexual? When he fails to stab his uncle while he's kneeling at prayer, is it just because he has a secret longing to stab him in some far more intimate and forbidden manner? Is that a line of thought we might dare to pursue during the rehearsal period?'

Oh, please, I thought to myself, let's not.

'Oh, of course. Sure. Naturally. The inverted nature of Hamlet's psyche has become a cliché of contemporary inter-pretation. We all know that his pathetic inactivity is due to his failure to face the truth of his own sexuality. Years ago Jean-Louis Barrault played him as a guy in love with Horatio.' (This came as a surprise to me and greatly increased my anxiety about the whole enterprise.) 'Balls!' Nan lit a Capstan full strength and let us into the secret of Hamlet. 'He was in love with Laertes.'

'But they hardly ever met,' I dared to remind her. The other actors seemed relieved that this novel thought would not affect the interpretation of their roles.

'Of course they hardly ever met in the play. Except to kill each other. Don't you find that illuminating?'

We thought this over in silence for a while. Then a plump man called Benson, playing the first gravedigger, whispered to me, 'Are you going to have to kiss Laertes, Philip?'

'Of course he's not!' Nan Thorogood's hearing was excep-tionally keen. 'The drip would never do anything as positive as that, thank you very much. The point is − and this is something I'd like you all to think about − that Laertes is the real star of this clichéd revenger's tragedy. Laertes hears that his father's been killed, so what does he do? Doesn't hang about. Doesn't sit around talking to himself. Doesn't go through a rejection of his girlfriend – which is nothing more nor less than ritual rejection of all women. Gets on his bike and comes straight home to be revenged! In fact he behaves like a man and not a mouse in mourning. Oh, by the way, you won't be wearing black, Philip. Not in my production.'

I wondered, later, what I should be wearing. 'You'll be dressed like you are. The typical undergraduate, growing up apologetically. That old tweed jacket, with leather patches, you've nearly grown out of will do. And a college scarf wound round your neck a few times. Oh, and don't forget your specs. Stick a bit of Elastoplast round them so they look as if you dropped them and forgot to get them repaired. You don't imagine you're going to camp about in doublet and hose, do you? Speaking the stuff as though it were *poetry*?'

Laertes, then, was the star part of this production and star parts are notoriously difficult to cast. Nan was still looking for the perfect brother to Ophelia, and in the early stages she read the part herself, a task she performed with virile intensity. Then she came up to me after rehearsal and spoke out of the corner of her mouth while lighting another Capstan. 'I saw you crossing the quad this morning,' she said, 'with a man I've never even met.'

When people say this sort of thing to me I always feel guilty, as though I were being accused of some serious but unconscious crime. I said, 'Oh, did you?' as noncommittally as possible.

'He *is* Laertes.'

'Oh, no.' I was suddenly positive. 'I'm quite sure he isn't.'

'Dark. Rather good-looking, don't you think?'

'It has never occurred to me.'

'Chap who looks as though he knows exactly where he's going.'

'I think we were going for breakfast.'

'I'm damn well going to nobble him for Laertes.'

'I honestly don't think you should do that.'

'Why ever not?'

'Well, to start with, he thinks that all acting's completely false.'

'Wonderful!' Nan's eyes lit up as she blew out a long plume of smoke. 'He sounds absolutely right for the part. Oh, what's his name, by the way?'

Not many boys from St George's got into Oxford in our year – only myself, Dunster and Porker Plumstead. As I have said, I had never found sums difficult. Dunster, in spite of his tendency to mutiny, had worked, as I always suspected, frenetically in secret. And Porker –? Well, of course, Dunster told me that Porker's father had put a large donation from Whittington's Bank at the disposal of the college library.

There had been times when I had secretly hoped that the end of my schooldays would be the end of my friendship with Dunster. I had fantasies of us drifting apart, meeting occasionally in the holidays, finding nothing much to say to each other and then forgetting to send a Christmas card. Although I had often longed for this outcome, I didn't believe in it and when I got to university Dunster was, as ever, at my side. He soon decided he didn't like Oxford. 'Why the hell do we have to spend our youth shut away in medieval dungeons? First St George's, now this.' Our college was small, built in stone which went gold in the sunlight, with a quadrangle of bright green grass and a huge clock of doubtful accuracy. From my top-floor room I could see the domes of the Radcliffe Camera and the Sheldonian. Dunster's room was on the ground floor, often in shadow. He managed to get through each short term without entirely unpacking his suitcase, so he lived in a gloomy chaos which reproduced as accurately as possible his home in Camden Town. 'Three years in a

dungeon,' Dunster decided, 'and the Master's an old faggot
with a Marcelle wave.'

'Dunster! You don't know that.'

'Of course I do. I looked him up in *Who's Who*: "Sir
Ninian Dobbs. Military historian. Hobbies: cooking and collecting miniatures. Unmarried." What do you think unmarried
means?'

'It probably means he hasn't got a wife.'

'Progmire, are you really a sort of Holy Fool? Or is it just
the act you put on to save yourself the trouble of finding out
about things?'

Sir Ninian Dobbs was a tall and distinguished figure whom
we sometimes saw presiding over the high table in hall. He
had an aquiline nose and admittedly carefully tended white,
wavy hair. 'I don't suppose he'll have much to do with us,' I
tried to reassure Dunster.

'With any luck. But if he starts inviting us to dinner, feign
illness.' He often used expressions which were appropriate to
the nineteenth century, which he was studying.

The college dramatic society was my escape route from
Dunster. I began to behave, like all university actors, in the
most actorish way possible. We thespians sat at the same table
in hall and I was careful to join in with dialogue like 'Did you
see that girl from St Hilda's in the Christ Church *Duchess of
Malfi*? It was absolutely *dire*.' Or 'I thought of going up for
Bartholomew Fair but now I'm not going to bother. They've
got a guy from Wadham who couldn't direct traffic.' Or
'Marcus Gravely thinks he's Pembroke's answer to Richard
Burton. Someone should give him a paper bag and see if he
can act his way out of it.'

Dunster, as I had suspected, couldn't take much of this and
soon moved off to another table where the discussion centred
on politics, economics and such subjects as Solzhenitsyn and
the invasion of Cambodia. I felt released and happier than I
had ever been. Dunster and I then met as equals and although

he listened to my chatter about the dramatic society with a pale smile of contempt, he realized that I had vanished into a world where he couldn't follow me. And I became tolerant of his pursuits, complimenting him on the articles he wrote for an assortment of university magazines denouncing Oxford and all it stood for, although I often got no further than the first paragraph.

'That weird woman in the trouser suit asked me to join the ac*tors*.' He emphasized the last syllable in what he thought was the way we talked.

'Nan Thorogood? She said she was going to ask you to play Laertes.'

'Who's he? Remind me.'

'A very positive type of person. I'm Hamlet. You'd have to kill me in the last act.'

'You mean pretend to kill you?'

'Well. Yes.'

'I told her straight out, old man, that the idea was absolutely ridiculous.'

In the end, Laertes was someone called Adams who read law. He had short, ginger hair, pointed teeth and a threatening smile. 'Suitably vulpine,' Nan told us triumphantly. But in spite of his promising appearance, he was a dull actor and I didn't expect him to cause me much anxiety.

'Going mad,' Ophelia said, 'makes me so bloody hungry.'

'I was thinking of eating in that Indian place in the Turl,' I lied casually. 'I mean, why not join me? We could discuss our scene.'

'I haven't got much money . . .'

'Don't give it a thought.' It was far into the term but I could manage a few curries by flogging my new copy of *One World Economics* in Blackwells' secondhand department; this would be particularly profitable as I hadn't yet paid for it.

When we arrived at the restaurant, although a sensationally

thin girl, she seemed prepared to tackle examples of all the Star of Bengal's limited cuisine.

'I don't know what your problem is,' she said when I confessed I still felt far from 'getting' Hamlet. 'You're marvellous in all the indecisive bits. By the way, why don't you have your glasses mended? I mean, the ones you wear in rehearsal?'

'Nan thinks Hamlet should have broken glasses. Remember?'

'Funny idea,' she said, meaning it wasn't.

'Also she wants me to do it without letting the poetry show. She wants me to say, "O, what a rogue and peasant slave am I" in a sort of low moan. I don't think it's written as a low moan. You know what?' I had seen looks of envy from two men eating in a corner and felt full of courage. 'I'm going to say the poetry on the night. When Nan can't do anything much about it.'

'That's the spirit!' She smiled up at me from her prawn vindaloo. My Ophelia's name was Bethany Blair and it would have been very strange if I hadn't fallen in love with her. 'But what's your problem with our scene?'

'Hamlet rejecting Ophelia. I can't see why any man in his senses would reject you.'

'He wasn't in his senses, was he? Anyway, he was pretending not to be.' There was a pause while she crackled a poppadum. 'Actually you don't need to say things like that.' For an elated moment I thought this was encouraging, that she meant my compliments were understood without being spoken. Then my natural pessimism returned and I felt that my flattery had displeased her. It would take some time and a fair number of oriental dinners before I discovered what I felt to be the truth.

When I drove Tash to her tutorial college on the morning of the board meeting, which was the start of all our present troubles, she was only three years younger than Beth had been when I first met her. They could easily have been mistaken for each other. Drowned Ophelia has been painted, pale with her red hair floating, looking perfectly at home in the water, but naturally remote from the problems of everyday living. Both Natasha and Beth had this look, so that you felt you admired their beauty through clear water or plate glass. The appearance was largely deceptive. These withdrawn pre-Raphaelite beauties could be as uncomfortable as Tash was in the car that morning, or as crudely unnerving as Ophelia in madness.

I found out all I could about Beth and much of it was surprising. She was the only child of an army major who'd retired to a small farm in the West Country. She could skin rabbits, strangle chickens, shoot pheasants, aid the birth of lambs and perform many tasks which would show me up as hopelessly incompetent, not to say, squeamish. You might have thought the fact that she bore such a striking resemblance to the Ophelia seen through the sentimental eyes of Sir John Millais, RA would have ruined her chances of getting the part. Nan could have been expected to go for a North Country revolutionary Maoist, or for a butch, overweight Nordic art student with a secret passion for Gertrude. Unexpectedly she made the obvious choice, only insisting that Beth should dress as a hippy in flowing Indian scarves and a head-band, and carry a sitar. This was far removed from the character of the only daughter of Major Jaunty Blair, whose bedroom at home was decorated with the rosettes she had won at gymkhanas and whose family freezer contained a fox's brush, wrapped in newspaper, which had been presented to Beth out hunting and which she had forgotten to have mounted.

I had no doubt at all what I felt about Beth, and as little idea of what she felt about me. We sympathized with each other, praised each other, did our best to cheer each other up; but this was the way with all actors as the terror of the opening performance drew near. In this she behaved no differently to me than she did to the rest of the cast. She smiled at us all and often laid her hand gently on our arms while she was speaking to us.

When I took her back to her North Oxford college after our dinner, she gave me her cheek to kiss, offering it with a vague politeness which made me feel she was thinking of something else. This good-night happened in the college entrance. I thought that undated girls were peering down from the windows above us and I only wished that we were putting on a better show. I wondered who else bought Beth tandoori chicken and took her home to this public farewell – Laertes, Horatio, King Claudius, or even the gravedigger? We went out quite often, although there were always plenty of dates she couldn't manage. We talked all the time, about our fears, the other actors and the awfulness of Nan. I thought she was less obsessed with acting than I was. It was just one of many activities which included riding, hunting, dancing and a certain amount of rough shooting with her father, Major Jaunty. Acting, Beth said once, was something she got into because a friend asked her 'and you might as well try everything'.

'Who was the friend?' I forced myself to ask.

'Oh, just someone I knew. He's not important.'

'How's *Hamlet* going?'

'I don't know. It'll probably be a complete disaster.' It was my way then, as now, to expect the very worst in the faint hope that things might not turn out to be quite as ghastly as I had predicted.

'Well, so long as you know that,' Dunster said cheerfully, 'you won't be disappointed.'

The extraordinary thing was that we had met at the Experimental Theatre's production of *The Ghost Sonata*. I had invited Beth, and Dunster was there with a girl who looked very young, had large breasts and seemed scared of him. He said her name was Prudence and that she had a taste for

Strindberg which he found ludicrously masochistic. When Beth asked him if he'd be coming to see *Hamlet* he said, 'I'm not sure. I may have an essay to write.'

'We're on for four nights.'

'I suppose that's what you hope.'

She took my arm then, something I was very glad Dunster had seen her do, and we went back to our seats. 'Is that a friend of yours?' she asked.

'Oh, I've known him forever.'

'He didn't sound like much of a friend.'

So the long, wet and over-excited summer term continued. There were no lazy afternoons on the river for us, no strawberries and Chablis in the sun. There were only glistening pavements and rehearsals and grey clouds. The heads of the philosophers round the Sheldonian seemed to dissolve even more rapidly in the rain, and cyclists pedalled even faster to avoid a soaking but arrived at lecturers with their hair plastered down and their notebooks soggy. Not only had we our unreliable memories, our minor talents, our nervousness to contend with but we had the added horror of an open-air performance. *Hamlet* in St Joseph's gardens was even more alarming than *Hamlet* indoors. We faced the doubtful future as courageously as we could and even arranged a first-night party in punts. We were not greatly encouraged by a brutal notice of *The Ghost Sonata*: 'A new terror has been added to death,' Paul Pry wrote, 'by the fear that we might be compelled to return to earth in a production as absurd as this. *The Ghost Sonata*, as the Experimental Theatre presents it, is not to be recommended to any audience, alive or dead.'

But we kept our worries to ourselves, hoped for the best and, as we sat at our table in hall, we told theatrical jokes. Benson, the gravedigger, knew most of the old actor-laddie stories and, a week or so before *Hamlet* was due to hit the turf, he told us what I now know to be one of the oldest of all. It was about the actor-manager who was asked if, in his opinion, Hamlet actually slept with Ophelia. 'When I was on tour,' he is supposed to have answered, 'I invariably did.' I don't suppose Benson thought for a moment about me and Beth when he told the story; but it gave me a vision of a new world, more likely to be fantasy than fact, with an old tradition which I was, I still thought, unlikely to live up to.

Chapter Four

I wouldn't want you to think that at the time of the run up to *Hamlet* I was totally inexperienced. I mean so far as sex was concerned. I've already made it clear that I'd done a certain amount of acting.

I'd met quite a lot of girls at parties, especially at those rather ostentatious affairs given by Porker Plumstead in his father's mock Tudor mansion somewhere to the north of Hampstead Heath. These do's always led to a good deal of panting activity in the corners of darkened rooms with girls from various highly priced London schools who danced invitingly to Joe Cocker records but showed an increasing reluctance as the new-found friendship developed. The first time I made love was to a Mrs Oakshott, who lived in a house in Gloucester Crescent and was a warm supporter of the Labour Party. My relationship with her – although it turned me from a worried virgin to a slightly more worried experienced person – is not something I am particularly proud of. It doesn't show me in a good light, but then if I confined myself to incidents that did that, I don't suppose this story would ever get told. If I'm going to make you understand it properly, I think you should know that when Beth and I got together I was someone who had lost his tenuous grasp on virginity in Mrs Oakshott's bathroom

'Marguerite Oakshott,' Dunster said, 'is a well-known figure of the Left. She has evenings.'

'Well, so do I. So does everyone. I have mornings too, as a matter of fact. And the occasional afternoon.' It was our final term at school and I was rehearsing *The Importance of Being Earnest*, so I had a tendency to shoot my cuffs, smoke Turkish cigarettes and speak in a languid drawl.

'I mean,' Dunster, unamused, explained as though to a child, 'she has evenings when all sorts of people get invited. Politicians. Famous journalists. TUC leaders. They discuss serious subjects.'

'How extremely frivolous of them.'

'Old man, when is that Oscar Wilde play over?'

'Next Tuesday.'

'Thank God for that. Mrs Oakshott's evening's in exactly two weeks' time. My dad was invited and he asked if he could bring me because I'm interested in politics. Now's he's going to be away doing a story about anarchists in Amsterdam. But she's said I can go and bring a friend. So I thought of you, Progmire, immediately. I'm trying to give you some idea of what the world's all about. My ambition is to educate you.'

In this last aim Dunster, I suppose, achieved some success. He was obviously extremely impressed with our invitation and had shaved and plastered down his hair with water. I wore my suit and a purple shirt, which I thought went with my Yellow Book period, although I doubt whether Oscar Wilde would have been seen dead in it. When I asked Dunster what he thought the party was going to be like, he had to admit that his father had never actually been to one of Mrs Oakshott's evenings, although he had been asked quite often. He thought someone probably gave a paper, after which there would be a free-ranging discussion over quiche and *vin ordinaire*. It might, he said, be a thoughtful gesture to bring a bottle. So Dunster and I arrived at Gloucester Crescent with a Carafino red from the off-licence.

'Children,' Mrs Oakshott said vaguely as we made our presentation, 'how terribly touching. But we do have our own stuff, actually.'

Even in the dimly lit sitting-room I noticed that her own stuff consisted largely of champagne. I caught a glimpse of the pictures – a couple of Lowrys, a Graham Sutherland, John drawings and something that looked suspiciously like a Dufy

– on the walls. The room was full of older men and younger women and they were laughing a good deal and talking in high, excited voices, no doubt about the Race Relations Act or the reform of the House of Lords.

'A tragedy your father couldn't come. I'm such a fan of his column in the *Listener*.'

'The *Guardian*.' Dunster was always a stickler for the truth.

'I love it, anyway. Now . . .' Mrs Oakshott looked around the room. She was, I noticed, a small, curvaceous, still-pretty woman with dark hair and bright brown eyes. She had a way of leaning back her head and trying to look down at us, which, as both Dunster and I were a good deal taller than her, was not a complete success. 'Now, shall I find you someone rather beautiful to talk to?'

'Is that Malcolm McCabe?' Dunster had spotted the one Labour Minister who still retained the respect of the Left, despite an uneasy compromise over private education. He was large, florid and Scots, with watery blue eyes and a mane of iron-grey hair. He didn't look, as he held court in a corner of the room, especially beautiful.

'Well, yes. But he seems a little occupied at the moment.' McCabe's audience consisted, I thought, of better-off girls from the Royal College of Art. Not to be deterred, Dunster moved purposefully in the direction of the politician. Mrs Oakshott squeezed my arm, murmured, 'See you later, cherub,' and I was left holding the bottle of Carafino. I saw Dunster work his way through the attendant art students and stand uncomfortably close to McCabe, who ignored him for as long as possible. I put our gift down among the superior bottles and no one spoke to me until a fairly friendly girl in a black dress asked me for a match and started to chat as I failed to make my lighter work. I looked terribly learned, she said, and was I going into politics? I was still trying to think of the correct Wildean answer to this line when another girl said, 'Come on, Michelle, the professor wants you,' and they went off towards a learned-looking fellow with a pale, domelike forehead, standing at the other end of the room.

'It's disgusting!' Dunster was back with me.

'Not necessarily,' I told him, although the distant professor did appear to be leading Michelle upstairs.

'McCabe. He was drinking champagne!'

'Quite a lot of them seem to be.'

'And so I tackled him about private education.'

'Well, you should know all about that. Seeing we pay fees at St George's.'

But Dunster was hard to disconcert. He went on with great intensity. 'I told him I felt thoroughly bad about that. I also said he ought to be ashamed of drinking champagne while the class system remains intact.'

'I bet that really got to him.'

'No, it didn't. That's the point. He said his brand of social-ism meant that champagne would be freely available to all. But until that bright day dawned, at least it would be available to socialist Cabinet Ministers. That man' – Dunster came to the inevitable conclusion – 'is completely false. I'm leaving.'

I might have gone with him if I hadn't wanted to go to the loo. I plucked up courage to ask directions of a lofty person in a dark suit, but he said, 'God knows. I only came with the catering.' So I started on a fatal journey up the staircase to the upper reaches of the house. Doors were open into darkened rooms and I heard, from one of them, the sound of suppressed laughter. Then I saw a light on gleaming tiles and went in.

Mrs Oakshott's bathroom, perhaps appropriately, was pale pink. It was comfortably furnished with fleecy rugs, book shelves and pots of dried-out petals. Either because I was in a hurry or because of some defect in the lock, the door wasn't fastened and I became conscious, as I washed my hands in the pink basin, that I was not alone. 'I do love those films where the chap takes the glasses off the librarian and she looks like a real woman, don't you?' Mrs Oakshott said as she removed my specs and put them carefully on a glass shelf. 'There now, you really look quite pretty.' I saw the world blurred, like an Impressionist painting, but it was clear to me that her shirt had become unbuttoned. She had a sweet, powdery smell which mingled with the rose petals – and the change in my life, such as it was, took place mid-way between the gold-tapped bidet and the end of the bath.

> 'So oft it chances in particular men
> That – for some vicious mole of nature in them,
> As in their birth, wherein they are not guilty,
> Since nature cannot choose his origin –'

It was quite early in the play but, in spite of Nan Thorogood's dire warnings and strict injunctions, the poetry showed through and I felt there was nothing much I could do about it. I heard my voice, nowhere near as incisive as Olivier's and much less melodic than Gielgud's, untrained, amateurish but still doing the same job. The rhythm of the words took me over and for those hours in St Joseph's gardens I forgot myself: Playing a character full of doubt, I was strangely certain; pretending to be a man beset with anxiety, I had forgotten my worries.

The day had started with unusual sunshine and we preened ourselves on our luck. Summer had begun at last, and especially for us. As we dressed, we were trying to cheer each other up, like a party of criminals waiting to come up for sentence. I felt short of breath and went to the loo frequently, unaccompanied. The play opened in low, evening sunshine with a cool wind flustering the trees. I saw my mother and father sitting together in the front row. They had brought a rug and I was grateful that my mother wouldn't have to put on the plastic pixie hood that I always found embarrassing. So the ghost, a pallid figure in a khaki greatcoat, walked in the daylight while we crowded in the JCR, the girls chattered and I stood in a corner trying to retch as quietly as possible. Then

I came on with the court but sat alone, like Dunster, I thought, in sullen isolation. 'A little more than kin, and less than kind': I heard my first line with surprise, as though it were spoken by someone a long way off. In due course I rejected Ophelia with ruthless determination, firmly believing that I had, according to tradition, slept with her but intended to give it up. As the daylight died and a colder wind stirred the branches, the pointed arches of the college were lit with the amber lights we'd hired at enormous expense and I welcomed the Players with what I thought was true princely condescension. And then, when I announced that the play was the thing wherein to catch the conscience of the King, I felt a heavy drop of water on my hand and the rain began to fall like muted applause.

The second half seemed timeless, like a dream. The rain stopped for a while and then set in heavily when Benson did his gravedigger jokes. The amber beams were full of water and the audience began to thin out. During 'Alas, poor Yorick' I saw my mother in her pixie hood. I took off my glasses when I put on the fencing mask and Laertes became an active blur as we fought, sliding on the wet grass. I didn't drop on the King like an avenging angel from a great height in the Olivier manner. I skidded towards him, full of purpose, and then let the venom do its work. When I died in the arms of Horatio, and as the four captains were bearing me to the stage, and the soldiers were ordered to shoot, I felt all my anxieties had been set at rest. The rattle of clapping from the wet survivors on the benches, although only just satisfactory by any theatrical standard, did nothing to diminish my confidence. I wasn't even worried about the party to come. It didn't occur to me that Beth would wander among the cast, laying a gentle hand on every arm, kissing most of them and treating us all as equals. I was still Prince Hamlet, although deceased, and Ophelia and I would go as a couple.

'It's stopped raining.' Laertes was looking up at the scudding clouds.

'To the boats!' Benson shouted in his gravedigger's voice. 'Women and children last!'

So off we set towards Magdalen Bridge, carrying macs and rugs, red plonk and an occasional bottle of whisky. Nan was among us, failing to dampen our spirits with congratulations like 'Well, my children, you got through it, didn't you? One day I might persuade you to act the *real Hamlet*. The grown-up version.' 'You mean the one where Osric falls for the ghost?' Benson asked. We knew we had done our own play. Nan, sitting alone in the rain, had suffered a severe disappointment, but we no longer needed her.

The actors were getting into punts, standing, rocking the boats on purpose, screaming in simulated terror, throwing in food and wine and scrambling to be together. I saw an empty boat and grabbed Beth's arm with some of the determination I had left over from my assault on King Claudius. 'Come on,' I said, 'that one's empty.' And I added, because we were still actors, 'Darling.' She got in and lay back on damp cushions. I looked round and saw that the rest of the cast were all accommodated in other boats. I sat beside her and covered her with a rug. She said, 'Who's going to drive this thing?' My heart sank as Laertes appeared from the darkness, stepped lightly on to the end of the boat and poled us expertly out into midstream, avoiding the punts with their loads of actors who tried to ram us. I held Beth's cold hand under the rug, she turned her face towards me and we kissed, disregarding the silently navigating Laertes. We lay still then and seemed to travel for a long time. I had no idea what was going to happen next.

Then I saw that the others had landed; there was a party going on and Laertes steered us towards it. Well, that, I thought, is the end of that, but when we were near the bank he jumped off, as quickly and as quietly as he had joined us. Neither of us moved and we drifted on, brushed by overhanging willow branches, into a cave of leaves where the intermittent moonlight was blotted out. We were stuck in mud and sheltered from the rain. I took off my glasses to kiss her properly. 'Beth,' I told her, 'I've been wanting to say this for so long.'

'Don't say anything,' she said. 'It'll be perfectly all right.'

'What do we do now? Ring the bell for the porter?'

'We climb in.'

'There's an easy way, isn't there?'

'Is that what you want?'

'I've always heard there's an easy way. A sort of formality. So that they can keep up appearances.'

'All right. We start up by the bicycle sheds.'

I followed him doubtfully. If there were an easy way of climbing into college, would it be in Dunster's character to take it? I didn't want to be with him on a mountaineering expedition without ropes in the darkness and persistent rain. I wanted to be alone, to remember what I now had to remember. I wanted a little peace and quiet to think of Beth making love, her competent hands, her body not altogether undressed under the blanket, her long hair wet against my face, her amused smile as we started, and the immense encouragement of her trembling later, and her small cry. Acting and making love, I knew then, were the two things I could do and forget my nature. And that night I had gone from one to the other without interruption, from death in the duel to another sort of obliteration in the boat under the willow tree.

The everyday Progmire, the one I know only too well, was still absent when we pushed the punt out of the mud and joined the party. Beth and I were careful to talk to other people and, as we separated, I felt we were even closer because of our shared and aloof performance. I was listening to a long complaint from Queen Gertrude about Nan's total failure to give her any direction whatsoever, devoting all her attention to Claudius, who, of course, needed it, the poor darling, and who looked, despite all our producer's efforts, less like a king than the manager of the local Abbey National. Then I saw, across the flames of the camp-fire lit on the edge of Parson's Pleasure, the pale face of Dunster, who was standing sharing a paper cup of wine with the large-breasted Prudence and looking at me with amusement.

'What on earth are *you* doing here?' I felt, as I had so often, that he had intruded on my private territory.

'Someone told us there was a party. So we thought we should come along. Do you want me to say, "You were wonderful, dahling"?'

'Only if you thought it.'

'Isn't the point of saying "You were wonderful, dahling" that you mean something entirely different?'

'Then don't say it.'

'I won't.'

In Dunster's presence feelings of anxiety began to return and I wanted some sort of reassurance from him. 'But what *did* you think of it?'

'I think' – Dunster looked more cheerful than I had ever seen him at Oxford – 'I need notice of that question.'

Beth and I went back in a punt full of people, singing and splashing with paddles. Laertes, the expert with the pole, seemed to avoid us and had gone off in a boat with Gertrude. I walked Beth to her college, silently holding hands. More sensible than me, she had managed to get a pass to go to the party. Before she rang the bell I said, 'We're going to do it again tomorrow.'

'Are we? I wouldn't mind.' She had her arms round my neck, smiling.

'Actually I meant *Hamlet*.'

'Oh, that too, I suppose.'

So I went back to St Joseph's and arrived, twenty minutes later, to find Dunster in the street without Prudence and the doors locked.

'Is this the easy way?'

'Casanova!'

'What?' Had Dunster guessed something? We climbed over the wall by the bicycle sheds and arrived on the flat roof of a building, some sort of outhouse. From there we could have scrambled down a tree into the small quad but Dunster would have none of it. 'You'd be bound to make the most terrible row. Breaking branches. The porter'd be out flashing his torch in a second. You may be bloody rich but I'd like to keep my money in my pocket. Look up there.' He pointed, up a steep, tiled roof which looked about as easy to climb as the west col of the Eiger. 'See that open window? By my calculations that's the loo on your staircase. Anyway, we can just ease ourselves in there and no one's going to hear us. Follow me, Progmire.'

So he started shinning up the roof, holding on to the bits of castellated masonry at its edge; and I came blindly after him, on my knees occasionally, and asking what the hell he meant by Casanova.

'He made a daring escape from prison. Across the leads of a Venetian roof.' Dunster was full of unexpected knowledge. 'Isn't he one of your heroes?'

'It *isn't* the easy way.' I was sure of it.

'Keep quiet, can't you? We're nearly there.'

I was always surprised by Dunster's agility. He was tall, angular and apparently uncoordinated, and he walked with loping strides and arms waving to express his strong opinions. But now he seemed to run up the tiles like a cat and stood gripping the top of an open window. As I struggled up to join him he slid the window up and whispered, 'Jump in. We're home and dry.' He stood aside to let me go first, like a sergeant launching parachutists into the unknown. I stepped out into darkness and landed more softly than I expected on thick carpeting rather than on lavatory tiles. The room felt more spacious than a loo and from somewhere in the middle distance there came the sound of regular, heavy breathing. 'Made it,' Dunster said as he landed beside me.

41

And then the bedside light went on and we were staring at the outraged figure of Sir Ninian Dobbs, sitting bolt upright in bed and wearing a hair-net.

'You noticed the hair-net, of course?' Dunster said at breakfast the next morning as we speculated on the amount of likely fines. 'That proved it, I hope, to your satisfaction.'

'What did it prove?'

'That I was absolutely right about him. Well,' Dunster added modestly, 'I usually am right about people.'

Chapter Five

'Sid Vicious,' Cris said, 'doesn't want us to do the *War Crimes* series.'

'I'm not all that surprised.' His wife Angie smiled at us from the other end of the dinner table.

'He has the sentimental affection for war of someone who's never really taken part in the bloody thing.'

It was a couple of weeks after the board meeting and the discussion which had started me off on the remembrance of Dunster Past. Cris had suggested a weekend at Windhammer then, and shortly afterwards the date was fixed. In the old days Beth had been puzzled by my fondness for the Bell-hangers. 'Cris needs you because you're bloody good at figures,' she used to say. 'He's not going to sack you if you don't travel miles to sit drinking gin with him and that elderly starlet. I don't know why you want to go, anyway.'

'Because I enjoy it.'

'Is that what you tell yourself? If you're doing that, I'll go and see Mum and Dad. I know you don't enjoy them terribly!' So we would go, on some weekends, our separate ways.

Windhammer, a ponderous statement of Gothic gloom built by Cris's ancestor in the 1850s, stood a few miles from the white beaches and treacherous tides of the North Sea. Icy blasts, after an uninterrupted journey from the steppes of Russia, besieged the walls and rattled the casement windows, but inside logs crackled in Arthurian fireplaces and the central heating rose comfortably to the vaulted ceilings of the bed-rooms. 'Great-grandfather made railway engines,' Cris used to tell me. 'I don't know why he saw himself as the Lady of Shalott.' There was still a gunroom where the weapons were

43

kept clean and oiled, and a stable; but Cris said he never went shooting and only used his horse for hacking across the flat countryside. 'I gave up killing things after the war,' he told me. 'It's made me an object of ridicule to the country set, but I can't say that breaks my heart. The great secret of living in the country is not to get on too well with your neighbours.'

The house was also warmed by the lady whom Beth called the 'elderly starlet'. Cris's wife Angie was once Angela Downing, star of a couple of dozen wartime movies. She still had the wide eyes, high cheekbones and the impertinent charm which had made her unflappable WRENS and steadfast heroines of the French Resistance irresistible. She always greeted me with a welcome kiss, steered me to the fireside and asked about my acting career. If she started on the gin and tonics a long while before dinner, and drank quite a bit with it, if her voice became a little thicker and her memory unreliable by the end of the evening, she was no less charming as she set an unsteady course towards her bedroom, shedding spectacles and magazines and shawls on her way. 'I suppose my lot enjoy drinking so much,' she used to say, 'because it was so bloody hard to lay your hands on a decent drop during the war.'

War was what we talked about that weekend at Windhammer. Fighting had started in the desert, or rather an enormous number of bombing raids had started, dropping missiles which were said to be capable of rounding street corners, creeping down stairs and destroying carefully selected military targets in Baghdad. Cris, unlike the rest of the safe civilian population of England, spent no time discussing the campaign. He was still thinking of the board meeting we had had before hostilities started.

'I'll say one thing for the war –' Angie held out her glass for a refill. 'The tide's gone down in this thing, darling. I mean, if it hadn't been for the war I might never have met Cris.'

'War was jolly good on the movies.' Her husband was

pouring wine, of which he also drank a good deal but with no apparent effect. 'Especially Angie's movies. That's where the war ought to have stayed. In the local Odeons. Everyone could have gone and watched Sergeant Johnny Mills being brave and Corporal Dickie Attenborough getting the screaming hab-dabs in the tail-end of the bomber, Angie making tea through the Blitz and actors with clenched teeth and monocles playing Nazis. Then they could have gone home and felt brave without anyone having to die.'

'He does talk nonsense!' Angie gave me the smile which had had such a devastating effect on Wing Commander David Niven in *Enemy Targets*. 'I was getting quite tired of going out with actors in uniform. I doubt if I'd've fallen for Cris if he hadn't been a real soldier. He was the only one who never talked about the war.'

'Actually,' Cris told me, 'she fell for me because I couldn't dance.'

'Most of the actors and directors I went out with were terribly keen on dancing.' Angie sighed. 'Round and round the floor. Fox-trotting away until all hours of the night. It used to leave me fit for nothing except a cup of Ovaltine and sleep. But when Cris took me out to dinner . . .'

'I told Angie I was absolutely no dancer,' Cris joined in. He and his wife enjoyed telling this anecdote as a team.

'He said he was no dancer but it was still early, so what about going to bed together?' Angie confided in me, not for the first time.

'I happened to have a room in the Regent Palace.'

'Actually he'd booked it before he even asked me out!'

'It only cost something like five quid.'

'Quite a lot of money for those days.' Angie was the careful one. 'And you know, the poor chap popped the question at breakfast the next morning.'

'And she said she supposed she liked me a bit better than the fox-trot.'

'Actually, I said I'd have to think about it very carefully and he'd better go away and ask me again when the war was over.'

'Absolute balls! She jumped at the suggestion. Couldn't wait. We got married before my leave was up. Special licence. In the Guards Chapel. During an air raid.'

'Did I ever tell you how we met?'

'No.' I lied, knowing that Angie would like to tell me again. Cris leant back in his chair and looked at his wife with considerable pride as she described how she hadn't known him from Adam when she went to some awful party in Kensington in aid of the Red Cross, and he came pushing past her with a glass of red plonk.

'Black market Communion wine, probably.' Cris filled in the details. 'At some of those parties people used to mix it with spirits and call it gin and altars!'

'He bumped into me and the stuff went all over my dress.'

'A total accident.'

'You don't believe that, do you, Philip?'

'No,' I reassured her, 'I don't believe it.'

'It was all done so that he could winkle my address out of me. He said he wanted to send me flowers.'

'I thought that was rather a gallant gesture?' Cris asked me to confirm his gallantry.

'Gallant gesture indeed! All he had in mind was rogering me. In the Regent Palace hotel!' Her eyes closed then, apparently in happy recollection of that night half a century ago. She was still smiling as Cris helped her to the staircase, picking up her dropped possessions and promising not to stay up too late talking to me.

After Angie had gone to bed we moved to the library, a long room with a stained-glass window done by some minor pre-Raphaelite, giving it a dim, religious appearance. There were shelves of leather-bound books – 'Great-grandfather bought them by the yard. They're on such fascinating subjects as the geology of Tibet' – and also Cris's larger, far more interesting, collection. There was an elaborate sound system and a grand piano at which Cris sat and played for a little. He broke the silence after the music arrived at its inevitable conclusion. 'A war crime is something that's done by the defeated. The Germans are supposed to have committed all the war crimes. We just liberated people, even if it meant killing large numbers of them to do it.'

'We're not suggesting that the Germans didn't commit war crimes, are we?' We were talking about history, a period which would seem as remote to my daughter as the Norman Conquest or the Napoleonic Wars, and I didn't know what surprises our proposed programme might contain.

'Oh, yes. Of course. They committed them.' He frowned and moved uncomfortably in his chair. Unusually for Cris, words weren't coming easily to him. 'Let me tell you something. We got to a little town when we were fighting our way up Italy. It doesn't matter where exactly. Anyway. Typical Italian town. Perched on a steep hillside. An old wall round it. Nothing much inside. A square where they had a market once a week. A church. A bar. A few narrow streets. No great paintings in the church. A place of no importance to anyone. Well, when we got there it was empty. Nothing. A ghost town. No sign of life. Flies buzzing over the meat going bad in the butcher's. Grocer's empty. Café deserted. And where a church had been, nothing.'

'Bombed?'

'Not as respectable as that. No. Some German had been killed. An officer. Not even in the town. Somewhere outside the walls. Anyway, that's where they found his body. Well, everyone in the village went to church on a saint's day. Men, women and children. Babies in their mothers' arms. So when everyone was inside, German soldiers locked the doors. They'd laid the charges the night before, we imagined. Their commanding officer yelled out some sentence of death over a loud hailer. That's what they heard instead of the Mass. Then the soldiers cleared off and everyone was blown to pieces, old and young – everyone in the village who'd gone there to pray.'

He shook himself, as though to escape from a memory. 'A small incident perhaps, but those people didn't start the war. Probably they had no particular interest in it, except for praying for it to stop. So they went to church and were blown to kingdom come. What the hell can you prove by killing people?'

I said nothing. War is something of which I have had absolutely no experience.

'That's why I want to do this series, in spite of anything Sid Vicious may have to say about it. I want people to understand. Look . . .' He went over to a desk in the corner and came back with a typescript, neatly bound. 'I'd like to know what you think of it. An outline for a series of six.'

As I took it, I saw Dunster's name on the cover and was filled with unreasonable foreboding. I read it in bed. It was clearly set out but contained no surprises. Lidice and My Lai, the French in Algeria, the Germans in Hungary, the Russians in Poland: the tales of horror seemed far away from the warm, fake castle in the flat countryside where the elderly couple, still in love lay sleeping, I imagined, in each other's arms. I wondered, now a new war had started, why Cris was so anxious to remember these old atrocities. As I finished reading and switched out the light, I realized there was something missing in that simple account of war crimes. It was the sound of anger and denunciation which I had been hearing since I was a schoolboy, the authentic voice of Dunster.

Chapter Six

The Absent Prince
by Paul Pry

No one was able to tell us where Prince Hamlet was last night. He was, perhaps understandably, staying on in college in Wittenberg to avoid the embarrassing proceedings which were going on in the gardens of St Joseph's. He did send an understudy, perhaps some remote relative of Horatio's who had once been in a school play. This unfortunate stand-in, referred to in the programme as one Philip Progmire, was clearly unable to afford a decent suit of mourning and came on wearing a well-used tweed jacket and jeans. He had also forgotten to have his glasses mended. Progmire's idea of acting seemed to be to stand about reciting the lines as though they were poetry or *familiar quotations*, a style of Shakespearian performance which you might think had long gone out of fashion, even in Denmark. His advice to the players was fairly well spoken; the only trouble was that he seemed unable to take any of it himself. Far from holding the mirror up to nature, he seemed to be holding it up to some hammy performance he once saw at the Old Vic.

It can't be said that the supporting cast was much help to the substitute Hamlet. Bethany Blair's Ophelia, straight down from Roedean, played the mad scene as though she'd had one too many glasses of claret cup at a May Ball. Her experience of 'country matters' was clearly confined to huntin', shootin' and fishin'. King Claudius and his 'lady wife' seemed a typical suburban couple, only slightly worried by the mortgage repayments and an outbreak of greenfly on the roses in the front garden. This pair of innocents probably thought that incest was something that Catholics burn in church.

Was there a bright spot in these gloomy goings-on, you may well ask? Just one. Paul Adams's Laertes struck exactly the right note of single-minded determination. He appeared to be the only passionate person at Court, although in this *Hamlet* the duel scene was about as exciting as a fight between an Olympic fencer and a short-sighted member of the Campaign for the Abolition of Sword-fighting.

It is worth noting that Nan Thorogood, who knows how Shakespeare should be acted, sat watching her production and was looking as unhappy as I felt. The gods passed their verdict by pissing on this production from a great height; it rained heavily in the second act.

'The little shit!'

We had bought the *Cherwell* at a newspaper shop in the Turl and were on our way towards the High Street and coffee. Beth was reading as she walked. The wind lifted her strawberry blonde hair and her forehead was furrowed.

'Who is?'

'Paul Pry!'

'It's not a good review?' I was beginning to get the message.

'Not exactly a rave. You could say that.' She aimed the *Cherwell* in my direction. I caught it and found the page. I only saw the headline, knew it would be a stinker about me and decided to spare myself the unnecessary pain of reading more of Paul Pry on Hamlet, and skipped to Ophelia.

'It's ridiculous,' I said.

'Oh, yes? I've been laughing ever since I bought the bloody thing.'

'You never even went to Roedean.'

'Of course I didn't! You don't think that idiot writes the truth, do you? He wouldn't even know what the truth was when he saw it. He's only interested in hurting people. Causing pain. That's what gives the little squirt his kicks.'

'Don't take it seriously,' I advised her.

'Seriously? Of course I don't take it seriously! I take it as being absolutely and entirely beneath contempt.'

'That's good then. We'll go and have a coffee.'

'What's the use of coffee! We'll go to the White Horse.'

After a large whisky Beth said, 'What're you going to do to him, Philip?'

'What did you say?'

'I said, what're you going to do to the little creep? At the very least punch his nose, I imagine.'

'All real pros get bad notices,' I told her, 'and they rise above them.'

'To begin with I'm not a real pro. And, to go on with, I have no intention of rising above it. One too many glasses of claret cup, indeed? I wouldn't be seen dead drinking claret cup. Look here. If you're not going to punch his nose for him, I will. I only know one thing. He's not going to get away with this.'

'Have another whisky.'

'All right. Then we'll plan the assault. What do you say we go and lie in wait for him? Both of us. May God forgive me if I don't knee him in the groin!'

I went to the bar and got her another whisky, hoping this would give her time to cool off. I made it a small one this time and put in a good deal of soda water. However, when I got back to the table where Beth was still crouched in fury, the cooling-off time had not been enough.

'We'll do that, won't we?' she said. 'Jump him in the dark and get a knee in there.'

'There's only a slight problem.'

'I don't see one.'

'We don't have the slightest idea who he is.'

'What on earth are you talking about? He's Paul Pry, isn't he?'

'That's what he writes under. I don't believe it's his real name.'

'You mean' – she looked up at me and I could see that her eyes had been full of tears – 'that the creep is hiding under an alias?'

'That's about the size of it.'

'Typical!' There was a pause while she drank. 'This whisky,' she said, 'doesn't taste as good as the last one.'

'I'm sorry.'

'But you'll find out who he really is, won't you?'

'I'll try.'

'You'll succeed. And then you'll do something awful to him. You promise me that?'

'Of course,' I said. Anything for a quiet life, but I had never kneed anyone in the groin before.

I found the office of the *Cherwell* on a top floor in Holywell. The editor was an eager, sharp-nosed, scurrying sort of person who seemed only to lack the courage to wear a green eye-shield and shout 'Hold the front page!' down a telephone. Long, flapping proofs were pinned up like Christmas decorations and in the background two mournful girls were pasting up pages in a martyred manner.

'Who is Paul Pry?' the editor said. 'I bet that fellow who played Hamlet would like to go and punch him on the nose.'

'Oh, I shouldn't think so,' I lied. 'It's just we'd like his name and college so we can send him an invitation to our next show.'

'Send the tickets here. That's the proper, professional way of doing it. And as for Paul Pry, you know we journalists never disclose our sources. Anyway, it's up to us to protect him from physical attack. Lots of actors threaten it. Come on, girls. The deadline's almost on us. We've got to get next week's paper to bed.'

When I left, the girls were plying their paste-brushes no faster than when I had arrived. I could think of only one other source of information.

'I mean, you write articles for all the magazines. You must know.'

'Must know what?'

'Who the little shit is who reviewed *Hamlet*.'

'I can't remember' – Dunster was looking at me with some

amusement – 'ever having seen you angry before, old man. Is this a breakthrough?'

'You think *I'm* angry. I'm almost completely calm compared to . . .' I hesitated.

'Compared to who?'

'Compared to other members of the cast.'

'You mean compared to Bethany Blair?'

'Naturally, she's extremely upset.'

'And you're upset because she's your girlfriend.'

'Well . . .'

'Oh, come on. Don't think it wasn't obvious. "There is a willow grows aslant a brook, That shows his hoar leaves in the glassy stream . . ." Don't look so pleased with yourself, Progmire.'

'No one could look pleased with themselves after that notice.'

'But you've got to admit, quite honestly, you weren't all that good?'

'Probably not.'

'But you wanted praise.'

'Of course I did. Everybody does.'

'So everybody expects a critic to lie.'

'Well, at least to look for the best things in a performance.'

'Why should he? Why shouldn't he look for the worst things if he wants to?'

'Because it's brutal. It causes unnecessary suffering.'

'To your girlfriend?'

'And to me, I suppose. If I've got to be honest.'

'Have you? I thought you didn't believe in honesty. Isn't honesty something rather beastly that hurts people's feelings?' He was sitting at his desk, among an indescribable mess of books and papers. There were at least three mugs of cold, half-drunk Nescafé and a paper plate smeared with yellow rice, a relic of some hastily snatched take-away, among the illegible, unfastened pages of an essay which had drifted on to the chairs around him and then fluttered on to the floor. He looked up and favoured me with one of his rare smiles.

'It's because you're my friend,' he said, 'that I expected so much more of you, Progmire. Because you're my friend I had to apply the highest possible standards.'

'You . . .?' Of course I should have known it all along. I had half guessed when I came into the room, but I put it past him. I was wrong. Nothing should be put past Dunster. '*You're* bloody Paul Pry!'

'A well-kept secret, don't you think?'

'So you wrote all that poison, about me and Beth?'

'Don't you understand, Progmire?' Dunster was still smiling as he explained it, as though to a child. 'I couldn't write something I didn't believe was true, just because we're friends. Could I?'

'I really don't see why not. It wouldn't've cost you anything.'

'It would have cost my integrity.'

'I don't give a fart about your integrity,' I had to tell him.

He looked at me then, very sadly, and refreshed himself from one of the cups of cold Nescafé. 'Progmire, you've always lived in a world of make-believe with absolutely no idea of morality.'

'Is it morality to make people miserable?'

'Sometimes it has to be.'

'If your precious integrity's so valuable to you, why didn't you get someone else to review *Hamlet*? Why not send one of those sad-looking girls from the office? They might have been glad of a night out.'

'They might not have told the truth. They might have thought I wanted them to go easy on my friend.'

'Oh, really?' I hope I sounded bitter. 'I'm sure no one could have suspected you of any decent, human, merciful feeling like that.' I had reached another point in my life when I was absolutely and entirely through with Dunster.

'I wanted to write the notice myself,' he said with maddening solemnity, 'because it was quite clearly my duty to do so.'

'"I was only doing my duty." That sounds like a sort of hangman's excuse.'

'Honestly, Progmire.' Dunster got up then and came over to me. He looked, as always, pale, overworked, untidy, uncombed, his long wrists and hands dangling from the sleeves of the jacket which had always been too small for him. 'I know you're a kind of actor, but don't try to dramatize everything. You haven't been sentenced to death. You've just got a bad notice. That's all. Perhaps acting just isn't your thing. I haven't written a word of criticism about your economics.'

I suppose I should have taken Beth's advice and struck him then. But I wanted to be out of the room, and I didn't want to touch him.

'You said we were friends,' I told him. 'Well, we're not any longer.'

'Why?' He was smiling again, maddeningly. 'Because you didn't get what you wanted out of me?'

'Because you've hurt someone I happen to love.'

'Nonsense. No one asked Bethany Blair to act Ophelia. If she didn't want to be criticized, she should've stayed at home reading the *Horse and Hound*.'

'Go and find someone else to be friends with,' I said. 'Some unfortunate bugger you can enjoy telling the truth to all the time. Give him my heartfelt sympathy, why don't you?'

I left him then. He was standing in the middle of the room looking, I was disgusted to see, not at all displeased with himself.

'Did you hit him?'

'Not exactly.'

'What does that mean? Did you knee him in the groin?'

'As a matter of fact I couldn't bring myself to.'

'What did you do to him, then?' Beth asked.

'I insulted him. I made him feel an absolute worm. I told him I never wanted to see or hear from him again and that our friendship was over. I must say, he looked pretty miserable about it.'

'Good.'

'Yes.'

'I'm glad your friendship's over. He was sorry about that, was he?'

'I think he realized exactly what I thought of him. Oh, and I told him he'd hurt the one person in the world I really loved.'

'What did he say to that?'

'Not much. He had a hangdog expression. All the arrogance had gone out of him.'

'So' – to my great relief Beth looked satisfied with what I'd told her – 'you made him suffer.'

'Absolutely. I made him suffer.'

We were in her college room having tea. She had bought a Swiss roll and chocolate biscuits, which were spread out on the rug in front of the electric fire. It was a treat, apparently meant for a returning warrior, although the battle had been bloodless.

'And you told him I was the one person in the world you loved?' she repeated, interested.

'And I meant it.' I took off my glasses, always, with me, a sign of sincerity.

'Well, then,' she said. 'I suppose we might as well.' She went to the door and locked it.

When we had made love and were lying together on her narrow bed she said, 'I don't think I'm cut out to be an actress.'

'Nonsense. You were brilliant.'

'No, I wasn't. I wasn't very good at all. I'm certainly not going to bother about the stage.'

'What're you going to be then?'

'Don't ask me that!' Her face had changed, or I saw it, as I lay beside her, from an entirely different angle. She looked like a furious child, much younger and less beautiful.

'I'm sorry.'

'Don't be sorry, for God's sake. Nothing. I'll probably be nothing. Why should we always be thinking about what we're going to be? What's it matter?' And then she was holding me tightly, her nails digging into my back, renewing our love-making with desperation, as though together we were gallop-ing away from a black and threatening place she never wanted to see again. At last she lay quiet, her hair spread over the pillow and her beauty, so far as I could see, restored.

In the time that followed the wounds inflicted on us by Paul Pry healed slowly.

Chapter Seven

There followed a period of freedom from Dunster. Of course I saw him. He seemed, as usual, to be everywhere. He was in hall when I had dinner with the thespians, he was in the street, in the White Horse, in the library when I went there to work, waving at me cheerfully from a distance. I didn't return his greetings and, in the vacation, when he rang me up at home I got my mother to tell him I was out. She hated lying and blushed like a young girl when she did so. She only undertook the task after I had shown her Dunster's notice of *Hamlet*. 'Pay no attention,' she said. 'He was probably jealous.' And she maintained her hostility to Dunster long after we had become, in some sort of way, reconciled.

My life was now centred entirely on Beth, whom I found a greatly preferable, but hardly more predictable, companion than my impossible school friend. For long periods, and for no apparent reason, Beth was aloof; she was busy with an essay, or writing home, or washing her hair. She wanted an early night or to be left alone for a week. Sometimes she went missing. Her room was empty and her friends confessed to not having seen her for days. Then, as suddenly, she would re-appear, tell me how much she had missed me, open my jacket and burrow inside it saying she hoped we would not be apart again. I'd take her to the Indian restaurant and she'd stop in mid curry so that we could rush off to make love – in her room, my room, or even in the battered Renault some friend who lived near her in the West Country had lent her. She was so impatient that she would start undoing buttons and zips as she drove, much too fast. I was, of course, flattered and delighted by this, although being a worrier I had visions of us being found impaled on some tree or lorry, stone dead with our zips undone. When we arrived at our destination she would control her impatience and proceed with the slow and deliberate expertise which always amazed me.

At the end of my second year I put my name down for a flat in a pink North Oxford mini château with a spire over the upstairs loo. I spent unnecessary days wondering how I was going to ask Beth to join me there, but as soon as she heard of it she assumed she was coming and asked Laertes and Gertrude to join us. My own acting career had peaked with *Hamlet*; it was then downhill all the way and I did pretty thankless roles, like Antonio in *The Merchant of Venice* – a miserable sod and not the sort of person you'd ever invite to a party – and Oliver de Boys, brother of the more famous Orlando, in *As You Like It*. Beth came to the thespian parties, gave us considerable encouragement but was no longer available for casting. I had hoped that when we moved into the flat everything would be different. It wasn't, altogether. Often she would go away in her car, saying she was meeting friends from home in London. Her departures were sudden and unpredictable, as were the times when she seemed remote, a strange girl who looked different as she sat, apparently drained of all energy, peering disconsolately into some bleak future she felt was inescapable.

She wanted to go to a May Ball, which I thought, with the expense of the flat and my mounting overdraft, would cost us too much. 'What the hell!' Beth brightened considerably at the thought of our poverty. 'We'll climb into Magdalen. You don't think I want to *dance* with all those rich twits, do you? Climbing in's the best part of the evening.'

She proved to be an altogether more reliable guide than Dunster. We drank a bottle of wine in the flat and then set off for the base camp under cover of darkness. Beth tucked up her long skirt, gave me her shoes to put in my pockets and we climbed from the roof of her parked Renault across some low battlements. I followed her white dress, climbing unsteadily,

while she seemed to move insubstantially as a ghost, a blur of
ectoplasm with long legs in tights. Then she dropped into the
safety of a shrubbery and held my hand as I scrambled down
after her. We joined a crowd going into a tent and there we
saw my other old school acquaintance, Porker Plumstead,
sitting mournfully in a corner with a cold collation on his knees.

'Progmire!' he called in the fruity upper-class voice he had
cultivated since leaving school. 'Why aren't you living with us
in the Cowley Road? We're all OGs together there.'

'Oh Gees . . .?' I was puzzled. 'Sounds like a lot of rather
outdated Americans.' Perhaps it was evening dress that made
me slip into my Noël Coward manner.

'Old Georgics. Have you entirely forgotten your school?
There's quite a nest of us. Self, your friend Dunster and one or
two others.'

'He's not my friend, actually.'

'Glad to hear that. He does make an incredible mess everywhere. You know what? He left his bloody pen in the marmalade. Odd sort of thing to do, wasn't it? But why aren't you
living with us?'

'I suppose I like it better living with Beth.'

'Beth?' He looked worried. 'I don't remember any Beth at St
George's.'

'No. This is Beth. She's a girl. In case you hadn't noticed.'

Beth had spotted an open bottle of champagne at Porker's
feet and was busily filling some used glasses she had found on
a nearby table.

'I say, Beth,' Porker confided in her, 'I've had a bloody
miserable evening. See this dinner jacket. Hopeless fit. I had to
hire it. And I'd had a specially beautiful one made at Hall's,
with sort of pale mauve lapels. My own design, actually. I say,
you two. Do have a drink.'

'Thanks.' Beth was looking at his upturned, discontented
face decorated with a touch of mayonnaise on the chin. 'We've
got one.'

'Well. This rather special D J arrived and apparently got left in a box on the hall table. And what do you think? Some wretched sneak thief got in and pinched it. Bit of a bloody cheek, don't you think?'

Beth gulped champagne and gave me a long and appealing look.

'Thanks for the drink, Porker. We'd better go and dance.' I was also anxious to be off.

'Certainly,' Beth said. 'After all, we paid all that money to get in.'

'But the mystery is – Well, you know what sneak thieves are. They're pretty poor, and thin, and out of a job, and probably never been to a ball in their lives. Well, what the hell would a sneak thief want with a dinner jacket with mauve facings?'

We left Porker then, unable to think of an answer to his question. We danced together for a little, but I'm not much better at it than Cris Bellhanger. Beth danced with a lot of other people, including Laertes, Osric, Horatio and Benson, the gravedigger. It was very late before she wanted to go home and I went to sleep quickly. I dreamed I was chasing her, a ghostly figure, across all the rooftops in Oxford. She was running very fast but her feet never touched the tiles. At last she rose high over the Radcliffe Camera and vanished into the night.

Some time after the May Ball we had a thespians' party in the flat, to which no Oh Gees had been invited. The next morning, leaving Beth sleeping, I wandered into the kitchen, put on the kettle and then went into the sitting-room to find some cups which I guessed would be filled with one-part cold instant coffee and two-parts cigarette butts. The curtains were still drawn, the room was dark and I had a strong feeling that I was not alone in it. My instinct was right. Dunster, looking pale and wearing his dark overcoat, was asleep on the sofa, having adopted the attitude of another pre-Raphaelite subject, the poet–forger Chatterton after poisoning himself. I kicked over an empty bottle and he spoke, 'Oh, there you are, Progmire. What time is it?'

'What do you mean, what time is it?'

'I just want to know the time, old man. It seems a fairly simple question.'

'And what the hell's the idea of coming in here, without an invitation, to sleep on our sofa? And waking up to ask the time, just as if you owned the place?'

'I just wanted to know' – Dunster was sometimes able to sound maddeningly reasonable – 'whether it's time for breakfast.'

'No, it's not time for breakfast. Anyway, no one here's going to have breakfast. They're probably all sick with hangovers. How did you get in here, anyway?'

'You left the window open. Don't you know that it's perfectly easy to climb up that ridiculous porch arrangement?'

I felt like giving up. I was surrounded, apparently, by urban mountaineers. At which point Beth came in, shivering in her dressing-gown, and said, 'Who're you talking to?'

'It's Dunster,' I said. 'You remember. Otherwise known as Paul Pry.'

She looked at him as he struggled to get to his feet and even performed some sort of bow to her. He spoke with rare courtesy. 'I hope what I wrote about your acting didn't cause you any sort of pain?'

'Of course it bloody did!' I made it clear to him. 'I told you. We all suffered outrageously.'

'Pain? Why ever should you think that?' I was amazed to see that Beth was smiling. 'I never took acting in the least seriously. In fact, I've given it up.'

'That, if I may say so, Bethany, is a wise decision. I congratulate you on your very sound sense.' I wondered why Dunster, that morning, was talking as though he were a character out of *School for Scandal*. I half expected him to say, 'Ma'am, your most obedient!' and bow his way out of the room.

'So, you see, I didn't mind at all about your notice. I'm afraid you upset Philip rather.'

'Oh, Philip's used to that. I've been upsetting him since we were snotty-nosed schoolboys together.'

'I wasn't all that upset,' I told him. 'As a matter of fact I don't read notices.' It was almost true as I had only managed a pain-filled glance at Paul Pry's verdict on my Dane.

'Oh, is that why you came to me in such a rage. After not having read it?'

'I was naturally concerned about Beth.'

'Well, I must say.' He smiled triumphantly at both of us, all pretence of humility gone. Dunster was himself again. 'You two show remarkable concern for each other. But just so long as I didn't offend either of you . . .'

'What do you think you're doing here?' I was determined to put Dunster back at his unusual disadvantage.

'That idiot Porker threw me out of the house. What's more, I can't get back. He's had the lock changed.'

'That doesn't surprise me in the least. I don't know why you went to share with him in the first place.'

'The poor fool was setting up a house for those he mistakenly believed to have been his friends at school. He's so obscenely rich that I thought at least it'd be comfortable.'

'And I suppose he chucked you out because of the appalling mess you take with you everywhere. Tell me, Dunster. Do you carry rubbish round with you in suitcases?'

'No. He chucked me out because I stole his dinner jacket.'

'You *what*?'

'There's this chap who lives in the basement. He's a protected tenant, so Porker can't get him out. Red Ned, they call him. He's a charge-hand up at the Cowley works. Mind if I have one of these?' Dunster was helping himself to someone's packet of cigarettes. 'And if you're making coffee . . .'

'Why on earth did you steal Porker's clothes?'

'I'm telling you. This Red Ned, for whom I have the most enormous respect, by the way, is involved in an unofficial dispute, so he and his supporters are getting no strike pay, although their claim is a 100 per cent justified. Well, he asked me to contribute to his fighting-fund.'

'So you contributed Porker's new tuxedo, with purple facings?'

'Well, not directly. I went and sold it at that Worn Again clothes shop in the covered market.'

'Dunster! That's theft.'

'Well, the tailor's chap left it in a box on the hall table. I had a look. It was such a ludicrous garment. People'd've come up to Porker and asked him to call them a cab. I mean, he'd've looked like a hall porter in it. So you see, I've very kindly spared him a great deal of humiliation.'

'But Porker's found you out.'

'Unfortunately. He spotted the damned thing hanging up in the covered market.'

'Is he going to turn you in to the police?'

'Naturally not. He'd only look more absurd than he does already: "Banker's son unwittingly donates ornate dinner jacket to striking car-workers". I could write a wonderful paragraph about it for the *Cherwell*.'

'I must say, he looked pretty sick at the May Ball. He'd had to hire one for the evening.' Beth smiled a great deal and often looked amused, but her laughter was a rare sound, full-blooded and louder than might be expected.

'Look here' – Dunster was clearly pleased by Beth's reaction – 'let me earn my keep by helping you tidy up. Some people,' he had the nerve to say as he looked round at the post-party confusion, 'do make the most ghastly mess of their places, don't they?'

'Earn your keep? What do you mean?' I asked him. 'We're not keeping you here, Dunster.'

'Of course you're not. And I wouldn't dream of asking. Red Ned promised to let me in the basement when he gets back from the meeting. Porker's mad if he thinks he's seen the last of me. Anyway, Prudence is buying me lunch to cheer me up. So, I'll just help you wash up and get the breakfast . . .'

I have to admit that Dunster was on his best behaviour that morning. He collected cups and glasses, he dried up and didn't break anything. He asked Beth about her home, her horse and her essay on Jane Austen. He was reasonably funny about the latent snobbery of his Marxist tutor, and Porker's increasingly desperate attempts to find a girlfriend. He even told me that he thought I made a 'very interesting Antonio' in *The Merchant* and if he'd still been doing Paul Pry he'd have come out and said so. As he left us he said, 'Well, my dear old Progmire. Thank God, we're friends again. I've felt something missing in my life without you.' And when I heard that, my heart sank.

After he had gone Beth said, 'As a matter of fact, your friend Dunster seems all right.'

'What do you mean. All right?'

'Well, quite entertaining, really. There doesn't seem to be any real harm in him.'

'Beth, you don't know the man. He's a disaster area. He's a minefield. He invites every sort of catastrophe. He's accident prone and his condition is highly contagious. My life has only been entirely happy since we stopped seeing each other.'

'Didn't you miss him?'

'Do you miss toothache?'

'Oh, Philip darling.' Beth was sitting at the kitchen table, eating toast and marmalade. 'I'm sure you're exaggerating.'

But, of course, I wasn't.

Chapter Eight

'I think it's about time I submitted you to the ordeal.'

'What ordeal?'

'The ordeal by fire and ice . . .'

'What's that meant to mean?'

'I think it's time you met my dad.'

'What about your mum?'

'Oh, she's not an ordeal at all.'

'Does he want to meet me?' I began to worry about a difficult confrontation when I might be asked about my intentions, or even about financial prospects. My only intention, I should have to say, was to hold on to Beth for as long as possible, which, at that time, I didn't expect to be forever.

'I shouldn't think he wants to meet you in the least. He doesn't often want to meet people. Anyway, not unless they've been Masters of Foxhounds. You haven't ever been one of those, have you?'

'Not so far as I remember.'

'Then he won't want to meet you.'

'Then why . . .?'

'I think it's only fair.'

'What's only fair?'

'That you should know the worst about me.'

So Beth drove me to Exmoor. The hedges were so high they towered over the roads which became green tunnels. We shot through little towns, full of gift shops and tea-rooms and elderly couples with rucksacks – the women in large flowered cotton dresses and the men wearing socks and sandals. Then we crossed the moorland and the wild ponies took fright, as I often did, at Beth's driving. We turned up a lane where a poker-work notice, suspended from a sort of wrought-iron gallows, announced Blair Cottage.

If this suggested a thatched roof and roses trailing across the porch, the truth was something quite other. It was less of a cottage and more of a house, and a gaunt, uncompromising house at that. At one time its plaster might have been bright yellow; now it was the colour of pale custard, baked and cracked with the passage of time. There were stables and a concreted yard but no flowers or flowerbeds, only a tide of gravel which flowed up to the walls. Our arrival produced an uproar of barking, yapping and over-excited squeals, together with feverish scratching at the other side of the front door. Beth said, 'Do you mind dogs?'

'I quite like them.'

'You're not going to like these.'

At which moment the door opened, apparently with some difficulty, and an uncomfortable number of small animals came plunging out, as excited as though they had been starved for a considerable period and Beth and I were two overflowing bowls of Pedigree Chum. One deafening white bundle of hair left the ground like a Scud missile and, aiming itself at my groin, scored a direct hit. Others stood on their hind legs and scrabbled with uncut claws at my trouser legs. It was true, as I had told Beth, that I have absolutely no objection to dogs *per se*. What I can't understand is why they all have such an irresistible desire to home in on my genitals. After the dogs came a tall, thin woman with reddish hair. In the shadow of the house I could have taken her for Beth's sister, even for Beth herself if my late Ophelia hadn't been standing beside me. And then, as she stepped out of the square of shadow, the sun hit her face unkindly and I saw a tracing of lines round her eyes like cracks on the varnish of an old painting.

'Hullo, darling,' she said to Beth, and to me, 'I'm Mike Blair.'

Michaela, Beth had told me, was her mother's name. Mike

was what her husband always called her. She was now lugging one of Beth's bursting holdalls out of the boot. Despite my protests, she started to walk up to the house with it. She was a woman who seemed used to carrying things. Beth walked with her arm round her mother's waist. Their heads were very close together, as though they were sharing secrets, but all I heard was: 'How are things?' from Beth, 'Much the same' from Mike, and 'I'm sorry about that' from her daughter as we walked into the house, the dogs yelping and bounding at our heels.

This was the first of many visits to Blair Cottage and I never crossed its threshold without being amazed at the high degree of physical discomfort to which the English sportsman is prepared to submit himself and his family. I had always imagined that hunting went with the blazing log-fires, crumpets for tea and steaming baths after a long run. Not at all. Chez Blair always struck a chill into my bones, even on the hottest of summer days. In the winter I felt I needed an overcoat to go upstairs and in the mornings Beth and I often found ice on the inside of the bedroom windows. In the sitting-room, among the ponderous furniture with its faded chintz covers frayed by the worrying of generations of terriers, the single bar of an electric fire illuminated plastic coals without producing a great deal of comfort. The light was shed by the dimmest of bulbs, often covered in thick shades on which hunting scenes were depicted. On my visits to her parents, I felt that Beth had gone into a cold country where I would always be a stranger. She understood this and between the icy sheets of her bed, surrounded by rosettes and silver cups and the photographs of her jumping her ponies at local gymkhanas, she was always especially and actively loving to make up for the Spartan nature of her home.

She was never able to tell me how her father, christened Jonathan, had acquired his nickname. Perhaps it was bestowed on him in some long disbanded mess as a cynical joke. I never saw him with his cap at an angle, sauntering along with his hands in his pockets or whistling gaily – my idea of jauntiness. The Major was short and square, with the wary and dangerous eye of an unpredictable horse and an expression of extreme discontent. He only cheered up slightly when talking to his daughter. They had, it seemed to me, a hidden understanding, although they never used anything like words of affection to each other. When he spoke to Mike, the Major's scowl was especially pronounced.

When I first met Jaunty he was sitting at the kitchen table, warming his hands on a cup of instant coffee and reading the local paper. He was wearing riding breeches, green socks and carpet slippers. One sleeve of his sweater was in an advanced state of disintegration, as though it had been chewed by rats or horses. At his feet lay a black lurcher which was, I was thankful to see, asleep.

'So Mister Progmire. My daughter got you down here all in one piece, did she? Amazing!' The Major had a curiously high, rasping voice and he always addressed me with sardonic formality.

'As a matter of fact, sir.' ('For God's sake stop calling him "sir",' Beth said when we were, at last, in bed. 'It makes him even more impossible.') 'Beth drives very well.'

'She drives as she rides. Like a maniac. You want a cup of Nescafé? It's watery and revolting. The odd thing is,' he confided in Beth, 'in bloody nearly thirty years of marriage your mother's never managed to give me a decent cup of Nescafé.'

Mike spooned the powder into a mug with a stoic smile and her husband turned on me with a serious accusation.

'I hear from Beth, Mister Progmire, that your family lives in Muswell Hill.'

'Yes. We've been there all my life.'

'Not much hunting country round Muswell Hill, I don't suppose?'

'Philip doesn't ride,' Beth said. 'So, for heaven's sake, don't go on at him.'

I was grateful to her. Some cousins had once persuaded me to go out with them in Epping forest. I had spent an anxious hour clinging to the animal's mane while it demonstrated the highly neurotic nature of all horses by trembling at the sight of babies in pushchairs and side-stepping nervously at the threat posed to it by scraps of paper. When my position had been made clear by his daughter, Jaunty ignored me and I drank some perfectly adequate Nescafé. He and Beth discussed the animals, the extraordinary love life of the Field Master of the hunt, and the 'jumped-up pox doctor' (in fact, Beth told me later, a heart surgeon from Bristol) who was turning the cottage along the lane into a 'kind of suburban knocking shop' complete with a 'vulgar little conservatory' and other signs of urban decadence. I do, as I have made clear already, worry about many things, some of them are unimportant, but Major Blair was a serious cause for anxiety. Only the thought that Beth was always on my side kept me relatively calm during the time I spent going through an ordeal as daunting as that faced by any of the great lovers of history.

That night we sat together in the Blair Cottage dining-room, which was decorated with parts of dead animals. The shrewd faces of decapitated foxes peered down from the walls and a stag's hoof ('It's a slot,' Beth corrected me later) set in silver was the centrepiece of the table. Jaunty carved us, with surgical precision, wafer-thin slices from a very small joint of beef. 'You're not a veggie, are you?' The Major's small, yellow eye regarded me with deep suspicion.

'No, Dad. Philip eats meat.'

'Thank God for that! We get the veggies out in force with the hunt. Wearing bobble hats. So bloody fond of animals that they string up wires for the horses to trip over and stub out cigarettes on the rumps of children's ponies. You know, I feel sorry for your generation, Mister Progmire. Bad luck, really. Born without a war to go to.'

70

'Do shut up, Dad,' Beth told her father. 'Philip and I aren't in the least interested in wars.'

'I pity you. I saw the last war coming. All the signs were there. Joined up. Lied about my age. Commissioned when I was twenty. Best years of my life, quite honestly. Soldiering.'

There was no reaction from Mike, dishing out the vegetables, to the fact that the best years of her husband's life hadn't included her.

'You don't know what's in a geezer,' Jaunty told us, 'until you've watched him advancing up a hill towards a few other geezers with machine-guns. The great thing about war is that it shows up character.'

'It seems a bit of an expensive way of doing it. Some people might rather stay alive than have their characters shown up!' Beth never seemed to take her father seriously.

'A lot of them were like that.' The Major was not smiling at me and yet his nearest eye appeared to wink. 'I'm sure you'd understand that, Mister Progmire. A lot of them much preferred to stay alive. A good many of them turned tail and ran. They keep quiet about that in the military histories. Anyway, that's why I feel sorry for geezers like you, Mister Progmire. You've never had your courage tested.'

'Don't you believe it. He's played Hamlet in St Joseph's College gardens. That's a bit like being under fire.' Beth showed me the consideration due to a foreigner in a strange land.

'No comparison!' Jaunty was certain of it. 'There's always been wars. Wars have been going forever. And how long's *Hamlet* been going?'

'Only about three centuries.' I felt something warm between my thighs, not Beth's hand but the lean head of the lurcher. Now awake, it was carrying out the usual doggish inspection of my private parts.

'I got my education in the barracks at Catterick, followed by a pretty hairy spell in the desert. Ever been in a tank,

Mister Progmire? Little tin oven. Desert heat. Geezers got trapped in those when they were shelled. The sands were crowded with pranged tanks and dead geezers still in them.' The Major produced a crumpled silk handkerchief as though, even in his icy dining-room, he sweated at the memory. 'After that a rather hairy time in Italy.' He seemed relieved to pass on to another campaign. 'Kick that bloody dog away if she's troubling you.'

'No. It's perfectly all right.' I pushed away the questing mouth and crossed my legs.

'If I had my way, this wimpish government wouldn't waste our money on universities. What the hell was wrong with National Service?'

Beth said, 'Come off it, Dad. You mean you'd rather I was a lance corporal for three years? Square-bashing!' I often wondered if the Major were playing an elaborate game, designed to deter his daughter's lovers. No one, I thought, could actually hold his opinions. In the end I had to admit that he probably could and did.

'What do you learn there, anyway, Mister Progmire? Apart from *Hamlet*?'

'Philip does economics,' Beth told him.

'Oh, yes? Are you going to be a banker?'

'I'm not sure. I'll probably end up as an accountant.'

For the first time Jaunty looked at me as though I were not a bobble-hatted vegetarian and hunt saboteur.

The next day it rained steadily. Mike and I sat in the kitchen and watched as Beth and her father put their animals into the lorry to drive off to the meet. Jaunty's mount looked enormous to me. It was a grey which snorted, tossed its head and backed in panic each time it approached the horsebox. At last Beth led the huge animal round the yard, patting its nose and apparently speaking to it in a conciliatory way. On the last lap it danced up the ramp for her. The Major slammed the door shut. For a moment he and his daughter hugged each other in triumph and I thought they looked like children after a successful game. Then they got into the lorry and drove away.

Mike said, 'I'm so glad Beth got to know you. It's a thoroughly good thing.' I was feeling a glow of appreciation when she added, 'At least I'll have someone to talk to when they're out hunting.'

We sat for a while in silence and then she said, 'You seem so calm. Beth's never been calm. Neither has Jaunty.' Calm! I wondered how Beth's mother could be so easily mistaken as I sat, a bundle of nerves, in that strange household, disconcerted by the Major, ill at ease with the dogs, deeply distrustful of the horses and even worried about the night to come, because it occurred to me that so much pleasure so easily given might vanish unexpectedly. As I thought of the future, I heard Mike's gentle voice telling me her troubles. 'It's not us that's extravagant. It's the horses. They eat so much and they're always ill. I can't understand it. Jaunty and I have hardly had a day's illness since we married. And Beth was never sick, not even as a child. But those great horses hardly draw a well breath. Their medical bills are quite terrifying. It's not just the vets. It's the physio. It's the injections. The ultra-sound. Sometimes I think it's a whole lot of fuss about nothing. I think those damn horses are hypochondriacs. Jaunty's almost dead with worry about it all.'

'But if they're so expensive, couldn't he give them up?'

'You don't understand. Jaunty wouldn't be Jaunty, not without horses. Do help him if you can spare the time, Philip. He seems to have the most terrible difficulty adding up.'

No more was said about help for Jaunty then, or for a long time to come. I read in the kitchen, keeping warm by the cooker, and the dogs, having grown bored, no longer abused me. Mike ironed a number of Jaunty's shirts and after tea Beth came back. Her jacket, waistcoat and even the white stock at her throat (she told me to call it a hunt tie) were spattered with mud. 'I fancied you when you went out,' I told her, 'but the mud's made it suddenly more urgent.'

'A lot of men say that.' Beth smiled. 'It's really rather disgusting of them.' Later she said, 'I think you've passed the ordeal.'

'You don't mean your father likes me?' I was incredulous.

'Oh, I wouldn't go so far as that. But he seems to think you'll do.'

It was not until I had paid Blair Cottage a number of visits that Jaunty asked me to help him with his accounts.

'I have this bloody man,' he said, 'who's meant to be an accountant. But he's in trouble himself. Woman trouble.'

I told him I was sorry to hear it.

'Two on the side and one at home who's threatening legal action. That is when she's not taking the law into her own hands, slashing his tyres and so forth. Anyway, he's up to his eyes in the smelly stuff, so he wants me to do my own VAT, work out my own expenses. I thought you paid these fellows to invent the expenses, at the very least.'

We were in his office, a small downstairs room which might have been used as a refrigerator. 'It's no use complaining,' Beth said, 'Dad simply doesn't feel the cold.' There was a bulging bureau, its top piled high with yellowing back numbers of the *Field* and *Horse and Hound* and its interior stuffed with forgotten bills, unopened bank statements and letters of almost pathetic complaint from the Inland Revenue. I took the whole lot into the kitchen, warmed my hands on the cooker and started, for the first time, a sort of filing system. Jaunty had decided to put all his faith in an undergraduate with a head for figures who had come into his home to make love to his daughter. After I had gone through his bank statements and made some sense of the scribbled invoices, I had a more or less clear idea of his financial situation.

As a matter of fact he was reasonably well off. The stables, built on a grander scale than the house, accommodated a number of horses at livery. His charges were high and might have brought him in a reasonable income if he'd had any regular system for sending out the bills. Most of the stable work was done by dedicated girls whose wages he'd forgotten to pay. Apart from the livery business he had his army pension, increased by compensation for a wound in his right leg which didn't seem to prevent him riding regularly to hounds. In addition to that his bank accounts showed a regular payment in, which I asked him to explain.

'Chap I used to soldier with. He took a shine to me. He knew I only had my pension, until I got this place and started the stables working. So he remembered me.'

'You mean, it's money he left you?'

'You could put it that way, I suppose. I say, aren't you sweating hot, sitting hunched up by that cooker?' He threatened to open the window but I told him I couldn't afford to have the scattered clues to his income blown away. In my researches at that time I never learned any more about Jaunty's useful source of income. My university economics course didn't include tax reduction schemes, but I had a bank manager uncle who told me that if Jaunty's stables became a private company he would save on his payment of bank interest. I don't know if he ever adopted this idea, but when I suggested it he looked at me as though I were the Delphic Oracle, and after that he often asked my advice on money matters and treated me with increased respect.

After we'd done our finals Beth and I took a punt and tied it up under the willow tree where I had first made love to Ophelia.

'It's all over,' she said.

'What do you mean?' I was worried.

'I don't mean us. I mean this part of it. Oxford and all that. You know when you asked me what I was going to be . . .'

'And you didn't want to think about it.'

'Well. I've thought about it lately.'

'So what is it then?'

'I suppose . . .' She was busy eating a greengage and now she spat the stone into the river. 'A wife and mother. Some sort of nonsense like that.'

'I never thought of anything so permanent.' I honestly hadn't.

'You mean you don't want to get married?'

'Of course I do.'

And as we lay on the worn, much-used velvet cushions she said, 'It wasn't to be expected that you'd be such a terrific hit with Dad.'

Before we left Oxford I had a letter from Dunster.

Dear Progmire

I bumped into Beth Blair the other day. I mean literally. She was crossing Banbury Road and I was coming back from a boring party on my bicycle. I managed to brake and it was only a minor sort of contact. I promised to pay for her tights. Anyway, she said she'd proposed marriage to you and you'd blushed a bit and said yes. She said that in the pub where I took her for a bit of a stiffener as she seemed rather shaken after contact with the bike. I told her that as your best friend over many years, in fact by my calculation, and discounting those insufferable actors you chose to associate with, your only friend, I had no doubt you would be asking me to be your best man. Now I have very little patience with the idea of dressing up in some sort of undertaker's suit and taking part in the sanctified sale of young women into slavery, or at least hard, unpaid labour in the kitchen as well as in the maternity ward. All the same, I told Beth, to whom I felt I owed something after the collision, which may have been caused because I was greatly preoccupied with the murder of Allende as I pedalled along, that I would hire the rig-out and make sure the ring was in my waistcoat pocket, and generally give you the moral support which you'd need if you weren't going to change your mind about thirty times on your way to the altar. She seemed absolutely chuffed when I agreed to do the necessary and said of course I could stay with her family and all I needed was a good deal of tolerance. It seems her father is a rather tricky piece of work so we ought to get on like a house on fire.

Don't bother to thank me, old man. The fact that you've actually made up your mind about something in your life simply has to be celebrated. See you in church.

Everlastingly yours
Dick Dunster

'Don't bother to thank him? I'll thank him to keep away from my wedding.'

'Don't do that,' Beth said. 'He seemed so excited about it all.'

'I'm not getting married,' I told her, 'for the purpose of exciting Dunster.'

'He's probably made all sorts of plans.'

'Of course he hasn't. He never makes plans at all. He'll miss the train and arrive late and he won't have hired the suit.'

'I don't suppose the suit really matters.'

'And he'll probably quarrel with your father.'

'That might be interesting.'

'Look. I don't want to stand up in church, vowing to love and honour you, or whatever it is, with the shadow of Dunster looming up behind me.'

'Then you decide it, darling.' Beth smiled and kissed me. 'You decide whatever man seems best for you.'

I tried to draft a number of letters rejecting Dunster's offer but they all sounded pompous. Dunster was right; years ago, when we were ink-stained schoolboys, we had taken each other for better or for worse, for richer or for poorer, in sickness or in health, and there was nobody else I had known better or for so long. To ask Laertes or Benson, the grave-digger, to do the job would seem an insult to our long past. Anyway, Beth didn't mind and to accept Dunster would probably be less trouble than turning him down.

*

'Nothing goes with Beth. No land, no cows. No diamond tiaras. You do realize that, don't you, Mister Progmire?'

'Of course I do.'

'I can't even give you much for a wedding present. There's a rather good saddle I might spare you, if you'd care for it.'

'I don't think so.'

'Not much use for it in Muswell Hill, eh?'

'No. Not much use for it there.'

'So. You'll have to keep Beth in the manner to which she's become accustomed.'

I can do better than that. I might even run to a decent central heating system – I might also have said that, but I didn't. In fact I said, 'Of course I will.' But with a second in PPE and no immediate job prospects I wasn't quite sure how.

'Beth needs a good deal of understanding. She's a lot like me.' I looked at the crafty, wrinkled face, the bald head and tufts of hair on the cheek-bones and I thought that nothing was ever less like Ophelia. We were sitting together after breakfast. Beth had gone into Tavistock with her mother to see about the bridesmaids' dresses and I was left at the mercy of Jaunty and the dogs.

'There is one thing I *can* do for you. And I'm pleased to have the chance of helping the young hopeful.' He leant back in his chair and looked at me in a manner which seemed vaguely threatening. 'How'd you like to work for a television company, Mister Progmire?'

'Well, of course . . .' I was more than a little astonished. 'I've been in lots of plays. I'm sure I'd be able to direct.'

'Not that exactly.'

'You don't mean acting?'

'God, no. Forget acting. You told me yourself you got slated by the critics. No. I mean in the accounts department. There's a fellow I know. He's a – Well . . . he's a connection of mine. I suppose you think I'm just an old fart who spends his time knee-deep in horse shit. Well, let me tell you, young

78

hopeful. I have connections. Everyone has, who's knocked about the world a bit.'

So that, strangely enough, was how I got started at Megapolis. Before then, I, Philip William Progmire, took Bethany Abigail Blair to be my lawful wedded wife. Dunster arrived the afternoon before the ceremony with his suit neatly packed in a box from Moss Bros. He was greeted by Beth's family with what I thought was unjustified respect. Even the dogs failed to leap at his crotch and slunk into their baskets, as though in the presence of a power which they, for some totally unknown reason, respected. That night I had a stag party among the oak beams and horse-brasses of the Jolly Huntsman which Jaunty insisted on attending. He sat next to Dunster and listened to him attentively, his head cocked and an ear occasionally cupped in his hand, as though fearful of missing any of the pearls of wisdom likely to drop from my best man's lips.

'I suppose you couldn't miss the stag party because you're so tremendously fond of stags?' Dunster suggested to the Major, and I became exceedingly anxious.

'Of course. Beautiful creatures. Everyone on the moor is extremely fond of them.'

'Is that why you keep on killing them?'

'Have to, of course. They need culling. For the good of the species.'

'So you're doing them a kindness, really?'

'Certainly we are.'

'Keeping down the numbers?'

'That's exactly it.'

'So you find one grazing peacefully and chase it for miles. Then you kill it when it gets into a stream to cool down.'

'Shot first, by the hunt servants. Then cut up, of course. That's the way it's done,' Jaunty agreed. In the pause that followed I hoped Dunster had done with the subject, but he had only been preparing the ground for attack. 'Would you agree, sir,' he asked the Major politely, 'that there are too many people in the world?'

'Yes, of course, there are. Lanes clogged up with little men driving with their hats on. Moor covered with trippers in the summer. Far too many.'

'Particularly old people. Some of them aren't much use, are they?'

'Dunster!' I tried an interruption. 'Has that bottle got stuck to the table?' My best man took absolutely no notice, but went on cheerfully.

'So, Major Blair. If you were to spot an old age pensioner on some lawn or other . . .'

'Say again?' Jaunty was, perhaps, feigning deafness.

'If you found an old lady sitting in the sun somewhere,' Dunster shouted, quietening the noisy table.

'I heard you the first time.'

'I mean, you might decide to cull her. You might get the dogs to chase her across the moor for three or four hours. Then, when she cooled her feet in a stream somewhere, the hunt servants could shoot her and cut her up?'

You've done it again, Dunster, I thought. I can't even get married without you coming down and starting a violent argument with my father-in-law. But then I saw Jaunty looking at me and, for the first time in our acquaintance, he was smiling.

'Your friend, Mr Dunster,' he said with apparent delight, 'is extraordinarily entertaining company. He must cheer up all you frightfully serious geezers at Oxford.'

'I do my very best,' Dunster agreed. 'It's not always appreciated.'

I got married in a cloud of pride and apprehension and I spent the evening in an alcoholic daze. Blair Cottage was warmed at last by the presence of innumerable bodies, young and old, beautiful and grotesque, some dancing, some clasped together in corners, some singing in the kitchen. There were hunt followers and Oxford thespians, Beth's countless cousins and Jaunty's band of creditors. Through it all Mike smiled patiently and Jaunty introduced my best man to all his friends and acquaintances as Mr Dunster: 'First really bright fellow ever came out of Oxford. Brilliant raconteur, this one. Quite brilliant.' I was standing with Beth and her mother when someone came and told us that the girl groom was taking a bath with both Polonius and Guildenstern. 'Oh, dear,' Mike said, with what I thought was admirable concern, 'I'm afraid there's never very much hot water.'

Later, very much later, finding the lavatory occupied by a number of people, I wandered out on to the gravel. I was standing there in the moonlight when I heard voices and saw some lights from the stable block. There was a crash and the sound of hoof beats on concrete and Jaunty's neurotic grey hunter appeared with a dark figure aboard. At first I took the rider, who wore a black coat with flapping tails, for a waiter, but I should have known better. As the animal trotted, with increasing speed, from the yard, the moonlight fell on the determined face of Dunster. I'm sure that my best man had never ridden a horse before, but he kicked it with his heels, held the reins with one hand and the mane with another, and went cantering down the lane. Then, to my utter amazement, the horse gathered its wits together, paused for only a moment and then took the dark, ill-omened figure of Dunster crashing through the twigs and branches at the top of a hedge and on to the moor. As I watched them hurl themselves into the shadows I was conscious of Jaunty beside me, holding a dark tumbler of whisky, and I waited for the inevitable explosion.

'My God!' he said, and I swear he was still smiling. 'You've got to hand it to him. Your friend Mr Dunster has spunk!'

Chapter Nine

All these things happened a long time ago, in and around the period of *Hamlet*, a performance, which like the acting out of my own youth, may not have been entirely satisfactory but which yet gave me a great deal of pleasure. Now I was Trigorin, a middle-aged author, 'charming perhaps but very inferior to Tolstoy'. By bullying the local businesses and incessantly begging for money, the Muswell Hill Mummers had built a small theatre, known to us, somewhat archly, as the Mummery. There we rehearsed, quarrelled, started up love affairs, had attacks of stage-fright and rare moments of triumph, and made most of our money from the bar and the sale of ice-cream in the intervals. We opened in January and came into immediate competition with the new hit show on television *Operation Dust Storm*. Generals strangely camouflaged, pointing at maps like schoolteachers, streams of tanks crossing the desert, spectacular firework displays and bombs with an unerring sense of direction and endless speculation as to what might or might not happen when the war really got going – these things provided the peace-loving citizens of Muswell Hill with a nightly entertainment far more spectacular and engrossing than *The Seagull*. The house on the first night was so thin that I had no difficulty in spotting Cris Bellhanger in the third row, next to the aisle.

'I enjoyed it very much. In all sincerity.' I had found him standing alone with half a pint of lager in the bar after the show. The actors were calling each other darling and pretending to be professionals. 'God, I was really down in the second act!' and 'What about the Bath chair wheels sticking? Didn't you notice? We had to slide Dennis out in it, and he weighed about a ton.' Standing still among so much fluttering Cris said, 'A man who can take a rational view of himself is a rare thing. I thought you managed that very well. I'll buy you a beer.'

We carried our half pints to a bench by the wall and sat under caricatures of leading Mummers, remote from the still over-excited actors. I said, 'This *is* a surprise.'

'You sent me an invitation.'

'I never expected you'd come.'

'That was a mistake. If you do something, you should expect the consequences. Angie'll be sorry she missed it, stuck in the country.'

'Just as well. She's a professional.'

'She's watching television. Reminds her of her old war films, I suppose. Only thing that's missing is Johnny Mills.' His smile concealed, I thought a deep feeling of revulsion at the sight of another army on the move. As an old soldier he was, in contrast to Major Jaunty, more of a pacifist than I could be sure of being. 'I wanted to talk to you,' he said, 'out of the office. I wanted to ask your advice. You know a good deal about drama.'

Around us the actors were getting ready for the first-night party. Madame Arkadina was taking the cling film off the sandwiches and sausage rolls. She was a large and muscular physiotherapist who approached Chekhov's play as though it were a patient complaining rather too much about a slightly sprained ankle. Nina, now wearing jeans and a Muswell Hill Mummers T-shirt, came staggering in with a box of wine and smiled at me as she eased it on to the bar. She was called Lucy and had just qualified as a solicitor. We had giggled together a little during rehearsals about Pam the physio's briskly common sense approach to the play.

'I don't know nearly as much as the professionals in the drama department at Metropolis.'

'That's rubbish. The last three instalments of *Social Workers* have been complete garbage.' Cris lowered his voice a little, although none of the actors was paying us the slightest attention. 'What I want to put to you, as a bit of an expert on the subject, is this. Drama and real life are totally different things, aren't they? Poles apart.'

'Well, not exactly.'

'Don't bother about all that "not exactly".' Cris was always impatient of imprecise language at board meetings. 'One is the truth and the other's fiction. Quite obviously.'

'Well, I shouldn't have said it was absolutely obvious.'

'You should never have acted Hamlet at Oxford. You seem incapable of coming to a clear view.'

'Well, there you are, you see.'

'Where am I?'

'Drama and life. They do get mixed up. From time to time.' And bring you some good times, I thought, until the curtain comes down and you discover it was just a play.

I looked over to where Lucy, my Nina, was opening the box of wine. She was talking to someone I had seen in the audience – a small man with a pale, bald head and a healthy growth of black beard, so that his face was like one in those old comic drawings which would make sense which ever way up it was. Lucy was smiling modestly at him as he left her and I thought he must have been saying something complimentary about her performance. He nodded a little nervously at me as he went out.

Cris said, 'Let's try to keep it simple, shall we? For the sake of the average punter who'll see *War Crimes* in the intervals between making love, or Nescafé or whatever.'

'All right.'

'What we're going to be making are documentaries. We want to tell it as it happened, don't we?'

'I imagine that's the aim.'

'Don't imagine anything. Plain, hard facts. That's what we're after.'

'Well . . .'

'None of your gloomy Dane doubts about it. If it isn't true, it's not worth doing.'

'I suppose not.'

'The people we've got working on *War Crimes*, I'm afraid, may have a remarkable talent for invention. I'm just nervous they might like a good story better than a real story. We want reporters, not artists.'

He didn't mention the name Dunster, but I knew who he was talking about. The excitement of the first night, the adrenalin generated by the challenge of performance, the joyful relief at having got through it, had drained away. I was left with the certainty that I was about to hear bad news. I didn't know then how bad. In fact I felt there was one thing Cris needn't worry about; so far as I was concerned Dunster was no more an artist than I was Laurence Olivier.

'I don't want anyone to start inventing for the sake of dramatic effect.'

'I suppose not.'

'It's particularly tricky, you see, when it comes to a war crime committed by our own people.'

'Were there some?'

'Of course.' Our audience was leaving the bar now and the excitement of the actors was growing. There was a pop and a cry of delighted concern as the first sparkling champagne-style bottle was opened and shed froth. 'They didn't get called crimes because no one was ever tried for them. Only the defeated commit crimes. But, oh yes, we did them. That's why I want a programme about one. It's the whole point of the series.'

Another bottle exploded. Konstantin, in love with Nina, played by a dark and soft-voiced young man in computers, arrived with his new Indian girlfriend. It seemed worlds away from the hidden crimes of an almost-forgotten war.

'They've got hold of a story about the Italian campaign. It's something I remember.'

'You told me.'

'It was an incredibly confused situation. So many groups involved. The German Army, of course, and the Allies. And then you've got German SS chasing Communist partisans, some of our SAS groups in the mountains, and the Italian fascists who were the real bastards ... Well, it's hard for someone of your age to get that lot sorted out. Hard for anyone, come to that.'

'I can imagine.' I was tired and my mouth was dry. I didn't want to hear about Dunster's problems.

'It would be so easy to get the wrong idea. Perhaps accuse an innocent person. We might do a terrible injustice, land ourselves in huge libel damages.' Cris smiled. 'That should worry the accounts department.'

'Is there a particular story?' I asked him.

'I've got an idea they've got hold of one. It concerns a Brit, I believe. Still alive. Chap who keeps his head down somewhere in the depths of the countryside. I wouldn't want us to trouble his old age for nothing.'

'What about a glass of bubbles?' Nina, the solicitor, approached us as we sat with the tide of the party rising around us. 'And wouldn't your friend like to stay for the bash?'

'No, no, thank you very much. It was a wonderful evening.' Cris lied convincingly and said to me, with his hand on my shoulder, 'You enjoy yourself.'

'What do you want me to do about what you've told me?'

'Nothing for the moment. I'll have to think about it. What we really need is someone completely sensible to keep an eye on it. We've got to be so careful. I mean, for God's sake. We don't want to commit another war crime, do we?'

'You think we might?'

'It's just possible. Is that the time?' He had taken out the gold watch he kept on a chain in his waistcoat and looked amazed at what it told him. 'Angie'll think I've dropped dead. Have a terrific party. You deserve it. I didn't mean to spoil your evening.'

'Good-night, Cris.'

He walked away from us and, when he reached the door, didn't look round but raised his hand in a sort of distant salute. I thought it a gesture of sadness at the prospect of going home to another war on the telly.

'I was terrible tonight.' Nina, otherwise Lucy, had taken Cris's seat after he had left.

'No, honestly, I thought you were very good.'

'You're lying. I was terrible.'

'Not a bit of it. You've got to remember, Nina was a bad actress. It takes a remarkable actress to play a bad actress well.'

'You mean, I was just a bad actress playing a bad actress? I just wish you could tell me the truth for a change.'

'I always do.'

'Now you really are lying.' She was right, of course. She was very young and had my daughter's uncomfortable knack of getting at the truth. 'Maurice Zellenek's a client of ours,' she went on, and the name meant nothing to me. 'I helped him over a house and he promised to be in this evening. He thought you were terrific.'

'You mean the little chap with all his hair under his chin?'

'You're so cool.' She looked at me in a complimentary sort of way, 'That's what I admire so about your Trigorin. All that suave, middle-aged charm.'

'That really was acting,' I told her. 'I'm not in the least cool. In fact I'm anxious most of the time, except when I'm playing a part.' What about being middle-aged? I was forty-three, perhaps twenty years older than her, probably older than Chekhov's writer when he seduced Nina in the play. My anxiety increased and, as soon as I reasonably could, I got up to dance with Pam, the physio. I'd had quite enough of becoming involved with people because we had met as characters in a play.

Chapter Ten

'There's absolutely no point,' Dunster had said that blustery spring morning – was it a few years or a lifetime before? – as we stood by the ruins of Alexandra Palace looking out over London. 'No point at all, Progmire, in us trying to hide the truth from each other.'

Since that day Dunster and I had hardly spoken. I had avoided him, although I don't know if he had taken any trouble to avoid me. Sometimes I got him on the telephone, but only by mistake. Sometimes we met outside his house, or in his hallway, but that was also by mistake. I have no great appetite for living through that day again. I have, you must understand, lived through it often enough on bad nights and long, empty afternoons in the years between. But that day, and the time before and after it, had an effect on the production of *War Crimes* and I must do my best to make it all clear to you. It's a story, I suppose, which has happened to a great many people. I just wish to God that it had never happened to me.

The one thing that everyone knows about memory is that every day of your childhood and youth remains stuck in your mind forever, while what happened last week is instantly flushed down the drain of forgetfulness. I can see myself, tormented with embarrassment, while Dunster heckled the little evangelical at Speakers' Corner with blinding clarity. So far as I am concerned Mrs Oakshott's bathroom fittings will be with me until the day I die. Every line and every moment of that damp and dour *Hamlet* is still present, for pain and consolation. But the time after I got my job at Megapolis, the years of marriage and living in Muswell Hill, have faded and slipped away in patches, like a wall painting in a poor state of repair. And it's bad luck that those greyish blots, where the damp got in, would no doubt have shown the best times: when Natasha was very young, and I started to work closely with Cris, and we bought the house in Grasmere Road. But if you were to ask me to remember exactly when Tash took her first staggering steps, or whose party it was at which Beth and I made up our first really serious quarrel under a pile of coats which were gradually removed by drunken guests who paid no attention to us, I would be hard put to remember. The brightest parts of the picture have vanished beyond hope of restoration.

Perhaps what I should do is just give you the facts as far as I remember them. I went to work in the accounts department at Megapolis under Gary Penrose, who was then a youngish middle-aged man with a moustache and hair just over his ears, a gold metal watch-strap and an expression of perpetual anxiety. Every morning he would ask me, 'How's your car going, Philip?' and look reassured when I told him that Beth's Renault was quite undependable in rain or frost or hot weather. Gary advised me on how to survive in the company. 'Don't try to be a high-flier. High-fliers are due for a crash at Megapolis. You know what I've got myself, when it comes to wheels? Toyota. Middle-management vehicle. You'll stick to middle-management vehicles, if you take my advice, Philip. And keep your head down.' Not long after I'd started work, to my surprise, Cris Bellhanger, in his shirtsleeves and braces, banged his tray down beside mine in the canteen. 'Welcome to the madhouse, Progmire.' He'd smiled at me. 'I hear you starred in *Hamlet* at university. You're just the type of fellow we need in accounts. Put a bit of poetry into the balance sheets.' I had no idea how he had got this information, and our conversation got me into some trouble with my immediate boss. 'Chattering in the canteen to the chairman of the Board is hardly keeping your head down, Philip. I say, he didn't mention anything about me and Andrea, did he?' Gary was having a flagrantly obvious affair with his secretary, a brisk, unsmiling person who was older and a great deal less attractive than Mrs Penrose, whom he used to bring to our annual dinner in the Connaught Rooms. Fear that this romance might become known to his wife was another cause of Gary's anxiety.

Beth and I had been lucky. When we found the house, my father lent me some of the money for the deposit and the rest came, astonishingly enough, from Jaunty. 'I have a few little goodies lying in various hidey-holes. No. I didn't tell you that when we went through the accounts. I thought it might come as a bit of a sweetener for Mister Progmire if he ever took on a girl who has to be ridden on a particularly tight rein.' When I asked Beth if she'd any idea that Jaunty had so much loose cash about him she said, 'The only way to get on with Dad is to ask him as few questions as possible. I wouldn't wish to know everything that goes on under that filthy old tweed cap of his.' I didn't inquire further. We decided that we could afford the mortgage repayments if we let off the top room, and our first tenant was Queen Gertrude, who'd come up to London to work in advertising. After her, our lodgers were all quiet, friendly and clean and, when Tash was born, ready to do occasional baby-sitting. Beth's black moods departed; she seemed, to my surprise and gratitude, content with life in Muswell Hill to an extent which I wouldn't have believed possible when we were at Oxford.

Dunster became a memory, one of the things we laughed about together: the eccentric, the stealer of Plumstead's dinner jacket, the too honest friend who gave us terrible notices, the lucky idiot who, totally unable to ride, jumped a hedge on Jaunty's hunter and didn't break his neck. He was writing articles for magazines and I would get an occasional blast of the Dunster anger and contempt from Africa, or Washington, or some town hall in the north-east of England. And then one evening, when Beth had taken Tash down to Exmoor, he rang up.

'Hullo, old man. It's about the room.'

'What room?'

'Your room, of course. Benson's wife's left him at last and his girlfriend's moving in with him. That's my reliable information.' It was true that our last lodger had been a quiet girl with tragic eyes who filled the unlikely role of mistress to Benson, the gravedigger. 'I'm absolutely bloody homeless. So I'll come round.'

'Where are you?'

'In the telephone box at the corner of your street.'

'Beth's away with her parents.'

'Don't worry, old man. I'll do us a fry up.'

He came with three bottles of Chianti and, for some extraordinary reason, I was glad to see him. It was as though I had gone for too long without the salt in the egg of my existence. We drank two bottles and I let him produce the smoking, partially blackened food and the heavy smell of bacon fat which was my memory of his childhood home. He was funny about the editor of the *Informer*, the left-wing journalist, who was apparently a closet golfer and a secret member of the local Rotary Club. He gave me all the details of the latest Washington sex scandal and described a helicopter journey with an army major who was terrified of flying and clutched a miniature teddy bear for comfort. He had, it seemed, penetrated the Church of England synod to detect some dirty work in the selection of a new archbishop; and lived with a gospel singer in Maryland to expose a racketeering faith-healer. He sat with his feet on a kitchen chair and said, 'I envy you, Progmire. My God. I envy your success.'

'What success is that?'

'You've got a home. A family. You've become a cheerful old Muswell Hill-billy. Damn it all, you're happy.'

'I suppose I am.' I was worried. Once you began to talk like that it might not last.

'And I, old man, haven't even got a roof over my head.'

'How did you manage that?' Not that, in Dunster's case, I thought it would be difficult.

'Living with this Jo Burton. Does the women's rights page in the *Informer*. Militant, my dear old Progmire. I can't tell you how militant this Jo person is. She locked me out of the flat because I wouldn't tell her I loved her.'

'Why wouldn't you?'

'It wouldn't have been true.'

'So you're out on the street?'

'All my stuff,' he said with dignity, 'is in the left-luggage department at Euston Station.'

'Then why couldn't you say it?'

'Say what?'

'Say you loved this Jo Burton. I mean, at least you wouldn't have had to move your stuff out. And she might have liked it.'

'Oh, Progmire.' He looked at me sadly. 'You have absolutely no sense of morality. Does that worry you at all?'

'As a matter of fact it's one of the few things that doesn't.'

'So are you going to let me your room?'

'I'll have to ring Beth.'

'That's what I thought. There's a bottle left.'

Later I telephoned and got Jaunty. He said, 'Are you drunk? I'll get Beth. She's talking to her mother.'

Beth said, 'Dad says you're drunk.'

'I miss you.'

'Did you ring up to tell me that?'

'Yes. And Dunster's here. He wants the room. I'm sure you think it's a terrible idea.'

'I don't see why. Provided he's good for the rent.'

'Are you good for the rent?' I asked Dunster.

'Old man' – Dunster looked at me sadly – 'have I ever let you down?'

So Dunster got his stuff – there was surprisingly little of it – from Euston Station and moved upstairs, where he lived rather quietly for about three months. He only came down in the evenings when we invited him, paid his rent regularly and seemed, so far as I could tell, to lead a life of celibacy. One day I came home from work and Beth told me he'd left for South America, where he was going to write some documentaries for television.

'Isn't that a bit sudden?'

'Apparently they'd just got the money together. He didn't expect it to happen so soon.'

'Have you seen his bedroom? I bet it's a tip.'

'No. It's remarkably tidy. And you know what?'

'What?'

'He's actually made his bed.'

We got postcards from various parts of the world, and I glanced through his articles. Then he wrote to tell us that his father had died and he had inherited the house in Camden Town which I used to visit as a boy. He invited us over for dinner some time, but a date was never fixed. I didn't see Dunster again until he rang me at Megapolis and said, if I was driving home from work, could I meet him at Alexandra Palace, as he had something to tell me which he thought I would want to hear? As it turned out, he was entirely wrong about that.

This was where we used to go when we were schoolboys and Dunster came to tea with me. We told each other that my parents had bugged my bedroom so we had to stand in the open air round the old Alexandra Palace to discuss the secret weaknesses and furtive misconduct of our friends and masters. It was there that we used to talk, looking out over London, near to the clouds, in a position in which we had always felt godlike, far above the small scurrying subjects of our ridicule and abuse. 'Down there' – Dunster would wave a schoolboy's hand with ink-stained fingers – 'is the house of ill fame into which old Dankwerts, the stinks master, is slinking on his way home. And, somewhere among the mist around Hampstead, Porker Plumstead is locked in the lavatory with *Health and Beauty.*' And we would smile tolerantly down on them, sure, at least, that we would never be quite as disgusting.

The most worrying sentence in the world to me is 'I'd like to have a word with you about something.' It leaves you in agonizing doubt about what exactly. The feeling of anxiety which started with Dunster's telephone call had increased during the long, slow drive through the north London traffic. Obviously he needed help. What was it? Money, shelter? An alibi, perhaps, for some crime of violence? By the time I had parked and was walking up the hill towards him, I had steeled myself to lock him in the boot of the car and spirit him out of the country.

The old glass palace of our childhood had been rebuilt in a more solid, less combustible version and there I found Dunster, standing under the reconstruction of a winged Victorian angel which was holding out a laurel wreath, as though to drop it on his head as some quite unmerited reward.

'For God's sake, Dunster. What's all this secret business? What do you want me to do for you?'

'Nothing for me, Progmire. I want to help you. I really mean that.'

He was looking at me with the slightly reverent concern of a doctor who is going to tell a patient that he has about three months to live. The 'poor old you' expression was mixed with the superior look of a man who knows that he's still as fit as a fiddle and likely to last forever.

'I'm not sure I need any help. Not just at the moment.'

'I think you do. In fact I think you always have.'

It was then that I got a feeling of doom, at the thought of being helped by Dunster. I should have been warned, turned, driven rapidly away and listened no further. That is what I ought to have done.

'You hide the truth from yourself, don't you, old man? You

tell yourself lies or just put off having to think about things. Well, what I want to tell you is that you can't put off thinking about it any longer. It's not fair to any of us.'

'Who's any of us?' Even then I had no real idea of what he was talking about.

'You and me, of course. And Beth.'

I knew then, as a matter of fact. I suppose it was the way he said her name as though he possessed it.

'What's Beth got to do with it?'

'Only that I'm in love with her. I told her that.' I felt a small glimmer of hope. Was it all an absurd fantasy, a Dunster dream of unrequited love?

'And what makes you think she's in love with you?'

'I suppose the afternoons we've been having together. Oh, for quite a long time now. And the weekends, when she said she was going down to Jaunty in the country. I told her she was absolutely wrong.'

'Wrong?'

'Not to tell you, of course. So far as I'm concerned not telling you was the only bad thing about it. But she didn't want to hurt you I suppose. I told her we'd all be far more hurt by lies.'

We had fought when we quarrelled at school, rarely, and so far as I was concerned, inefficiently, struggling together, filled with impotent rage, pulling hair and pinching. I'm not sure how I attacked him then. I couldn't have punched him neatly on the jaw like John Wayne in a saloon bar. I couldn't even, as Beth had once advised me, have kneed him in the groin. But the lovers, the mothers with pushchairs, the girls sharing crisps and giggling together, the small dog that jumped up at us, saw two grown men grappling – one with his arms flailing, the other in retreat until he was by an iron railing and lay back against it, smiling.

'Well done, old man!' Dunster said, out of breath. 'That's just how I'd hoped you'd react.'

I left him. I was not in the business of fulfilling any of Dunster's hopes.

'You'll feel better now,' he called after me. 'Now you know the truth. Of course you will! You can live life as it really is. Not as you hoped it was going to be. We can all feel better. Now we're honest with each other. Just take the truth out and look at it. Cope with it. You can't kid yourself, old man. You can't go on pretending that nothing exists unless you like it . . .'

There was probably more but I didn't listen. I got into the car, slammed the door and drove away, down to where I lived. I wished to God the last half hour had never happened and that I could have lived on, even in my ignorance, forever.

Chapter Eleven

When I got home after my fight with Dunster on the parapet of Alexandra Palace I was astonished by the appearance of normal life continuing. If I hadn't expected to find the house burnt down, utterly destroyed, I thought it would be empty, my wife and child gone and a note left on the kitchen table. But Beth was cooking the supper and Tash had her homework spread out and there was no sign of a note anywhere. The place was warm and inviting and smelt gently of stew. Beth said, 'You're late.'

'Yes,' I said. 'I met Dunster.'

She was peeling potatoes, with an apron tied over her jeans, wearing one of my shirts with the sleeves rolled up. She seemed as beautiful as on the first day I met her, perhaps more beautiful after twenty years, with a few small lines at the corners of her eyes and no sign of grey in the strawberry hair. She was thin and straight-backed and competent, and seemed so uninterested in my meeting that I was able to hope again, with wild optimism, that the whole confession was a Dunster fantasy.

'He asked me to meet him at Alexandra Palace. He had something he wanted to tell me.'

'Damn!' Beth blasted my hopes forever. Our daughter, said, 'Do be quiet, you two. I've got yards and yards of history.' She was going to be as beautiful as her mother and on the whole we got on very well, although she was inclined to boss me about. Tash was always keen to involve me in her homework, which I found hard to cope with after a long day in the accounts department.

Anyway, I went upstairs, as I always did when I got back

from work, and hung up the accountancy suit and put on a sweater and a pair of cord trousers. Back in the kitchen Beth had got the white wine out of the fridge and poured a glass for each of us.

'I suppose we ought to talk.' It was the last thing I wanted to do.

'Later.' Beth emptied her glass quickly. 'When Madam's gone to bed.'

'That won't be for *hours!*' Tash assured us. 'Not with all this work I've got to do.'

I suppose it was hours. It seemed like a lifetime. We ate stew and mashed potatoes and cabbage and finished the bottle of wine. Tash demanded my help on an essay she was writing about a day in the life of a Norman peasant, but she rejected most of my suggestions with contempt. It was strained and pointless, like a game of cards with the warders to fill in time until the hour of execution. At last Tash started to pack up her books very slowly, made herself a mug of chocolate with enormous deliberation and performed a prolonged, dramatic exit. Her mother and I sat down on opposite sides of the kitchen table.

'I'm sorry.' Beth looked at me and smiled faintly.

'Sorry it happened?'

'Sorry he had to tell you. I was afraid he would.'

'He wanted to boast?'

'Not that. He's got this terribly awkward thing about telling the truth.'

'Is that what you like about him?'

'Do I like him?'

'Don't you?'

'I'm not sure liking comes into it, exactly.'

'Then why . . .?'

She didn't answer but went and got another bottle of wine and started to open it.

'Do you love Dunster?' It had never, in my life until then,

occurred to me that I would have to ask her such an extraordinary question. She pulled the cork and refilled our glasses. She pushed mine towards me. She was as gentle and solicitous as she had ever been during all our good times together.

'I can't explain. It's something in me I don't like particularly. I'm rather afraid of it. It almost horrifies me. It's what I feel out hunting, or with my father. What do you think it is?'

'God knows.' She sat and looked at me as though she really wanted an answer. I had none to give her. Every word was like a barefoot step across broken glass and I had no wish to stand still discussing the view.

'Danger? Is that what it is? I suppose it might be what makes me feel close to my father. I mean, you wouldn't really expect anyone to like my father, would you? Not in the normal course of events.'

There was no answer to that. I said, 'Is there any chance it might be over?'

'Not much chance, I'm afraid.' He's infected her, I thought, with his awful habit of telling the truth. Then she looked down into her glass and said, 'I don't want to leave you, Philip.'

'Then don't.'

She shook her head slowly, red-gold hair under the big bright light that hung over the kitchen table. 'I couldn't stay here. Not after he's told you.'

'You mean, you might've stayed if he hadn't?'

'I don't know. Yes. I suppose I might.'

'Is that why he told me?'

'How can I tell? Perhaps he thought you ought to know.'

'How bloody considerate of him!' I wanted to be angry with her also. I wanted to shout at her, storm, break glasses. I couldn't. There crept over me, like a disease, a fatal understanding of how she felt. I finished my wine; it tasted of nothing and was useless as an anaesthetic.

'Now that's happened,' she said, 'I'll have to go.'

'I'm asking you to stay.'

'Not now. Don't ask me that now. You can't.'

'He didn't mind sharing you. Not for all that time. He put up with you being with me, didn't he? He compromised. Made you tell lies. Let you be dishonest. He's not so bloody pure and truthful, is he? Dunster!' I remember that I was standing then, and shouting too, probably.

'I'll have to leave,' she said. 'It can't go on.'

Then I felt as if I'd been crying into the wind, alone on a beach with nobody listening. I also thought I'd aged at least ten years since Dunster told me.

'No, I'll leave,' I said. 'You'll need the house.'

'I don't want to take anything that's yours. Nothing.'

Not yourself? but I didn't say that. I said, 'Not Natasha?'

'Natasha's ours,' Beth said. 'Of course we'll share her. She needs both of us.'

So that was it. It was over. What was left were the arrangements, practical and boring and heartless. When I went upstairs I pushed open her bedroom door to look at Tash. She was asleep on her back, with one arm over her head and her hair spread out on the pillow – as she had slept as a small child and as her mother slept. I loved them both as much as ever and I thought I always would. That was why I behaved as I did, in the events which were to come.

When the arrangements had been made, when we had parted and I was living alone in the house, and I had spent the weekend at the Zoo and the Natural History Museum and the cinema and the Hard Rock Café with Tash, overfeeding and over-entertaining her but not knowing what else to do, I was sitting alone in the canteen at Megapolis when the chairman in shirtsleeves once again put his lunch down beside mine.

'Cheer up, Philip. It may never happen.'

He was unloading his tray when I said, 'I'm afraid it has.'

There was a silence while he laid out his fish and chips methodically, his roll and butter, his bottle of beer, and I cursed myself. Now both my parents were dead, I had no one to tell, and I hadn't meant to tell Cris.

'Your marriage?'

'How did you know?'

'Well, I didn't think it could be the share price, or even that bloody awful series about hairdressers I should never have let them do. You know they wanted to call it *Who Did You Last?* Well, I stopped that, at least.' There was a silence. I could think of nothing to say to him.

'Is it for good?' he asked.

'Yes. For good and all.'

'No hope?'

'I'm sure not.'

'Sometimes no hope's better. At least you know where you are. You want one of these?' He was pouring his bottle of beer carefully.

'No thanks.'

'It just might not be the end of the world.'

I had nothing to say to that either. I didn't believe it. Cris took a long chip in his fingers, dipped it in tomato ketchup and ate it thoughtfully.

'We've entered those ghastly hairdressers for the Golden Comedy Goblet. Can you imagine anything worse than the International Small Screen Festival in Nice?'

'Not much,' I had to admit, although there was something – an empty house in Muswell Hill with its bedrooms full of memories.

'Absolutely ghastly. I've got to go, of course. Can't get out of it. So you'll have to come with me.'

'I couldn't.' I didn't want to be given treats, like Natasha, to take my mind off the truth of the situation.

'You must.' For once Cris sounded like a commanding officer. 'As the representative of the accounts department. Keep some sort of check on my expenses.'

The Small Screen Festival was all that Cris had expected. Nice was full of flags, posters, parties and television executives from all over the world doing deals in restaurants and on the beach with bored blondes at their elbows. Girls in bikinis, peering through square helmets in the shape of television sets, processed down the Promenade des Anglais together with the local firemen and police bands and floats depicting scenes from the Great Soaps of All Time. Cris and I saw one show, a Belgo-Argentinian co-production of a musical in which Donna Quixote was an ex-Miss Argentina and Sancha Panza a fat Flemish comedienne. After it, and before the VIP champagne supper in the Negresco that followed, Cris said, 'Let's flee to the hills.'

He deferred to me elaborately as the Controller of his Privy Purse and asked if we could afford the Colombe d'Or in St Paul de Vence, provided he promised not to waste any more of the company's time watching television. I agreed and we spent the next few days eating on the terrace as the white doves circled round us, drinking pink wine by the Léger mural. I went to bed early and slept late, sinking quickly into the blank oblivion in which people are said to take refuge from disasters such as the death of those they love. I can't say I began to recover, but there were moments when I sat in the sunshine, listening to the doves and smelling the wood smoke and the lavender, and almost forgot to be unhappy.

On our last evening, as we sat outside the Café de la Place drinking coffee and watching the old men play boules, Cris said, 'We all change in time. We all become somebody different.'

'What do you mean?'

'In a while, perhaps only a short while, you'll be a different Philip Progmire. Not the one who was married to Bethany. Another one altogether. Made up of quite different experiences.'

'I doubt that.'

'Oh, not that you'll lose those years when you were married. They'll be there always. But it'll be as though they happened to someone else.'

A little flock of girls passed, chattering, with bare arms and sweaters round their shoulders because it was chilly after dark. Boys with rackets played against the old town wall. Their tennis balls vanished into the darkness and then bounced back under the street lights.

'Do you want to talk about it? Your marriage, I mean?'

'No,' I said. 'Not really.'

'Are you sure it's over? Is she with someone else?'

'Let's change the subject. If you don't mind.'

So I never told Cris about Dunster and Beth, not even years later, when he first mentioned *War Crimes*, and gave me the scripts and told me who had written them. Dunster was something I didn't want to mention, like a shameful disease, until, in the end, I had to.

On the plane back to London, Cris passed me his copy of *The Times*. 'Another bit of bad news for you,' he said. '*Hairdressers* won the Golden Comedy Goblet at Nice.'

THE QUESTION

Chapter Twelve

A few weeks after I opened in *The Seagull* with the Muswell Hill Mummers (the notice in the *Advertiser* was rather like one of Trigorin's own: 'An agreeable and competent performance but not a patch on Jonathan Pryce'), I got a telephone call while I was trying to put the best possible face on the year's drop in advertising revenue.

'Perry Gryce here. As I think you know, I'm produce-directing *Crimes*. Could we have the smallest possible natter?'

'What about?'

'The powers that be,' said Peregrine Gryce mysteriously, 'think we ought to meet and talk. I'm in the Malibu Club and I thought it might interest you to buy us both lunch.'

'I don't know. It'll take me about an hour and a half to get to Soho.'

'Of course. You're in the Isle of Dogs, aren't you? I always avoid the place myself. But I think you ought to come. Seems Lord God Almighty suggested we should meet.'

'Really . . .?' I must have sounded dubious.

'Don't worry, luv,' he reasoned with me. 'There's nothing born again about Perry. I was talking about the chairman of the Board.'

As the taxi crawled through Limehouse and we sat staring at the backs of lorries along the Commercial Road, I couldn't stifle a feeling of excitement at the thought of entering what I'd been led to believe was the very heart of show business. At last we turned into Soho and drove down past the Boy's boutique and the peep-shows, past the arcade where displaced children from the North spent their days playing computer games and their nights in doorways, and the multi-language newspaper shop, to the discreet entrance of the Malibu Club.

The bar was filled with men swathed in linen, lying back in armchairs giving interviews. The little lights of recording machines glowed on the coffee tables in front of them. Opposite them eager girls held notebooks to make sure no word of wisdom was lost. As I passed, I caught snatches of deliberately quiet, self-controlled dialogue. 'So we had a deal with Paramount but when we talked story they didn't see the project in quite our terms, so we went . . .' I am ashamed to say that all this excited me, voices from a world of professional drama I had always yearned for. Through what I found to be rather beautiful waitresses in bow-ties and black trousers, a hand waved at me, a wrist enclosed by a heavy gold chain. At the zinc counter, lit by a blue neon strip and perched on a high chromium-legged stool, so that he looked like a gnome seen by moonlight, sat Peregrine Gryce, producer of *War Crimes*, with a bottle of champagne nestling in an ice-bucket beside him.

'Philip, hi!' he beamed at me. 'Welcome to the great big world outside the accounts department.'

A drink at the bar gave me chance to inspect the Gryce outfit. His jacket was also made of floppy white linen, but the trousers had a sort of buttercup-coloured tartan pattern, while his striped cotton shirt was set off by a deep-blue waistcoat decorated with white flowers. He was a lean, lantern-jawed man with cropped grey hair and small, gold-framed spectacles.

'I suppose,' he said, when we sat down to lunch, 'it's all a bit of a treat to you, being invited out by the creative side.'

'It's something that's always interested me,' I admitted.

'Has it really, Philip?' Peregrine Gryce sounded supremely uninterested in my career as he studied the menu. 'You don't mind the Philip, do you? As it seems we've got to work together?'

'Have we?'

'Well. In a manner of speaking. Caviar blinis. You could

hide them away somewhere, couldn't you, in the budget?'

'No' – I thought it was about time to assert the authority of the accounts department – 'I don't think I could.'

'My, you are strict! All right, then. It'll have to be the warm monkfish salad and the grilled breast of duck with saffron rice and lentils. And Philip . . .'

'Yes?'

'Could I give you a bit of advice? If you really want to go into production give that dreadful, grey accountant's suit away to some hard-up Member of Parliament. A bottle of Ngatarawa Sauvignon? Can Megapolis rise to that, do you think?'

When I had written off the New Zealand white, Peregrine spoke on the subject which seemed to interest him most.

'I have a creative job and so I need to dress creatively. Every morning I open the wardrobe and what am I searching for?'

'Clothes?'

'I am searching for *myself*. I am trying to create some sort of distinctive harmony. Also I want to send Perry out into the great wicked world feeling confident, well loved and full of that particular joy in living which comes from a really expensive cashmere cardigan.'

'What was it exactly you wanted to meet and talk about?' I didn't know how long I could sustain this discussion of the dressiness of Peregrine Gryce.

'Of course, a few years ago, I was an absolute sucker for mid-eighties monochrome chic,' he went on remorselessly. 'It was all unstructured suits, everything from the same place, if you understand me. I suppose there was a certain purity about it. But now I feel free. I've taken off. I mix and match. I shop around. I'll go for separates: Cerruti, Armani or Issey Miyake.' His voice sank to a confidential whisper. 'You might not believe this, but I got the waistcoat, Philip, from an Oxfam shop in Godalming!'

'All right,' I promised. 'I won't tell anyone.'

'The shirt is Romeo Gigli.' Now he obviously felt on safer ground.

'I'll take your word for it. But how can I help you over *War Crimes?*'

'I don't know, Philip. I don't know, luv, honestly. Just at the moment, it seems to me, we're in deep trouble.' His confidence, in spite of his clothes, seemed to have drained away. I looked at him and he seemed even smaller, a shrunken elderly man dressed in a way that was far too young for him.

'Oh,' I said, 'and why is that?'

'Script trouble. It usually is.'

'Who's your writer?' I asked, as innocently as possible.

'A person who wears a tweed jacket with leather patches.' Contempt seemed to cheer Peregrine up. 'He must think they're coming back in.'

'How did you find him?'

'Unnerving.'

'No. I mean, how did you come to be working with him?'

'Oh, *that*. Well, Dick Dunster sent us this idea, written out, in handwriting. Of course we didn't read it. I mean, who reads handwriting nowadays? I don't believe they teach it in schools any more, do they? Anyway, then he called round. At my office. Streetwise Productions. We're just next door to the Malibu, so convenient. And he made a terrible fuss, shouted at everyone. Shouted at me. Explained the idea, war criminals of all nations, and demanded an immediate answer. Well, really to get rid of him, I said I'd try it on a few people. He said, 'All right. I give you two weeks and then I sell it to the highest bidder.' I didn't believe he had any bidders, but at least he went. Well, then. About ten days later I was having lunch with your director of programmes.'

Gary Penrose, by dint of keeping his head down, had risen soundlessly in Megapolis. He continued, despite his eminence, to avoid trouble and drive a Toyota.

'Gary said to me, "Perry," he said, "we need a newsworthy

public affairs programme for late-night viewing to improve our image and our ratings." He asked if I could come up with something. To be honest with you, my mind was a complete blank. I looked round the room. This very room, as it happens. There was some exhibition of old photographs round the walls. All war scenes, you know. Faces smeared with camouflage paint under helmets, rows of corpses, a child crying in a burnt-out village. What's his name? The guy who does these things? All black and white and grainy. I hadn't noticed them when we sat down to lunch, but then I said, off the top of my head, "We've developed six really brilliant eps on war crimes." A few days later Gary rang me up to say he's happened to mention it to your chairman, who was particularly keen on the idea.'

'I know,' I said. 'Cris wants to do it.'

'And for some reason he wants you to join me as associate producer. He thinks you'd welcome a chance to get out of accounts.' I was grateful to Cris for the suggestion, but could I stand any sort of working association with Dunster? I wanted to find out more.

'You said you were in trouble. What sort of trouble exactly?'

'This Dunster's got a final story which he regards as his great scoop. So far as I can gather, he's only told me this. Mind you, I haven't seen a word on paper. It's about some British bad behaviour in Italy. You know, up in the mountains. Peasant town perched over precipices, place crawling with partisans and Italian fascists. Runaway prisoners of war, brave British SAS dropped by parachute, and the wicked Germans. It could be a fun location.'

'All right,' I said in my best down-to-earth accountant's voice, 'what do you need me for?'

'Your artistic in-put, of course. Goes without saying.' The expensively dressed gnome opposite me smiled mockingly.

'Balls. What do you really want?'

'Dick Dunster has got all these bright and shocking ideas of what the Brits in the mountains got up to, but he won't tell us his sources. And your chairman is dead keen that we check extremely carefully on this one. It's obviously a bit of a mine-field, politically speaking.

'It probably is.'

'But, as I say, Dunster refuses to tell us where he got the story from. He's quite cagey about what it is, too. At the moment I've only got the vaguest idea. And he said if we don't do the one about the Brits in the Apennines, we can't do the series.'

'I suppose that would be your bad luck.'

I looked round the room. At some of the tables the inter-views were continuing and the red lights of tape-recorders glowed by the side plates. On the walls fashion photographs were now being exhibited. Models, standing with their legs apart and facing a high wind, had ousted men in combat gear and crying children. War was something we didn't want to think about too often or brood about for long. But we were being led back on a surprise trip to a long-forgotten battlefield by a man who seemed prepared to tell us nothing at all about what we might expect to find when we got there.

'So,' Peregrine Gryce said, 'are you for the job?'

'I don't know. I'll need time to think about it.'

'I suppose you're a bit wary of leaving a nice safe desk in accounts. Is that it?'

'Something like that,' I told him.

Chapter Thirteen

Although I had been offered a job as associate producer, I took my preferred option and did nothing. That is to say I stayed quiet, kept my head down and got on with my work. Tash came for her weekends and we went to the movies and had lunch at the Indonesian restaurants in Muswell Hill which she liked, and I willingly put up with Deng Deng Goreng and beanshoots for the pleasure of her company. During these visits Tash was in charge, cooking, on the evenings we stayed in, elaborate and rather good meals which she never washed up, employing a process which she called 'leaving it in to soak'. I asked regularly, trying to drain my voice of all emotion, about her mother, and she would answer automatically, 'Beth's all right,' and pass on to other subjects.

We hardly ever mentioned Dunster, mainly because I couldn't bring myself to say 'How's your step-father?' I hadn't seen him since the wedding. Beth had remarried in Camden Town register office and invited most of the old cast of *Hamlet*. Dunster had written with an extraordinary suggestion. 'I don't exactly know whether a best man's called for in the civil ceremony, but I wouldn't want anybody else but you, Progmire, old man.' I read the letter in the kitchen, dropped it into the tidy-bin and arranged to take a trip up the Nile at the time of the ceremony. Most of the other passengers found that Egypt had an appalling effect on their stomachs and I sat alone on the deck of a boat which by then bore a striking resemblance to the *Mary Celeste*. I watched the muddy banks, the villages with their biblical appearance and television aerials, glide past and tried not to remember the punt under the willows, or the icy, rosette-hung bedroom in Blair Cottage.

*

Not long after my lunch with Peregrine Gryce, I got a telephone call from Major Jaunty Blair. He regretted the way we had 'drifted apart' and suggested a meeting: 'What about a spot of dinner at my club?' I should have declined the treat. My continued involvement with Beth's family was like picking at a scab which should have been allowed time to heal. I didn't want to talk about her, hear about her, or be made to remember. All the same I went.

I had expected to find Jaunty half asleep in a leather armchair under a painting of the Battle of Inkerman in some dusty retreat for retired officers of the British Army, but I was mistaken. Dandini's, when I managed to find it tucked away behind Shepherd Market, had a white tie, top hat and silver-knobbed cane over the door, depicted in neon strips that had failed in patches. The doorman was a pale young man in a braided jacket many sizes too large for him, who was leaning against a wall playing, what we used to call at St George's, pocket billiards. When I asked if Major Blair was in the club he said, 'There's only one old guy here yet. You better go and ask him.' Inside there was a lot of crimson flock wallpaper, stained in patches, pink-shaded lamps, tables round a minute dance floor and a number of dispirited girls in white ties, tails and fishnet tights engaged in low-key gossip. Jaunty was at the bar. When he saw me he drew back his lips and gave a low growl. I was reminded of the dogs at Blair Cottage that used to leap for my groin.

'God, this place has gone off. Everything's gone off. Tracy!' This emerged as a bark at a girl at the far end of the counter who was very slowly polishing glasses. She was blonde with a face, I thought, like that of a very young white mouse. She was suffering from a severe cold and in the intervals of polishing dabbed at her nose with a tiny bundle of pink Kleenex. A closer view of her seemed to calm Beth's old father a little. 'Another large G and T for me please, Tracy dear. And one for my guest.'

I said I'd prefer white wine and the girl was delighted to tell us that they didn't do white wines, not by the glass and it'd have to be a bottle.

'Oh, come on, Tracy!' Jaunty's grin looked savage but it was meant, I suppose, to be ingratiating. 'I've been a member here long enough, haven't I? And you always used to do it by the glass, didn't you, for any guest of mine?'

'Anyway, I'm not Tracy.' As the girl advanced on us I saw, on the large plastic notice fixed to her lapel, the word, Tina. 'We haven't got no Tracy.'

'Tracy gone!' There was, in the Major's voice, a terrible note of doom, as though the meaning had also gone out of his life. 'But you look so exactly like Tracy.'

'I don't know, do I?' The girl was pouring gin from an upturned bottle on the wall. 'I don't know what the girl might have looked like. Now. Do I have to open a bottle of white?'

'No,' I reassured her, 'I'll have a gin and tonic as well.' I didn't want to add to her problems.

When the drinks were poured things began to look up for my host. A big-breasted and motherly person carrying two huge menus in scarlet covers with gold tassels came up smiling and said, 'As soon as you're ready, Major dear. I've kept a nice table for you and chef's put on the *caneton à l'orange*. Your favourite.'

'There you are, you see.' Jaunty shot me a look of triumph from over the top of the menu. 'They know me here. You know how to look after me, don't you, Marion?'

'Marcia.' She smiled tolerantly and looked, I thought, like the nicest kind of hospital matron. 'And will it be your usual, Major? It's the Barolo, isn't it?'

'The Barolo Italiano.' Jaunty was now almost cheerful. 'And another couple of generous gins, old girl. Prawn cocktail to kick off, Progmire? We're here to enjoy ourselves!'

'Thank you, young man.' Marcia smiled at my host, took

our menus and left us, a kind, top-heavy woman walking unsteadily on shiny high heels who had managed to remember Jaunty.

Later I was looking round at the Dandini club where we were almost the only diners. Three brawny men in suits who looked like plain-clothes police officers were having dinner with an elderly man similarly dressed. They were listening to his stories, laughing at his jokes, and I thought he might have been a retired superintendent and that it was some private reunion of a few privileged members of the Vice Squad. The duck *à l'orange* had not been hatched out long enough in the microwave and the Black Forest gâteau lingered cloyingly on the palate.

Jaunty said, 'They know me here, of course. Know me well. I've only got to breathe the word and they'll make you a member. No other reference needed!'

'I don't really think so.' Why did I feel, obscurely, that I didn't want to disappoint Jaunty? 'It's a bit off my beaten track. I mean, it's rather a long way from Muswell Hill.'

'It's a bloody long way from Exmoor but I've been a regular for years. I come here on leave, you might say, when things get a bit rough on the front line.' I wasn't sure what he meant by the front line, but I thought it must be the altogether peaceful presence of Mike. And then Jaunty gave me another of his unnerving grins. 'I should think you might find a place like this pretty useful, living the sort of life you do now.'

'What do you mean exactly?'

'A geezer on his own. Unmarried. I don't need to spell it out, do I, Progmire?'

'Is that why you asked me here?' I felt a wave of depression. Was that the way ahead? Tina with a cold or Marcia leading me gently and tactfully into the geriatric ward?

'Well, no. Not exactly.'

'Why, then?' Tina had taken a tray of drinks over to the Vice Squad. As she set down their glasses, she bent her knees in a curious bobbing motion and smiled at their greeting.

'It's about my blessed son-in-law. The new one, that is. He shouldn't be doing that job.'

'Which job is that?'

'The one he's got on for your people. I tried to tell Bethany. It's a war he knows absolutely nothing about. Too young for it. Most people are. Only just a few of us left. Only a very few of us understand what it was like exactly.' He looked at me in a way he never had before, as though he was asking me to feel sorry for him. He filled my glass. 'Barolo.' He rolled the word round his mouth with a sort of relish. 'Reminds me of Italy. Not that we got it there in those days. Horse's pee mixed with red ink and paint-stripper. That's what the peasants gave us if we were very lucky. That was our tipple in those far-off days.'

'Which far-off days were those?' I asked the question reluctantly, feeling that each word was a step further into a plot that no longer concerned me. But it apparently concerned Beth and so I asked the question.

'Winter of 1944. In the High Apennines. Bloody bleak and bloody dangerous. The King of Italy had surrendered, but Mussolini was still kicking about in the north. Allied armies fighting their way all up the peninsula, which was a complete waste of effort, quite honestly. Germans fallen back on Florence, and in the hills . . . Well, all sorts of odds and sods.'

'Partisans, mainly communists,' I told him. 'Italian fascists and some British SAS sections, dropped by parachute. Oh, and the Germans of course.'

He looked at me suspiciously, as though I was trying to trap him. 'You seem to know a lot about it.'

'I know something.'

'Not how we felt, though, do you? None of you peace babies know that. Look, I wasn't much older than you both were when you put on that show at Oxford. What was it?'

'*Hamlet.*'

'Not much older than that when I was an army veteran. We'd fought across North Africa. We hadn't been home for – Oh, it seemed as long as anyone could remember. We were shagged out, tired of each other, tired of sleeping in our clothes. Most of all we were tired of being scared to death every waking hour from what I remember.' His hand was unsteady as he raised his brandy glass. For some reason, in the tacky surroundings of the Dandini club, wartime terror had returned to him. This was an entirely different Jaunty from the old man who had told me the army taught him everything he knew, and that war was the finest university. 'Italy was the end, as far as I was concerned. The end of the bloody line.

'To be absolutely honest with you, Progmire. I never understood what we were meant to be doing there. They dropped us in between the communists, who were busy getting ready to take over after the war, and the worst of the fascists, who were a gang of murderers on the way out. And then there was the German Army. Bloody good fighting-machine, you've got to hand it to them. What were we meant to do with six men and a boy? Frighten them out of their wits? Cut off their retreat? Best we could do was to keep our heads down, hide in some cave or in the pigsty of a peasant who'd betray you for the price of a bottle of grappa.'

So this was the setting of one of Dunster's scripts: the High Apennines, which Peregrine Gryce had said would make a 'fun location'. This was the drama to be created by actors and extras and cameramen, which Jaunty Blair had acted out for real a lifetime ago. He took a gulp of brandy, coughed as it hit his chest and growled on. 'Do you think everyone fought that scrap entirely according to the Queensberry Rules? Or the Geneva Convention, come to that? Do you? Do you think if they'd've bagged a group of Musso's cutthroats, they'd've built a nice comfortable prison for them and arranged for Red Cross parcels to be sent in? Do you honestly think they did that?'

By 'they' did he mean 'we'? I felt I was going to get some

sort of confession and had no idea what I should do with it. I looked down and saw Jaunty's gnarled hand on my arm. He was looking at me beseechingly and I was reminded of all the animals he had hunted.

'An old geezer has nothing to do with what he was as a youngster, Progmire. We all change completely. We haven't got the same bloody fingernails. Our hair falls out. Our teeth aren't ours any more. You can't hold an old man responsible. Not for what happened when he was a different mind in a different body and scared shitless. Do you catch my drift, Progmire? Do you see what I mean, old son?'

'I'm not sure I do.' What struck me most about this speech was that he had called me son, as though Beth and I were still together. But then he brought me back to reality.

'Your friend Dunster,' he said, 'can charm the birds out of the trees.'

'He's not my friend exactly.'

'No. No, of course not. Not under the circumstances.' Jaunty seemed cheered up for a moment, and then his gloom returned. 'He got me talking one night, over a jar at Blair Cottage. Got me talking about the old days.'

'When you were someone else?'

'When we all were. Perhaps I had a jar too much, I don't know. We got out some old maps and started talking about that time in the mountains. He seemed so bloody interested. Led me on, I suppose. Not that I told him anything, not anything sensational, believe me. But perhaps I set him off, inventing. And I want to tell you this, Progmire. He's got nothing to go on. No evidence at all, you understand? No use him poking about and trying to find a story.'

'Is that what he's doing?'

'Something he can sell for your geezers to put on the box. That's what he's after. You've got to tell your lot. There's nothing in it. No truth at all.'

'I'm an accountant. Not the programme controller.'

'I know but you have the ear of the bloody management. And you can tell –' Jaunty was gripping my arm now. I could feel the surprising strength of his old fingers. 'You can tell my present son-in-law, tell your successor . . .'

'I haven't got his ear. I haven't got any part of him.'

'He'll listen to you. No bloody good my talking to him. Tell him he's just asking for it, that's all.'

'Asking for what?'

'Disaster. For himself. For the whole family. You'll put a stop to it, won't you?'

'I can't promise anything.'

'You'll do it, won't you? You'll do it for Beth?' He leant back in his chair then, less rattled, sure of his ground. 'After all, you owe me something.'

'Do I?'

'Have you forgotten? Who found you your job? All those years ago. I had this connection at Megapolis.'

'Yes, of course. So you did. I was very grateful.'

The Major finished his brandy and his eyes seemed to film over, as though he'd lost interest in the entire subject. The ex-superintendent, or whoever he might have been, had left his table and was at the bar chatting to Tina. He had an impressive head, like the damaged bust of a Roman emperor, with a nose that had been broken at some time in his career and iron-grey hair as a fringe to his naked scalp. He looked in our direction, as though curious about what we were doing together. A few other couples had arrived and music for dancing came unsteadily out of a speaker in a corner of the room, like warm water dripping from a rusty tap.

'Look here,' the Major said. 'If you've got something else on, I really don't want to keep you.'

'I must get back.' I wanted to go to sleep and try, for a night at least, to forget everything he had told me.

'Sure you don't want to stay? That young Tracy behind the bar looks as though she might be friendly.'

'No, really. Got to work tomorrow.'

As I left the Dandini club, a middle-aged couple, looking at each other hungrily, were bopping to a crackling tape playing, 'In the jungle, the mighty jungle, the lion sleeps tonight.' I saw the Major get up and leave our table, and I thought he was about to join the man who had been eyeing us from the bar.

Chapter Fourteen

After this meal certain conclusions were, I'm sure you would agree, obvious. Jaunty, in his cups, had hinted at some discreditable incident in the Apennines. Dunster had received this information eagerly, researched it further, touched it up a little and was about to produce a story in which Beth's father – a man who, for reasons best known to herself, she loved – was to be accused of a war crime, heaven knew how serious, during the Italian campaign in 1944. Cris wanted me to join that sartorial enthusiast Peregrine Gryce in an effort to control Dunster, an activity which required the hopeless optimism of King Canute giving orders to the tide.

I had woken early and lay waiting for the grey start of the day. Then I decided to drive to work before the traffic, but at half past six the container lorries were already rattling down to the Angel and queuing where the road was up. From the car radio I learnt that the oil wells were flaming in Kuwait and that half-starved Iraqi conscripts were surrendering. Soon the war would be over and quite soon forgotten. Nothing would be left but the choking clouds, the burnt-out and twisted buildings – and the uncomfortable revelation that those we fought for hadn't been much better than the enemy. When Natasha was my age it would be a part of history, the names of generals and places and participants buried, as were the details of the Italian campaign, in a few books which not many people read. There would be other fears, different sufferings, to fill the *Today* programme. As I was driving, I was thinking about Beth, wondering whether she knew about Dunster's script and if there were any way of preventing the Jaunty story being beamed into ten million homes.

I got to Megapolis far too early and had breakfast in the canteen among the security men and a few people who'd come in for the early chat show. And then I waited for Cris to come in and tell me, I hoped, exactly what I ought to do.

'Jaunty Blair!'

I was sitting in the conversational part of Cris's office and he was standing looking out over the river, showing me his back in its white shirt and crossed braces.

'As a matter of fact he used to be my father-in-law.'

'I know,' was what I thought Cris said, and I was puzzled because I'd never told him. And then he turned slowly with the sun behind him making a silvery halo on his head, his face in shadow. 'He told me when you and Beth got married.'

'How long have you known him?'

'Since 1942. He arrived in Egypt with the yeomanry. One of the new boys. I was sent back from my regiment to give them some basic training in tank warfare. That's when I first met young Second Lieutenant Jonathan, usually known as Jaunty, Blair.'

'Young?'

'Four years younger than me.' It was hard to believe. Cris was straight-backed, hardly lined. Jaunty's face was etched like a map of Spaghetti Junction, his hands peppered with those brown marks which are said to be signs of approaching death.

'Of course, I didn't really get to know him then. I was a desert rat who went over to the Special Air Service regiment. Jaunty had the best of the war in Egypt. We were actually winning in his time there. But he got trapped in a burning tank. Lucky to get out alive. After that he said he had a sort of horror of closed spaces. So he was keen to get into the SAS. Fresh mountain air, that's what he said he was after. No more being cooked in a tin oven in the desert.'

'You were up there, in the Apennines together?'

'Some of the time. Only some of the time. The situation was pretty fluid, if you understand me. But, yes. I suppose that's where we got to know each other a little better.'

I had got up early and the sofa was too comfortable. My eyelids were heavy during his account of an ancient campaign, but now I was awake to a situation that seemed inexplicable.

'You met Beth. Often. We came to stay with you. When we were together.'

'Which is why I understand, I think, exactly what you felt about her.' His smile was gentle, as always. He moved then, to sit near me.

'She never said you knew her father.'

'Perhaps' – Cris carefully straightened the trade magazines and the heavy marble ashtray on the glass-topped table between us – 'her father never told her about me.'

'And you never told her you knew Jaunty.'

Cris was still smiling, which encouraged me in my unusual role as a cross-examiner.

'No point in opening up old wounds. The truth of the matter is, Jaunty and I never got on particularly well together.'

'I can understand that.'

'We parted on pretty bad terms, as it happens. Let's say we didn't see eye to eye on the way wars should be fought. That is, if you have to fight them. Then he wrote to me. Out of the blue. It was rather a pleasant letter. He said we'd been through some hard times together and had our differences in the past. Well. That was putting it mildly. But his daughter was marrying a young economist, a man with a terrific head for figures who'd played the part of Hamlet at Oxford.'

'Jaunty wrote to *you*? I mean, I know he wrote to someone at Megapolis. I imagined it was someone in accounts. But when I asked Gary Penrose about it he was a bit vague. Said whoever it was must have left.'

'I suppose it was such a curious idea.' Cris looked up at me again. 'The Hamlet of the balance sheets! I found it irresistible. Or did I admire Jaunty's cheek, asking me for a favour? I told Gary to get you in for an interview.'

So I had been Cris's choice from the start, because of what I'd done before he met me. I said, 'There's something I should have told *you*, long ago. I suppose it's just that, well, since Beth and I broke up I don't like talking about him.'

'Just as I don't like discussing Major Jaunty Blair.' He gave the military rank a mocking emphasis.

'I suppose,' I said, 'something like that.'

Cris lay back in his chair, his legs crossed, his hands clasped across his stomach. 'You're talking about Dunster, of course.'

'You know?'

'Naturally. When he was doing this job, I made a few inquiries.'

I suppose I should have expected Cris to know everything. 'I really can't explain why I didn't tell you that Beth left me for Dunster. I should've told you as soon as you said he'd written the scripts.'

'Don't worry. I can understand exactly why you didn't.'

'And now,' I said, 'Dunster's found out what Jaunty got up to in the war.'

'Is that what you think?'

'That's what I know.'

'Tell me.'

Cris moved again and sat in a more official position behind his desk and I gave him a condensed account of dinner with my ex-father-in-law at Dandini's. This was followed by a silence. Then he asked me, 'Do you think Jaunty's frightened of being exposed?'

'Don't you?'

'I suppose it's likely.'

'And you must know what it's all about.'

'I've got an idea or two. I'm not sure until I know what Dunster's written.'

'But it could be very bad for Jaunty?'

'What I can't understand is, now Dunster's married your Beth' – Cris frowned – 'why the hell should he want to call her father a criminal?'

'If you knew Dunster, you wouldn't wonder about that. He has a habit of telling unpleasant truths about his nearest and dearest. It makes him feel heroic.'

'An odd sort of character.'

'Unusual. Yes. I think you might say that. Peregrine Gryce asked me to be an associate producer on *War Crimes*. He wanted me to check Dunster's sources. That was your idea, wasn't it?'

'I can see we should never have asked you.'

'Why?'

'It was too much to expect.'

'I might want to stop him doing any more harm. To the company. And to Beth.'

'Do you think you'd have any sort of influence over him?'

'I might do something. If I spoke to both of them.'

He looked up at me. 'You're still concerned about Beth, aren't you?'

'And always will be.'

So I moved from accounts on to the production side. I was now in the world of make-believe – or drama that was telling the truth. I would have to discover which when I became associate producer on the *War Crimes* series.

Chapter Fifteen

'I'm afraid Perry's not here.'

'Shopping?'

'On a recce for a new series of *Neighbourhood Watch*. *Crimes* isn't the only thing we're doing at Streetwise, you know.' The tall and determined woman was Pippa Marching, Peregrine Gryce's PA, who looked as though she'd been the captain of cricket at Cheltenham Ladies College and no doubt served Peregrine with undying loyalty. She had been trying to put me in my place ever since I told her I was the new associate producer.

'You mean, you're the chap Megapolis put in to keep an eye on us? We're just don't know what they're in such a panic about. Perry's last six productions came in way under budget.'

'It's not the money I'm concerned with,' I said. 'It's the artistic quality.' At which she gave me the sort of look the man who comes to read the meter might get if he'd suddenly offered to do an audition for Musician of the Year.

'I'd like to start by going through the files.'

'I suppose you can,' she conceded, after a long moment of doubt. 'But don't get them in a muddle, will you? Perry's very particular about his files.'

The offices of Streetwise Productions looked like an extension of the Malibu Club next door; the same white walls and chromium, the same cream sofas and blown-up stills and prints by American photo-realists. Peregrine Gryce's certificates of nomination for various awards were framed in gold. Pippa Marching banged me up in a small room with an interesting view of the dustbins outside the Malibu kitchens. Then she left me alone to discover exactly what Dunster was planning to do to Jaunty Blair.

The files had been divided into various countries. Some of them contained scripts I had read in Cris's country house, their second or third drafts, long research notes and treatments. The slimmest was THE BRITISH IN ITALY, with most of the work apparently still to be done. I sat looking at the cover of it for a while, listening to the traffic and the kitchen noises, breathing in a faint smell of left-over monkfish and decaying vegetables. But the telephone didn't ring, no one brought me a coffee, and so I had nothing to do but open the brown folder.

The first thing I found was a large-scale map of the territory between Florence and Bologna, with a place called Pomeriggio ringed in felt-tipped pen somewhere in the brown-shaded part of a mountain range. Then there were photographs: the main street and square of a small town, and a rough path leading precipitously up to what seemed to be a pile of rubble on a promontory perched high over a valley. There were also five pages of the chronology of the Italian campaign from 1943 to 1945, and no more than a page of somewhat inaccurate and much corrected typing. BRITISH WAR CRIMINALS? was the heading, and I felt grateful, at least, for the question mark which didn't seem entirely characteristic of Dunster.

'Victorious armies never commit war crimes, because if they're victorious no one dare call them criminals.' The thought had been Cris's, but the words were Dunster's:

But what exactly happened in the town of Pomeriggio in the High Apennines on that long-ago Sunday in the autumn of 1944? It was the Feast of Santa Magdalena in Lachrimae, the village's patron saint, traditionally celebrated in the Chiesa Nuova, which was, strange as it may seem, the older of the two churches, built in the fourteenth century on the edge of a precipice just above the village and only used on one day a year. Certain facts can be established. A German SS officer had been found garrotted in a field outside the village walls just before the massacre of Pomeriggio. On the saint's day, the whole village processed, in the evening, up to the Chiesa

Nuova carrying banners, candles, the saint's statue and her Holy Relic – a fragment of her little finger in the Reliquary. Half-way through the service the church was dynamited, presumably with a timing device. The building was reduced to rubble and Pomeriggio to a ghost town. the incident has passed into history as yet another German outrage, a savage reprisal for the murder of one SS officer.

I remembered what Cris had seen in Italy, a town deserted and a mined church. Could it have been the same town, in the same campaign? Cris had certainly blamed the Germans; Dunster had a different solution.

'*Fact*' he went on:

Two escaped British prisoners of war were shot by the Italian fascists in Pomeriggio's square only a week before the massacre. Had someone in the town betrayed their hiding-place – a cave high up above the Chiesa Nuova? There was certainly one British SAS (Special Air Service regiment) team in the area and probably more at the time of the massacre. 'Those commandos didn't fight' one veteran campaigner told me [and here I recognized a quotation from Major Jaunty Blair] 'by the Queensberry Rules or the Geneva Convention.' Such teams contained a demolition specailist, used to blowing up munition dumps or supply centres. An ancient, little-used church would present no problems to such an expert.

I have researched this incident thoroughly [Where's the research? – someone, presumably Peregrine, had scrawled in red biro] and I have been fortunate enough to meet an ex-officer who was serving in the SAS in the area around Pomeriggio at the time. [Who? – from Peregrine] For very understandable reasons he wishes to remain anonymous. [We'll need an affidavit from him if we're to go on with this – Peregrine] I am also on the track of at least one witness still living in Italy whom I intend to visit. [Bring back statements, certified by a local notary] From these and other reliable sources [What sources?] I have been able to piece together the truth. [Here the red biro had merely placed a large question mark]

The SAS team knew that some villagers had betrayed our escaped prisoners. They may also have known that the fascists used the deserted Chiesa Nuova as their headquarters and for occasional meetings. They undoubtedly knew that everyone would be in the church on the Feast of Santa Magdalena [Can you prove this? Peregrine asked] and on no other day in the year.

Are we simple-minded enough to believe that taking reprisals was a form of warfare only practised by the Germans? Revenge fulfils a basic human need. The town was responsible for the deaths of two Britons, and so the town must pay the penalty. That is exactly what we did to Pomeriggio in the High Apennines.

It might be argued that there's no point in punishing a town unless you let everyone know who's done the punishing. [What about that? – Peregrine] The answer is that the town was extremely isolated and the SAS team responsible was moved back to Maltraverso immediately after the incident.

Historians of the campaign, and many people at the time, were misled by the murder of the German officer, which seemed to give the SS a motive. I think I know who strangled the German. [You know everything, don't you? Then why don't you tell us? – Peregrine] It was no one from the town.

I read all this through twice and then sat for a long time, postponing my involvement in a massacre that had happened so long ago, the repercussions of which seemed likely to last forever. Then I lifted the phone and asked Miss Pippa Marching to get me a line. 'Dial 9 and do it yourself,' she rebuked me smartly, and so I called the number I usually avoided and heard Beth, sounding, as she always had, surprised and slightly out of breath.

'Hullo.'

'Oh, hullo. Is Dunster there?' Not Dick, not your husband, never anything but Dunster.

'He's abroad.'

'Not by any chance in the High Apennines, somewhere to the north of Florence?'

'He might be. It's not the sort of thing he tells me much about.' I had a sudden hope that this was a criticism, but she sounded perfectly satisfied with the situation. 'I suppose he may ring me, or just turn up. Why do you want to know? Is it about Natasha?'

'No. Tash is the least of my worries.'

'So why did you ring up? You don't usually.'

'I've been thinking. We might have lunch.' In fact I had only just thought of it.

'Because he's away?' I could imagine her smiling as she said it, but I knew it was no real encouragement.

'Because I have something very important to tell you.'

There was a silence, so long that I thought she had left my voice on the hall table and abandoned me to go about her business. At last she said, 'Where are you?'

'Soho. We could go to Sophia's. Could you make it at one?'

'All right then.' She rang off and I put down the telephone. It had seemed, when I came to do it, almost too easy.

Sophia is the small, grey-haired, soft-voiced Italian who makes Piero's in Greek Street such a pleasure to visit. Beth and I used to go there when we came up to the West End to a theatre or cinema, and because of that I hardly ever go there now. Sophia greeted me warmly when I arrived at ten to one and there I sat, crumbling bread and drinking too much white wine, until Beth arrived on the dot of half past. I rose to greet her, feeling just as I had when she walked into the Indian restaurant in the Turl when our love affair had just started – no different at all.

'I'm sorry.' She smoothed the back of her skirt and sat down. 'I don't know what happened to the time.'

'That's all right' – I found myself lying – 'I haven't been here long, really. I had a busy morning.'

Sophia brought another bottle of Orvieto and said, 'It's wonderful to see you together again.' She went away smiling and neither of us said anything to disillusion her. We were silent because I couldn't think of how to begin, and then Beth said, 'You've got something to tell me? I'm very glad.'

'Why are you glad?'

'Aren't you going to marry one of those Mummers of yours? I thought that was what you had to tell me.'

'Would you like it to be?'

'Of course. It'd be better all round. I'm sure Tash would like to see you settled.'

It was as though this beautiful, red-headed woman I loved so much had become a kindly aunt, hoping that I would put the dangerous days of my youth behind me and get married and start a family. Settled indeed! For a moment I was almost pleased to have news to disturb her.

'I have to talk to you,' I said, 'about Dunster.'

'What about him?'

'He may be about to write something that's going to cause a lot of pain and suffering.'

'Well,' Beth said, 'he usually does.' She caught sight of herself in the tarnished mirror by our table. Her long, pale fingers pushed back her hair. It wasn't so much that she sounded as though she had lost interest, but she was retreating behind that wall of vagueness which I knew so well.

'It's a bit more serious than the notice he wrote about our *Hamlet*.' I tried to imagine that we were back at Oxford, discussing another Dunster outrage.

Beth said, 'You were upset about that, weren't you?'

'And you,' I said, 'wanted me to knee him in the groin.'

She was still looking at her reflection, smiling at herself as though she didn't believe me.

'This isn't just a bad notice,' I told her. 'He's going to write about something your father did, or what Dunster thinks he did.'

'What Jaunty did?'

'Something terrible. In the war.'

'Well, most people did terrible things then, didn't they? That's what they got called up for.'

'But not to massacre an entire town. In a church!' If I had wanted to shock her, I failed. She had abandoned her reflection and was looking round the restaurant as though for ways of escape.

'Jaunty didn't do that.' Her voice was a sort of a shrug, less a denial than a deliberate retreat.

'I don't know. I told you, Dunster thinks he knows.'

'I suppose none of us knows what happens. In wars.'

That year's war had finished quickly. The short burst of desert fighting was over. An almost bloodless victory, one of the newspapers had said; most of the people dying being assorted Arabs killed in air raids, or retreating, or slaughtering each other. If we cared so little about them, why should we concern ourselves with what happened in a scarcely used Italian church almost half a century ago? Perhaps I shouldn't have cared if Beth's father hadn't been attacked, or if Dunster hadn't been the attacker. I said, 'Do you imagine Jaunty wants a film made about him, suggesting he's a mass murderer?'

'No,' she agreed, 'I don't think he wants a film about him at all.'

'Then, can't you stop Dunster?'

'If I could stop him,' she said, 'I don't suppose I'd be with him now.'

And that, as far as I was concerned, was the bleak and honest truth of the matter.

'I'll have to see Dunster when he gets back,' I told her. 'I'll have to talk to him.'

'I'm sure he'll be glad to see you.' And then we went on to discuss other things: Tash and her A-levels, her chances of getting into Manchester University which she thought was going to suit her much better than Oxford – a place she was sure would be too 'false' for her tastes. This was an expression I was afraid she had learnt from her step-father. We kissed in the street when we parted, a small, polite tribute to the past, and then she was gone, walking quickly towards the Tube. Whatever drama was going to be put on, Beth, it was clear, wasn't up for a part in it.

Chapter Sixteen

It was Wednesday when I had met Beth and for the rest of that week Peregrine was away somewhere in the north of England, and Dunster didn't come back from Italy. Pippa Marching treated me with unyielding suspicion and I had nothing to do but sit in my cell and worry about how I was going to deal with Dunster. The more I thought about it, the more slender and unsubstantiated the story of the massacre seemed. At the best moments I felt sure that I could make him see reason and drop it, and then I had to remind myself that reason was something Dunster found invisible. On Friday I gave up and told Pippa I was going home early, news which she received with no interest whatever. Sunday was going to be my birthday and I had invited a selection of Mummers to lunch. On Saturday I went shopping for this occasion. I was going to give them smoked salmon, roast pork with apple sauce, and an open tart that I bought at Pierre's Pâtisserie in Muswell Hill. I meant to think about anything but Pomeriggio and the Feast of Santa Magdalena in Lachrimae.

The party consisted of Pam, the physio, who had played Madame Arkadina, and her husband, Dennis, the dentist. There was Martin, the bank manager, who had directed *The Seagull*, and his wife, Muriel, who did our publicity. Ken, who had played Konstantin, came with his girlfriend Ranee; and finally there was Lucy, the solicitor. I had not meant to ask her, afraid that my dramatic seduction and abandonment of her in the play might start a friendship at a level for which I was not prepared. However, she came into the Mummery bar when I was asking Pam and Dennis and it became impossible to leave her out. When not excited by the aftermath of a performance, she was a quiet, methodical girl with short, dark hair and attentive, watchful eyes. I thought she would do well in her chosen profession.

Martin and Muriel brought champagne and the others parcels. Lucy's was wrapped up in pink and green paper with a matching card. I opened it and found a bright yellow silk shirt of the sort which might have decked out Peregrine Gryce. I stood holding it, wondering exactly what idea she had of me and how much it must have cost her, when there was a ring at the door bell and there was Natasha, wearing an old pair of jeans with a carefully cultivated hole in the knee, accompanied by a stocky boy who she said was George. She looked disappointed to find the place full of Mummers, as though I should have been celebrating my birthday alone with the Sunday papers. All the same, she gave me her presents: a single rose, a packet of incense, a piece of soap in the shape of a woman's bottom and a small model aeroplane. George had brought a bottle of Spanish wine, for which my thanks were effusive.

'Mum remembered it was your birthday,' Tash said. 'So she suggested we came over.'

'That was nice of her.'

'Anyway, George wants to get into television. I told him you could be a big help. Now you're an associate producer. George thinks that all television's crap and he wants to do something about it.'

George said, 'Television's the language of the future. No one can write a novel after George Eliot and poetry's completely finished. So are the movies, except for Roger Corman. So it's over to you, Mr Progmire. You should be speaking for *now*, but all you're doing is making crappy costume dramas about maids in Edwardian country houses.'

I tried to explain that it was a long time since *Upstairs, Downstairs* – and that hadn't been made by Megapolis – anyway. And that up to now I'd been in accounts and hadn't had much of a chance to speak the language of the future. At which George looked at me with considerable pity.

'Associate producer.' Dennis, the dentist, who had a perpetual and artificial suntan, and glasses hanging on a chain round his neck, spoke with the quiet, concerned voice which he used to ask which tooth was giving the trouble. 'Isn't that something of a departure?'

'Philip's gone creative,' Pam, the physio, explained. 'It's what he's always wanted.'

'Producers and directors' – as Muriel spoke, she blew out a little cloud of cocktail biscuit – 'I can never remember the difference. Isn't the producer the chap that looks through the camera and says "cut"?'

'No, darling. That's the director.'

'Really?' Dennis, the dentist, looked astonished. 'Is it *really*? What does the producer do then?'

'I suppose,' I told him, 'he worries about things.'

'Oh, well.' Dennis raised his glass to me. 'Congratulations and happy birthday.'

They all drank. George looked at me and said, 'At your age, Mr Progmire, you must spend a lot of your time thinking about death.'

'It's a theory George has,' Tash explained. 'People over forty think about death a lot.'

I said, 'I don't think about it much more than when I was seventeen.' That had been true – before we started to do the *War Crimes* series.

'Who gave you this, Dad?' Tash was holding up the yellow shirt. 'Isn't it a bit of a positive statement?'

'Nina brought it.' The Mummers laughed and I corrected myself. 'Not Nina, of course! Lucy, it was incredibly kind of you.'

'You can always change it.' Lucy was calm and practical, unfazed by my daughter.

'I wouldn't dream of changing it. It's extraordinarily . . . elegant.'

'I thought it was right for an associate producer. Bit showy for a Trigorin, perhaps. You dad was a wonderful Trigorin,' Lucy told Natasha. 'Are you an actress too?'

'She did Hermia in the *Dream* at school,' I told them, if only to get these disparate elements of the party together. 'She was remarkable.'

'Don't boast about me, Dad. It's *so* embarrassing.'

'I never really *got* Arkadina.' Pam was peering anxiously about the room, as though still searching for this elusive character. 'There was something wistful about her that I could never quite catch.'

'I would call it wet.' The dentist had the same view of Chekhov that Nan Thorogood had of *Hamlet*. 'What a hopeless collection of wallies! That's what you couldn't get, Pam. The wimpishness. We're a couple of medics, you and I. Practical people. You have to have a bit of energy to be a physio.'

I wanted to tell them that Chekhov was a medic also, but I was too concerned with Natasha's look of terminal boredom. This turned to contempt as Lucy said, 'Nina had enough energy to run away with a man who didn't really love her. That was a pretty positive thing to do.'

I saw Tash look inquiringly at Lucy when she said this, and so to change the subject I asked, 'You're sure Mum didn't mind you coming over? Leaving her alone, I mean.'

'Oh, she's not alone. Dick's back. He flew in from Bologna early this morning. He's terribly excited.'

'Is he?' The one thing I didn't want to hear about was Dunster's excitement.

'He woke us up to tell us he'd got the entire story for his latest script. And he says he's absolutely thrilled to be working with you.'

And as she said that, they were all there, uninvited, at my birthday party: the SAS and the Germans, the Italian fascists, the singing procession carrying the Saint, Beth, Jaunty, Dunster. The lot.

*
137

The phone rang very early on Monday morning, the second day of a new year in my life.

'Progmire, my dear old man. Great news! We're going to be working together again.'

'I hear you had a successful trip.' I hadn't remembered us working together before.

'You've no idea just how successful. We've got something absolutely stunning on our hands.' I should have known that it couldn't be good news.

'You'd better come into the office.' As associate producer I was, after all, meant to be in charge of Dunster. 'You can tell me all about it.'

'This is a bit too sensitive for the office, Progmire. Besides, I don't want to run into that swinging little sixty-year-old in the funny clothes. Have you seen his wife? She's a little old lady in a tweed skirt and a twin set. Funny, isn't it? Look, I've got a bit of serious research to do. Just to dot the i's, you understand. Why don't you meet me there? Shall we say eleven o'clock?'

'Meet you where?'

'The Imperial War Museum. Where else?' He was laughing as he put down the phone, no doubt at my extraordinary inability to guess where he was going to be.

I decided that I wouldn't go, that I would wait until he came into the office in a normal and businesslike way. There was something ridiculously theatrical in our meeting among a collection of old weaponry and relics of forgotten wars, but 'theatrical' was a word of powerful attraction to me. Having first rejected the idea of going at all, I started out far too early and reached the river by ten o'clock. By a quarter past I was crossing Lambeth Bridge in sunshine, with light shining up from the water. I drove up Lambeth Road and parked on a meter in front of an imposing domed building exactly forty minutes early for my appointment with Dunster.

I had no alternative but to sample the entertainment offered.

The engines of death and destruction were set out in the sort of chic surroundings usually associated with modern American art. Small fighter planes dangled from the ceiling like mobiles. Battle-scarred tanks were mounted and shown as though they were abstract sculptures. The air was filled with discreet officer-class voices, recorded on tape, whispering the virtues of the Churchill tank or the Focke-Wulf bomber. I stood before an ancient, beautifully polished, double-decker bus which had rattled up to Ypres and the Somme on a free ride to the slaughter. Enticing notices pointed to the World War I trench 'complete with sounds, smells and other special effects'. Somewhere Neville Chamberlain was telling the nation we were at war, somewhere else soldiers were singing 'Roll out the Barrel'. In a hidden corner, no doubt, Dunster was dotting the i's of history. I went and sat in the canteen and had a coffee among parties of uncontrollable schoolchildren for whom war was a welcome day out. Then, still having time on my hands. I bought a ticket for the Blitz experience.

So I sat in the darkness of a mock-up air-raid shelter, listening to the excited whispers of German tourists. 'My name's Charlie,' said a recorded Cockney accent, 'and I've been an air-raid warden down this street for the last couple of years. And I wouldn't be surprised if they don't come over tonight.' The sirens started whining and another voice in the darkness said, 'Enjoying the war games, are you, Progmire?' Dunster sounded young, eager and fatally enthusiastic. 'I saw you bolting in here for safety.'

We left together before the All Clear. 'Don't you like it?' The attendant looked disappointed. Dunster told her it was hugely pleasurable but we had business to attend to. 'What I suggest,' he said as we walked under the fighter aircraft, 'is that we go outside to talk.'

Two mammoth naval guns protruded over the circular flowerbeds in the museum's garden. As we walked down the gravel path towards a seat we were back to our boyhood when we had pretended my parents' house was bugged and we had to talk in the grounds of Alexandra Palace. And the strange thing was that, now we were together, I was almost pleased to see Dunster. Years had vanished for a moment and it was as if I had seen that familiar figure in a flapping coat, with long, uncovered wrists, running towards me with some secret of the prefects' room to tell, or a scandal among the staff to reveal. Today, however, Dunster was dressed differently. The jeans were familiar but they were topped by a black leather jacket, decorated with zips, which gave him a military appearance, perhaps adopted for the work in hand.

'We're going to make the most sensational programme together!' he promised me, as we found a bench to sit on.

'Are we?'

'The snappy little dresser . . .'

'Peregrine?'

'When he's not deeply concerned about spilling coffee on his cashmere, Perry worries about how we're going to make the last war interesting to "nowadays". I suppose he means to the ordinary, down-to-earth chap in the male boutique.'

'How do *you* want to make it interesting?'

'It's not the *war* we're on about.' Dunster's eyes were bright with enthusiasm, his forehead pale and a lock of dark hair, untouched with grey, still fell across it. He clutched at his knees, as though to prevent himself from jumping up in his excitement. 'It *is* about nowadays. It's about the old men that run our lives. It's about them being murderers.'

'Isn't that a bit exaggerated?'

'You wait, Progmire. You wait until I tell you what I've found out.'

'I've read the story,' I assured him, 'of the church blown up.'

'Of the massacre?'

'If you want to call it that.'

'Oh, I do. I certainly do. A reprisal for two British prisoners, betrayed to the fascists.'

'That's your theory.'

'It's a lot more than a theory, old man. I've got the evidence. Do you want to know who put me on the scent?' He was hugging himself now, his hands nursing his elbows, rocking with delight. 'Our mutual father-in-law.'

The March sunshine was thinner than I had thought and I felt cold. A middle-aged man came jogging by, music from a Walkman plugged into his ears. He wore a T-shirt with Madonna's pout stretched across his pigeon chest and bright-green shorts. His thin legs ended in purple trainers. I wanted to get up and go, away from Dunster and this absurdly peaceful garden with two great guns mounted over it.

'Oh, yes,' Dunster said. 'Major Blair is a great source of information.'

'Jaunty took me to dinner,' I told him. 'He said the war crime was done by a young man, and he's not that young any more. Everyone changes, he said, over the years. For once I thought I understood him.'

'I don't think you did, quite.' Dunster seemed amused.

'What do you mean?'

'I mean, Jaunty didn't have anything to do with it. He was in the SAS section, that's true. But he was left behind, back in the caves above Pomeriggio. Jaunty wasn't in that select little group of hand-picked murderers. Only four of them did in the church.'

'Thank God for that!' I had never thought that I would feel grateful to Dunster.

'You're relieved for Jaunty?'

'No. For Beth.'

'Why?'

'She wouldn't like a scandal involving her father.'

'Don't worry your head about Beth, Progmire. Jaunty didn't do it but, of course, he knows who did. You want to know how I got him to tell me?'

'Go on.' Now I didn't mind what I discovered.

'I was talking to him one night, quite late, actually. We'd gone down to stay. I'd brought a bottle of brandy and we were drinking the stuff. Well, I knew we were doing this series and I wanted to know if Jaunty had any stories about the Italian campaign – and if he'd ever heard of Pomeriggio. I think he rather likes me, in a sort of way.'

I thought of Dunster in a tailed coat, jumping a hedge when he couldn't ride. I remembered Jaunty's look of admiration.

'He started to talk about what happened. He also began to look very important. You know, the way people do when they know something that nobody else does? And then he said, 'Bloody bad luck for the poor buggers that went to church that day, but it's been a wonderful little nest egg for Jaunty.'

'What on earth did he mean?'

'Didn't you ever notice? Jaunty's tight as hell, of course. But if it comes to it, he always seems able to produce a bit more cash than you'd expect from an army pension and looking after a few horses. He helped Beth and me out of a bit of a hole once.'

And contributed to the down payment on my house. I also remembered ill-kept cashbooks and chaotic accounts in Jaunty's office, and bank statements that seemed healthier than could reasonably have been anticipated.

'I asked him what he meant' – Dunster was smiling – 'and sloshed the four-star Remy about a bit. He said two things that I remember. One was "Silence is golden, old boy. Silence is the equivalent of a golden handshake." The other was "The fellow who commanded that church parade has always been good enough to look after Jaunty. And Jaunty's always been suitably grateful."'

So blackmail wasn't a young man's crime, something done in a vanished age, but a source of continuing profit. Would Beth have to discover that about her father? 'So who was paying him? Did he tell you?'

'Not directly, no. I couldn't get that out of him. I've found out now, though. That's what's going to make our programme so sensational. Forget Megapolis. Any company would take it on.'

'What do you mean, forget Megapolis?'

'The party that did for the church was very small.' Dunster was now sitting with his legs stuck out, his arms crossed comfortably, staring at the ground between his feet. I can still see him and hear his quiet, careful, dangerous voice. 'Only a young captain, a sergeant, the demolitions specialist and a Lance Corporal Sweeting, who helped hump the gear. Sweeting went missing some time after the incident. He was a deserter who took up with an Italian girl and her family hid him. He never came back and he's still there – an old man who speaks Italian, calls himself Andreini and owns a small café in a backstreet in Maltraverso. That's who I went to see.'

'What did he tell you?'

'Only what I'd already figured out, long ago.'

'What?'

'The captain in charge is now one of the great and good, of course. A pillar of the establishment. A chap who controls what we see, and suggests what we should think, on so many questions of political morality.'

I wanted to shout at him, Keep quiet, Dunster! For God's sake don't say any more! But I waited.

'He's your boss, Progmire. Sir Crispin Bellhanger. The Santa Magdalena's Day murderer.' He was looking at me then, smiling in what appeared to be perfect happiness.

'Balls!' was what I said, after a long silence.

'Congratulations.'

'That is complete and utter rubbish!'

'At last! I've found something you feel strongly about.'

'Is that why you made it up?'

'Don't lie to yourself, old man. And don't let him lie to you. I happen to know it's the truth.'

'And I know it's not.'

'Have you been out and found that old soldier in the High Apennines? Perhaps you've spoken to the sergeant?'

'I don't need to.'

'It might be difficult, anyway, seeing that Sergeant Blaker was killed later in the war. I'd like to know if you've found the demolitions specialist. I think I've got a lead to him. But we're supposed to be working on this project. Perhaps we could investigate it together.'

'There's nothing to investigate. I know Cris.'

'Such touching loyalty. You've always been such a simple soul, old man!'

'He's not a murderer.'

'Oh, I don't suppose he's ever called himself that. He was just doing his patriotic duty. Avenging the deaths of those two thoroughly good chaps, Troopers Ashley and Pickering, who'd been handed over to the fascists.'

'He couldn't have killed women and children. In a church. Forget it, Dunster.'

'How do you know what people are capable of? In a war? You've never been in a war, have you?'

'Neither have you.'

'But I haven't got your simple faith in the morality of the chairmen of television companies. I can imagine exactly how it happened.'

'Your fatal imagination.'

'We'll get the facts. Find the man who planted the explosives. He'll confirm who gave the orders.'

I thought of an irresistible argument. 'If Cris had been guilty of anything like that, would he have been so dead keen to do a series about war crimes?'

'Yes.' No argument seemed likely to stop Dunster. 'Of course he would.'

'Why on earth?'

'Have you never heard of the need for confession? Murderers

have it. They hang around police stations. They offer to help the police with their inquiries. They make witness statements. In the end they have to give themselves away. Don't you know that's what happened? Sir Crispin Bellhanger's been longing to tell the world about this for years.'

'For almost half a century!'

'It's a long time to keep a secret. Too long for your friend Cris. Your hero.'

'I don't have heroes.'

'I forgot. You don't, do you? Nothing so positive as that.'

There was a silence and I could only repeat, 'It's just something he wouldn't do.'

'You weren't sure Jaunty wouldn't.'

The answer was no, I wasn't sure. But I didn't give Dunster the pleasure of hearing me say it.

'Beth told me. You got terribly steamed up, for you, Progmire. You thought I was on the verge of exposing the galloping Major. You thought she'd mind dreadfully. Do you think he's a more likely killer than your boss in the office? That doesn't say much for your opinion of your ex-wife's family.'

Was Jaunty so entirely different from Cris Bellhanger? The answer was yes, but, again, I didn't want to say it. I didn't want to argue with Dunster. I wanted to be rid of him and his awful, smiling certainty. I said, 'I've got to get back to the office. I'll have to talk to Cris.'

'You mean warn him?'

'Tell him what's happened.'

'I'm sure he'll be interested.'

'And I expect it'll be the end of the series.'

'You're going to kill the story?' Dunster was laughing now.

'Don't you think it's gone far enough?'

'Oh, no, not nearly.' The joke, for Dunster, seemed to be getting better all the time. 'Not nearly far enough.' And then he was serious again. 'You can't stop it now. There's no way you can stop it.'

'I can try.'

Then I got up and left him, sitting on the bench under the guns and enjoying the situation. I walked quickly to the gate and got into my car, but Dunster wasn't far behind me and as I started the engine, which responded with a complaining whine, I saw him unfasten a crash helmet from a motor bike as formidable as Jaunty's horse. This was a new interest in his life, which I supposed he had bought with his earnings from Cris Bellhanger.

I had told Dunster I'd try to stop him. At that time I thought I could.

Chapter Seventeen

'Good news! You've got Sir Percy Blakeney.' Dennis, the dentist, picked up the spectacles that hung round his neck, elevated them to his nose and looked at me closely, as though doubting whether I was an appropriate choice for the Scarlet Pimpernel in the light-hearted romp that was to be the Mummers' big autumn production.

'And we'll be playing opposite each other again,' Lucy said in her quiet and businesslike manner. 'I've got Marguerite. Martin was trying to get hold of you to tell you all about *Pimpernel*.'

'I'm sorry. I've been out of London.' I had been down to Windhammer and had called in at the Mummery for a drink, hoping to find something to talk about other than long-ago deaths in the High Apennines. So I discovered that I was to play, for the first time, a positive hero engaged, despite his languid and flippant manner, in springing aristocrats from the guillotine. I would be raising a weary eye-glass and saying lines like, 'Odds my life, Lady Blakeney! I have spent the entire morning in the perfection of me demned cravat.' Dunster would have found that entirely ridiculous, but then I no longer cared what Dunster thought about anything. I was now at war with Dunster. I had talked to Cris and made up my mind that, at whatever cost, Dunster had to be defeated.

When I had paid my first visit – and I hoped to God it was my last – to the Imperial War Museum and got back to the Streetwise office, I had found Peregrine Gryce agitating because on his return from the North of England I wasn't waiting in my cell, staring at the back wall of the Malibu Club, breathing in the smells of last night's dinner and eager for instructions. 'Pippa tells me you've been looking through the files. I hope you've come up with some ideas?' 'Yes, I have. I've also been talking to our writer.' 'And did you manage to get any sense out of him?' 'I don't think so. I hope not.' 'Tell me.' 'I'll tell you what I can, after I've spoken to Cris. Pippa, get me Megapolis, will you? The chairman's secretary.' Miss Pippa Marching looked at Peregrine for confirmation and then made the telephone call. You have seen from this passage that I was, in some ways, a different associate producer. It was as though Dunster, riding away on his huge black motor bike, had left me some of his determination to act, whatever the consequences. I felt frustrated when Pippa got me through to Megapolis and I discovered that the chairman was spending a couple of days at Windhammer, when once I should have been relieved at the postponement of an almost impossible meeting. I left Peregrine Gryce protesting at my going to Cris over his plaintive little head and I took a taxi to Liverpool Street Station.

I sat in the corner of a dusty railway carriage, looking out at the trailing farewell of London, the back gardens full of weeds and broken toys and grimy, lean-to greenhouses, and the new but already shabby suburban stations. Then came the flat countryside on the way to that sham Gothic castle which Cris treated, as he did so many things in his life, as some sort of a modest joke. I wondered exactly how I was going to ask the man who had given me my job, and taken me away to forget my pain over Beth and Dunster, and who had always been more like an exceptionally companionable father than an employer to me, whether he happened to recall having taken part in a massacre.

My life, as you will have understood by now, has been much concerned with the performing arts, not to mention make-believe. Only Dunster, my former friend and long-time enemy, has shunned pretence and invention and shown an unreasonable addiction to what he felt to be the truth. My own

happiest moments, at Oxford, at Megapolis and with the
Mummers, have been theatrical. Drama surrounded me, so it
wasn't a surprise to discover that what had kept Cris at home
was a touring opera company's performance of *Così fan tutte*
in the baronial hall of Windhammer for the benefit of Angie's
favourite charity, the local branch of the War Widows' Association.

When I arrived she greeted me even more warmly than
usual. She kissed my cheek and made the small noise of
'mmmnyah' as her lips departed. She was clearly as excited by
the preparations going on around her as she had been when
she first came on to the set in Pinewood Studios to act the part
of an intrepid ATS girl in the war her husband had been
fighting in bitter reality. She stood in the hall and watched
curtains being hung, lights set up, props assembled. She organized cups of tea and sandwiches with the efficiency of a
film unit caterer as the singers went through their exercises
and the small orchestra tried out the more difficult moments
in the overture. Cris was with her working, as always, in his
snow-white shirtsleeves and blue braces, and he was still smiling
when I told him we had to have a serious discussion on the
subject of war crimes. 'We'll go outside and talk,' he said.
When he told Angie we were going to look at the garden, she
said she wouldn't come with us because of early clouds of
midges.

There were sheets of butter-yellow daffodils and white nar-
cissi in the rough grass under the beech trees. The first azaleas
were coming out in the borders and there was the start of
blossom and fresh green leaves on the tall Japanese cherries.
As we walked away from the house we heard the faintest
sound of the quartet 'May the Wind be Gentle'. As you can
see, the setting couldn't have been more inappropriate for the
business in hand.

Down the broad, grass walk between the long beds of
flowers preparing for their annual display, I started on my

story and Cris listened. I tried to tell him all I felt about Dunster, how our lives together had seemed a long, comical-tragical preparation for that morning's meeting. We stopped in a grassy circle, surrounded by a tall yew hedge, with a moss-covered sundial in the centre – a place as quiet and private as a room. There I told him about Dunster's account of a late-night, brandy-inspired conversation with Jaunty. I said Jaunty had spoken about a dynamited church packed on a saint's day. Jaunty had nothing to do with this atrocity.

'Of course not,' Cris said, 'the Germans did it, after one of their officers was found strangled.' So it *was* the same church, the same ghost town, that he had told me about after dinner as we sat together and he had played the piano. I was troubled by that for a moment but then relieved. Cris's simple sentence sounded a hundred times more convincing than Dunster's over-excited account of Jaunty's drunken confidence, or his contact with an unnamed deserter gone native in the Apennines.

'You said my ex-father-in-law fought the war in a way you didn't approve of?' I asked Cris, postponing the final question.

'I couldn't be sure but I had my suspicions. That garrotted officer had the mark of Jaunty about him. We shouldn't have held that against him, only it had such terrible consequences.'

'So Jaunty's section was there when the incident happened.' I knew it was ridiculous to try to protect ourselves by calling it an incident.

'Oh, yes. He was well established over and above Pomeriggio at the time.'

'And you?' I had to ask.

'We'd had a job to do, further south, towards Monte di Speranza. We only joined up with the support group, Jaunty's lot, after the church business was over.'

Relief again, a tide sufficiently strong to allow me to launch the great attack. 'Dunster says Jaunty told him you were there, before it happened.'

'Does he?' Cris's eyes were blue and clear, their corners wrinkled by his customary smile. He seemed not in the least perturbed.

'And that Jaunty said you commanded the church parade.'

'Me and who else?' Cris asked, without a pause.

'I'm not quite clear. Three or four others. A sergeant who was killed later.'

'Blaker.'

'And someone who deserted and married an Italian girl. Dunster's been to see him in Italy.'

'Lance Corporal Nathaniel Sweeting. "Natty Suiting" I used to call him because he was always such a bloody mess. He must have a defective memory after all those years on the run. Or one that can be altered if the price is right.'

It hadn't occurred to me that Dunster might have paid for his information. I might once have thought that for him to do so would have been out of character; now I was prepared to believe him entirely ruthless. But I still had to say, 'There's even a suggestion that you've been paying Jaunty all these years – I suppose to keep him quiet about what happened. I went through his accounts once, and he does seem to have some mysterious source of income.'

'Me pay Jaunty Blair?' Cris seemed to find the idea entirely comic. 'I'd rather contribute to the Pit Bull Terriers' fighting-fund. Please don't ask me to explain Jaunty's finances.'

'No. I wouldn't.' By now I felt able to smile. I had been worrying about Cris's pay-off to Jaunty going into my down payment on Muswell Hill.

'There might be a hundred explanations. Good, bad or indifferent.'

'Of course there might.'

'Well, then.' Cris was standing with his hands in his pockets, his face turned up gratefully towards the sun. 'The whole thing's the most complete and utter balls, then, isn't it?'

'That's exactly what I told Dunster.'

'I'm sure you did.'

'As a matter of fact,' I assured him, 'I didn't believe it for a moment.'

'Your friend's just looking for a sensational story.'

'He's not my friend. He's my enemy. And I'm sure that's what he's after.'

'Yes.' Cris looked down at the grass now, at the carefully shined brogues planted firmly apart on the short grass. 'We'll have to think what we ought to do about it.'

'I'll do anything,' I told him. 'Anything I can to kill this absurd story.'

'We'll talk about it when we're back in the office. Meanwhile, you will stay tonight, won't you? You wouldn't want to miss the Mozart.'

So, that evening I sat next to Cris and Angela Bellhanger and listened to the opera which informs us that our personalities are irrelevant, and indeed interchangeable, that one lover is really quite as good as another, that all women do it and it all comes to the same thing in the end. And this hard lesson is set to music of such perfection that war crimes slipped out of my mind for a little while. I even forgot to worry about Cris letting it all wait until we met again in London, which seemed a rather too laid-back way of dealing with the problem.

After lunch the next day, and after no further discussion, Cris drove me into Norwich to catch the train. When he'd stopped the car he said, 'What do you think we ought to do?'

'I think you ought to ditch the series.'

I had made the proposal and Cris agreed. He said, 'Not because of me, you understand. I can cope with whatever anyone cares to throw at me. But I don't want Angie upset. Not in any way.'

'Of course not.'

'Do you think we might offer Dunster some other sort of work?'

'We might try.'

'You sound doubtful.'

'Once he's set on something he's hard to shift. But I'll certainly try.'

'You do that. Let me know how you get on, will you?'

And as I opened the car door he said, 'That *Così*. Bloody marvellous, wasn't it?'

'I thought they did it very well.'

'I mean *what* they did, not how they did it. It was saying, what's it all matter in the end? Isn't that it? What's it all matter, anyway?'

Then we said goodbye and I caught the train back to London. I rang Dunster's number from Liverpool Street and Beth answered. She told me he was out and I wondered whose memory he was ransacking now.

'I've been with Cris,' I told her. 'I wanted to let Dunster know as soon as possible. Our series has been cancelled.'

'That's a pity.' She sounded only moderately disappointed. 'He's just bought himself this ghastly great motor bike.'

'I know. I've seen it. And the jacket to go with it. He must be celebrating his perpetual adolescence. Oh, and could you tell him, we're going to try to find something else for him to work on. Will you tell him that?'

So I took the long journey back to Muswell Hill and called in at the Mummery to have a drink. That night, for the first time ever, I slept with Lucy, my ex-Nina, my coming Lady Blakeney. It seemed that the crisis caused by Dunster had awoken me from a long reverie into a burst of activity on all fronts. But I'd better explain exactly how it happened.

We sat drinking in the bar and one by one other Mummers turned up. Martin, the bank manager – whom I had to thank for Sir Percy – and his wife, Muriel, came in with Pam, the physio, who said I looked 'tremendously tense' and began to knead the back of my neck in a way which made me feel I would settle for the tension. Her dentist husband was not altogether pleased by this attention and he asked Pam, rather sharply, if she couldn't leave her work behind when she visited the Mummery bar. Finally, Ken, who had played Konstantin, came in with his girlfriend Ranee. They wore identical gold bracelets on their slim wrists and looked at each other with melting eyes. They were so obviously in love that they seemed like creatures from another world, one of which I had inhabited so long ago that I had almost forgotten it, and I found myself looking at them with a kind of envy.

We talked about putting on the French Revolution with the small cast at our disposal and the problems of guillotining people. I let the familiar, safe conversation lap over me like bathwater after a hard day. 'What you need, young man' – I knew Pam called even her most geriatric patients 'young man', so I wasn't flattered by this, although I was relieved that she had stopped digging her fingernails into my neck – 'is a square meal. What about us all going to the Swinging Bamboo?'

'Do you know the story about the two girls who went for a Chinese?' Dennis, who had been drinking pink gins, spoke a little indistinctly. 'The poor fellow died.' Nobody laughed and he explained how it had sounded quite funny when a patient told it to him.

'You probably had your fingers half-way down his throat.' Pam was in an unsympathetic mood. 'You didn't hear it properly.' Ranee turned large, sad eyes on the dentist and said, 'That is a most terrible story!'

I sat opposite Lucy and watched her eating rice. She lifted very small morsels to her lips and ate with her head on one side like a bird, perhaps the seagull I had fatally wounded in a play. I felt that sharp moment of lust which Trigorin must have known to be irresistible and finally unimportant. I remembered promising myself that I would never again become involved with anyone who had been my lover in a play, but that night the declaration of war with Dunster had separated me further from the memory of Beth. It was as absurd to imagine that we were Trigorin and Nina, as that we should become that melodramic couple, Sir Percy and Lady Blakeney. I was an associate producer in television and she was a solicitor. The evening could start from there. Lucy said, 'You look tired. Overworked?'

'Not too much work. But it's got a little difficult.'

'More difficult now you've gone over to the artistic side?'

'The trouble's not artistic. More, well, perhaps more legal, actually. I may be needing your advice.'

'Oh, you can have that any time. It might help to talk it through. You might be able to see it in proportion, whatever it is.' She looked at me with all the wisdom of her youth, not a bad actress, not a wounded seagull, but the commonsense lawyer she was.

I had walked from my house to the Mummery, which was only a few streets away. Lucy had driven me to the Chinese restaurant and eventually she drove me home, as though I were her date and she were seeing me safely back to my front door. I asked her in for a drink. As I poured white wine I felt ashamed of my sitting-room, not because it was a tip but because it was too neat, the home of someone who had lived alone too long, who was too fussy about putting books and records back in their places and was too set in his ways.

'Well,' Lucy said, 'aren't you going to tell me the problem?' She sounded very judicial, like a schoolgirl playing Portia. She sat in an armchair, her legs crossed; her fingertips even seemed in danger of coming together like a lawyer's at the start of a conference.

'No,' I decided. 'I'd think we'd better go to bed together.'

'Really?' She still had her young lawyer look. 'I thought you'd never get around to asking. Can I finish my wine first?'

'Of course you can. There's no special hurry.'

'No.' She was smiling now. 'There doesn't seem to be.'

While she was finishing her glass, the phone rang. I picked

it up knowing what to expect. 'So you've chickened out of *War Crimes?*' Dunster said.

'We've decided to cancel the series. I told Beth, the chairman's going to suggest another subject for you.'

'No thanks! I don't want to be another recipient of Bellhanger bribes. You can tell your chairman to save his money. He'll probably need it, by the time I've finished with him.'

'What're you planning to do?' I did my best to sound unconcerned.

'Don't bother your pretty little head, old man. I'll be working by myself from now on.'

He put down the phone then. A minute later it rang again. It was Cris's secretary to say that the chairman was organizing a special meeting of the Board for tomorrow afternoon. He particularly wanted me to be there.

'You're very busy,' Lucy said.

'A little. Just at the moment.'

'Was that the difficult business you started to talk about?'

'Yes. But it can wait until tomorrow.'

Upstairs Lucy undressed methodically and put her clothes, neatly folded, on a chair. She joined me in the bed where I had spent the years with Beth, but there was none of my ex-wife's faintly musky, red-headed smell, nor her scarcely controlled frenzy. Lucy was sensible, patient, considerate, generous, and yet, in spite of her cool and casual acceptance of my invitation, still a little formal. In complete silence, only breathing lightly, I felt she was giving me the advice she had promised, in a way that was far more valuable than any lecture on the law of libel. When we had come to rest and I had her head pillowed on me she said, 'Of course you don't love me, do you?'

'What do you want me to say?'

'Exactly what you feel.'

'It's because of Beth. I'm not sure if I can ever be in love again.'

I had told her the truth, just as Dunster would have done.

Chapter Eighteen

There we were again, around that great, black marble sarcophagus, the Megapolis boardroom table, high up over the river with views of cranes and long-untenanted office blocks, and warehouses tarted up into flats. Floating restaurants for business lunches gently chugged up towards the Thames barrier. The directors, having rushed their lunches and spent an hour in the traffic, looked as though they wished they hadn't come to an extraordinary meeting for which they weren't prepared and hadn't got written down in their diaries.

They sat, stony-faced and silent, from Charles Glasscock, the youngest member, a solicitor by profession, through to Lady Helena Mendip, a retired headmistress, who often talked a good deal of gruff commonsense, and Barnum, known as Barney, Fawcett, a wealthy old manager of touring companies, pantomimes and summer shows, who was meant to be a fountain of wisdom on the entertainment industry, and Sydney Pollitter, with his hands folded in his lap and his eyes turned up to heaven in the attitude of an ancient cardinal about to embark on a peculiarly unpleasant process of excommunication. Only Gary Penrose, who had risen without trace to become managing director, did his best to smile as he shuffled through his papers. I sat beside Cris and tried to settle my nerves by thinking, with gratitude, of the night that was past.

'I thought we should meet' – the chairman was his usual brisk and cheerful self, although he hadn't on this occasion, stripped down to his braces – 'so that I can explain the position we have reached on *War Crimes*. Simply this. I have decided to cancel the project. My reason for doing so is something I shall have to go into in a little detail. Then I hope you'll all agree that I have taken the only possible course.'

'Chairman' – Sydney Pollitter coughed, tugged at his ear lobe and started up his engines – 'I know that with your usual fairness and courtesy you will forgive what many of my colleagues, perhaps all of my colleagues' – here he gave a slightly wolfish grin around the table – 'may well think to be a trivial, perhaps uncalled-for, and it may even be stigmatized by some as an impertinent, observation, but I had some considerable doubts about that particular programme when you first laid it before us.'

'Yes, Sydney.' I was, as ever, astonished by Cris's patience and self-control. 'I do remember.'

'I knew you would, Chairman. I knew that with your amazing grasp of every tiny detail of whatever concerns us at Megapolis you wouldn't fail to recall that supremely unimportant moment of my, perhaps ill-phrased, interjection. But I must say this in all fairness and honesty to my colleagues, and to you, Chairman, of course. Please, all of you, do laugh me to scorn if you so desire, but the very first time I heard the words War Crimes I scented danger.'

'Then you'll be very glad, Sydney, that the programme's been ditched.'

'That, Chairman, is a matter of profound relief to myself. Of course, I do not speak for colleagues. Colleagues are perfectly capable of speaking for themselves. They will undoubtedly do so far more lucidly and effectively than I can pretend to. They have the eloquence. So. *War Crimes* has been ditched, to use our chairman's terse and pithy expression. "All well and good", that may be said when it comes to the turn of others. What arises is what, if any, public explanation should be given?'

'I wasn't intending to give a public explanation.' Cris was now ignoring Sydney and turning his full charm on the ex-headmistress, who appeared to soften a little. 'I am intending to outline the course of events to the members of the Board, in confidence.'

'I am rebuked by the chairman.' Sydney Pollitter looked round at the colleagues with a smile of considerable satisfaction. 'The chairman rebukes me and he is perfectly right to do so. I do most respectfully suggest that the chairman be allowed to address us without further interruption.' Whereupon the colleagues who had been silent throughout looked somewhat bewildered. Cris said, 'Thank you, Sydney,' and embarked on his statement.

He spoke clearly, crisply and without notes. He told them he had wanted to do the *War Crimes* series to show the senseless cruelties that all sides might commit in a war. He had wanted to include a British atrocity, if such an event could be proved to have occurred. He was familiar with the massacre at Pomeriggio because of his service with the SAS in the Apennines. He had no doubt that the church was blown up as a reprisal for the death of a German officer. He had been concerned when he discovered that the scriptwriter might suggest that this outrage was in fact a British reprisal because two of our escaped prisoners had been handed over to the fascists. He had then asked Philip Progmire, who knew the writer personally, to take over as associate producer. He wanted to be kept informed of the script's progress so that he could prevent potentially dangerous inaccuracies.

Only yesterday Progmire told him that he had seen the writer, Richard Dunster, and it was clear that this man thought he had discovered who had given the orders to blow up the church on a saint's day when almost the whole town had gone there for a service. The suggestion was that it was he, then a young captain in the SAS, who was responsible for this ghastly event. He hoped that the Board would accept his word that there was not the slightest truth in that allegation. He believed that war was always tragic but he had never overstepped what are generally called the 'rules of combat'. In the interests of truth and to maintain the high standards of our documentary output, and in no way to protect his own reputation, he had cancelled the series. Other than that, he intended to take no further action.

I thought that the headmistress was about to open her mouth in warm agreement but there were sinister signs from the other side of the table. During his chairman's speech, Sid Vicious had produced a letter from an inside pocket, unfolded it carefully and adjusted his spectacles to read again what I suspected he knew by heart. He now pulled his ear and thanked the chairman for his statement, which was as full and frank as they had all known it would be. 'However, I have had a letter, and from the word or two I have been able to have with colleagues over the telephone I think we have all had this same communication.'

There was a murmur of assent round the table. And then the long-winded interrupter said the few short words which made my heart sink. 'It was delivered to each of us this morning. Personally. By motor bicycle.'

'Well, what's it say?' Cris asked. 'This precious letter?'

'The chairman didn't receive a copy?'

'Not so far as I know.'

'And you would know, Chairman, had you received it. Undoubtedly. That is indeed strange. Then perhaps colleagues would like me to read it out, so that it may be incorporated in the minutes. I promise to do so quite without comment or digressions, whether tedious or no. Chairman, may I proceed?'

'In your own time, Sydney.' Cris was calm again, even smiling. I couldn't join him.

'The heading is Streetwise Productions and the date today. It is signed Richard Dunster.' Sid Vicious gave a further jerk to his ear to speed him on his way:

Dear Member of the Megapolis Board
Today you will be told that my *War Crimes* series is to be cancelled.

This is because I have obtained incontrovertible proof that your chairman is himself a war criminal who, up till now, has managed to avoid arrest. You will have been told of the destruction of the church at Pomeriggio. Captain Bellhanger thought up, planned and commanded that operation. Its sole intent was the murder of almost the entire population as a punishment for betraying escaped prisoners. There can be no doubt that this is the truth. I have interviewed a Major Blair, who served in the SAS with Bellhanger, and Lance Corporal Sweeting, who now lives in Italy. One of the other members of the squad who performed this atrocity, Sergeant Blaker, lost his life later in the war. I have not yet interviewed the explosives expert. When I do so, I have no reason to think that his evidence will not bear out all that the other witnesses have told me.

I am determined that this information shall be made public, if not by television then through some other medium. You, as members of the Board, may agree that the truth cannot be suppressed and may decide that the series should proceed as planned. Whether or not you do so, I am completely dedicated to the cause of justice for the innocent inhabitants of a small Italian town. Perhaps, in his heart, your chairman will agree and intends that my work shall be his public confession. Yours sincerely [etc.]

The style was appallingly familiar. These were the sort of words I had been hearing throughout my life, but those days were a rehearsal for this final blast of moral outrage, the explosion calculated to do the maximum possible damage. That they were read out in Sydney Pollitter's high snuffle made them no less the voice of Dunster. And as he sat listening to them, I had never admired Cris so much. He looked as detached as if someone were reporting on the sale of videos and T-shirts in the Megapolis gift shop. When the letter had been read, even Sydney was silent for a moment, impressed by the enormity of the charges.

Then Cris said, 'Very interesting. But pure fiction.'

'Speaking for myself and I hope for the rest of us' – Lady Mendip spoke as one accustomed to take a hard line with unsubstantiated allegations of snogging in the music room – 'I am prepared to accept our chairman's word entirely. If he tells us that it's fiction, then that's the end of the matter.'

There were sounds of approval led, unexpectedly, by the ever vocal Sydney. 'I will second Lady Mendip's excellent motion, if I may. We unhesitatingly accept the chairman's complete denial of these shocking allegations.' Was that it? Could we gather up our papers and leave the black marble? Could I ring Lucy and suggest the Muswell Hill Odeon? Apparently not. Sydney still had another trick up his sleeve. 'However, that can't be quite the end of the matter, can it? The chairman said this letter was interesting. He said so, of course, with that complete fairness we have come to expect of him. Now, I am no lawyer. I am a man of figures and accounts, tedious matters, perhaps, in the view of some around this table. Here I speak purely as a layman but is this letter not also a flagrant libel? Through the Chair, of course. I turn to Charles Glasscock for legal advice.'

'Clearly libellous.' The youngest member enjoyed his moment of glory. 'I have no doubt that would be the advice of any reputable counsel.'

'I will be shot down in flames by Charles if I am in error on this point, Chairman, but does not the sending of this letter, this very morning by motor-bicycle rider, amount to publication of the libel?' Sid Vicious, who denied all knowledge of the law, looked extremely knowing.

'Publication has occurred,' Glasscock the solicitor told us, 'and further publication is apparently threatened.'

'There now, Chairman.' Sid leant back and looked at Cris as though congratulating him on having won a much-coveted award. 'You have an unanswerable case. You will also have the full support of colleagues, many of whom are far more learned in these matters than I could ever pretend to be, in issuing a writ immediately.'

For the first time in that long meeting I thought Cris

looked troubled. He stared down at the table, took in a deep breath and then began to collect up his papers.

'Thank you, Sydney. Thank you all for your support. I will, of course, have to consider my position carefully, very carefully indeed. No doubt I'll take legal advice. Well, thank you all for coming in at short notice. Let's hope I shan't have to trouble you again.'

'A final word, Chairman, while you are considering the matter, as indeed you must. And this is spoken, I do hasten to assure you, in the spirit of true friendship and lasting respect. If no action is taken on this wretched letter' – at which Sydney liberated his ear lobe and brought a large hand down smack on the offending document – 'a terrible slur will remain on the reputation of our chairman and of course' – and here a note of almost religious awe came into the Pollitter voice – 'on the good name of this great company, Megapolis Television plc.'

'That's right!' Barney Fawcett, a stout and elderly man, had the cheeky schoolboy face and unsettled hair of the hero of the William books I used to read as a child. 'This business has got to be put a stop to. Who is this fellow Dunster? Some sort of leftie agitator? Let's see how he'll stand up in court. Not too well, if you want to know my opinion.'

'One doesn't like to resort to the courts, of course. But it may be that the threat of proceedings will be enough to force an apology.' The trouble was that Lady Mendip had never met Dunster.

'I would like to see a writ issued and served tomorrow,' young Charlie Glasscock said, and I thought he would also like his firm to be instructed to do it.

'Why tomorrow?' Sydney Pollitter began a little, snuffling giggle at his own final joke. 'Why not deliver it this afternoon? By *motor-bicycle* rider!'

'The spirit of true friendship!' Cris had taken his jacket off when we got back to his office and was pouring two large whiskies. 'When Sid Vicious starts to talk to me about true friendship I can feel the knife tickling my shoulder blades. You understand what he was doing?'

'It was fairly obvious.'

'He thinks he's got me in a corner. Sue for libel or give up your job.'

'You think he wants it?'

'Of course. And he wants the golden handcuff the company'd give him. A big lump of money to induce him to take on the job he's been angling for this last ten years.' He put his legs up on the sofa as though he were intending to sleep off his troubles, clutching the chunky glass of dark liquid for comfort. 'I've a good mind to make him a present of it. Our precious directors would probably have him, or he'd go on talking until they gave in. Board meetings mean being bored by Sydney Pollitter.' Something was happening I had never bargained for. It seemed I was seeing Crispin Bellhanger, who took to command so easily, in a rare and unexpected moment of defeat.

'You're not going to resign?'

'What's the alternative? Days in court. Headlines in the papers. The hopeless business of trying to prove things that all the witnesses have forgotten, even if they're still alive and talking. What's that going to be like for Angie? No. I've got a good mind to jack it in. Perhaps they'll let me run that little touring opera. Now that's a nice, peaceful job for an old soldier.'

'It wouldn't stop him, you know.'

'What did you say?' Cris seemed far away in the world of whisky and Mozart.

'If you give up, it's not going to stop Dunster. He'll be cock-a-hoop. He'll say your resignation proved him right. He might even get the newspapers to agree with him.'

He turned his head slowly to look at me and seemed amused. 'What's your advice? What are you telling me to do?'

'He's got to be fought,' I told him. 'He's got to lose.'

Cris swung his long legs down from the sofa, put his glass on the coffee table and looked at me with an entirely new interest.

'Something's changed you, Philip.'

'Perhaps this has.' This, or too much of Dunster. Perhaps it was also the fact of Beth receding in last night's lovemaking in the bed that hadn't been hers for so long. Or was it seeing Cris cornered and taken off his guard?

'You seem to have become quite ruthless.'

'I've had enough of him.'

He stood up and went to his usual position, looking down at the water with his back towards me. He emptied his glass slowly and said, 'All right. I'll go and see the lawyers. You know so much about it now. Would you be good enough to come with me?'

'Anything,' I told him. 'Absolutely anything I can do to help.'

Chapter Nineteen

I started this account by telling you about my chronic anxiety and that I could always find something to worry about, even if it were the way I seemed to worry about nothing at all. This feeling was a perpetual handicap, a pain I grew used to and lived with but which was always there, like an unloved companion I couldn't ignore. The morning after the board meeting I woke up and felt that something had gone seriously wrong because I was not really worried any longer. And the worrying thing was that this had happened at a time of great anxiety, when I had started to fight against an enemy I now knew to be implacable for the honour and reputation of a man I knew to be innocent. Perhaps these uncharacteristic decisions had suppressed my worries like some strong pain-killer, or at least a placebo. I really don't know how else to explain it.

I had been to the Muswell Hill Odeon after the meeting at which Sydney Pollitter had performed his delicate manoeuvre, and I woke up with a dark head beside me on the pillow, which may have helped to explain my alarming absence of doubt. As I went downstairs to make the tea, the phone was ringing. It was Cris who said the top libel QC, Robin, or Robbie, Skeffington, was finishing a case in Hong Kong and couldn't see us until Monday. He hoped I'd be able to fit that into my diary. He sounded cheerful when we said goodbye and, as I spooned the Earl Grey into the teapot, I wondered why I wasn't particularly worried by the extraordinary fact that Sir Crispin Bellhanger had taken my advice.

For the rest of that week events were suspended. I called in at Streetwise and told Peregrine Gryce that, although the series had been cancelled, all the work he had done would be paid for and I was taking possession of the files as Cris's lawyers had asked for them. 'I must say, Philip' – he was looking extremely sulky – 'nothing's gone right since you came on to the artistic side. Why did you want to get us mixed up with lawyers? Lawyers simply don't understand the creative imperative. Also they dress so terribly badly. Rather like you, actually.'

'I didn't get us mixed up with lawyers. Dunster did. Have you spoken to him at all?'

'I keep leaving messages but he doesn't return my calls.'

'He's probably busy trying other forms of expression. He seems to have lost his faith in television.'

'This mess with Megapolis has shaken mine, rather.'

'Goodbye then, Perry. We may meet again some time.'

'Oh, I don't expect so. I imagine you'll sink back into accounts. You do look just a tiny bit out of place in Wardour Street.'

Miss Pippa Marching didn't look up from her copy of *TV Quick* to return my parting salute.

Tash came for her weekend. On Sunday night she cooked me a surprisingly good dinner – a cheese soufflé and roast lamb – and left the kitchen looking as though we had been entertaining a group of some forty-five drunk and starving teenagers. As we sat over our coffee, getting on, I thought, rather better than usual, she said, 'What's the matter, Dad? Have you become a hippy or something?'

'Have I changed as much as that?'

'I mean, have you taken to wearing these?' She put her hand in her jeans pocket and pulled out a pair of green earrings which I had last seen decorating Lucy.

'Where did you find those?'

'Top shelf in the bathroom. Didn't you notice?'

'I should have done but I've had a lot to think about.'

'It wasn't the pallid job who gave you the inappropriate shirt, was it?'

'You mean Lucy? She was my Nina.' I don't know why I felt I had to add that as some sort of an excuse.

'I don't care what she was of yours. I'm just not going to make friends with her.'

'It'd be nice if you could.'

'Horrible! So many people at school have to do it. Go to awful chatty lunches with their father's girlfriends. So they can discuss Dad as though he were a difficult child they were both crazy about, really. And so the girlfriends can be told his marriage was breaking up anyway and it's not their fault.'

'It had broken up long ago. And it certainly wasn't Lucy's fault.'

'No. I know.' She looked thoughtful and then she said, 'I don't think I'll be coming to stay with you again, Dad. Not for some time, anyway.'

'Why ever not?'

'It's about Dick. He says you sacked him. You and that boss you seem so terribly fond of.'

'I think he sacked himself.'

'He wants to tell people about your boss being a war criminal.'

'He's got that idea into his head. It's not true.'

'He says there's people to prove it.'

'Let's see how they stand up in court.'

'Grandpa Jaunty's one of them.' Her use of that familiar childhood name made me feel how closely, and how uncomfortably, I was related to the Major, who was now a hostile witness.

'We'll have to see what he says too.'

'Dad.'

'Yes?'

'What're you up to? Are you really just protecting your job? Or the establishment? Or something?'

'Is that what Dunster says?'

'Well, yes.'

'And what does Mum say?'

'She says I can make up my own mind about what I want to do.'

'So you want to stay away from me?'

Tash, like her mother, was vaguely retreating to a prepared position. 'Dick believes things so passionately. You know, there's a sort of purity about him. I don't want to be disloyal to him.'

'Only to me.'

'It won't be forever, Dad. Anyway, you don't care about things like loyalty, do you?'

'And I don't believe in things passionately?'

'Well, do you?'

'As a matter of fact, yes. I believe quite passionately in not charging around the world causing people unnecessary pain.'

'Dick would say that the pain's very necessary.' I hadn't convinced her. 'Justice has to be done.'

'That's what's going to be decided.'

When she went to bed she asked me to come and say good-night to her. She put her arms up and fastened them round my neck, reluctant to let me go. It was how she had behaved when she was a child, but I didn't build too many hopes on it. I knew she would keep away from me and that I should be presumed guilty, at least until the case was over.

'By the way,' I said, as I drove her to college early on Monday morning, 'how's George?'

'Oh, I sent him away to stay with his mother for the weekend. It'll do him good. He can get rid of some of that embarrassing affection he seems to feel for everybody.'

'Robbie Skeffington. Done all the right things. Scholarship at Eton or somewhere. Next year's chairman of the Bar Council. Bound to get his bum on the High Court Bench in the next year or two. Terrific track record in libel. Managed to screw half a million from the *Daily Planet* for that Tory Minister in

the gay wedding case. You couldn't do better than Robbie.'
Sitting naked in bed beside me and sipping tea, Lucy had
talked like an old lawyer, seasoned in the courts, weighing up
barristers' reputations over port and walnuts. When she was
discussing the law, she adopted a tone of infallibility and
became condescending to outsiders like me. This, I discovered,
was a characteristic of lawyers in general and of Robin Skeffington, QC in particular.

From what Lucy had told me I had expected to meet some
tall, smooth-haired operator with a voice like a coasting Rolls
and well-tailored charm, a man who would purr at juries and
deal tactfully with the judge. Robbie Skeffington had none of
these so-called civilized qualities; he seemed to be a creature,
when you first met him, who had only been house-trained
with difficulty. He was small and hirsute and his eyebrows
met in a single black line across eyes which would glint, as I
later discovered, with such ferocious cunning that I wondered
why the highest tribunals in the land placed so much faith in
him. I never saw him woo the jury; what he could do was
jostle them into accepting his most caustic comments and his
most contemptuous treatment of opposing witnesses.

He was a most untidy man. He sat at a desk on which
briefs and books were balanced to form insecure towers and
he had Dunster's habit of keeping a half-drunk cup of tea
cooling at his elbow. His fingernails, on some occasions,
almost matched his black brows and he was a great biter of
pencils. During all our meetings and throughout the trial itself,
he either ignored me or treated me as though I were incapable
of understanding what was going on. I soon came to the view
that the only thing worse than having Robbie Skeffington on
your side was having him against you.

On our way up to the dizzy heights of the legal profession,
on which Robbie sat like a gargoyle perched on top of a
cathedral spire, Cris had not gone to young Charlie Glasscock,
the solicitor on the Board who had looked longingly at the

case, nor to Megapolis's regular lawyers. He had consulted his family firm of Fanshawe, Glover, Mandelow & Singleton, who had advised the Bellhangers since their ancestor made his fortune out of steam engines and built Windhammer. Our case was in the care of Justin Glover, whom even the telephone girls called young Mr Justin. He was in his late thirties, prematurely balding and he looked at life through strong, gold-framed glasses. His apparently cheerful, even flippant manner covered a deep anxiety which I was able to recognize and often share. I was later to discover that his frequently haunted expression was caused not by the demands of his legal practice but by a distracted wife and four talented but temperamental children, all under the age of ten. He had introduced us to our leading counsel rather as a nervous keeper might approach the cage of some rare but dangerous animal, inviting us to look and marvel but not to get our fingers too near the bars of the cage.

'This is a most wicked libel and the damages will be immense.' Like the early saints Robbie Skeffington seemed to have been born without any talent for doubt. In that respect, I thought, he was fairly matched with Dunster.

'There's some suggestion in the letter to the Board,' Justin Glover dared to remind our leader, 'that there may be an attempt to justify the charges.'

'Is there any truth in them, Sir Christopher?' Robbie used the tone of respectful commiseration with which he would always speak of his client to the jury.

'It's Crispin, actually.' Cris hated being called Sir. 'No truth whatever.'

'Then let them try it, that's all. If they attempt to justify they'll inflame the award enormously.'

'Damages,' Cris said, 'aren't really the point.'

'They are always the point. In any libel action. You must really allow your legal advisers to advise you.' Robbie made a gesture, almost knocking over a pile of papers, which embraced not only Justin Glover but Marcus Beazeley, his junior barrister. He really was tall and elegant and no doubt had a Rolls-Royce voice to use if Robbie had ever allowed him to open his mouth, and was to sit through our case with an air of complete detachment. 'Immense damages will be the measure of your high reputation. What is a man but his reputation? What are the words Crispin Bellhanger? Without reputation they are a meaningless jumble of syllables. They might mean a man of straw, a fraudster, a layabout, a nobody. Add reputation and those syllables mean a much-decorated ex-officer, a gentleman who fought heroically for his country, a patron of the arts, a chairman of a great public company, a tireless worker for a number of charities, a force for good in the community. That's your reputation, Sir Crispin, and if the jury values it at less than half a million I shall consider I've cocked it up!'

At this, Robbie retired behind his papers. 'What a prize ass that scruffy Stuffington is!' Cris, who made a point of getting our QC's name wrong from then on, said afterwards. 'Perhaps that's what you need when you get involved in a libel action?' Now he said, 'This fellow Dunster hasn't got a penny. Philip Progmire can tell you that.'

'Progmire?' Robbie looked straight at me and I felt invisible. 'Which one is Progmire?'

I owned up.

'And you're from Mr Glover's office?'

'From my office,' Cris said. 'He's worked on the project. What's more, he knows Dunster and the whole history of this case.'

'My name's *not* Progmire,' Robbie told us, I thought unnecessarily. 'I don't know Mr Dunster, although I may make that gentleman's acquaintance if he's rash enough to enter the witness-box. I may not know the whole history of this case. Yet. But I imagine it's my opinion you're paying for – and not Progmire's – and I have to tell you that as soon as I opened the papers I smelled a winner. I got a sniff of very substantial damages indeed. I form a view when I first get my nose near the papers and I'm not often wrong. Is that your experience too, Mr Glover?'

Cris said, 'What's the point of immense damages if we can't recover them?'

'Recovering them is Mr Glover's business. It's a purely mechanical matter. Summonses, judgements, possession orders. The bargain basement of the profession. No need for you to concern yourself with that, Sir Crispin. You are shopping at Harrods. I fully expect you to top my record damages from the *Planet*, when the Junior Minister for Communications was alleged to have gone through a ceremony of marriage with a man from the Department of Trade and Industry. God send us a respectful judge and a more than half-witted jury and I am confident, sir, that we shall do it. Would you agree with that, Mr Glover? We shall overcome!'

Cris, Justin Glover and I left the Temple and walked down Fleet Street, a place that seems dead now all the newspapers have packed up and departed for glass towers on the wharves round Megapolis. In time those papers would be full of the case of *Bellhanger* v. *Dunster*, but then they had only reported that a writ had been issued because of a letter to board members concerning the chairman's war record. Cris led us into El Vino's. The journalists had left there long ago to sit by their computer terminals down a traffic-clogged road far from the centre of government, the theatres and cinemas, the clubs and the sources of scandal. Now the lawyers were in sole possession of the wine bar: large, sombrely dressed figures who laughed loudly at the memory of things that had only seemed funny because they had happened in the hushed and oppressively serious courts of law. As we found a table among the mahogany and legal caricatures of the back room, some of the barristers smiled and raised their hands in greeting to

Justin Glover, hoping that he would send them work. There was a pretty, dark-haired waitress who reminded me, for a moment, of better things, like Lucy. Cris ordered a bottle of the house champagne. 'Not to celebrate the half million we'll never see but because we're out of that legal badger's set. I thought that if he called me Sir Crispin again, I'd plead guilty just for the pleasure of depriving him of a brief.'

'Robbie has an extraordinary effect on juries.' Justin Glover did his best to sound reassuring.

'And a pretty devastating one on clients.'

'Robbie's a fighter. You've got to allow him that.'

'Now you're reminding me of all I didn't like about the army.'

The girl came back and started to tussle with the champagne cork. Cris helped her and as he filled our glasses, I said, 'About the damages . . .'

'I won't ever try and get them out of him. However much they give us.'

'I'm glad about that.'

'Because of Beth?'

'Yes,' I said. 'Because of that.'

'No costs, no damages.' Cris raised his glass to me. 'They're not worth the trouble of enforcing.'

So it was agreed, as I'd felt sure that it would be, given Cris's good sense and generosity. And I said I'd give Justin Glover a full account of all that I knew about Dunster and the story which had apparently started with my ex-father-in-law. He wanted to know if the Major would give evidence and, if he did so, what he was likely to say. I told him that Jaunty's behaviour was quite incalculable but that Dunster was now part of his family and that he'd been impressed by our opponent's first ride on a horse.

A week later a privately printed pamphlet, setting out Dunster's version of the events at Pomeriggio, was distributed, free of charge, to all the employees of Megapolis, other television companies and most newspapers. Justin Glover told us that Robbie had been delighted at this development; it now being certain that the amount of damages would break all previous records.

In due course Dunster's solicitors filed their defence. It alleged justification and accused Cris of having commanded the party that blew up the church full of praying civilians. It also said that 'shortly after this incident, the plaintiff said to a fellow officer, Lieutenant Jonathan Blair, "We will have to say that the Germans did it."' So the field of battle was defined, and the opponents prepared for war.

THE TRIAL

Chapter Twenty

'He's upstairs,' Beth said when she opened the door of the house in Camden Town. 'You'd better come up.' The square looked peaceful in the sunlight; the traffic boomed in a familiar way from Kentish Town Road. Beth's greeting was not hostile, and yet I felt I had crossed into enemy territory. As the door shut behind me and she led me up the staircase, I wondered if I should ever have undertaken this twelve o'clock mission to Dunster.

When his father died, Beth's husband – that was how I had to think of him for the purpose of this visit – had come in for the whole house, including the lower floors which used to be let out to the couple from the *Financial Times*. The place looked reasonably tidy and the heavy and perpetual smell of burning bacon and fried bread had been banished. I tried to concentrate on something other than Beth, in jeans and a white shirt, her hair pulled back and tied with a small scarf, her face pale and free of make-up, walking in front of me. I might once have embraced her, put my hands on her breasts, kissed her pale face as she arched back towards me. Such conduct was now out of the question and quite inappropriate to my mission.

The top room with windows looking out over the rooftops and back gardens, where Dunster's father had written his articles and Dunster worked now, was far less of a tip than I had expected. There were relics of the past: signed caricatures of Michael Foot and Nye Bevan; photographs of John Dunster, younger than his son was now, shaking hands with Castro and Tito and Mendès-France; shelves of Fabian pamphlets and Left Book Club publications in battered yellow jackets; a

179

Tribune poster with the headline THE END OF THE ESTABLISH-
MENT *by John Dunster*; and the old upright typewriter on which
such forgotten diatribes were written. His son had added his
own trophies: a fax machine and a word processor, books piled
up against the wall and, blocking out the light from the windows,
a bulging filing cabinet and a few hundred copies of what I could
recognize as the pamphlet which he had entitled SIR CRISPIN,
WAR CRIMINAL: FROM A MASSACRE TO MEGAPOLIS.'

Dunster was sitting behind the big writing-table as we came
in. He rose to greet me, smiling in the way a head of state
might have welcomed a journalist who, after prolonged nego-
tiations, had been granted an interview.

'A herald' – Beth's husband was clearly on top of his form –
'come with a white flag and an offer of surrender! Is the
distinguished old fart you work for prepared to admit the
game's up?'

Beth said, 'I'll go and put the coffee on.'

'No, you'd better stay.' I stopped her. 'This is important
for both of you. It's about the damages.'

'Please, old man. Have a seat.' Dunster waved me to an
upright chair in the middle of the room. Beth moved some
books, sank on to the cushions of a disintegrating wickerwork
armchair and began a close study of her fingernails. Dunster
sprawled behind his table and hit a thin paper knife on it, as
though it were a tuning fork. I saw a map on the wall with a
red-headed pin marking Pomeriggio. He seemed to be enjoying
the whole thing like a military operation.

'There aren't going to be any damages,' he said, 'because
your lot aren't going to win.'

'Robbie Skeffington's forecast is half a million plus costs.
You've got no way of paying that – either of you.'

'There's no way we're going to have to.'

'That's what I came to tell you. It's just possible that Crispin
Bellhanger won't enforce the damages. He's not really interested in money.'

Dunster looked at me with considerable amusement and said nothing.

'I don't want to see you lose Beth's home, Tash's home. Your home, come to that. I don't want to see you bankrupt and put out on the street and I don't think Cris does either.'

'Yippee! He's cracking up!' When the words finally came from Dunster they did so with a whoop of delight.

'He's prepared to behave extremely generously. I wish you could understand that.'

'Generously? Not bloody likely! He's on the run! Of course he is. He knows he can't win and he wants to buy me off. Just like he bought off Jaunty, and you too, Progmire. He's promoted you to be the chairman's yes man and spokesperson on delicate missions.'

'It's not a bribe. It's what I think he'll do whether you go on with the case or not.'

'Then why did you come here to tell me about it?'

'In the faint hope that you could understand what sort of a man Cris is. And when you understand that, you might wonder whether you ought to go on hounding him.'

'You mean, let him get away with murder? Just in case I lose an old house in Camden Town, which is a damn sight too big for us, anyway. Is that the honourable way you want me to behave?'

'It's not a case of honour.'

'Oh. What is it, then?'

'Just . . .' – I looked at Beth, appealing to her – 'commonsense.'

'You mean it's sensible to give up fighting, at the moment when the enemy's starting to retreat?'

'Can't you see?' I asked Beth directly now. 'You're both running the most ghastly risk!'

She had found a fingernail which wasn't to her liking and had been chewing it without embarrassment. Now she stretched out her hand, looked critically at the back of it, and considered the result.

'It's his case,' she said. 'He'll make up his mind about what to do with it. From what you say, it does sound as though we're winning.' I had come to offer them a way to avoid annihilation, and found them united and poised for victory. I stood up, out of patience with Dunster's limitless self-assurance.

'A word before you go, old man. You tell your boss to stuff his damages. He'll never get them, anyway. And you know why? Because we're going to win. We've been told that by Ken Prinsep and he doesn't act for clients he doesn't believe in. "This is a truth that has to be told." That's what he said. And the jury're going to have to accept it.'

Later Lucy told me there's no such thing as a barrister who believes in all his clients. He'd go off his head if he tried to generate so much faith.

'You'll have heard of Ken?'

'I don't believe so.'

'Oh, Progmire! You do live in a world of your own, don't you? He's the leading radical barrister and he's prepared to take on my case for £200 an hour, which is nothing. Juries love him. And they can't stand being patronized by that awful little old-public-school creep, Skeffington. Ken says he spends his time hanging round the Sheridan club and brown-nosing the judges. Old man, that's the lot you've got in with. Trust you to join the establishment just as it's on the way out.'

I couldn't resist glancing at the *Tribune* poster on the wall and saying, 'Your father thought that's what it was doing quite a long time ago now.'

Dunster gave me a look full of pity and said, 'You know, for a moment, I thought you'd read our manifesto and come over to join us. You see I'm constantly trying to think better of you, Progmire.'

Despite my protests, Beth came down the stairs to see me out. I said, 'Tash says she's not coming for any more week-ends.'

'Yes. She told me that.'

'What did you say?'

'That it's her life. She must make her own mind up about what she does. I think she was pretty annoyed about your girlfriend too.'

'What do you think about that?'

'I'm really glad.' After all those years I still felt a faint pang of disappointment as she said, 'I told you. It'll be a great relief to see you settled.'

'Are you settled?'

'Of course we are.'

Don't be quite so sure about that, was what I restrained myself from saying. We got down to the front door and Beth opened it.

'You know I only came here to help.'

'You shouldn't bother. He doesn't need that.'

'What does he need?'

'I suppose for people to believe in him.'

'And this Ken Prinsep's prepared to do that for £200 an hour.'

'You weren't always like that, Philip.' Beth also looked at me regretfully. 'You weren't always thinking about money.'

The landslide that started when Dunster threw the first stone was slow, ponderous and inescapable. It moved, however, at varying speeds. Sometimes it would take a great lurch forward and the earth would tremble. Sometimes it hung suspended, scarcely moving, with only small fissures to betray the underlying upheaval. Then we could travel on, avoiding the potholes and cracks in the roadway, as though the disaster area didn't really exist. I drove to the Isle of Dogs, moved back to my old desk in the accounts department and supervised the budget of a new and quite uncontroversial series about the world's great art collections. Cris and I hardly discussed the libel action and the subject never came up on the agenda at board meetings. I did notice, however, that Sydney Pollitter became more flattering than ever to Cris and treated him with the sort of reverent concern usually reserved for those whose days are numbered. His colleagues on the Board went through our business with only the smallest hint of embarrassment.

Natasha no longer visited and I spent the weekends with Lucy. We cooked and shopped together, went out to the Odeon or drank in the Mummery bar – but our relationship was a curious one. It seemed, like the long-awaited battle between Cris and Dunster, to hang suspended in time. Most affairs are restless; like history they can't stand still. They must be forever moving, upwards towards some deeper understanding or down to a final crash from which you can hope to escape with only minor injuries. Lucy and I stayed at the point we had reached when she first took off and neatly folded her clothes. I didn't tell her I loved her and she didn't refer to the subject again. Whatever she may have felt for me was curiously undemanding and I hadn't reached the point of worrying about that either. We made love. We didn't quarrel. We didn't seem to find much to argue about. It was as though all my emotions, hopes and fears were fixed on the trial that was bound to happen, and that my time with Lucy was a safe haven of ordinary life.

Nor did our friendship excite much comment among the Mummers, who were used to a changing of partners in an elaborate formation dance as one production gave way to another. Sex, indeed, was one of the main reasons why new arrivals in Muswell Hill, which otherwise offered few opportunities for romantic meetings, wanted to join our group. Martin, the bank manager, used to take great trouble at auditions to weed out those candidates who, he said, were more interested in the parts of fellow actors than those created by any dramatist. Once accepted into the company, however, your life was your own, and indeed a certain cheerful promiscuity was felt to be the mark of a professional, like using Leichner

numbers 5 and 9 and buying the *Stage* every week at the Tube
station. When I turned up in the bar of the Mummery with
Lucy there were few comments, although Pam did draw me
aside to ask, 'Are you sure she has a sense of humour?' and
said, 'If she'd been a mature, experienced and really *physical*
type of woman I might have felt just the tiniest bit jealous. But
as it's only Lucy, I honestly don't mind at all.' Dennis, the
dentist, said, 'You seem to be pretty well rooted in that girl,
Philip.' So at least I felt like a healthy tooth.

It was Lucy who told me all about Ken Prinsep. 'Bit of an
odd background,' she said. 'Born in Canada. Rich family of
biscuit manufacturers. Went to Yale Law School in the
flower-power era. Took part in protests in the South. Did
some human rights cases after he joined a law firm in Chicago.
Then decided that England was the only place where justice
was incorruptible and went to Cambridge to read Law. Got a
First but had some difficulty finding chambers. The English
legal hacks probably felt he took it all a bit too seriously.
Finally got into a radical set we brief sometimes – they special-
ize in things like terrorism and porn. The litigation partner
says he can be brilliant, but he was behind the door when tact
was handed out. Also that he can't quite get on the same
wavelength as some of the judges.'

'It sounds as though he'd suit Dunster.'

'Perhaps. But he might get too involved in the case. He
might be too much on Dunster's side, if you know what I
mean.'

'Not exactly. Can you be too much on the side of someone
you're defending?' Was I too much on Cris's side, for instance?

'Oh, yes. Our litigation partner says that can be very dangerous.'

A few days later I was sitting in my office, staring out of the
window and wondering if Cris had heard any more from our
lawyers, when the telephone rang and a surprisingly deep and

resonant voice said, 'Is that Mr Progmire? Maurice Zellenek here.' He pronounced it Morreece in the American manner, although he didn't have an American accent. 'I had the pleasure and privilege of seeing your Trigorin, Mr Progmire. A young lady in my lawyer's office was kind enough to obtain a ticket for me.'

I vaguely remembered a man who had been talking to Lucy after the first night, a stranger to the Mummers with all his hair at the wrong end of his face.

'Mr Progmire. Your Trigorin was quite something.'

'Well. I suppose it was. Something or other.'

'I was led to believe that you are a modest sort of person. That's a mistake, let me tell you. In our business modesty gets you nowhere very much.'

I wondered what I was meant to say. That I was the greatest Trigorin since Stanislavsky? And what did he mean by 'our business'? Sitting in front of a pile of accounts and awaiting a difficult libel action, I was still ridiculously pleased to be told that I was a part of the world of entertainment, for that must have been what it was. Grocers and dentists don't talk about 'our business'.

'I'm not sure I was a wonderful Trigorin, but it was very kind of you to telephone and tell me so.'

'The purpose of this call is not just to congratulate. The purpose is to suggest we meet and talk. Talent is a kind of rarity these days, especially among men in middle life. I shall be away in Hungary for several months. May I look forward to calling you on my return? Shall we do lunch?'

'It would be a pleasure.'

'No, sir, Mr Progmire. The pleasure is entirely mine. "A subject for a short story." Unforgettable, the way you handled that great line.'

Mr Zellenek then left my ear and I sat looking at the river and wondering if the call were not a practical joke organized by Dunster as some obscure form of revenge. However, when

I told Lucy what had happened, she said that her client Zellenek had been greatly impressed in my acting, was surprised to find I was an accountant and had asked for my telephone number. 'I didn't want to tell you that,' she said, 'in case he didn't ring and you'd've been disappointed.' I thought that this was very considerate. 'He's got some big project for next year,' Lucy said. 'I think it's a series for Channel Four.' Was he really going to ask me to go into 'the business'? Would Mr Zellenek finally release me from the world of budgets and balance sheets and set me up forever on the creative side? I allowed myself to toy with this idea for a little while until there was a distant murmur of thunder and the case of *Cris* v. *Dunster* took another lurch forward.

Chapter Twenty-one

I drove down to Exmoor, as we had so many years before when Beth decided that it was time I went through 'the ordeal by fire and ice'. My destination was, once more, Blair Cottage; other than that I had no more idea of what I should find, or how I should be greeted, than when Beth first drove me, far too fast, along the seaside road and then inland, between the tall hedges and through the little towns with their gift shops and boarding-houses and cream teas, towards the moor and the parents I had never met.

Dear Progmire
In the past you have appealed to me as a geezer who could see further through a brick wall than most other geezers. You sorted out my personal and business affairs in double-quick time, if you remember, and I thought, there goes an old head on a pair of youngish shoulders. I have never had much luck with so-called professional advisers. Solicitors and accountants seem only interested in drink or women (or both) and in sending exorbitant bills. So I thought I'd ask your advice as I have done in the past.

My problem is legal and business mixed, so it should be up your street. Mike's away, getting her mother into a home at the moment, so if you could motor down here tooty sweet, say Thursday morning, we could go up to the Old Huntsman for a ploughman's after our chinwag.

I would be much obliged if you'd say nothing about this to my daughter, Beth, her husband – or anyone else, come to that. I'll keep an eye skinned for you around midday.

Sincerely
Jonathan Blair (Major, Retired)

This unexpected letter, in spiky, unpractised handwriting,

much crossed-out and clearly the result of considerable thought, had arrived in an envelope marked PERSONAL AND EXTREMELY PRIVATE. In spite of Jaunty's instructions, I took it to Justin Glover, whom I had seen a number of times since our first conference, feeling in need of a certain amount of advice myself.

Robbie Skeffington had plunged us into such a hot certainty at the start of the case that the time was bound to come for cooler feelings and I found our solicitor in a state of increasing apprehension. 'The key witness,' Justin told me, 'is obviously going to be Major Blair. If he goes into the witness-box and says Sir Crispin commanded the operation, we can only attack him on the grounds that he's trying to save his son-in-law's pocket. Robbie'll do that with wonderful brutality, of course. But it may not be enough to destroy the old boy's evidence. It's something we ought to be worrying about.' Then I showed Justin Glover the letter and he said I'd better go and find out what it was all about, as it might do some good and he didn't see why it should do any harm.

So I left Muswell Hill and Lucy around dawn and at exactly a quarter to twelve I passed the gallows on which the notice Blair Cottage swung and drove down the rutted path to the stable yard and the house sitting uncomfortably among the gravel. I parked and got out of the car as the baying started and the task force of assorted dogs leapt for my genitals. It was like old times.

The back door was open. I stood on the step and rang the bell, which made a loud, high-pitched buzz and produced no Major. I waited and then crossed the threshold into the kitchen, setting off a hysterical reaction in the dogs who leapt, yelped, barked and bounded as though I were an escaped axeman who had called to murder Jaunty. I did my best not to give these animals the satisfaction of seeing how nervous their welcome made me. I had come a long way on an important mission and I was determined to complete it.

The house was as cold as I always remembered it, as though the dark furniture, the shiny lino and the dun-coloured wallpaper gave off their own particular chill. The kitchen floor was well stocked with boots, slippers, dog bowls and the small mess of a half-trained puppy who had been over-excited by my arrival. There was a plate on the table which had held bacon and eggs, a half-full packet of Mother's Pride and an almost finished mug of Nescafé. The number of dirty dishes in the sink testified to the time it had taken Mike to get her mother into a home.

I went through the kitchen into the hall. Most of the interior doors were open. I saw Jaunty's office, with the bureau bulging as ever with papers, some of which had floated to the floor. On the carpet, handy for the sitting-room sofa, there was a whisky bottle, a glass and a saucer full of the butts of small cigars. I went to the foot of the stairs and, having no desire to inspect Jaunty's bedroom, I called into the shadows, 'It's Progmire!', which seemed, in that empty house, rather a foolish thing to say.

There was no answer and I went out towards the stable yard. The dogs were delighted to see me leave the house and their clamour sank to sullen growls as they returned to the kitchen. Only the old black lurcher, who had slept throughout the excitement on a patch of blanket beside the cooker, trotted out after me.

The long, mournful faces of silent horses peered over half doors, looking as though they had been waiting a long time for some attention and had become resigned to the lack of it. But there were some signs of activity around the stable yard: a bucket filled, a hosepipe pulled out and the door of the tack room swinging open. The big lorry stood with the ramp ready for a nervous horse to be induced to step inside. It was then that I first heard a faint and distant sound, a weak hint of thunder but more metallic and not so far away. One of the lorry doors left open was banging, I thought, and not shutting properly. And then it came again, closer and more insistent. But what attracted my attention was the lurcher whining.

It had left me to go up the ramp and it was standing looking into the shadows, making sounds of distress. There was straw on the floor of the lorry and the darkness smelt of horse piss. I was about to turn away, drive down to the pub and try phoning later, when there was a fainter boom and a weaker rattle. It seemed to come from in front of me. I could see more clearly now and there was a short ladder propped up against what looked like a pair of large cupboard doors over the back of the driver's cabin. There was no mistaking it now, the rattle of the bolted metal, and over the lurcher's concerned whining the faint sound of a human voice in panic.

I have never – I don't suppose many people have – rescued from a coffin someone who has narrowly escaped being buried alive. All I can say is, the experience can hardly have left its victim in worse shape than that in which, on that quiet morning, I found Major Jaunty Blair. He emerged from his tomb, where saddles and horse blankets and other bits of equipment were stored, wild-eyed and grey with terror. His forehead was shiny, his wispy hair soaked with sweat and plastered to his head, his hand, as he grabbed my arm, strengthened by an accumulated frenzy of terror. It took him a long time to summon up the will to be helped down the ladder. Then he stumbled into the open air, coughing and spluttering as though he had forgotten how to breathe.

'Thank God you came, Progmire! Thank God for you! Always a friend.' The Major looked up at me, trembling with gratitude, rather like one of his dogs, I thought, who had been cruelly treated. 'Always had this horror. Rat in trap. Locked in. Bloody tank. Hot as hell. Tank on fire. Locked bloody in! Saw them everywhere. Tanks full of dead geezers.' He was nursing his arms and his elbows, as though they were bruised as he had thrown himself against the door, struggling for freedom. He talked breathlessly, in bursts like random gunfire. As he got to the end of the ramp he vomited.

*

I did a great deal for Jaunty that day. I cleaned him up. I helped him to the sofa where he stretched out. I soothed him with whisky and hot tea. I made him baked beans on toast, which he said was all he could face for lunch. I was there to find things out for Cris. The incident itself remained a mystery. Jaunty said he had been going to take his horse Montgomery to a local show where he would be ridden by a whipper-in to parade the pack of hounds. He had collected the saddle and various accoutrements and was putting them in the space over the driver's cabin, which he mysteriously called the luton. As he was doing this, some bloody fool must have come into the lorry, shut the luton's door and bolted it from the outside. Perhaps they thought that was funny. They might have thought the war in the desert bloody funny, and being trapped in a tank a real hoot, being suffocated in a red-hot box fucking entertaining. At this point Jaunty became incomprehensible and had to be brought back to a serious consideration of the problem with whisky.

Who could have done it? Fiona was the girl groom, he told me. She was meant to come over and help with the transport of Montgomery. She was a sensible girl most of the time. Worked long hours for the love of horses and didn't keep bothering him for more money like some of the more mercenary little bitches. God only knew who was rogering Fiona at the moment. Could be one of the hunt servants. Could be some mad joker with a bloody warped sense of humour who'd never seen the inside of a tank or gone soldiering. Could be . . . Yes. He had Fiona's telephone number. It was on a bit of paper pinned to the wall of the office.

So I went off to ring Fiona, who sounded sensible, shocked and totally puzzled. She was going to come with someone called Charlie Riggs and drive Montgomery over to the show in the lorry, but that wasn't planned to happen until two o'clock because Jaunty was having lunch with a visitor from London. That was me, wasn't it? She didn't really know why

Jaunty should have been putting things in the luton around midday. She'd been with Charlie Riggs all the morning, riding across the moor. She'd never known him to be capable of a practical joke, let alone the cruel one which had terrorized Jaunty. There is only one other thing worth recording about this conversation. During it, I was looking out of the office window and I saw a red Cortina come bumping down the lane and into the stable yard, where the lorry was still standing with its back down. The car stopped, turned round slowly and then drove back past the house towards the main road. For a moment I had a clear view of the driver, an old man with broad shoulders and the look of a bald emperor. It was a face I knew I had seen before but, on that extraordinary afternoon, I couldn't remember where.

After I had spoken to Fiona I went back to my patient and told him what she'd said. He shook his head and lay in silence, staring up at the ceiling, until I reminded him that I had come not to rescue him but because he had sent for me.

'Don't know what to do. That bloody geezer of Beth's. Must have got the wrong idea. Something I said to him. Got hold of the wrong end of the stick.'

I said I was glad to hear it. I was careful not to sound hopeful too soon.

'Poured brandy into me. Got me talking. About the old days. About the war and so on. Up there among the Eyeties.'

I said I knew he'd done something like that.

'Now I hear he's causing trouble for your boss. For old Cris Bellhanger. A bloody good geezer I went soldiering with. Is he causing trouble?'

The old man lay in riding breeches with his boots off, the sleeve of his sweater disintegrating and his shirt open to display the white hairs on his chest, his face a slowly relaxing mask of fear.

I said yes, and that Dunster was causing trouble.

'So many bloody fools about nowadays. Is he still on about that business of the church?'

Yes, I told him, that was what he was on about still. It was the understatement of the year. 'Did you tell Dunster that Cris had said to you, "We must say the Germans did it"?'

'Can't remember all I told him exactly.' Jaunty shook his head. 'But the Germans did do it. We all knew that. German captain in charge gave the order.' The cold house suddenly seemed warmer, the dark sitting-room filled with sunshine: He held out his empty glass but I didn't refill it, not being sure of him yet.

'How do you know that?'

'Didn't I tell you?'

'Never.'

'I ended up in Austria. Major Blair, Allied Administration. Stamping out the black market – bits of it, anyway. Sorting out war criminals. That's where I found out who did for those poor devils who went to church. Bad idea, going to church.' He gave a ghastly sort of a smile. 'Can be extremely dangerous.'

It all sounded so simple. Too simple perhaps, but I didn't want to ask questions that might throw doubt on what was Cris's clear defence. What Jaunty had said was already enough for me to fill his glass again, but I still wanted to know something. 'So was the German officer put on trial?'

'We never quite caught him. Slippery bugger. Got away with it. Well, all it needed was a promise to fight communism, plus a big slosh of money. In the proper quarters. None of it came my way, I have to tell you. Not a dollar for Jaunty. Not that I'd've taken it. I'd have had the geezer tried and shot. Might feel differently now. Much water under the bridge. Gallons of bloody water!'

Some of it still didn't fit, particularly the bit that had once led me to suspect the Major himself.

'When you took me out to dinner, that night at Dandini's . . .'

'Super place, isn't it? Go there a lot, do you? Now you're a bachelor again?' The whisky had done a remarkable job: there was a flush on his cheek-bones and the small, yellowish eyes he turned on me were glinting. 'Is that smashing girl still there? That little Tracy?'

'You told me that an old man isn't responsible for what he did when he was young. You said he was quite different then, different fingernails and teeth and so on.'

'I remember,' the Major nodded. 'Yes, I remember saying that. Too bloody true.'

'So no one should be blamed for what they did years before.'

'Right! That's what I said.'

'Who were you thinking of when you said that?'

There was silence. He looked back at the ceiling. For the first time since I had rescued him from the tomb he seemed almost relaxed.

'Was it the German captain?' I suggested.

'That's right, Progmire. You've got it. Spot on!'

'Why were you worried about him?'

'I keep my ear pretty close to the ground – or I did in those days after the war. When I was in the Allied Administration. And after.'

'What did you hear?'

'Rumours.'

'What sort of rumours?'

'About our Kraut friend who did the job at Pomeriggio. Finally got away to England. We've given him hospitality, that's my belief, for all these years.'

There was a question I felt it dangerous to ask, all the same I asked it. 'What else did you hear about him?'

'Well. He changed his name, of course. Arrived here as Lewenstein. Now goes under the name of Llewellyn and runs a large garage somewhere in the Cardiff area.'

'And his fingernails have changed?'

'You've got it, Progmire. Spot on. After all these long years, let him rest in peace.'

'But you did say . . .' – I took my final risk – 'that if Dunster unearthed the true story it would be a disaster for all the family?'

Another car had driven up and the dogs were barking in a muted sort of way, as though it were a formality they had to go through even for friends. The Major was still examining the ceiling carefully. 'Of course,' he said at last. 'It would have been extremely awkward for me if Dunster had told that story. After all, I knew where the German was and I never told anybody. I want your advice, Progmire. That's why I asked you here. Should I . . . Should I tell them now?'

'Of course. You must tell Crispin Bellhanger's lawyers.' And then Fiona called out from the kitchen. The girl groom came in with Charlie Riggs and after that I got little further information from Major Jaunty Blair.

I am an accountant and not a lawyer. If I had had any proper legal training, or perhaps if I had not been so elated by a story which exculpated Cris, I should not have left Blair Cottage without a signed statement from Jaunty. Instead of getting that, I wasted the rest of my time there in looking after the old rascal and allowed the most precious evidence – for this is what it seemed to be at the time – to slip through my fingers. 'Don't blame yourself for a moment,' Cris said afterwards. 'You did absolutely all you could and I shall be forever grateful.' Of course he would say that, out of pure kindness, but I went on blaming myself even after the trial was over.

I did ring Justin Glover. I drove into Dulverton as I'd offered to replenish the stock of whisky, and I telephoned from the post office. I recounted the whole story and Justin said he was a little disorganized at the moment as Theodora, the six-year-old, was having 'the old ear trouble, only worse' and his wife, Jenny, was getting into a bit of a lather about it and he'd probably have to slip off home early. He'd fix up for someone to come down in the next day or two and he hoped to get Jaunty to swear an affidavit, or at least sign a proof of evidence. He congratulated me and then asked who the hell I thought had banged Jaunty up in the luton.

'God knows.'

'I suppose someone might've played a practical joke?'

'I don't think it was the girl groom. Or her boyfriend. They seemed genuinely upset. I don't know about Jaunty's other acquaintances. Some of them might be rather dubious.'

There was a silence and then Justin Glover said, 'I hope it isn't going to be one of those sort of cases.'

'Which sort of cases?'

'Witnesses being got at. Anyway, thanks, Philip. I'll get someone down to him as soon as possible.' As it turned out, as soon as possible was far too late.

When I got back to Blair Cottage, Fiona and Charlie Riggs went off with Montgomery to the show and I managed to call Mike at her mother's house in Chester. Jaunty, I told her, had had an accident, the lorry door had jammed and he's been shut in, which upset him rather. He was a good deal better now. 'Don't want to speak to her.' Jaunty waved a dismissive hand from the sofa and said in a harsh and penetrating whisper. 'The woman'll only fuss. Just tell her to get herself back down here tooty sweet. Plenty for her to do, what with the mess she's allowed the place to get into.' As a result of constant recourse to the medicinal whisky bottle Jaunty was not in a very good condition to receive Mike, so I told her there was no desperate hurry. She said she'd get up to London that evening and stay the night with Beth, which of course meant spending the evening with Dunster. She could get to Taunton quite early the next morning and Fiona would drive over and meet her train.

'Bloody women!' Jaunty said. 'There're never anywhere when you need them. You're not going to leave me alone here tonight, are you, Progmire?'

'Well, I had thought of driving back quite soon.'

'I'd honestly rather you didn't. For God's sake, wait until Mike gets herself down here.' He looked up at me and once more I thought of an animal at bay, which he had hunted. 'Do that for me, won't you, Progmire? After all, you can't say I haven't done my bit for your boss.' That was true, so I agreed with reluctance.

Around six o'clock Fiona and Charlie came back with Montgomery in the lorry. She told Jaunty that his horse had performed magnificently with the hounds. Later she helped me get his supper. He ordered baked beans on toast, now with two eggs and two rashers of bacon. This meal was over-ambitious. He pushed it away half-eaten and told us, 'Get me up to bloody Bedfordshire!' Charlie Riggs and I supported him up the stairs and into a room where the bed hadn't been made during Mike's absence, clothes were on the floor and the ashtray on the bedside table was overflowing with small cigar butts. We got him undressed with difficulty and left him with relief.

So I slept that night, as I had once done so happily, in Beth's small bedroom, among the rosettes and books on the care of ponies, and the photographs of the child and teenage Bethany clearing jumps or receiving cups at gymkhanas. I felt tired and slept well, confident that Dunster was defeated and Cris out of trouble. In the morning I took Jaunty a cup of tea. He lay awkwardly in bed, one arm thrown up across his forehead as though to ward off a blow. When I put the tea beside him, he opened one suspicious eye and said, 'The bloody woman not back yet, I suppose?'

'The train gets in at eleven. Fiona's going to meet her.'

'I think I'll stay in bed. Tell you the truth. Don't feel quite the ticket.'

'Rest,' I said, and sat down beside him. 'You probably need it.' I also thought he'd got the most prodigious hangover. 'Only I just meant to ask you. When you wrote to me . . .'

'Got you down because you can see a bit far through a bloody brick wall.'

'Well, were you going to ask my advice about whether you should tell our solicitor about the German captain?'

''Course I was. I was going to give them the whole story. If you advised me to do so, Progmire. I honestly wanted to help old Cris. No need for that. Bloody uncalled for and out of order.'

'No need for what, Jaunty?' His voice had become faint. I sat nearer to him, eager to learn the truth.

'No need for what happened. No need for that at all. I wasn't about to let down Captain Cris.' Then his one open eye closed and he told me no more about his imprisonment in the luton.

I went downstairs and read back numbers of *Country Life* and was bored to death with stately homes and Stubbs paintings, Royal Worcester and breeding Palominos, when Fiona drove up with Mike.

'It came as an awful shock to him,' I told her.

'It would do. Jaunty wouldn't like to be shut up in anything. It was the tanks, you know.'

'Yes.'

'The tanks in the desert. That war! It's amazing how long it takes some people to get over it.'

'Amazing.'

'How on earth did it happen? Has he told you?'

'No,' I said truthfully. 'He hasn't told me that at all.'

'Beth and I were wondering why on earth did he ask you down?'

'He wanted to ask my advice about something.'

'About this wretched law case?'

'Yes. About that.' Mike was growing old. She was vague and probably quite innocent of all knowledge of Jaunty's affairs. But she had been with Dunster and I thought it better not to tell her anything more. So, for the last time in my life, I said goodbye to Blair Cottage.

Justin Glover's representative didn't go down for two days.

When he telephoned from the station, Mike told him that the doctor was with them. Jaunty had had a stroke in the night. He couldn't move his right arm and had totally lost the power of speech.

I wrote a long letter to Beth saying how sorry I was and explaining most of what had happened and how I had done my best to look after her father. I got no answer; the lines of communication between us had virtually broken down.

Chapter Twenty-two

The *Informer* is a weekly magazine which was started long before the last war and even before people like Cris and Jaunty were born. Its circulation has been falling steadily over the last decade and its brand of earnest, puritanical and self-righteous socialism has made it acceptable only to a dwindling number of lecturers, social workers and school teachers. The book reviews are still pretty good, however, and the theatre criticism excellent. For that reason a copy was usually to be found in the Mummery bar and I was on my way through a lot of statistics on glue-sniffing, and a lengthy denunciation of the government's policy on food additives, towards an assessment of the latest *Hamlet* at Stratford, when I came upon a piece headed THE BATTLE OF POMERIGGIO: THE ESTABLISHMENT CLOSES RANKS.

The facts of the libel were set out and the progress of the action reported. Cris was depicted as one of the much-favoured 'great and good', a liberal millionaire who had a large country house, belonged to the best clubs and knew all the 'best' people. Dick Dunster, 'no stranger to *Informer* readers', was the first investigative journalist to expose this hollow man who, 'through his sway over Megapolis TV, exercises considerably more power over the nation than his close friend the Prime Minister'. 'Sir Crispin Bellhanger,' the article continued, 'is nothing more nor less than a war criminal who, after half a century on the run, has at last had his collar fingered.

'The vital witnesses in the forthcoming trial,' the writer went on, are old soldiers and no doubt the powers that be will try every possible means of silencing them or persuading them not to grass on such a prominent member of the old boy net. The pressure on witnesses, so the word goes in legal circles, is being applied by Sir Crispin's confidential assistant, a shadowy accountant named Philip Progmire, who, although an enthusiastic amateur actor in his spare time, shuns the limelight in his professional life. His personality is said to be so negative that one Megapolis executive mentioned that his colleagues often start confidential conversations before they have noticed that Progmire has, in his unobtrusive fashion, "slithered into the room". He recently visited a retired army officer who was to be an important witness for Dunster's defence, travelling all the way down to the West Country to do so. Speculation is rife as to what was said on this occasion, but the hard fact is that this tough old campaigner, ex-desert rat and hero of the SAS, was so alarmed by what the devious Progmire had to tell him that he suffered a stroke and may now be incapable of giving evidence for either party. All of which only goes to show that when it comes to behind-the-scenes manipulation, the "great and good" have fewer holds barred than any of us.'

Lucy, sitting beside me and holding a pint of beer that seemed too heavy for her thin arm, said, 'You're jolly lucky.'

'Why?'

'You've been libelled too. You ought to be able to collect some wonderful tax-free damages from the *Informer*. Who wrote it? – Laurence Anderson Ertes. What an extraordinary name. Do you know him?'

'Well, I think I might.'

'Who is he?'

'Usually known by his first two initials. L. A. Ertes.'

She shook her head slowly, not understanding, and took a gulp of beer.

'Laertes,' I told her. 'Although he never played the part. There was talk of offering it to him.'

'A friend of yours?'

'Of course. It takes a close friend to write stuff like that about a person.'

Curiously enough I didn't feel hurt or worried or even particularly angry. Being angry with Dunster, in any event, seemed as futile as raging at the rain that fell each day when it was meant to be summer, or yelling curses at the traffic in the Commercial Road all the way to work, or railing at the fact of death. In a way I was proud of being identified with Cris, and coming in for this attack made me feel that I had atoned, to some extent, for my negligence in not taking a signed statement from Jaunty Blair before the great silence descended on him.

We had a calm conference in Justin Glover's office. Robbie Skeffington had written an opinion saying that we should issue another writ against the *Informer*. Cris, of course, was all for moderation. He said the *Informer* had a very small circulation and was hardly worth powder and shot. I had absolutely no desire to sue anyone or be involved personally in what seemed to me the horrors of litigation. In the end we decided that Justin would write a letter to the *Informer* denying any interference with witnesses and threatening immediate proceedings if any repetition of such a suggestion were to take place. I left the conference glad that Cris felt in a strong enough position to exercise such restraint. It was true that our principal witness, the one who might well have won the case, was now lost to us, such was the unsuccessful result of my so-called interference. But as Theodora's ear had cleared up nicely, Justin promised to devote all his energy and resources to the search for an Austrian refugee who was now a Mr Llewellyn, running a garage outside Cardiff. This was the war criminal who, as I now knew, had ordered the massacre at Pomeriggio. As for Dunster, it seemed that he had fired yet another random volley into the air and had wounded no one.

Then I got a handsomely embossed card telling me that Marguerite Oakshott would be At Home from 6.30 p.m. onwards on Thursday week. On the back was scrawled in green ink: 'Do try to come, and bring a friend. It's been *centuries*! M.'

I don't know how most men feel about their first experience of sex. I can imagine one of those articles in the Mr Chatterbox column of the *Sunday Fortress* in which various famous persons are rung up and asked to describe this particular incident in their lives. There would be little photographs of footballers, novelists and, probably by now, cabinet ministers (it'll soon be bishops) who would say: 'How can I ever forget that time in the bicycle sheds, or in the long grass, or when we broke into the cricket pavilion, or in the front room by the Christmas tree when her parents were asleep upstairs – when I felt terrified, or liberated, or completely inadequate, and when Red Annie from the check-out, or whoever it might have been, was so wonderfully understanding?' Such people would no doubt leave us to think that so modest and wryly described an initiation had led to a long line of successes which had helped them in their ambition to become stars of the Mr Chatterbox column. One thing I'm sure about is that none of these famous persons, however distinguished, thinks of the first woman who ever made him completely welcome without some degree of gratitude and she will never be forgotten.

I have already made it clear that I am not particularly proud of my seduction by Mrs Oakshott in her pale pink Gloucester Crescent bathroom, but, looking back on it after so many years, I feel that, on the whole, it was kind of her to take the trouble – especially on a busy night when she had a house full of guests.

Lucy said, 'Who is this Marguerite Oakshott?'

'A strange sort of woman. Rich and supposed to be left-wing. She's got an original Dufy. Her parties were quite interesting, I seem to remember. It might be fun to go.'

'I suppose it could take your mind off this great libel action.'

But, as it so happened, it didn't take my mind off that at all.

The house was familiar, but not so Mrs Oakshott. Who was this charming, totally respectable, grey-haired lady in her sixties who greeted me as though she were a devoted auntie, welcoming her favourite nephew home from a long spell in the tropics? She had fought no battle against time, surrendering her neck to loose skin and her eyes to wrinkles, but she still smelt of sweet powder, her breasts were still plump and her ankles slender. She still leant back on her heels and tried to look down on us – an exercise which her shortness made impossible – but now she was peering through thick-rimmed spectacles. I thought her acceptance of old age creditable, although it made me feel as though I had lost my virginity an alarmingly long time ago.

She kissed me and said, 'Great to have you back at one of my parties. And who's this you've got hold of?'

'Lucy Cattermole,' I told her.

'Sweet. Really very sweet and, I should have thought, rather suitable. It's time you settled down. I want to get all the dirt from you about this great war crimes trial, now you've become so famous! Are you really the *éminence grise* of Crispin Bell-hanger? And don't you think he must have done *something*?'

'I'm quite sure he didn't,' I said. 'And I'm not in the least famous.'

'He was always so modest, even when he was a child,' Mrs Oakshott, who sounded as though she had kept in close touch with me all my life, told Lucy. 'Didn't you read all about him in the *Informer*?'

'Yes, I did,' Lucy said. 'He's thinking of suing them.'

'How tremendously exciting! You must tell me everything that's been happening to you. Now we've found you again.'

'I was wondering how you managed that?' I was a long way from buying the house in Muswell Hill on the night that Mrs Oakshott and I met on the bathroom floor.

'That friend of yours . . .' she said, peering vaguely past me at some new arrivals. 'Oh, my God! Did I invite them?'

When she had left us Lucy said, 'Is she related to you?'

'I'll tell you about it some time. Let's go and find a drink, for God's sake. We needn't stay long.'

The place was full of those people that any girl journalist working on the Mr Chatterbox column would have rung up to ask not only about their first sexual experience but about their ten best books, their favourite films, the way they spent Sundays, what they thought of a common European currency, where they took their holidays and what they customarily had for breakfast. Their faces were either well known from newspapers or television, or vaguely and maddeningly familiar, like the people who come and greet you and know all about you but whose names you have forgotten. They looked, these well-nourished, smiling men and younger – but not quite so young as they would like to be – women, as if they were all closely related. They were like a family, all the members of which were bored with each other, had grown to hate each other and yet had to go on meeting, on and on, because every evening was yet another family reunion at the opera, or some embassy or other – or at Mrs Oakshott's because she was rich and knew them all, even though they might not have recognized her husband who was quite uninteresting and worked for a bank. And I thought how desperately they hoped to meet someone new, anybody who would tell them things they hadn't heard before, even someone like me, whose claim to fame was having played a few leading roles with the Muswell Hill Mummers and having been mentioned, in an extremely unfavourable manner, in that week's *Informer*.

I also knew that Cris's reputation would be totally unsafe in their hands. The story of the Pomeriggio massacre had come to them like an extra treat in a dull season, a promise of something more dramatic than federal Europe, or a Cabinet reshuffle, to speculate about and get to know its inside story. But just as unsuccessful plays and bad books and disastrous marriages provided more pleasurable conversation – and were easier to make jokes about – than hits, or masterpieces, or people who lived happily together, so the great libel action would only be interesting if Cris were guilty. For that reason he already was guilty for them, because there was never any smoke without a fire, and because once something terrible had been suggested, or written about in a newspaper, it had better be true as life would become so very dull if it weren't. I felt a stab of pity for Cris, who was going about his business and home to Windhammer, caring for Angie and listening to Schubert, in the belief that the case in court would decide things one way or another, when this laughing, champagne-drinking, canapé-eating tribunal had decided that he was already guilty as rumoured.

As we stood holding our glasses, Lucy looked round and whispered the names of the faces she recognized. She then covered her mouth with a flat hand, like a child suppressing a giggle, as she recognized an extremely distinguished-looking elderly gentleman whom her firm had defended on a serious fraud charge at the Old Bailey. 'I sat in court for three weeks with him, but he won't recognize me. Our litigation partner says clients never do.' Then a penetrating girl's voice squealed, 'Lucy Cattermole! I can't believe it!' and there was someone called Amanda with whom Lucy had been at school and who had come with her dad. As they went on a brief trip down memory lane I started on the familiar journey to Mrs Oakshott's bathroom.

There were couples sitting on the stairs and the front door kept opening to admit more guests. I had obviously been invited to one of the Oakshotts' more all-embracing parties. Of course I had more than half expected, almost known, that Dunster would be there. Perhaps I thought he would be there with Beth and I wanted to prove something to both of them. I wanted to show her that Lucy and I were now a couple, an item, and getting on perfectly well, thank you. And I wanted to show Dunster that he had drawn no blood at all, that his most vicious lunge, designed as a rapier to the heart, hadn't even grazed the skin. The suggestions in his article were so absurd they could only produce laughter, not pain. Perhaps it was childish of me to wish for this demonstration but it was at least part of the reason for accepting Mrs Oakshott's invitation.

The pink bathroom revisited produced no sort of drama. As I left it there had been another intake of new arrivals and an all-too-familiar voice called up from the hall, 'There you are, old man! I thought you might be here.' He came bounding eagerly upstairs towards me. I waited for him on the landing, not wanting to talk to Dunster in the middle of the party.

I told him his latest article was the most ludicrous in a long line of absurdities.

'*My* article? Bright of you, old man. You saw through my little joke.'

'It wasn't hard. And it wasn't tremendously funny either.'

'You spotted me as Laertes.'

'Don't flatter yourself. You're nothing like Laertes.'

'Don't you think so?

      . . . I, with wings as swift

      As meditation or the thoughts of love,

      May sweep to my revenge.'

Dunster didn't often quote poetry.

'Laertes didn't say that. Hamlet said it.'

Two women, look-alikes, red glossy lips and white breasts crammed into black cocktail dresses, came towards us arm in arm and one said, 'Are you two guarding the door or something?'

We moved aside to let them into the bathroom to gossip or whatever they had to do. Dunster was leaning against the wall of the landing, looking at me with his most intolerably amused expression.

'You remember when they wanted me for Laertes to your terrible Hamlet?' He now seemed proud of this fact. 'That was what I was thinking of when I wrote the piece for the *Informer*.'

'You do surprise me. It read as though you thought I was a person who went around terrorizing witnesses.'

'Well, Beth is extremely upset about what you did to poor old Jaunty. You must have scared the wits out of the old devil.'

'Where is Beth?'

'Not coming.' He looked at me. 'She didn't want to meet you.'

The noise of the party rose several decibels. A girl sitting on the stairs started to laugh helplessly, no doubt at a wonderfully new piece of gossip. A man came up to try the bathroom door and went away frustrated. I tried to convince Dunster of the absurdity of his ideas.

'Jaunty Blair was about to make a statement which would have cleared Cris completely. Do you honestly think I wanted to stop him doing that?'

He still looked back at me with that infuriating amusement, as though he knew everything and I were a child who couldn't understand.

'I don't think there's any end to the dirty tricks Bellhanger's lot would get up to. He was trained to that sort of thing in the war. Bloody well trained too. You're just his newest recruit, old man. Perhaps you're not fully involved yet. He may not tell you everything.'

'What's that mean?'

'I expect Cris's lot had it in for Jaunty, for some reason or another. Maybe they scared him into making that very favourable statement you're talking about and went a bit too far. But Jaunty's not their number one target.'

'Who is then?'

'Who do you think?'

'I've no idea.'

'Me.'

I looked at him and tried my own superior smile. Dunster, I thought, you never cease to overestimate your own importance.

'I'm not kidding myself. I'm a thorn in Cris Bellhanger's

flesh. I'm out to get him. Of course, he wants to get me first. It's perfectly natural.'

'You're joking!'

'It's not really funny, old man. I live in a rather quiet sort of square.'

'I know exactly where you live.'

'I came out of the house. Yesterday morning. Quite early. I was crossing the road to get to my car. Some maniac in a red Cortina came round the corner and drove straight at me. I just managed to jump between the parked cars, but it was a bloody near thing. Luckily the milkman came pottering round and he scarpered.'

The party and the party noise now seemed a long way away. I think the girls in black dresses came out of the bathroom and pushed past us. Down in the hall an early leaver was shouting goodbye. I said, 'Did you get a look at the driver?'

Dunster was smiling now, more confidently than ever. 'Why, old man?' he asked me. 'Is he a friend of yours?'

Chapter Twenty-three

That night I couldn't sleep. I usually find that people who tell you that end up by also giving you detailed accounts of their dreams, or they have lain beside you dead to the world while you were careful not to breathe too loudly in case they woke up. I'm sure I did, in fact, sleep for a bit on the night of Mrs Oakshott's party, but I also spent quite a lot of time downstairs, listening to the World Service on the kitchen radio and worrying.

It was the red Cortina that started it all off. I saw a red Cortina turning round in Jaunty's yard. Could it have been to liberate him, or to discover if he'd learnt whatever lesson his incarceration in the luton was meant to have taught him? A red Cortina was driven at Dunster in Camden Town, if Dunster were to be believed. It was not that he told deliberate lies – he might have seemed more human and fallible if he did – he merely made huge assumptions which then became Holy Writ, part of the unchallengeable Gospel according to Dunster. And yet I had never mentioned the red Cortina at Blair Cottage to him. Was its presence in both places too much of a coincidence?

I made tea in the cold kitchen. Some listener to the World Service in Africa was requesting 'Spread a Little Happiness' with a dedication 'to my cousin Joseph Okimbo in the Department of Justice'. There must be millions of red Cortinas, one of the most common cars in the country. One belonged to a tourist who'd lost his way and turned round at Blair Cottage. Another to a careless, or even dangerous, driver in a hurry, going round a square in Camden Town. And then I had a memory of something I hadn't thought of in connection with either of these two incidents. When Jaunty had taken me to dinner at his appalling club, when he was troubled and wanted me to help him avoid trouble, there had been a man dominating one of the other tables. I began to remember a large, elderly man with a bald head fringed with grey hair and a broken nose who had been at the bar when we left and who had, perhaps – or was I imagining it from a great distance – exchanged looks with Jaunty as I was leaving. The car turning in Jaunty's yard had been driven by a bulky, elderly man, who looked like a Roman emperor.

If this was the same character, who was he? I had thought in Dandini's that he might have been an ex-superintendent of police, out with members of the Vice Squad. Then I remembered that Lucy said that she had noticed that policemen, and those who committed serious crimes, looked, when young, like professional footballers and as they grew older they acquired the same bulky respectability, so that in the court canteen it was often difficult to tell them apart. Had a professional killer been hired in the case of *Bellhanger* v. *Dunster*? What had he been hired to do and who the hell did I suppose had hired him?

Lucy and I were patrials of Muswell Hill. My parents lived there, as did hers, in Coniston Road. When she passed her solicitors' exam and got her job as an assistant in a firm which did a good deal of crime, she went on living in her mother's house (her parents had long been separated) and when we slept together she often walked over, or took a short bus ride, from her place to mine with a bag slung over her shoulder. By now my wardrobe contained some of the sombre and businesslike clothes appropriate to her profession, as well as the jeans, sweaters and T-shirts she changed into in the evenings. We weren't really living together. There was an unspoken agreement between us that we were not committed to each other in that way, and perhaps never would be. Lucy came to me on visits, and her mother, whom I met quite often in the Mummery bar and who helped out in the ticket office, would often speak wistfully of the time when Lucy would be leaving home and starting a family, like her brother Seb, to which Lucy would say, 'Not yet, Mum. You'll have to put up with me for a few years yet!' On the nights when she did stay with me, I often drove her early to the City on my way to work, just as I used to drive Tash to her tutorial college. On that morning, when I was stopping and starting down the Farringdon Road, I asked her a question about something which might have arisen from time to time in the legal profession.

'I suppose there must be contract killers about?'

'Plenty.' Lucy yawned.

'How much do you think they charge?'

'Oh, I believe you can get a pretty decent job done for about two grand. Were you thinking of bumping off Dunster?'

'Not Dunster.' I was squeezing my way past a lorry the size of a building, which was bringing us yoghurt from Dieppe. 'I wouldn't pay him the compliment.'

'Stop! You're going through a red.'

I braked hard and the man behind me tooted an indignant protest.

'You are tired, aren't you?'

'Exhausted.'

'Still the case?'

'Yes.'

'It'll be over. That's the thing about law cases. They finish and then you get a result. It's always a relief, whatever it is. It's the waiting that does for people.'

It would all be over. By then, perhaps, it wouldn't seem to matter very much. But it wasn't over yet. Not by a long chalk.

Cris had gone into the viewing-theatre early to see an episode of *Social Workers* that had a scene in it in which Sue O'Donnell, a central character, who had just recorded her first single, has it away with Peter, one of her clients who is on probation after a conviction for thieving motor cars. The incident takes place on a deserted Cornish beach during an illicit and un-professional weekend. As a result of it, Sue O'Donnell's career is put in jeopardy over several episodes – for who should be out birdwatching on the cliff top than old 'Meanface' Maguire, JP. But I expect you'd rather I spared you further details. Gary Penrose, scared almost equally of his wife and the Broad-casting Standards Council, had wanted Cris to see the episode. He sat through it patiently and I, who had come in late, sat behind him. When the lights went on he said, 'Old Meanface can't have been on the lookout for waxwings. They don't have waxwings on the Cornish coast. You could make it guillemots. It'll mean re-dubbing the line and playing it off his face. You could use another few feet of that rather boring sex scene.'

'You don't think the fuck scene goes too far?' The director, a sprightly old man who always wore jeans and trainers and had been doing *Social Workers* longer than most people could remember, had received so much advice on the subject that he was now totally confused. 'Gary thought we might get com-plaints.'

'We probably will but we're not in the business of censor-ship. Anyone who is reduced to getting his pleasure by watch-ing two actors who probably can't stand each other having make-believe sex on a draughty beach in long-shot deserves our sympathetic consideration. All right. Is that all you wanted me to see?' Cris was uncharacteristically abrupt and seemed de-pressed. I said I had something else to discuss with him so we let Gary and the producer and director of *Social Workers* file out, no doubt pleased to have got away with their scene intact. Then Cris said, 'Awful, isn't it?'

'You mean the case?'

'No. The stuff we have to churn out. We'd just got our hands on a half-way decent subject and we had to cancel it.'

'But about the case . . .'

'Don't you lose sleep over it, Philip. It's not your case, after all. I'm grateful for all you've done.'

'Dunster's been on to me again.' To accuse you of hiring a man to kill him was what I should have said. But I couldn't come out with his latest extraordinary suggestion, not as Cris and I sat close together in the small, stuffy viewing-theatre, having watched a copulation as remote and unreal as the idea of the chairman involved in a plot to murder the boy I had been to school with, the man who had removed from me the wife I continued to love. I had to find a more oblique way of disproving the charge and setting my doubts to rest. I went back to something that Dunster had told me in the garden of the War Museum. 'He's narrowed down the party he says blew up the church. You and three others. That's going to be his case. We ought to be prepared to deal with it.'

'That Rottweiler of a QC we've hired, that Roger Stuffington, or whatever he calls himself, he'll deal with that.'

'But I'd just like to get the facts clear in my own mind, in case Dunster gets on to me again. You said you'd gone somewhere to the south of Pomeriggio when it happened.' I had never thought the day would come when I should be cross-examining Cris like a barrister, even though I was avoiding the direct question.

'That's right. Just north of Monte di Speranza.' Cris looked amused at my new role.

'What did you go down there to do? I mean, was it anything to do with explosives?'

'Yes. Now you come to mention it.'

'What? But if you can't remember . . .'

'I can remember exactly. A German supply store. Quite a successful mission.'

'Who did you take with you?'

'Those three chaps.'

I felt a surge of excitement, as though I were getting near

some truth, although I didn't know what it was or even if it would be the truth I wanted.

'That was the sergeant who died and the lance corporal who deserted. Natty Suiting?'

'Suiting was what we called him. He was so untidy. Remember?'

'Yes.' I remembered everything that anybody told me about the case, perhaps too much.

'Who was the third?'

'The fireworks man himself. The big bang expert.'

'The demolition specialist.' It was the man Dunster was trying to find, the one he said he had a lead to. 'What was he called?'

'Lester Maddocks.' The name meant nothing. 'I'm not sure where any of this gets us.' Cris got up then, out of the soft stall where I had often snoozed during Megapolis productions. He stretched, an old man whose limbs grew stiff if he sat for too long in one position, and took a little confined exercise, like a prisoner pacing his cell. I looked up at him as he stood in front of the white screen that had no picture on it, and asked if he could describe the dynamiter.

'I watched him carefully enough, laying his charges and setting his fuses. He was young. Of course we all were.'

'Big?'

'Yes. The burly sort. Big chest and lots of muscles. Light on his feet, though, for such a heavy chap. I believe he'd done a certain amount of boxing, amateur nights round the East End where he came from. He was hoping to get into the profession when we all got back from the war.'

'Justin Glover's going to have to try to find him. He'll be an important witness.'

'I suppose so.' Cris sounded uncertain. Then we fell silent. Cris was right, it wasn't my case. All the same I asked my last question.

'Do you remember if he had a broken nose?'

'Not when I knew him. I don't think so.'

And when you knew him, I don't suppose he had a red Cortina either, I thought in an irreverent moment.

I did something that I thought I'd never do in my whole life. I went back to Dandini's club.

It hadn't changed, or improved, in any way. The pale doorman was still leaning against the wall with his hands sunk deep into his trouser pockets. Once more he asked me to sign the book, which seemed to be the only formality needed to confer immediate membership. There was a girl behind the bar, neither Tracy nor Tina but a pretty and panic-stricken brunette whose label introduced her to the empty room as Nerys. She was only too anxious to pour me a dry white wine, but searched for the bottle, the glass and the corkscrew with trembling hands, knocking things over and whispering 'Sugar!' to herself, as though the bar were packed with important customers, all waiting to be served. She said she was new there, very new, and had never heard of a member called Lester Maddocks.

That day I had called Justin Glover, not to tell him what Dunster had said to me outside Mrs Oakshott's bathroom but to see how he was doing in his hunt for witnesses. He said he had spoken to Cris, who had given him the names of the men he was with 'doing the other job when the Germans blasted Pomeriggio'. He knew Sergeant Blaker was dead and they were doing their best to find Maddocks, the demolitions expert. The deserter in the Apennines wasn't going to present too much of a problem. They had traced an old man, born in England, running a bar in Maltraverso, who now called himself Andreini. There was only one slightly worrying thing. They were having absolutely no luck in finding a former Austrian refugee who used the name Llewellyn. An inquiry agent had been round numberless garages in and around Cardiff. Llewellyns were extremely thick on the ground but none of them seemed to have any connection with Austria, let alone Pomeriggio. They were checking voters' lists and trying to get something from the immigration authorities. They were also going through the Public Record Office. If that failed they would look up the old intelligence files in the Ministry of Defence. 'Cris knows someone in the MOD.' I thought how that sentence would enrage Dunster if he ever heard it spoken. Justin Glover said he hoped to have some good news for us soon and rang off.

I could have left it all to him. I could have said, 'Dunster's got an idea that Cris is trying to kill him.' I could have asked him to find Lester Maddocks because I had a terrible suspicion that he was a hit man employed by Justin Glover's distinguished client. I didn't say any of that. I wanted to find out the truth for myself and decide what to do about it. It was the sort of positive decision which I didn't, up till then, believe it was in my nature to take.

'I remember you, don't I, dear? Didn't you come here with the old Major? We don't see a lot of him nowadays. All right, is he?'

'As a matter of fact he's been ill.'

'Has he, the naughty old darling? Nothing serious?'

'Yes, it is rather.'

'Let's hope he gets better soon.' Marcia, known to Jaunty as Marion, had arrived at work, got into her black fishnet stockings and, after these preliminary greetings, asked me if I'd like to order. In return I asked her if she often saw the group of men who had been drinking together the night I was there with Jaunty, in particular a large man with a bald head and a broken nose – at which description Marcia laughed.

'Why, dear? You getting married or something?'

For some extraordinary reason I thought of Lucy with a pang of guilt. What did this Marcia know about me? 'No. Why ever do you ask?'

'Weddings. Funerals. Taking out some new young bird you

want to impress. That old chap's got limos for all occasions. He's always trying to get us to recommend them to our customers. But they're not all the limo type, to be honest. Not those that we get in here.'

'Do you have his address? I suppose I might need a limo some time.' Need one for what? Marriage, death or just to impress a young bird and lead her to believe I was the sort that owned a Roller with a chauffeur in a cap? The kindly Marcia was now hunting behind the bar, clicking her tongue and accusing Nerys of having moved everything around, and then telling her to just keep calm dear when Nerys broke a small, pink glass giraffe. They searched through cards from members and staff on holiday, from a Day and Night Visit-U massage service, afternoon hotels, adult cinemas and suppliers of exotic underwear. Lodged between a bottle of blue Bols and a china donkey wearing a sombrero they found the well-thumbed card of Cupid Cars: LUXURY LIMOS OUR SPECIAL-ITY. DINE, WINE OR WED IN STYLE. The address was Allenby Mews off Inverness Terrace in Bayswater, and you could no doubt die in style with them also.

So I went in search of Cupid Cars, only a short taxi ride from the Dandini club in Mayfair, on a quest which seemed to be proving almost too easy. The next stage, assuming I was able to meet Mr Maddocks, was likely to be more difficult and, as the taxi drove up between the darkness of the Park and the glitter of lights in the trees in front of the Dorchester, I rehearsed various conversational openings, ranging from 'Have you got a small and unostentatious Rolls in which I might get married to a young solicitor with criminal connections?' to 'Who paid you to shut up Jaunty and try to knock off Dunster?'

Lucy had told me about the allegedly legal operations which criminals use as a cover. With the small thieves and petty burglars it's window-cleaning; minor East End gangs run mini-cab businesses; and it's only those who earn the attention of the Serious Crimes Squad who go into limos. I thought of all this as the cab turned down Queensway, past the bright lights of Greek restaurants, Asian grocers' shops, newsagents who sold newspapers in all the languages produced by the Tower of Babel – and soft porn which could do without words altogether – and we were in striking distance of Allenby Mews. Looking down it I could see, in the shadows, two or three Rolls-Royces parked close to the wall, but no red Cortina. I paid off my driver and walked down the cobbles towards a light shining from the office window of Cupid Cars.

I knocked and, getting no encouragement, pushed open the door of a room in which three elderly men in dark suits were playing cards under a glaring strip-light. On a side table their chauffeur's caps stood among a mess of used take-away boxes, sandwiches packaged in plastic triangles, paper cups, beer cans and Coke bottles. Their faces bore the sullen expression of men who would tell you that the recession is worse than any bloody politician is going to admit, that the Americans aren't coming this year and most of their regular clients have gone bankrupt, anyway. They would probably say this as they drove you with your bride away from the wedding. Hanging on the wall was a large, pink, naked doll, equipped with a silver cardboard bow and a quiver of arrows. I wondered who, in this melancholy firm, had spent time decorating Cupid.

I said, 'Is Mr Maddocks about?'

'Who's he?' The eldest card-player might just have been old enough to have fought in the war. He was a thin, old man with the long face and tragic eyes of the Middle East, an Arab or an Israeli.

'Isn't he your boss? I've got a complaint to make.'

'What complaint?'

'One of your cars broke down at my wedding. I've written four times and got absolutely no satisfaction.' My powers of invention amazed me.

'Mr Loughborough's our boss,' a fat driver said. It wasn't a warm evening but he was sweating and had a bunch of Kleenex on the table beside him. 'You must have wrote to the wrong bloke, Mister.'

There was a door with a frosted-glass pane at the end of the room. Behind it there was a light and the sound of a telephone ringing. A deep, indistinct voice could be heard answering it.

'Could I speak to Mr Loughborough, then?' An outraged and inconvenienced bridegroom wouldn't have left without seeing the top man.

'You can't speak to him, no,' the fat driver said, and the third man, of whom I have no clear recollection except that he had a dodgy eye which might have made his left turns erratic, added, 'On duty.' At which moment the door opened and the big, bald man with the broken nose came in. He was wearing a white shirt and the trousers of a suit held up by braces, which was Cris's working outfit.

'There's a job for you, Jack,' the man whose name might just as well have been Loughborough said to the sad Middle-Easterner. 'Pick up 9.30 Launceston Place, W8, over to the Savoy Grill and wait as long as you're needed. Who's this?'

'Bloke that's come to complain about one of our bridals.' The fat driver spoke before I could introduce myself.

'Was it the white Roller or the Bentley?' the boss asked.

'It was the white one.'

'All right, then. You'd better come in here.' He stood aside and let me go past him into the room, then he shut the door.

'I'll just take a few details. Do have a seat, Mr –?'

'Progmire. Philip Progmire. I work for Sir Crispin Bell-hanger.'

He sat at a desk in front of a row of telephones which didn't ring very often. On it was a framed photograph of a couple with three children, standing under a blue sky in some sunny spot. The man in the photograph also had the features of a younger, less battered Roman emperor, but his nose was unbroken.

'Am I right in thinking,' I said, 'that you're Lester Maddocks? An old soldier from the SAS?'

'The name's Loughborough,' he said and sat back in his chair looking at me. His voice was very soft, with only a trace of the Cockney accent he must have taken to the war with him. His statuesque looks gave him a noble appearance and his broken nose might have been caused by the weather on the stone over the centuries since the birth of Christ. 'I hire out Rollers and quality cars.'

'And during the war, you fought in Italy?'

'What's it matter where I fought? It's a long time ago. Now, what's this about a breakdown in one of our wedding vehicles?'

'You were with Cris, weren't you? Sir Crispin Bellhanger?'

In the silence that followed, the man I had called Lester Maddocks opened a drawer and got out a tube of mints. His hands were enormous, but he used them delicately, first to peel off the silver paper and then to put one in his mouth. Then he said, 'Who are you? And don't give me a lot of shit about a wedding that never happened!'

'I'm someone who works for Cris.'

'How do I know that?'

'You do know who Cris is, then?'

'Don't try to be clever. You'll find you've made a mistake if you came here trying to be bloody clever.' He spoke quietly, but his hand on the table closed into a fist.

I wanted to convince him that we were on the same side, so I offered him a lie. 'Cris asked me to speak to you,' I said.

'Oh, yes?'

'He's told me about it.'

'About what?'

'Your team in the Italian mountains. You and Captain Bellhanger and Sergeant Blaker, now dead. Oh, and Lance Corporal Sweeting.'

'What you know about Sweeting?' The big man behind the desk looked unconvinced.

'Everyone called him Natty Suiting. Because he was always in a mess. Didn't he stay in Italy?'

There was a small, muffled report. Tired of sucking, he had cracked the mint between his teeth. 'Someone's putting about a lot of lies.'

'Cris asked me to have a word with you about that.'

One big hand came towards me, with a mint squeezed in the offering position. 'Do you care for a curiously strong?' he said, an offer which I didn't like to refuse.

'And Blaker?' he asked me.

'Killed later, so Cris told me.'

'He wasn't a brave man, Blaker.' Maddocks leant back in his chair. For the moment he seemed at ease, no longer threatening. 'Always scared of it. Perhaps that's why he got it. And as for old Natty . . . Took up with a nice bit of local crumpet, old Natty. Gone to live in sunnier climes. Like my son and my grandchildren.' He looked at the photograph on his desk with pride and then at me. We'd all've done anything for Captain Cris. If you work for him, I expect you know the feeling.'

'Yes. I know the feeling. And you're still working for him?' I asked the question and sat, dreading his answers.

'Freelance,' was what he said, after a long silence.

'What's that mean?'

'It means . . . I want you to tell Cris I'm doing my very best for him. I'm doing what I can, in his interests. You tell him that.'

Did that mean Cris hadn't given any instructions, issued any orders and knew nothing whatever about the movements of the red Cortina? I was more than ready to believe it.

I asked, 'What exactly should I tell Cris you've done for him?'

'There was Jaunty.' He had put the silver paper back neatly and was rolling the tube of mints backwards and forwards along the desk, making the only small sound in the room.

'Jaunty?' I prompted him.

'He was putting about some funny things. I think I got him to straighten out his story. We all know as it was the Germans done it. We know that, don't we?'

'That's what Jaunty told me.'

'Will he stand up in court?'

'I'm afraid not. He's had a stroke since then. He can't speak.'

'I'm sorry for Captain Cris. Personally I never could stand the Major. Cocky little bastard. That's all you could say about the man. Well, then, if Jaunty won't stand up in court . . .'

'He won't.'

'Best thing is, make sure that mad Dunster bloke can't stand up either.' He gave me a small, friendly smile and before I could answer the telephone rang again. He picked it up, cradled it like a violin and went on rolling the mint packet as he spoke reassuringly to the phone. 'Yes, sir. Yes, Mr Godstowe. Pick up at Launceston Place. And after the Savoy Grill, down to the country. The Bellavista Hotel in Haywards Heath. I'll tell the driver, Mr Godstowe. Of course he'll be glad to do it, sir.' He scribbled a note in pencil. 'Any time, Mr Godstowe. Cupid Cars is here to serve the customer.' He put down the phone carefully and looked at me. 'Is that what Captain Cris wants, that bloody madman not able to stand up in court? Is that what he sent you down to tell me?' He was as willing to do a violent crime for Cris as he was to see that Mr Godstowe was able to impress his bird by taking her to Haywards Heath in a Roller.'

'No,' I told him. 'That's not what Cris wants at all.'

'It's not?' The big man's face clouded over. He looked puzzled and, once again, dangerous. 'What's he want then? His Lordship?'

'Not for you to mess things up.' My moment of courage seemed entirely out of character. 'Thanks to what you did to him, Jaunty can't give evidence.'

'What I did? I meant to help out Cris.'

'All the same, you haven't, you haven't helped him at all. And he doesn't want anything to happen to Dunster.'

'Not to that madman?'

'Of course not. If it did, by any terrible chance, who do you think'd get blamed? It'd be Cris, wouldn't it?' For some reason I wasn't afraid then. There seemed no risk in it. 'Who else do you think they'd blame?'

He thought it over and gave himself another curiously strong peppermint, but this time he didn't offer me one.

'What's the Captain want me to do then?'

'He wants you to come to court and tell them that you were all away doing that other job when the church was blown up. Just tell the truth. That's all the Captain wants done.'

Loughborough, or Lester Maddocks, or whatever his name might be, or was going to be, made a small, thoughtful sound sucking his peppermint. At last he spoke. 'Can't be done.'

'Why not?'

'Me? Come to court?'

'Yes. It won't be particularly difficult.' Much easier, I felt like saying, than trying to knock one of the parties off with a red Cortina.

'Be questioned, like. About all I've ever done?'

'I don't know. I suppose they might ask you about your record. That is, if you have one.'

'Not that. I'm not talking about that. There's things that happened so long ago. When we was all young lads. That's all over now. Well, no one ought to hold you responsible for that.' What Jaunty had said in Dandini's his assailant was repeating in the office of Cupid Cars.

'What do you want me to tell Cris?'

'Tell him I've tried to help all I can, in my own way. Freelance. But I can't undertake to come to court and answer questions about it. Not at my age. I can't answer questions about all that we did so long ago.'

'I'll tell Cris, and I'll see what he has to say about it.' I stood up. He was looking at the photographs on his desk.

'You do that. And say at my time of life a bloke feels like joining his family for the chance of a bit of sunshine. The more so, tell the Captain, since my wife passed away and there's nothing to keep me in the old country.'

'I'll tell him that,' I said. 'And I'm sorry about Mrs Maddocks.'

He stood up then. I had suddenly gone too far and I remembered a picture I'd had in a childhood history book: a chained bear, baited past endurance, rearing on its hind legs and striking out with a huge, fatal paw. 'Don't you use that name now' – he spoke in a scraping whisper, more dangerous than any shout – 'not here. Understand me, sonny? Not anywhere. Tell Cris I always got respect for him. Not for whoever does his errands.'

I felt him watching me as I turned and went out through the door. I knew he was still standing behind his desk as I closed it behind me. I crossed the room with the card-players in it, trying not to break into a run.

'Governor sort you out all right, did he?' the fat one asked.

'Yes, thank you.'

I walked as quickly as I could across the dark cobbles and up to find the glare and double-parking of Queensway and the welcoming light of an empty taxi. When I got home I half expected to find a red Cortina waiting outside my front door. It wasn't. I went into the kitchen and took off my jacket. My shirt was cold with sweat and my hand was unsteady. I made myself a cup of tea and poured in the brandy Megapolis had given me for Christmas. When I had taken off my clothes and put on pyjamas and a dressing-gown, I rang Lucy's number.

'She's here, Philip. I'll just go and call her. I think she tried to ring you earlier. She was worried about you,' her mother said.

Not half as worried as I've been about me, Mrs Cattermole, was what I didn't say.

Lucy said, 'You were going to ring me at eight or something,' and then, realizing that she sounded too much like a long-suffering wife, 'not that it mattered at all. I'd've had to stay in working, anyway. Did you do anything exciting?'

'I think I discovered how it must have felt to be in the war.'

'He's probably got a string of convictions, and for some reason or other he's scared to death of coming anywhere near a law court,' I told Cris when we met in our solicitor's office.

Justin said, 'It doesn't sound as though he'd make a particularly good witness. All the same, I do think I'll have to see Maddocks. Let's hope he hasn't gone the way of Major Blair.'

I don't suppose that the old Cockney ex-pugilist Roman emperor went Jaunty's way, but we never discovered exactly which way he went. When Justin Glover called Cupid Cars he was told that a Mr Jamir had already taken over the business. Mr Loughborough had gone abroad and no one had any idea of his destination. He might now be playing with his grandchildren on some golden beach, or setting up another little business anywhere from Cape Town to California.

So we were left with Lance Corporal Nathaniel Sweeting, known as Natty Suiting, known as Signor Andreini, who was waiting for us at the Bar della Luna in a small town in the Apennines.

Chapter Twenty-four

'It's absolutely terrific,' Justin Glover said, 'to be going abroad without Jenny and the children. This really feels like a holiday.'

We were sitting side by side on a flight to Bologna, business class, and I thought of the bloody awful string of events which had combined to produce this rare feeling of happiness. The inhabitants of Pomeriggio had died, a person called Dunster had been born to bring about unmitigated disaster, Jaunty had lost the power of speech, a hit man had been compelled to off-load his Rollers and flee the country, and Lance Corporal Sweeting had deserted – all so that Justin Glover could fly to Italy, unencumbered by his nearest and dearest.

'The moment we leave home,' he said, 'they start asking how long it'll be before we get there. Mind you it was touch and go whether I could make it.'

'Was it?'

'Deirdre, that's our mother's help, didn't get back till two in the morning and she'd had a terrible row with her boyfriend, so she overslept. And the baby Augustus is in trouble with his gnashers and the twins were quarrelling over a broken Walkman and Theodora did mention her ear again – but she does that every morning when it's PE, which she hates. Understandable, really. It was touch and go, as you can imagine.'

'How did you manage it?'

'Well, Jenny was shouting at me from the top of the stairs and asking if I thought that Sir Crispin Bellhanger was more important than her and the children. You know what I said?'

He had started on the complimentary champagne as we crossed the Channel and was now in a confiding mood.

'No. Tell me.'

'I said, "At the moment, I'm afraid, yes."' He was smiling at the memory of his moment of daring. 'You see, I was careful to put that in, "at the moment". I mean, this case will soon be over and naturally Jenny and the children are more important to me in the long run. Over the years. She'll understand that, won't she, when she has time to think about it?'

'Let's hope so.'

'All the same' – Justin had now got himself worried – 'I think I'd better ring her this evening. If we can find a phone.' We might have been going into the depths of the jungle where communications were by tom-tom only. 'How many nights do you think we'll be away?'

'Didn't we say two?'

'Oh, I told Jenny three. I thought we might pop along to Florence on the way back.' Then his face cleared and the holiday spirit returned. 'Imagine the pure joy of seeing the Uffizi without having the children in tow!'

We booked in to the Hotel Internazionale in Bologna and met Dr Picchioni, a notary employed by Justin Glover's firm to take any sworn statement the former lance corporal might care to make. We had dinner in a restaurant not far from the Neptune fountain, and Justin Glover telephoned before he left the hotel. During our tortellini he was sunk in gloom.

'Things all right at home?' I asked.

'Actually, no.' And then he brightened up and said, 'I don't suppose we'll be able to ring from Maltraverso, will we?'

Dr Picchioni was small, neat and unexpectedly young, wearing a dark suit and tie despite the stifling Italian summer. He spoke impeccable English and treated us with a sort of amused suspicion, as though he knew exactly what game we were playing. He had already been in touch with Natty Suiting. 'He is frightened to death,' he said, 'that he'll be arrested as a deserter.'

*

I drove the car we hired at the airport out of Bologna and on to the motorway to Florence. The road was built high over great gorges and kept plunging into the blackness of tunnels and emerging into dazzling sunshine. The mountains towered above us, stony slopes which the snow had covered for much of the time that Cris and his men fought their secret battles behind the Gothic Line held by the Germans. I got the bit about the Gothic Line from the guidebook Justin had bought for the occasion. It also told us that the Apennines bred wolves, so that the sheep were guarded, on the lower slopes, by very large and savage dogs. Some wolves, it seems, might still be about, but bears, present in Roman times, were to be found no more, nor were wild goats. Maltraverso is a small town used as a winter resort by those with a taste for mountains. The Hotel Gandolfo, one star, was closed during the month of August. Otherwise the town seemed to be of no special historical or architectural interest. The Bar della Luna received no stars whatever.

When we had taken the Maltraverso turn-off and the road was climbing steadily towards the grey peaks, we passed a collection of small signs pointing up a steeper, narrower road and there I saw the word I had learnt to dread – Pomeriggio.

'The scene of the crime,' Justin said, and added, apparently in case I didn't understand English, 'the *locus in quo*. Do you want to go and take a view?'

I didn't but I said, 'Do you think we ought to?'

'Might as well.'

So I started to climb towards the sky, along the edge of a precipice which led down to the service stations and the motor-way, which were, as we drove up higher, shrouded in a mist which might have been a cloud. The road was lined with dramatic warnings of danger, hairpin bends, steep ascents, uneven surfaces and there were no white lines. We were also warned of rocks falling on us from the cliffs above. 'CADUTA MASSI' – Justin, still in holiday mood, was laughing at his little joke – 'wonderful name for an opera-singer!'

What was Pomeriggio? A village or a town? The guidebook, once again, was silent on the subject. It had an old and crumbling wall but inside its arches only a small square, a church, a post office and one steep main street. There was some sort of municipal building, so perhaps it was the capital of a small area of the rocky and precipitous countryside. Cris's description was forever stuck in my mind and I expected a ghost town, with a street only prowled by uncared-for dogs and cats, doors banging in the wind. Whatever toll the massacre had taken of the small population, life had returned to Pomeriggio. Women were crowding the few shops and men, perhaps not as old as in other towns but old enough to have stopped working, sat on chairs outside the café ordering nothing. Across the street a banner hung advertising a forthcoming Festa di L'Unita; no doubt there would be coloured lights and stalls in the street and young men and girls dancing. I doubted whether anyone in Pomeriggio knew that an English court was about to decide who had blown up their church and murdered their relatives almost half a century before and I wondered how much any of them would care.

We drove round the walls and found the unmade road leading to the place in the photograph I had seen, it seemed years ago, in the office of Streetwise Productions. On a rocky promontory, once the site of the Chiesa Nuova, there was an iron cross over a plaque. Dr Picchioni translated: *In honour of the people of Pomeriggio, murdered by the German Army of occupation in the Church of Saint Magdalena in Tears, 23 October 1944.* They had not been entirely forgotten because there were fresh flowers at the foot of the cross. Justin Glover took a photograph of the inscription 'for whatever evidential value it might have'. Then we drove away from Pomeriggio and I have never been there since, although the sight of that bleak spot where a church full of people was once blown into eternity is impossible to forget.

'They can't hold it against me now. Not what happened all

those years ago. That wouldn't be fair, would it? Not that the army was fair to me, not always.'

I had heard it said so often that it seemed to have become a sort of theme song, the introductory music instantly recognizable whenever Pomeriggio was mentioned. Jaunty had said it, and Lester Maddocks, and now Signor Andreini – disowning all responsibility for the actions of Lance Corporal Sweeting – was taking up the all too familiar melody.

He had a face like a puzzled sheep, a turned-down nose and bewildered eyes, crowned with a woolly mat of grey hair. He was shapeless and clumsy and he had cut himself shaving. There was blood on his collar, although his white shirt was otherwise carefully laundered and ironed. What surprised me most was his voice; it was a middle-class bleat, rising at times to a high note of complaint, at others inviting us to join him in laughing at his own misfortunes.

We sat round a table near the 'Toilette' in the shadowy recesses of the Bar della Luna, away from the sunlight and the zinc bar, the hissing coffee-machine and the big glass doors letting in the sunlight. We were shut away behind a white coffin full of ice-cream and a glass cabinet in which the cakes and *paninis* were ranged like geological specimens. On the wall a glossy print 'Christ, the Light of the World' looked gravely down on us, the Pope smiled in a knowing fashion and the Maltraverso football team looked grimly determined.

'I was a hopeless sort of a soldier, anyway. My father was terribly disappointed when I didn't get a commission. Dropped my rifle on the parade-ground. I was always doing things like that so I had to go in through the ranks. "Rank outsider", that's what my father called me. I don't think he was joking. What I'm trying to tell you is this.' Words came pouring out of him; it was as though he had spent years in solitary confinement. 'I was always hopeless. I never managed to please them, even when we were in the mountains when you wouldn't think they'd have been bothered about all the rules and regulations. And I was always losing things. Or not keeping up when we started to run. You see, I'm sure they were glad to see the back of me. So they wouldn't hold it against me now, that I wandered off, as you might say. I don't think I could stand prison. Not at my age. Prison must be very much like the army. Don't you think it must be like that?'

Natty Suiting was not talking about the deaths of the church-goers but about the fact that he had abandoned his previous existence in favour of the calm, grey-haired woman who sat watching us, unable to understand a single word we were saying. She must once have been as urgently desirable as their youngest daughter, a girl with long, naked arms, shiny black hair and brown eyes, who was laughing as she served a group of admiring young men. The choice between her and carrying on a terrifying war with Cris and Sergeant Blaker, now dead, and Jaunty Blair must have been a clear one. He was right; it would have been hard to punish this elderly Italian for what he might have done when he was someone else entirely.

'We haven't come about your desertion,' Justin Glover said. 'No one wants to see you in prison, Mr Sweeting.'

'Signor Andreini.' He smiled round at us apologetically but insisted on his new identity.

'I beg your pardon. Mr Andreini,' Justin corrected himself. 'You have absolutely nothing to fear from us.

Natty seemed reassured and was silent for a moment. Then he looked at me and I thought I detected, behind the sheep-like innocence, a sort of cunning, which he might have picked up during long years of running the Bar della Luna. 'Well, then,' he said, 'what *are* you interested in exactly?'

'My firm acts for Sir Crispin Bellhanger.' Justin Glover took charge of the meeting. 'It's been suggested that he was in command when you and Sergeant Blaker and another man called Lester Maddocks blew up the church.'

'There ought to be a pardon issued. A free pardon. From the Queen or someone like that.'

'You mean a pardon for blowing up a church?' Justin Glover's voice had acquired a note of professional irritation.

'I think,' I said, 'Signor Andreini is still worried about the desertion.'

'Desertion? You couldn't call it that. I was no good to them. No good at all. I was just' – Natty invited me to join in the joke – 'just relieving them of my company. I did that one night. I ran then. You can't believe how I ran. I got here and the first person I met was Constanzia.' He looked across at the old woman and stopped smiling. 'She was outside her house. It was very early in the morning and she was filling a bucket from a tap. I made all sorts of signs to her. I was hungry and tired and she took me in. Her and her family. I couldn't understand it. I'd never had much success with girls in Dorking. That was where we lived. My father was a head-master. Very keen on the army, my father. I remember he gave me toy soldiers at Christmas and I never played with them. They always got broken though. Now I think Constanzia and her family knew the war was ending and they wanted me to marry her and take her to England. But I couldn't go back, could I, because I'd broken the law? You understand. Constanzia never picked up any English. Other people taught me Italian. I took to it quite easily. Well, I didn't have much choice.

'My father's dead, of course. But I've got a married sister in Dorking. I'd like to go back. I'd really like to. I'm getting tired of all this Andreini business. I'd like to be myself again. Not pick up where I left off. I could never do that. You mentioned Captain Bellhanger. He could help in my case, if anyone could.'

'I think he wants you to help in his,' I told him.

'Let's hope we can help each other. The man who was here before you, he promised he'd look into my case. Let on he'd get questions asked in Parliament. I had high hopes, but he's done nothing whatever about it. Just my luck.'

So Dunster had sat there, in the shadows at the back of the
Bar della Luna, by the *paninis* and the ice-cream and 'Christ,
the Light of the World', and offered the one bribe that meant
anything to its owner. Knowing Dunster, I didn't believe that
he'd offered it deliberately or with intent to deceive, but he
was enthusiastic and had promised too much, over-excited by
being told the story that, above all others, he wanted to hear.

'Would Captain Bellhanger help with the free pardon side
of things? Would he? He was always kind to me. You know he
called me Natty Suiting, because I was so hopeless with the
spit and polish.'

'I don't think we can promise anything.'

'But?'

'What?'

'There's always a "but", isn't there? You can't promise me
but . . .'

'I feel we can go so far as to say this –' Justin Glover, who
didn't, it seemed, intend to come all this way just for a trip
round the Uffizi, offered his sweetener in the most judicial
language possible. 'My firm would represent you in any ap-
plication you wish to make to the proper authorities. And I've
no doubt Sir Crispin would be prepared to give you a good
character and speak highly of your war service. That is, until
you saw fit to leave the army.'

'I told you I promised to take Constanzia to England. I've
disappointed her and I'm not sure she's ever forgiven me, to
be quite honest with you.' Signora Andreini sat with her hands
folded in her lap, gazing into the middle distance without
expression. 'That's the trouble with me, I'm afraid I disappoint
people. I suppose I disappointed Captain Bellhanger too, that
night I ran away. It's very decent of him. He wants to help
me, do you say?'

'Our client Sir Crispin Bellhanger tells us' – the lawyers'
phrases sounded more than usually ridiculous in the back of
the bar where the proprietor was lost in dreams of Dorking –

'that on the night the church was blown up he and you and the others were destroying an enemy ammunition shed some miles to the south of Pomeriggio.'

'Let me get you chaps a proper drink.' The cheerful Natty now became an expansive host. Business was suspended while the smiling girl from the bar brought us a bottle of grappa. Justin Glover didn't take a sip until he had asked the half-a-million-pounds' worth of damages question.

'What we have come all this long way to ask, Signor Andreini, is whether you can confirm Sir Crispin's account of the events?'

'Of course I can. I remember that ammunition dump. I left one of the bags behind there. Well, it was only an empty bag. We'd brought the charges in it. Sergeant Blaker was absolutely unreasonable about it.'

'So you had nothing to do with the affair at Pomeriggio?'

Natty poured himself another grappa, knocked it back and looked round at us, his sheep's eyes full of innocence. 'Do I look,' he asked plaintively, 'like a chap who goes around blowing up churches?'

'So it follows that Sir Crispin had nothing to do with it either?'

'Of course it does.' At last he said the words we had come to hear: 'Everyone knew the Germans did it.'

So Justin Glover and I, unencumbered with children, stopped off at Florence to look at the pictures. Walking past the 'Primavera' I remembered, as other pictures had made me remember, Beth's face and was filled with a sudden bitterness at the thing that had parted us, which was the same, irrational, irresistible force that had taken us to Italy. Soured by this unwelcome moment of recognition I said to Justin, 'You don't think old Natty Suiting's going to do us the slightest bit of good, do you?'

'Why not? He's made a statement, signed and certified by the notary.'

'You know perfectly well why he did that. He thinks we can get him some sort of amnesty.'

Justin Glover stood still, surrounded by virgins and nymphs dancing in paradise. 'Let's face it' – he was giving his best dry, old family solicitor performance, which was fairly absurd, I thought, in someone younger than I was – 'Andreini isn't going to come to England to give evidence until he knows he's absolutely safe from the possibility of arrest. It's an obvious precaution for us to make sure his position is cleared up before the trial starts.'

'You mean, it's an obvious inducement to him to say what we want him to say?'

'Robbie was right when he told you to trust your legal advisers. Lawyers have to live in the world as it is, Philip. Not as we might like it to be. You'd be much better off leaving the practical side of things to us.'

Which coming from a man whose family life was in such chaos that he could only escape from his house with difficulty, struck me as a bit rich.

Chapter Twenty-five

'We like Lucy.'

'So do I.'

'We wouldn't dream of interfering. Not in any way. But Angie was saying how glad she was to see you settled.'

'I don't think I'm that exactly. Perhaps I won't ever be. Not again.'

'You're living in the past.' Cris was the man who had, that autumn, the best reason for visiting that unhappy region. 'You've got to put all that behind you. My God, she's young though, isn't she? Just imagine anyone having all that future! The thought of it makes me feel quite dizzy.'

It would have made me dizzy too if I'd thought about it. Everyone, it seemed, wanted to see me settled: Lucy's mother and Angie, Mrs Oakshott and Beth, especially Beth. I was glad that I had brought Lucy for the weekend at Windhammer, glad that everyone seemed to like each other, but being settled wasn't a subject I felt able to pursue. So I asked if there was any more news about the case.

'Nothing much. We found out who was the German captain in the Pomeriggio district. Got it out of the MOD information files. Well, the Minister will do almost anything to get his face on television.'

'Does the ex-captain own a garage?'

'I'm afraid not.' Cris smiled, as though the evidence were completely unimportant. 'His name was Kreutzer. Captain Ernst Kreutzer. No relation to the sonata.'

'He went to Wales?'

'Not as far as we know. He went back to Hamburg and became a headmaster. He retired and died there ten years ago.'

'So Jaunty was telling us a load of rubbish?'

'Jaunty was never going to be a reliable witness.' That was the verdict on the man who couldn't lie any more, for better or for worse.

It was near the end of September, with low, welcome sunshine and air touched with freshness and the smell of bonfires. We were walking the long way round through the woods while Lucy and Angie sat by the logs in the mock baronial grate and waited for us to join them for tea. As the trees ended at the edge of a field, a pheasant rose with a great fuss and chatter from a tangle of brambles and bracken and flapped off into a clear sky. 'I sometimes wonder,' Cris said, 'whether to take up shooting again.'

'I thought you'd decided against it.'

'Such a contradiction! People who know about animals, understand them, really get to love them in a way, are those who kill them. Foxes aren't specially likeable little brutes, but huntsmen get a sort of respect for them. My old father was that sort. Always noticed the leaves or the water moving and he'd sniff at the wind and know which way the birds'd fly – and he killed things a lot. I suppose the truth of it is, with a gun in your hand you become one of them. Red in tooth and claw. I don't know whether I'll ever do it again. I suppose I might.'

So we started the walk back, across the flat countryside, and Cris asked me about Natasha. I told him what I knew, except for her decision not to visit me again. 'She's got a boyfriend who knows everything.'

'Everything about what?'

'How to run a television company. Oh, and about death.'

'What's he know about that?' Cris was smiling.

'That when people get to my age they practically think of nothing else. As a matter of fact, I don't think about it at all.'

'Neither do I. No point in it. You know what I believe? We're born with a clock inside us. It's set for the time we're going to pop off, and it can't be altered. Absolutely nothing we can do about it, so why worry?'

And when we came in sight of Windhammer among the trees of an open stretch of parkland he said, 'Rotten luck on Angie we could never make children. Perhaps that's why we're enjoying having you here. You and your Lucy. You must bring Natasha down some time too, if she'd ever agree to it.'

I said yes, although I didn't think she ever would.

Nothing could have been so unperturbed, so apparently imperturbable, as Cris that weekend. He made my anxiety ridiculous, and I worried about having worried so much about a possible Dunster victory. And yet, when I thought about it on that calm walk through the woods in the autumn sunshine, there seemed no real danger of Dunster leaving the battlefield crowing with victorious delight and Cris being convicted of an atrocity. Natty Suiting was no longer, for whatever reason, a witness for the defence. Jaunty would never enter a witness-box again and whatever he'd heard would be forever locked inside him. And there was something else. When Dunster lost (I no longer said, even to myself, *if* Dunster lost), would Beth's eyes be open at last? Would she see what she had taken on, an addict who gets his highs by causing wanton suffering to the innocent in the heady name of public morality? Was that the hope that kept me going, as well as my concern for Cris, during the long months of waiting for the trial? And was it that faint possibility, that result which nothing she had said or done gave me any particular reason to hope for, which still made me reluctant to settle – which meant, I suppose, settling for Lucy?

'Did you take her there?' Lucy asked when I said we might go down to Windhammer for the weekend.

'Who?'

'Your wife, of course.'

'Sometimes. Beth didn't like it very much. She used to go off and see her parents.'

'Why didn't she like it?'

'She couldn't understand why I was so fond of Cris and Angie.'

'Was she jealous?'

'I don't think so. She just thought it was a bit creepy, for anyone to be fond of his boss. I tried to tell her I'd've liked him whoever he was.'

'Will they compare us? Her and me, I mean.'

'Of course not.'

'You're sure?'

'Absolutely. That's not the sort of thing they do. I know they'll like you very much.'

'I suppose it'll be interesting' – Lucy was still hesitant – 'to meet someone who's going to be in a really important case.' So Cris was a sort of star to her. To the up-and-coming young solicitor, big criminals, bank robbers and murderers were stars, as were those cool gamblers who played for enormous stakes in libel actions. I said, 'Forget the case. He may not want to talk about it at all.'

'What on earth am I going to wear?'

'Don't worry. There's absolutely nothing smart about Cris and Angie.'

When Cris and I got back from our walk they were sitting on the sofa, looking at old photograph albums. Their heads were close together, one dark and smooth-haired, the other blonde going grey; a woman at the start of her life and another getting to the end of hers, laughing together over some story of Angie's about her life in the old days of British movies. 'Not a casting couch in sight when we were doing *Sound the Alert*, not when we were playing girls in the ack-ack emplacements. As my friend Cissie Watts said, "You'd be lucky if you got a casting sandbag." I'm joking, of course. The director was Ronnie Deering and he had no interest in any starlet without a beard or a moustache and a dirty great pint . . .' The word floated across the room as we came in and then

Angie twisted round on the sofa to greet her husband, while Lucy went on turning the pages of the album, smiling in amazement at a world that was so unlike anything she had ever known.

'It was a war, wasn't it? I mean, bombs were dropping on London. Knocking down houses. Killing people. She lived there and Cris was away fighting. Listening to her you'd think all they did was to make jokes about it.' Lucy was lying in the bath, the steam rising round her; long white legs and a triangle of black hair. Her eyebrows were arched upwards but she spoke in admiration rather than criticism of Angie.

'She's like that. Cris took it more seriously. He hates it now.'

'And we won't ever know how we'd've behaved. In a war.'

'Aren't you glad about that?'

'I suppose so.' Cris had sent us upstairs with a bottle of champagne to drink while we got ready for dinner. She put out her hand for a glass blurred with steam and icy wine. 'It's funny, though. When I was looking at all those photographs I couldn't help envying her. It can't have been dull, can it? I'm sure she wasn't afraid of anything. Except insects.'

'Insects?'

'Didn't you know? It seems they really upset her. That's why she wouldn't come out for a walk with you. "Awful buzzing things, hurling themselves at your face the whole time. I think you and I can do without that, can't we, Lucy?" That's what she said. All those stories about the things they got up to out watching for fire-bombs on the roof of Pinewood Studios and she's scared to death of horseflies!'

After dinner Cris sat down at the piano under the big stained-glass window in which a pre-Raphaelite girl stood palely loitering while a young knight knelt at her feet. The girl was dark and not red-headed, Jane Morris and not Elizabeth Siddal, and I felt no pang of regret on that untroubled weekend.

He was playing I don't know what – Schubert, Chopin, something he knew by heart and could do without the music, with an apologetic but insistent melody. Suddenly he struck a different chord, grinned and pounded the Steinway as though it were a pub piano. The tune was familiar; my father used to sing it in the car on family outings, and then, in a clear, unexpectedly young voice, Angie began to sing as I had never heard her sing before:

> 'There'll be bluebirds over
> The white cliffs of Dover
> Tomorrow when the world is free . . .'

She got up and stood leaning against the piano and gave us a performance at the end of which we clapped. Then her husband called out, 'Come along, everyone. Sing along with Angie.' So we took our drinks and stood by the piano too and did our best to join in songs I only half knew and Lucy didn't know at all. I realized exactly where we were, in a London pub during the war, with Cris on leave and Angie back from a hard day on the set. We went through all the tunes of the time: 'Run, Rabbit', 'We're Going to Hang Out the Washing on the Siegfried Line', 'Somewhere in France with You', 'You are My Sunshine', 'Lili Marlene' and 'Wish me Luck as You Wave me Goodbye', which Angie ended with a high operatic trill. 'Well done,' Cris told her. 'Almost as good as Gracie Fields!' At which Lucy delighted him by saying, 'Who's Gracie Fields?' He played another great crashing chord and went into 'Yesterday', to the strains of which, I suppose, Lucy might just about have been born.

'One thing I'm sure about,' she said as I turned out our bedside light, 'he couldn't possibly have done what they say he did.'

'I know,' I said. 'The idea's ridiculous. So we're going to win, aren't we?'

'Of course.' She gave me her considered legal opinion. But

Chapter Twenty-six

I had never been in a court of law before Cris's trial opened, not even to contest a parking ticket, and I don't know if you ever have. Although no one escapes a visit to the doctor or the dentist, or a punishment session with some such beefy physio as Pam from the Mummers, not everyone has seen the Great British Legal System at work. I must say it came as something of an eye-opener to me.

I expected a solemn, ecclesiastical atmosphere, a silence in which the slightest cough would be greeted as blasphemy and everyone would sit in reverent awe as the judge and the barristers held forth. In fact Queen's Bench Court Number Five, in the Law Courts in the Strand, was packed to bursting point by a constantly changing body of spectators, and it reminded me of nothing more awe-inspiring than a section of Victoria Station during the rush hour. The wigged official seated under the judge was making telephone calls; there was constant whispering, coming and going and the passing of notes; Justin Glover's articled clerk didn't bother to disguise the fact that he was reading a novel; Marcus Beazeley, our junior counsel, was finishing off *The Times* crossword; and Mr Justice Sopwith, a small, impatient man, was furiously polishing his glasses and looked like a frustrated commuter waiting for his train. Most of his interjections were made in the tone of someone who is dictating a letter of complaint to the management. Robbie Skeffington, our learned leader, always referred to the judge as Hugo Sopwith, reassuring us by making it clear that they had known each other for years and were probably at school together.

The jury sat like passengers resigned to the fact that they

wouldn't get home that night, or indeed for a considerable time to come. Only one gaunt young man, wearing a grey cotton jacket, a thin leather tie and carrying the *Guardian*, had the look of a Dunster supporter. Otherwise they seemed a middle-of-the-road lot, though none of them looked quite old enough to have fought in the war.

Robbie, on his feet and opening our case, had none of that cool authority that might have been expected from the next chairman of the Bar Council. He stood, a small, hunched figure, whose gown was constantly slipping off his shoulders, pausing to yank it back, or to blow his nose, or slide up his wig and scratch his forehead, or lift his glasses to hold a document as close as possible to his unaided eyes. His opening speech was like a knock-up before a tennis match. He only really got going when the scoring started and the cross-examinations and the arguments began. His opponent Ken Prinsep, not being a QC, sat in a bench behind Robbie. He was making notes industriously throughout the opening speech and he seemed the only one of the lawyers to be taking the case entirely seriously. He was tall, broad-shouldered and with regular, handsome features which made him look more like a comic-strip hero, Superman with glasses, than a civil rights lawyer. He spoke with a barely detectable Canadian accent, something the judge found irritating; but then Ken, who would rush in where even Robbie might fear to tread, irritated Mr Justice Sopwith for most of the trial.

'This Richard Dunster, members of the jury' – towards the end of his speech Robbie enlivened the knock-up with a fore-taste of some of his meaner strokes, skimming low over the net – 'this small-time scribbler, journalist and television script-writer, of whom you may never have heard, took it into his head to publish a sensational story for fame and money. It was money he took from the very man whose reputation he was to slur. Not even Judas, members of the jury, stooped to collect his thirty pieces of silver from the Master he betrayed.'

Looking down the long bench in front of the barristers I could see Dunster in profile at the far end. Beth was next to him, then came his solicitor, then Cris, then Justin Glover and then me, at the furthest extreme from my one-time school friend and enemy. His lock of hair was flopping over his forehead, the collar of his seldom-worn dark suit was turned up at the back, his tie was loose and exposed his shirt button, but on his face was the look of triumphant joy which I had seen when some despised master finally lost his temper with him in class. To be compared with Judas by Robbie Skeffington, QC was a huge compliment to Dunster. He took it, I'm sure, as a sign of the weakness of our case. Cris, who might have been thought to have come out best in the Skeffington comparison, seemed, by contrast, miserably embarrassed.

'No doubt the defendant Dunster thought he'd further his career by publishing these lies. Perhaps he'd be seen, in his unappealing trade, as a fearless journalist. He might have tried to enhance his reputation by destroying someone else's. Members of the jury, it will be for you to decide, at the end of this extremely painful trial,' said Robbie, who looked likely to enjoy every minute of it, 'whose reputation has survived intact and whose lies in tatters. The life or death of a great public figure, members of the jury, that is the issue you have to try. I will now, with the assistance of my learned friend, call our evidence. The first witness will be Sir Crispin Bellhanger.'

Cris stood in the witness-box, tall and unworried, and took the oath in a voice that was quiet enough to make everyone in court stop whispering and listen. He added the first touch of dignity to the proceedings and the jury looked more confident once he had arrived on the scene. Yes, he was Crispin Henry Bellhanger. He had fought in the last war and had been awarded the Distinguished Service Order and the Military Cross and was three times mentioned in dispatches. He had served during the North Africa campaign in the yeomanry and then in the Special Air Services regiment. He had been parachuted into Italy in the autumn of 1943. Robbie's manner in eliciting this evidence was that of an old family retainer who smiled and gave a little bow of delight every time his master came out with some impressive item in his history. I knew that this was annoying Cris almost beyond endurance but he managed to control his irritation.

He told the story I knew by heart and he told it well. He blamed no one openly, not the villagers who had betrayed our prisoners, nor even the German captain who may have been under the intolerable pressure of battle fatigue. He seemed anxious to remove the unfortunate impression of a Judas Dunster. Perhaps the defendant was an inexperienced script-writer who had been misled by some wild rumour, or had not entirely understood a story he had been told. At this, Dunster looked, for the first time, wounded. Cris thought he might, himself, have been partly responsible by commissioning a series designed to show that everyone might be capable of atrocities in time of war. He had, of course, been hurt by the circulation of the libel among his colleagues on the Board, and this had made his position as chairman difficult. He had no doubt, however, that he would survive; after all he had survived the battles in the desert and the stealthy operations behind the German lines in the mountains of central Italy. 'Thank you very much, Sir Crispin.' The old retainer bowed and added, as though apologizing for the unpleasant and ill-mannered visitor who would be the next to arrive, 'Just wait there a moment, would you? If you'd be so good.' Then Robbie sat down and fell to cleaning his nails with the sharpened point of a pencil, and Justin Glover on my right whispered, 'My God, if all witnesses were as good as that we'd win every case. No doubt about it.'

'Sir Bellhanger . . .' I don't think Ken Prinsep meant to say it. It may well have been a slip of the tongue, brought about by the strain of having to launch an attack on an almost perfect performer in a court crammed full of journalists and expectant lawyers. He was probably over-eager, overworked and over-prepared, but the judge's rebuke rose to a high pitch of intolerance, after he had ostentatiously checked the name of the offending barrister on the list in front of him.

'Mr Prinsep . . .'

'My Lord?'

'You will be so good as to use his proper style and title when addressing this witness.'

'I'm sorry, my Lord.'

'I am prepared to make some allowance for your ignorance in these matters. I understand you did not receive your education in this country.'

'I received a good deal of it here, my Lord.'

'Call him Sir Crispin Bellhanger,' Robbie hissed audibly. He grinned like a merciless old tom-cat offering a momentary respite to a bird of whom he fully intends to make a good meal later.

'Sir Crispin' – Ken turned, his intensity undiminished – 'I didn't mean to offend you. Anyway, not quite so early in my cross-examination.'

'I'm not offended in the least. I've always felt the title a little ridiculous. Anyway, most people call me Cris.'

'We will keep to the correct style and title, please, in my court.' The judge looked startled and somewhat betrayed. 'Now let's get on with it, Mr Prinsep. Do you have some questions for this witness?'

'Just a few, my Lord.' Ken shuffled his notes, page after page, I imagined, of carefully prepared interrogation, the work of several all-night sittings. 'You know the name of the German captain in the Pomeriggio area at the time of the massacre?'

'I do. He was a Captain Kreutzer.'

'You were able to find that out?'

'I thought it might be helpful to the court to do so.'

'Not helpful to your case?'

'Not particularly.'

'You see, I'm going to suggest to you that you have all sorts of information made available to you, as a member of the establishment.'

'My Lord. Perhaps my learned friend can help me.' Robbie was on his feet behind me, clearly not in need of any help at all. 'What exactly is it that my client is alleged to be a member of?'

'I am not at all clear, Mr Skeffington.' The judge managed a faint smile in our direction which changed to a pained frown as he turned his attention to Ken Prinsep. 'What do you say the witness belongs to?'

'The establishment, my Lord.'

'But which establishment do you mean? You must make yourself clear, you know. You might be talking about anything from a gentleman's club in St James's to ordinary licensed premises.'

Justin Glover and Marcus Beazeley led the sycophantic laughter. Robbie, who had subsided into his seat, shook with silent mirth. Some members of the jury smiled, others looked solemnly puzzled.

'I am suggesting, my Lord,' Ken Prinsep replied with a self-control I couldn't help admiring, 'that this witness moves in the corridors of power. He has many friends and supporters in government departments, including the Ministry of Defence. So it's easy for him to find out all the facts about Pomeriggio.'

'Perhaps my learned friend could help me just once again.' Robbie was on his feet and hitching up his gown. 'Did his client not know the name of the German captain?'

This led to a whispered conversation between Ken Prinsep and Dunster, which caused the judge to close his eyes and lean back as though suffering from terminal boredom. At last he could bear it no longer and asked, 'Well, Mr Prinsep. What's the answer?'

A few more whispers and Ken straightened up to say, 'My Lord. My client is a very experienced journalist.'

'What on earth's that go to do with it?'

'He has been able to find out the name of the German officer, my Lord.'

Robbie stared triumphantly at the jury and the judge said, 'Very well, then. Your client and the witness are in the same sort of establishment, whatever that may be. Now, may we please move to some issue of importance in this case.' I looked at Dunster then: his jaw was clenched, his pale face set and, at having been called a member of the establishment which included Cris, he looked more deeply wounded than he did at any other stage of the trial.

It was, I thought, to Ken Prinsep's credit that he recovered from a disastrous opening and put his case carefully and energetically to Cris. The witness was patient, courteous, didn't either seek the help the judge was prepared to give him or seem grateful for it, and kept to the account he had always given me. He was nowhere near Pomeriggio on the night when the church was blown up. He and three other men destroyed a German store in an old farm-building at least six kilometres away on the road to Monte di Speranza.

'Did you get back some time after midnight?' Ken Prinsep asked; he was clearly getting towards the high point of his case, the part of the evidence on which Dunster's hopes were centred, and he found it hard to keep a note of excitement out of his voice.

'I think it was quite late, yes. I can't remember the exact time.'

'You joined the rest of the section?'

'Yes.'

'They were camped in the caves up above Pomeriggio?'

'That's right.'

'Did you return in the company of Sergeant Blaker, Maddocks, the demolition expert, and Lance Corporal Sweeting?'

'I did.'

'Did you have an Italian guide with you?'

'No. The Italian partisans had given us the information about the dump and we found our own way there. It was relatively easy.'

'When you got to the caves, did you find Lieutenant Blair awake?'

'He was awake, yes.'

'Were there sentries posted to guard the position?'

'There would have been, naturally.'

'Did your companions, that is to say Sergeant Blaker, Maddocks and Sweeting, go off to another cave to sleep?'

'So far as I can recollect, they did.'

'Did you then have a conversation with Lieutenant Blair?'

'I can remember that. Yes.'

'Sir Crispin. Before you spoke to Lieutenant Blair, did you know that the church had been blown up in Pomeriggio?'

The official under the judge stopped telephoning, the whispers ceased; Robbie looked deliberately unconcerned, like a gambler with a high stake at risk waiting for the roulette wheel to stop spinning; and Dunster, a few yards below the witness-box, stared intensely up at Cris, as though willing him to give the answer he wanted. There was a pause, only slightly longer than usual, and Cris said, 'No. I knew nothing about it until Lieutenant Blair told me. Apparently he'd heard about it from a partisan scout who'd come up from near the town.'

'Just a moment.' The judge was writing laboriously and when he'd finished Ken also summoned up all his powers of suggestion to ask what was by then a pretty hopeless question. 'I have to put it to you, Sir Crispin, that you knew perfectly well who'd blown up the church and you told Lieutenant Blair that you and your party had done it.'

'No.' Cris was smiling now, perfectly at his ease. 'There is absolutely no truth in that suggestion.'

'Absolutely no truth . . .' The judge was writing with evident satisfaction.

'Do you remember if Trooper Midgeley was one of the sentries on duty outside the cave that night?'

'I'm afraid I can't remember that.'

'Really, Mr Prinsep.' The judge was clearly bored as a spectator and came trotting briskly on to the field of play. 'We're talking about a night almost half a century ago. A no doubt confused and dangerous night in wartime. Is Sir Crispin really to be expected to remember the name of every soldier and exactly where he was posted?'

'Then perhaps this will remind him.' Ken Prinsep spoke like an excited conjuror about to astonish us all. 'May Mr Derek Midgeley come into court?'

'You have no objection to this, Mr Skeffington?' the judge asked hopefully.

'No, my Lord.' Robbie was careful to look unconcerned by any trick his opponent might be capable of playing. 'I have no idea what this is all about. But if my learned friend thinks that it might possibly help his case, then I have no objection.' He shrugged his gown back on to his shoulders and sat.

The sepulchral voice of the usher was calling outside the court, 'Mr Derek Midgeley! Derek Midgeley, please!' Then the courtroom door swung open and Mr Midgeley marched in under the usher's orders and came to attention in the well of the court. I suppose he was old; he looked ageless: a lean, cadaverous man with receding hair, a high, bony forehead and an expression of gloomy severity. His face was pale as plaster, in which two deep cracks ran from his nostrils to his mouth. In another existence he might have been a militant Puritan, retired long ago from Cromwell's Ironsides, one who had marched with sword and Bible against the frivolous Cavaliers. He had on a dark-blue business suit, shiny with age, and some sort of badge in his buttonhole. He was the only one of all the witnesses who looked like an old soldier and when he said the word Midgeley I expected him to add his rank and number.

'Just stand there, Mr Midgeley, would you, where the

witness can see you?' And Ken Prinsep told him, 'You won't be called on to speak until later.'

So Midgeley stood and looked up at Cris. It was a long, hard stare with very little warmth or forgiveness in it.

'Is that Trooper Midgeley?' Ken Prinsep asked Cris.

'It's rather a long time ago. He's changed a good deal since we last met.'

'I expect we all have, in the last forty-odd years.' The judge got some obedient laughter.

'But I believe that's Midgeley, yes.' Cris smiled down at the silent witness and got no reaction.

'If he says he was near enough to you and Lieutenant Blair to hear these words from you – "We must say the Germans did it" – how would you feel about that, Sir Crispin Bell-hanger?'

'I should wonder how he came to give evidence that was so far from the truth. I should be prepared to believe that he was mistaken and not telling a deliberate lie.'

The judge wrote that down carefully and Derek Midgeley was about-turned by the usher and marched out of court, but not before Robbie had subjected him to a minute inspection.

'See that, Glover?' our leader whispered to Justin. 'CND badge in the buttonhole. Get hold of their membership lists. Find out all you can about him. Clearly a nutter who doesn't like war.'

The day in court was over. We struggled out into the mosaic-floored corridors and I headed, with some urgency, through the door marked Gentlemen in Gothic lettering. As I stood facing the porcelain, the door was pushed open and Dunster looked in. Anyone else, me included, would have beaten a hasty retreat. Not so Dunster. He stood beside me as though we had never had a quarrel in our lives and seemed, all things considered, quite extraordinarily cheerful.

'Brilliant, wasn't he?'

'I don't think we should discuss the case.'

'Oh, come on, Progmire. At least have the guts to admit he was brilliant.'

'Cris gave his evidence very well. Yes. Probably because he was telling the truth.'

'Not your boss. Your boss was hypocrisy on oiled wheels. That's how I'd describe his evidence. No, I mean Ken. Totally fearless. Absolutely dominated the proceedings.'

'The judge doesn't seem to like him much.'

'Tactics, old man. Brilliant tactics. Ken's got the judge to expose himself as a boring and entirely prejudiced old fart. I think the jury have got the message.'

'Do you, really?' I moved away from him to wash my hands. It was a ridiculous scene; we might have been back at school, hanging about in the bogs.

'Tell you one thing, old man' – Dunster was zipping himself up with a look of complete satisfaction – 'we're going to make a far bigger impact with this story in court than we'd ever have done on television.'

Chapter Twenty-seven

Queen's Bench Court Five became a way of life; I went there instead of to the office and in the evenings I discussed the day's work with Lucy. I sat, each day, helpless to alter the course of events. I kept looking at the jury and worrying if they didn't think that the very enormity of the charge against Cris meant that it had some truth in it, and how impressive the surprise witness, Derek Midgeley, might be when he came to give evidence.

The odd thing about those days in court was that they seemed to have nothing much to do with the facts of the case. Pomeriggio – the procession of men, women and children, singing, carrying candles, walking slowly to their death – had never seemed further away and more lost in the pages of history. What we were concerned about were the judge's questions, Robbie's cunning re-examination, or the futile and counter-productive attack Ken made on a general, long retired, whom we had called as a witness to Cris's character. Looking back to those long mornings and sleepy afternoons I seem, in all the time taken by the laborious and highly expensive investigation, to have learnt nothing new about that night in the Apennines. No question was finally answered and no new layer of truth revealed.

Trying to remember the so-called courtroom drama, much of it has vanished, as unmemorable as lessons at school. Pictures come back to me. I can see Dunster staring at every witness with ferocious or friendly intent, trying to exercise some sort of remote control over their evidence; Beth looking beautiful, calm and detached; Robbie hitching up his gown; the judge's furious little puffs at his glasses before he polished them; Justin Glover arriving gloomy and exhausted after another family crisis, gradually cheering up as he listened to other people's troubles. These things come back to me most clearly, but the important moments of the trial are harder to remember. I have to think hard before I can hear the questions and answers that seemed so dangerous or conclusive at the time.

'Mr Sweeting. You were visited in Italy by my client, Mr Dunster.' Someone, no doubt Justin, had tricked out the ex-trooper in a genuine natty suiting which made him look ill at ease. He had told his story to Robbie, much as he had to us in the back of the Bar della Luna, grinning at the jury with a mixture of bravura and guilt, like an elderly, awkward schoolboy who has been caught doing something moderately disgusting and is doing his best to brave it out. And then Ken Prinsep had risen to the attack.

'Yes, of course.' Natty seemed to notice Dunster for the first time. 'Thanks for reminding me.' He was the most cooperative of witnesses. 'He was the other one who came out from England to visit me. I seem to have got quite popular lately. I can't believe that they just came for the grappa at the Bar della Luna!' He looked hopefully round the court, waiting for the laugh that never came. 'Mr Dunster rang me from Bologna and then came over. It was a Friday. No. I tell a lie . . .'

'Please, Mr Sweeting, be careful.' Ken Prinsep gave a strong warning.

'It was a Saturday.' Natty looked contrite and this time did get the ghost of a smile from the jury.

'Don't bother about whether it was a Friday or a Saturday. Did you give him an account of what happened, that night when the church was blown up?'

'Oh, we chatted away about a lot of things. He was my first visitor from England, oh, for a long time. That's how I remember it.'

'Did you make a statement to him, about the church?'

'Mr Prinsep!' The judge, who had been silent during Robbie's examination, could contain himself no longer. 'Am I to understand that your client has been around collecting statements from witnesses?'

'He visited Mr Sweeting in Italy, yes, my Lord.'

'For the purpose of discussing the question the jury has to try?'

'Is your Lordship suggesting there was any harm in that?'

'Harm, Mr Prinsep? I don't know about harm. We shall have to see how the matter develops. I don't know what the situation is under other jurisdictions, with which you may be more familiar, but litigants in *this* country leave it to their solicitors to go round collecting evidence.' He made it sound an eccentric and revolting occupation, like someone pulling out their own teeth.

'My Lord, Mr Dunster's visit was some time before these proceedings started.'

'So he *wasn't* collecting evidence?'

'He said he wanted a good story,' Natty volunteered to help the judge, who was acting, in a way which even the Mummers would have found over the top, the part of a man completely mystified. 'It was for a film he was making.'

'For a *film*, Mr Prinsep?' Mr Justice Sopwith tried to do for the noun what Dame Edith Evans had done for the handbag.

'Your Lordship will remember' – there was, in the soft Canadian voice, only the slightest tremor of desperation – 'that Mr Dunster discovered the truth about Pomeriggio when he was researching a television film he was writing.'

'Of course,' said the judge, who did seem to have forgotten. 'I remember that perfectly well.'

'He wanted a good story for his film, sir. He was interested in finding out if our side hadn't done things as bad as the Germans did. That's what interested him, as a film maker, from what I remember.'

'If our side hadn't done what sort of things?' The judge looked puzzled.

'Well, breaking the rules of the game if you know what I mean.' Natty looked embarrassed. 'The rules of war, I think they call them.'

'Did he ask you to tell him if the British committed a war crime?' the judge asked and Natty agreed, while Ken leant over for one of his whispered conversations with Dunster. Then he surfaced again and turned his horn-rimmed spectacles on Natty.

'That's not entirely correct, is it? He just asked you to tell him all you knew about the incident.'

'Did he?' Natty did his best to look interested, an attempt which wasn't wholly successful.

'And you told him clearly that you had helped Captain Bellhanger and the other men blow up the church.'

'Is that what he says?'

'Exactly. Did you tell him that?'

Now Natty looked across to me and Justin. No doubt he was trying to tell us he was sorry for the answer he was about to give. He knew he was a bit unreliable, the one who always made a mess of things, but he hoped we'd go on liking him all the same. 'I suppose I might have done.'

'You might have done!' Ken was staring at the jury as he repeated the words; it was his first wholly successful moment in the trial. And it was the point at which he should have sat down and shut up, but he had to go on to ever-diminishing effect. 'Where were you when you might have told Mr Dunster that?'

'We were in the back of the bar. I suppose we were enjoying ourselves. As I say, I don't often get anyone from England to talk to. He bought a bottle of grappa.' Jaunty Blair, I remembered, had recalled the facts as Dunster wanted them with the aid of a bottle of Remy Martin.

'And you said that Captain Bellhanger had ordered you to do it?'

'Mr Dunster said that was the story he was after, yes. For the film he was doing. I thought it was just like those ones we had in the war: *Night Fighters*, *Girls on the Square* and *London Defiant* ... Things like that. What was the one they had on at the Odeon, Leicester Square?'

Ken tried another smile on the jury. 'I don't think most of us were around then.'

'Pity. That was a good one.'

'Never mind about that.' Ken did his best to reassemble his scattered winnings. 'The fact is that you may well have told Mr Dunster that Captain Bellhanger was guilty.'

'He *might* have, Mr Prinsep.' The judge was displeased.

'Yes, my Lord.'

'You said he *may well* have. We must be careful here, mustn't we, to be entirely accurate about the evidence?' At which Ken Prinsep sat down, no doubt unwilling to risk further questions.

'How many did you have?' Robbie hitched himself and his gown up to re-examine.

'How many what, sir?'

'Grappas!' Robbie boomed like a cannon, making the jury blink.

'Maybe we saw off half a bottle.'

'Just the two of you? You and Mr Dunster?'

'The two of us, yes.'

'Grappa's pretty strong, isn't it? Stronger than whisky?'

'It was a bit of pretty good stuff, yes. Local grown.'

'And you thought he was making a cinema film like those you saw at some picture palace? A work of fiction. With an invented story?'

'That's what I thought, sir. Yes.' Natty had obligingly answered the question before Ken Prinsep could get to his feet to object.

'No doubt you were feeling a bit cheerful and you thought you'd give this nice gentleman who'd come all the way from England exactly what he wanted?'

'My Lord. I object. My learned friend is cross-examining his own witness.'

'He's simply asking him to repeat what he told you. Yes. Carry on, Mr Skeffington.'

'But was there a word of truth' – Robbie glared at the jury, inviting them to share his outrage – 'in this fictional story?'

'Oh no, sir. Not a word of truth, sir.' Natty looked round as though amazed that anyone should have taken him seriously. 'It was just he thought he could make a better film out of it. If he put it that way round, you see. I'm sure he really knew that it was the Germans, all the time.'

'My Lord. Might this witness be released?' Robbie was no doubt anxious to get Natty as far away from the court as possible, in case he gave us any more surprises. He went, but not back to Maltraverso. Apparently the Ministry of Defence had lost all interest in his past desertion. His wife Constanzia was waiting for him outside the court and he was free to keep his promise and take her, after so many years' delay, to visit Dorking for the first time in her life.

'Mr Dunster. You wrote a letter containing this libel to every member of the Board of Megapolis?'

'I wrote a letter containing the truth about the chairman's past.'

'What you thought was the truth?'

'What I know was the truth.'

'This letter was calculated to cause Sir Crispin the maximum possible embarrassment.'

'I imagine all criminals are extremely embarrassed, when they get found out.'

No one except Dunster smiled. Robbie let that one go for the moment and went on with his cross-examination. 'When you wrote that letter, your allegations were already known to Sir Crispin?'

'I expect Progmire told him.'

'Mr Progmire did. So you thought it likely he'd cancel the series?'

'I knew that he would. He'd hope for a cover-up.'

'And when the series was cancelled you'd be out of a job.'

'What do you mean?' Dunster looked genuinely puzzled.

'I mean, you wouldn't get any further payments from Megapolis.'

'Oh, I see what you're getting at. That hadn't occurred to me.'

'So it was because you were angry with the chairman that you wrote to the Board, and then sent this wicked pamphlet round to everyone working at Megapolis?'

'I wanted them to know the truth.'

Throughout this cross-examination I could only marvel at how little Robbie Skeffington, QC understood the witness he was attacking. The immense harm done by Dunster didn't come from the fact that he was a liar, or a cheat, or a crook – like the other shady litigants Robbie was used to showing up in their true and unattractive colours. He had to deal with a witness who believed all he said. Our leader should have opened fire with, Mr Dunster, are you not a man who is passionately and selflessly devoted to the truth? That was the most damaging indictment that the ingenious old QC could have possibly thought of.

'You are a journalist, aren't you?'

'Yes, I am.'

'With ambitions to be a *successful* journalist.'

'No. I distrust success in any profession. It usually goes with compromise and dishonesty.'

The QC and the High Court judge looked at him with displeasure. Only Ken Prinsep gave a brisk nod of agreement.

'Come along now, Mr Dunster. Be honest with us.'

'I have every intention of being honest. With or without you.'

'You know perfectly well that every journalist is after a

sensational story.' Robbie ploughed on like a tank, ignoring all insults.

'Sometimes, I suppose, the truth is sensational.'

'So that is what you were after, a sensation?'

'That is not what I was after.'

'And in the unlikely event of your winning this case you hope, don't you, Mr Dunster, to become famous as the journalist who exposed a British war crime? Just tell us, have you already signed a contract with your publishers? Or is that a question you'd prefer not to answer?'

'You're right,' Dunster said calmly, and the judge, who had closed his eyes during the last few questions, opened them with newly awakened interest. 'I prefer not to answer.'

'Because you *have* signed a contract?' Robbie asked with considerable satisfaction.

'No. Because I find your question utterly contemptible.'

I don't know how the jury reacted and it may be a fatal flaw in my character that, in spite of a lifetime which should have taught me to know better, I felt an uncomfortable stab of admiration for Dunster. Robbie was like the executioner, as he lit the fire, asking St Joan if it wasn't true that she was only doing it all for the money, a possible new scene in the play we had done at the Mummery with considerable lack of success.

The cross-examination then droned on, all one long afternoon and up to lunchtime the next day. It became a prolonged exercise in mutual misunderstanding, which left Dunster unaffected and Robbie worse tempered than usual. No one seemed to understand the witness any better at the end of it, but then they hadn't had a lifetime's study of Dunster forced upon them.

'Are you Sir Ninian Dobbs?'

'I am.'

'One-time Professor of Military History and Master of St Joseph's College, Oxford?'

'That is right.'

'Author of *From Sicily to Surrender: The Italian Campaign 1943–1945*?'

The former Head of our college, long since retired, was a wasted, stooping figure, his hands trembling but his white hair, yellowing like old paintwork, was still luxuriant and carefully brushed. It seemed that all our lives, mine and Dunster's, were a journey towards this trial, including the night we had arrived, uninvited, on this old man's bedroom floor. Ken Prinsep, examining him, asked him, 'Have you ever heard of the massacre at Pomeriggio?'

'Oh, yes. There were, unfortunately, a number of such outrages, when reprisals were taken against a civilian population.'

'Do you know who the German commanding officer in that area was at the time?'

'Oh, yes. It was a Captain Kreutzer.'

'After the war there were a number of trials of war criminals?'

'Yes, there were.'

'Have you been able to discover whether Captain Kreutzer was ever prosecuted for a war crime?'

'I have made sure, my Lord, that he never was.'

Robbie's cross-examination was short. 'And have you ever heard it suggested before, in any document not prepared by Mr Dunster, that this crime was the work of anyone connected with the British Army?'

'No, my Lord. I have not.'

'Thank you, Sir Ninian Dobbs,' Robbie said in a voice which meant 'That's seen you off, I think'. As the witness shuffled cautiously from the box, with a tentative foot searching for the step, a trembling hand feeling for the rail, the usher brought me a note scribbled by Dunster. 'How do you imagine I got the old fart to come here? Do you think I threatened to tell the world about the hair-net?'

*

At two o'clock in the afternoon on the tenth day of the trial Ken Prinsep called his last witness. When he entered the box, Mr Midgeley declined to take the oath, to Robbie's obvious delight.

'Is that because you have no religious beliefs?' The judge was disapproving.

'No, indeed. My religious beliefs are too profound to be used for such a purpose as this.'

Mr Justice Sopwith, although not best pleased at the suggestion that God would not care to take part in the proceedings in Queen's Bench Court Five, said, 'Very well, then you may affirm,' and ex-Trooper Midgeley told his story. He did so in flat, nasal tones which betrayed no shadow of doubt on any subject. When he had finished, Robbie Skeffington rose to cross-examine.

'Mr Midgeley. You are a member of the Campaign for Nuclear Disarmament?'

'Indeed I am.'

'And have been for many years?'

'Yes.'

'And also of the Peace Pledge Union?'

'Yes.'

'Does that mean you're against all forms of war?' Robbie was a great one for spelling things out; he didn't have much respect for the intelligence of juries.

'I am completely and utterly opposed to war in any shape or form.'

'When did you become a pacifist?'

'I think I became sure of my beliefs when we were fighting in Italy. After I was demobilized I decided to do all I could to stop anything like that ever happening again. I have devoted my life to the cause.'

'By "anything like that", you mean war?'

'Yes, indeed.'

'Any sort of war?'

'Any sort. Whatsoever.'

'Even ordinary, legitimate fighting . . .?'

'I don't believe there is any such thing as legitimate fighting. The conception of a just war is denied in the Ten Commandments.'

'Mr Midgeley. I don't think we need you to come here and give us Bible lessons.' Robbie had, in fact, been the first to introduce the Scriptures into the case.

'I thought you needed exactly that, Mr Skeffington: "Thou shalt not kill." Had that one slipped your memory?'

The jury smiled and the judge told the witness he mustn't ask learned counsel questions, whereupon Derek Midgeley looked disapproving, as though he was now convinced that the proceedings were profoundly irreligious.

'So even the heroic actions of soldiers in defence of their country would be called a war crime by you?' Robbie deftly steered clear of the Ten Commandments.

'"All they that take the sword shall perish by the sword." Matthew 26, verse 52.'

'So, in your view, all warlike acts are criminal acts?'

'It is not my view. It is the view of the Holy Bible, as I am trying my best to remind you, Mr Skeffington.'

'So, ever since you joined this Peace Pledge Party . . .' Robbie, delighted at having persuaded the witness to be at least moderately rude to him, carried on cheerfully.

'Union.'

'What?'

'It's called the Peace Pledge Union. That's its correct title.'

'Mr Midgeley. Let's not trouble the jury with unnecessary detail.' Robbie gave us his patient and long-suffering look. 'Let's get down to the vital issues in this case. Ever since you joined this pacifist pressure group, you have done your best to persuade us all that war is a horrible and brutal business.'

'I should have thought that was obvious.'

'That it turns ordinary people into criminals.'

'It leads them to do terrible things. Yes, indeed.'

'Then this case must have come to you as a heaven-sent opportunity.'

'I don't know what you mean.'

'Oh, come, come, Mr Midgeley. You're an intelligent man.' As Robbie said it, intelligence sounded like a serious character defect. 'Here was your great chance to tell the world that even such a decent, honourable character as Sir Crispin Bellhanger might commit a terrible atrocity in time of war. Now, wouldn't that be a wonderful bit of pacifist propaganda?'

'That thought never occurred to me.'

'Oh, come on, Mr Midgeley. Don't you write a regular column for *World Peace*?' Robbie picked up a magazine with well-acted distaste. 'I won't bore the jury with this, my Lord, but Mr Midgeley is the author of a monthly diatribe against war. If Sir Crispin is guilty, that will really give you something to write about, won't it?'

'I only came here' – Mr Midgeley was not going to fight back, no doubt on principle – 'to tell the truth as I remember it.'

'As you remember it! And can you swear that you remember Sir Crispin's exact words, spoken in the middle of the night, nearly half a century ago?'

'He and Lieutenant Blair were talking about something that had happened in the town. Bombs had been planted in the church. Captain Bellhanger said, "We must say the Germans did it."'

'So you believed he was responsible for a terrible crime.'

'I'm afraid I did.'

'So did you accuse him to his face – or just denounce him to his superior officers?'

The answer, when it came in the flat, gloomy tone, was strangely chilling. 'I was prepared to leave Sir Crispin Bellhanger to his conscience and to the final judgement. I didn't think any man-made punishment could be more severe than that.'

'Isn't the truth of the matter' – Robbie clearly had no interest in any law courts other than in the solid and earth-bound building we were occupying – 'that you did nothing because you weren't sure of what you heard?'

'Not sure?' The witness seemed puzzled by the suggestion.

'Oh, I've no doubt you've persuaded yourself now. You're sure you heard something which comes in very useful for your peacenik propaganda. But might his words on that night have been "The Germans *must* have done it"?'

'"The Germans must have done it",' Mr Midgeley repeated the suggestion; his thoughts were, no doubt, a long way away, in a cave on the cold mountainside. And then he said, as though he were quoting Holy Writ, 'No. Indeed not. "We must *say* the Germans did it." I feel sure of that.'

'But you weren't prepared to swear to it on that Holy Bible you set such store by, were you, Mr Midgeley?' Robbie grinned triumphantly at the jury and sat down.

When I think back to those days, the sight of Mr Midgeley in the witness-box is the last thing I can clearly remember. The closing speeches, Ken's attack on the establishment, frequently interrupted from the Bench, and Robbie's diatribe against Dunster, listened to in respectful silence, were predictable. More unexpected was the judge's summing up, which was perfectly fair, perhaps, as Robbie suggested, because the old friend whom he now called 'Soppy' Sopwith, revealing another layer of intimacy, kept a wary eye on the Court of Appeal. The jury must give what emphasis they thought right to the evidence of Mr Midgeley, his Lordship told them. He had seemed very certain but it was all a long time ago. They must also remember that the German captain had never been prosecuted and that Lance Corporal Sweeting had clearly told two contradictory stories. If the plea of justification failed, the amount of damages was a matter entirely for them. They shouldn't go wild with someone else's money, but could they imagine a more serious libel on a man of the highest possible reputation? They should go to their room now and take all the time they needed. No one was going to hurry them in any way.

Cris and I spent the next hours drinking too many cups of coffee in the canteen under the Gothic arches. During that time he seemed unworried. He was entertaining, talking about everything except the case and he treated our long wait as a minor irritation, like a delayed flight from Heathrow.

At last the jury came back. To my surprise the young man in the cotton jacket and the leather tie had been elected foreman. He announced that they had found in favour of the plaintiff, Sir Crispin Bellhanger, and awarded him £500,000 worth of damages. It was a sum no doubt far in excess of the worldly goods of all those who had died at Pomeriggio.

When we came out of court we had to push our way through a crowd of reporters. Dunster was addressing them as though he had emerged victorious. Beth was standing on the edge of the group, silent, expressionless and remote. I went up to her and said, 'I'm sorry,' but she turned away from me and didn't speak. When I last saw her she was managing a smile for the journalists, as she stood by her husband's side, her arm linked in his.

Cris said, 'No celebrations. Absolutely no celebrations of any sort.' He nodded a brief goodbye to Robbie and then we walked with Justin to the back entrance of the Law Courts, the one that leads into Carey Street. 'I'm going down to Windhammer now,' he said. 'I promised Angie I'd bring her a full report. Then I might take a bit of time off. That'd be all right, wouldn't it, Philip?'

I couldn't imagine why he was asking my permission, but I said that was exactly what I thought he should do. All the cheerfulness with which he entertained us while the jury was out had drained away. Since the verdict he had been looking pale and now he seemed almost like the ghost of his old, upright, military self. When we got to the Carey Street entrance he said, 'Don't bother about me. I'll find myself a taxi. Thanks for everything.'

As he walked down the steps, one of the photographers spotted him and several of them ran forwards, their cameras flashing. He walked on, stopping for no one, and, as he went, raised his hand to us in a sort of salute. I never saw him again.

THE ANSWER

Chapter Twenty-eight

There are certain productions in which everything goes wrong, mainly ambitious ones in which the Mummers try to do something spectacular and create a vivid theatrical moment. For these we call on the services of Mr Webber who runs the Handyman shop in Muswell Hill. Greeting every challenge with a cheerful 'No probs!', Mr Webber, with all the tools at his command, made us a revolving bed for Feydeau, the end of a swimming-pool for Alan Ayckbourn and an indoor menagerie for *The Wild Duck*. These devices, as temperamental as the most nervous actors, all performed admirably at the dress rehearsals and were subject to alarming attacks of stage-fright when in front of an audience. The water, I remember, once mysteriously gurgled away from the swimming-pool; the bed spun round long before its cue or remained sullenly immobile; and the rabbits, on a special Senior Citizens' matineé, escaped from captivity and bounded into the stalls.

Mr Webber's guillotine looked magnificent when erected. Its hardwood blade was painted to imitate steel and it slid down to decapitate the small band of aristos in the spectacular opening that Martin, the bank manager, had produced. The victims were to kneel with their backs to the audience, the blade would fall and a dummy head drop into a basket which would then be held up in a dim light by Harry Smithson from the Aurora Garage. On our opening night Mark, a stylist from Crowning Glory, playing the First Aristocrat, knelt in position and the blade resolutely refused to descend, in spite of pulls, jerks and whispered imprecations from Harry the executioner, and his *sans-culotte* assistant, Colin from the fishmongers. After all his efforts had failed, they were moved to improvise.

'*Sacrebleu*, Citizen!' Harry said. 'Madame Guillotine is a tired old whore. She's not coming down for anyone else this evening.'

'All right, Citizen Executioner' – Colin was not to be upstaged – 'we'll get the rest of them aristos done over tomorrow.' This exchange got a bigger laugh than any of the subsequent proceedings.

After this the Mummers never quite recovered their nerve. Chauvelin (Dennis, the dentist) cut a whole page of dialogue in his scene with Marguerite and, when he had realized his mistake, went back on it, an unnerving situation which Lucy dealt with admirably by adding the line, ''pon my little life, Citizen, how you oft times do repeat yourself!' I had managed to cope with Sir Percy without forgetting the words or falling over the furniture, but had been early alarmed, while in my disguise as an old hag, by the sight of the bald-headed Mr Zellenek, the film producer, in the front row. My future as an actor, my first chance to do something as a professional, hung in the balance, at the mercy of Mr Webber from the Handyman shop. I found myself thinking about various subjects unconnected with the French Revolution, such as whether Mr Zellenek, if he wanted me badly enough, could help me to an Equity card, so my poem about the 'demned elusive Pimpernel' went off at half-cock. I tried to make up for this by plenty of play with the eye-glass and inane upper-class laughter, but I could see Zellenek leaning forward, staring closely up at the stage, his brow furrowed with anxiety.

In Act Two things began to settle down; that is until I had to make an entrance into the Lion d'Or tavern near Calais, where, unknown to me, the villainous Chauvelin is eating soup. Sir Percy's arrival is signalled to the audience by his whistling 'God Save the King' outside the tavern door. Chauvelin utters the line, 'The Pimpernel!' and I enter, or I should have done if the door hadn't stuck, and I was pushing desperately, whistling a longer, fainter and even more out-of-tune

version of the national anthem. Once again the invention of
the Mummers was called upon. Chauvelin called for Brogard,
the ghoulish hunchbacked landlord (someone called Pete Per-
shaw in life insurance), and said, 'Citizen Landlord, there is a
passing wayfarer demanding entrance,' – something the audience had been aware of for quite a while. Brogard said, '*Mon
dieu*, my wife has left the key in the cellar!' and went off to
fetch it. As soon as he was gone, the door gave up all resistance
and I made a precipitate entrance before Chauvelin could pull
his hat over his eyes in case I recognized him.

Instead of a party in the Mummery bar I had invited the
cast back to my house. I wanted to be occupied, to forget
those long days in court and everything to do with Dunster,
even that defeat which I had every reason to believe he would
come to think of as a triumph. The case had died out of the
newspapers, Cris was still in retreat at Windhammer and I
had taken the afternoon off to run through my words and
prepare for the party. Despite the disasters the Mummers were
cheerful, relieved that we'd got through it somehow, their
glands still bubbling with adrenalin.

'I think we got over the reluctant guillotine bloody well!'
Harry, the executioner, was satisfied.

'All that about the old whore not going down on anyone
else. I mean, I don't think Baroness Orczy would write a line
like that.'

'"Coming down", that's what I said.'

'We haven't *all* got filthy minds, Mark.'

'Sorry about our scene, darling.' Dennis, the dentist, let his
glasses swing round his neck and put a hairy and short-sleeved
arm round Lucy's shoulders.

'It was fascinating' – Lucy liberated herself when it was
polite to do so – 'like an action replay on television.'

Mr Zellenek had left as soon as the play ended. Lucy said,
'I'm sure he'll call you. I know how interested he is.'

'Not after tonight.'

'You were perfectly fine, in the circumstances.'

'Oh? Thank you very much.' I suppose I am a natural Mummer. Anything but exaggerated praise sounds like an insult.

'Cheer up, anyway. They loved it, didn't they?'

'Oh, yes. They had a marvellous evening. Particularly when the door stuck.'

'Let's have a drink.'

I began to enjoy the party. After all, when I came to think about it, a stuck door in the last act of *The Scarlet Pimpernel* was nothing much compared to what I'd lived through. I was, I thought, amazingly lucky to have that as the present number-one worry. Even if you added Mr Zellenek's rapid departure to it, you couldn't describe it as a grand-scale cause for anxiety. Anyway, it was probably insane to think of going into the profession at my age.

Mark, the stylist, had brought his Madonna tapes and the Mummers were dancing with varying degrees of skill and enthusiasm. Dennis, the dentist was singing along with 'Like a Virgin', and then the telephone rang and Pam, the physio, picked it up.

'It's for you,' she said. 'Justin someone or other.'

I went to the phone in the kitchen, away from the noise of Mummers celebrating.

'Where've you been?' Justin sounded disapproving, as though I had been wasting my time in some frivolous occupation. He was probably right.

'We had a first night. And now we're having a party.'

'Oh, you were *acting*!'

'Yes, I'm afraid so.'

'Well. I didn't want to leave a message. It's something I felt I had to break to you. Before you hear it on the news or read about it in the papers.'

'What is it, for God's sake?'

And then he told me.

When I put the phone back on the kitchen wall, I was shivering. The room seemed to have become darker and the music loud, strident and unendurable. I had no idea exactly what Justin's news meant, and I was afraid to guess.

'It was an accident.'

Yes, my dear, darling Angie, yes. I'm sure it was. Of course it was. What else could it have been? – Even to say that, to agree as fervently as that, might have seemed to cast doubt on her statement of a simple certainty.

'A horrible, stupid, unnecessary accident.'

We were sitting side by side on the sofa in the library at Windhammer, under the pre-Raphaelite stained-glass window, by the silent piano and elaborate sound system. I held her hand, as it seemed a natural thing to do. Angie looked like a young woman who had stumbled at long last into old age.

'The doctor said it was an accident. And they said it was an accident on the television news, and in *The Times*. Did you see *The Times*?'

'Yes. I saw all the papers.'

'He should never have taken up that wretched shooting business again.'

'He told me he was thinking of it.'

'He told you that?' Was she grateful for a small piece of evidence to back up everyone's interpretation of that terrible event?

'He told me that before the trial,' I assured her.

'Dr Megarry said that when people kill themselves with a shotgun they put the muzzle in their mouths, then they reach down to pull the trigger. They're usually standing up or sitting when they do it. With Cris it wasn't like that at all.'

'In the papers it just said it was an accident. That's all it said.'

'He'd gone down on his hands and knees. He'd got under a hedge and pulled the gun after him. Some sorts of guns can go off, apparently, if you do that. Dr Megarry shoots a lot round here. He knows all about it.'

'Yes,' I said. 'I'm sure he does.'

'A bloody stupid accident.'

'No one's suggested anything else.' No one had, but I could think of someone who very well might, someone who could say that this event justified him and proved that all he'd said in the case he had lost had been the truth, the whole truth and nothing but the truth.

'Of course it was an accident,' Angie repeated. She looked at me, wide-eyed and innocent. 'What else could it be?'

'Nothing,' I said. 'Nothing at all.'

'Such a terrible waste,' she said. 'Such a waste of Cris.'

'Cris wasn't wasted.' It's so much easier to console than be consoled. 'He had a long, marvellous life. We all had so much from him, you more than any of us. This can't take that away. Not all the years you've had together. Not all the years I've known him either.'

'He wanted me to stay young, you see. He'd fallen for me when I was young and that's how he wanted me to be always. Young and rather helplessly heroic. But, as a matter of fact, I'm old and frightened of insects. They even get indoors.' Her hand flapped at the air round the sofa which, so it seemed to me, was completely insect-free. 'We're battling against nature in here.'

I had arrived by the earliest train and I said yes, of course, I'd stay for lunch and for the night if that was what she wanted. I poured her a large gin and tonic and she became braver, less prone to slap at imaginary insects. When we went into the dining-room I took her arm; she needed help and she walked stiffly, much more slowly than usual.

'You remember that evening when you and your girl Lucy were here and we all sang silly old wartime numbers?'

'Of course I remember.'

'Cris was so happy that night. I don't think I've ever seen him happier than that.'

Before I left Windhammer I said Lucy and I would come down and stay with Angie again, as often as we could. I'm sure I meant it, but I knew that our visits would diminish and she would be left, like so many people who are old and unhappy, for most of the time alone.

I went back to London and took a taxi to Megapolis from Liverpool Street Station. There was a gloomy excitement about the place, which seems to be the usual reaction to news of death. I tried to avoid most of my colleagues and the pitying looks they gave me. I sat at my desk, doing nothing, lost and lonely, staring straight in front of me. Then I got three phone calls: good, bad and extraordinary.

The first was from Mr Zellenek, who said he was sorry he'd had to rush away 'to call LA', but he'd had a fantastic evening, my performance had triumphed over all technical difficulties and would I lightly pencil in a Tuesday in three weeks' time for a lunch at the Malibu Club? My mind was on other things but I saw no particular reason not to accept.

The second was from Sydney Pollitter. 'I want to say this in all sincerity, without any desire to flatter you, Progmire, or bullshit in any way, that you were the closest to him. You sat on the steps of the throne, as it were, and I was far away in the ante-chamber. What a terrible loss to Megapolis plc and to England! Words cannot express the sense of utter deprivation one feels, at such a moment.'

Then shut up and leave me alone was what I wanted to say. But Sid Vicious gave me some Shakespeare.

'. . . and the elements
So mix'd in him that Nature might stand up
And say to all the world, "This was a man for all seasons!"'

'"This was a man!"'
'What?'

'Mark Antony about Brutus. He simply says, "This was a man!" Nothing at all about "for all seasons".'

'Of course. How well you put it. "This was a man!" By the way, Progmire . . .'

'Yes, Mr Pollitter?'

'Have you heard any whispers, any sort of buzz going around, about a possible new chairman of the Board?'

'Nothing at all. It's very quiet around here.'

'Of course, Cris Bellhanger would be a pretty hard act to follow.'

'Impossible. Must rush now. Goodbye.' I put down the phone, feeling it would take a long, hot bath before I was thoroughly clean again.

Then Justin Glover rang and said something extraordinary. 'I've got a letter here for you from Cris Bellhanger.'

'What do you mean?' For a wild moment I thought Cris might be alive, but Justin explained.

'I'd sent him a packet of things to sign. Documents about his property. He must have posted them back on the day of the accident. The post's ghastly and they've only just arrived. One of them's an envelope for you. It's marked PRIVATE. TO BE OPENED BY NO ONE EXCEPT PHILIP PROGMIRE. I'm to hand it to you personally.'

'What one earth can it be?'

'I can't imagine. Why don't you call in on your way home and find out?'

So I left Megapolis and drove to Justin's office in Lincoln's Inn. He told me that Cris had given him final, written instructions not to enforce the damages. Then he gave me my envelope. I saw Cris's handwriting and I signed for it. I took it back to Muswell Hill with a message, so it seemed to me then, from beyond the grave.

Lucy had gone out to a legal dinner with one of the partners in her firm and I was glad to be alone. I sat in the kitchen

with Cris's envelope on the table and looked at it. Then I
made myself a cup of tea. Quite a while after that, I poured
myself a drink. I felt as I had when exam results arrived, or
the letter telling me whether or not I'd got into Oxford; I
wanted to postpone the possibility of bad news as long as
possible. At last, despising myself for such a prolonged hesita-
tion, I picked up the envelope and tore it open. I pulled out a
wad of Windhammer notepaper covered with Cris's handwriting, clear and bold like everything about him.

When I first read the letter I think I was just listening to
Cris's voice. I could hear him as clearly as though he were
with me, having come into the room in a mysterious and
miraculous fashion. Then I read it again, and again. At last I
knew everything, the simple explanation of all that had
happened. I didn't yet know what I thought about it. The
front-door bell rang. I pushed the letter into the table drawer,
among knives and corkscrews, and went to answer it.

It was an autumn evening, and already dark. He stood in a
long black coat, his collar turned up, his hands deep in his
pockets. He looked, to my surprise, far from triumphant.

'All right,' I said to Dunster. 'He's dead. What the hell do
you want now?'

'I'd like to talk to you, old man. I did try and phone you
but you were out somewhere. Spare me a bit of your time.
The fact is, I'm worried.'

Chapter Twenty-nine

I could have slammed the door in his face. I could have assaulted him, taken him by the throat, perhaps more effectively than I had in the garden of Alexandra Palace when he told me about Beth. There was a moment when I felt I could have killed him. But to attack Dunster then would have been to support a conclusion about Cris's death which I was sure he'd come to already. I needed to know what he thought and what further plans he had for destruction. So I stood aside and I let him into my house.

'So long since I've been here.'

'Yes.'

The light was on in the kitchen and the door open. He walked in and sat at the table. I was standing.

'You're comfortable here, are you, Progmire? Natasha says you've found a girlfriend.'

'For God's sake. Is that what you came here to talk about?'

'No. I heard what happened to Bellhanger.'

'I expect everyone did.'

'They said it was an accident. Is that what it was?'

'Yes. It was an accident. No question about it. Is that what's worrying you?'

'Not exactly.' I should have known that. I should have known that any idea of his having driven a man to such desperate lengths would only have satisfied his appalling sense of justice, but he asked no more questions. Instead he surprised me by saying, 'It's that bugger Midgeley.'

'Midgeley?'

'Yes. He's changed his mind. Changed it completely. I'm

not sure what I ought to do about it. I say, old man. I couldn't have a drink or something?'

It was the first time, I swear it was the very first time, in my life that I had heard Dunster say he wasn't sure about anything. I was so surprised that I poured him a drink from the bottle on the table.

'He's going to write an article about it in that bloody *Peace* magazine of his. He's written to the judge. He's written to the Home Secretary. God knows what they're meant to do about it. Aren't you having one yourself?'

'Not now.' I didn't want to drink with him and I had to give my full attention to the conversion of Midgeley.

'When that ghastly little barrister of yours suggested that what he heard was Bellhanger saying, "The Germans *must* have done it," he began to have his doubts.'

'He seemed absolutely sure in court.'

'In court he was. Now he says he didn't have time to think, or pray about it. Apparently he's done a lot of thinking since. And praying too, come to that.'

'And he's not so sure?'

'It started like that. Now he says he's positive that your man's version was right.'

'I don't see that it matters much. The jury didn't believe him, anyway. If they had, you wouldn't have lost the case.' I was delighted to be able to remind him of that, at least.

'It matters to him. He says it matters to his conscience. And, of course, the point is, old man, it matters to me.'

I sat down then, opposite Dunster at my kitchen table. I felt exceptionally calm. He was hunched over his drink. The light fell on his face, which seemed, at that moment, a mask of anxiety.

'Why are you so bothered? The case is over. I saw the solicitor today. Cris had instructed him not to enforce the claim for damages, or costs. It's exactly what I told you.'

'I'm not worried about that. I'm worried about the truth.'

I said nothing. I sat waiting to hear more. What did he think the truth was, exactly?'

'You never talked to Midgeley, did you? No one from your side got at him?'

'We never set eyes on him. Not till he turned up in court.'

'Yes. That's what he said. And you haven't seen him since?'

'Of course not.'

'He said that too. He said no one persuaded him to change his story.'

'Why should we bother? After all, we won.'

'I was so bloody sure it was true.' Dunster was holding his glass tightly. He lifted it to his mouth and seemed to force himself to drink. 'I had all the evidence. I had what Jaunty told me and what Sweeting told me. And I had Midgeley.'

'And Jaunty changed his mind and so did Sweeting. And now Midgeley has too.'

'Yes. He's the worst. He was rock hard, and now he's gone back on it all.'

'Perhaps it just doesn't do to be too certain. You know I found Lester Maddocks, the explosives man?'

'You never told me.' Dunster seemed hurt that I hadn't taken him into my confidence.

'Why the hell should I? You were against us.'

'What did he say?'

'He confirmed Cris's story. He said the Germans did it.'

'Then why didn't you call him as a witness?' Dunster sounded hopeful.

'That was all explained in court. He'd gone missing, out of the country.' I looked at Dunster and summed up against him. 'So now no one says Cris was guilty. Not one single witness anyone's found. That fact is, old man, you never had a bloody case at all!'

There was a long silence. I could hear the kitchen clock ticking and a police siren somewhere quite far away. I felt I had scored a hit but I never expected the astonishing result.

'Do you think,' Dunster asked me, 'that I may possibly have been wrong about it?'

'Completely wrong. Utterly wrong. I always knew that. I always told you so. You wouldn't listen. You wouldn't be put off. You had this idea about Cris. This fantasy.'

'Fantasy?' He said the word as though he loathed it.

'Total fantasy.'

Another long silence. Dunster had something to ask and I wasn't about to help him to ask it.

'And it really was an accident? What happened to Bell-hanger?'

'I've told you that. The doctor says it was an accident. Everyone says so. Cris had won the case, hadn't he? He'd got everything to live for. At least your stupid mistake didn't kill anybody.'

'A stupid mistake? Do you honestly think that's what it was?'

'Of course. I've got no doubt about it.'

'Then what can I do?'

'You said you were worried.'

'I am, old man. I am, quite honestly.'

'I think you should be. What can you do? You can't do anything. Except worry about it. Worry about it for the rest of your life. I'm sorry. That's all I can say. Good-night, Dunster.'

He'd finished his drink. He stood up and went to the door. Before he left, he turned round and looked at me reproachfully. 'Old man, we've known each other for a long time.'

'Too long.'

'I came in good faith. I expected a bit more of you.'

'You made another mistake. You had no right to expect anything.'

When he had gone, when I heard the front door bang after him, I opened the table drawer. The letter was there, among the cutlery. I took it out carefully and read it for the last time.

Dear Philip

You are the only person in the world to whom I can write this and I feel, after all these years, that I have to tell someone. When you have read it I know I can trust you to destroy this letter, and never to say a word about it to anyone. Angie, of course, must never get to hear about it.

I don't know how I can explain the way we felt during the Italian campaign. We were all tired, past the point of exhaustion. The war was four years old then. Most of us had fought across the desert. I'd done a bit in Yugoslavia. Now we were fighting a battle we didn't really understand. After all, the Italians had surrendered. Why couldn't we forget Italy and get on with the French invasion? What was the point of all that bloodshed? A lot of the men were disenchanted, some near the point of mutiny.

But that's not the whole story. You don't know what it's like to be fighting in a war. I pray to God you never learn. There's fear and boredom and anger and an awful sense of unreality. What've you done that anyone should be trying to kill you? Why should you, aged twenty something, be dragged off to kill people who never did you any particular harm? Then it becomes unreal. They aren't people you're killing but a sort of abstraction called 'the enemy'. The enemy are nothing like you, of course. They're brutal, without feelings, and the best thing is for them to die in large numbers. At least, that's what you're meant to think.

I want to tell you what happened at Pomeriggio. We knew that the local fascists, a collection of brutes who made the German Army seem like the Peace Corps, met in the old, disused church, the place they called the Chiesa Nuova. We'd kept a watch and we saw them go in there at the same time every night. They kept a few supplies there and they'd get together and plan some new bit of devilment.

So our plan was to mine the church and blow up the fascists. Strangely enough, they didn't take the trouble to guard the place properly when they weren't using it. They didn't have much stowed there anyway, so I suppose they didn't bother. We got all the explosives packed as soon as it got dark. Maddocks, our explosives man, revealed a not unexpected talent for picking locks and, as I say, the church was deserted until the fascists showed up, which was regularly at 9.30, after they'd enjoyed a good black-market dinner.

We got a timing device fixed for 9.45 and then we retreated up to a high point where we could watch the fireworks. You may think it strange that we should want to see a number of people blown to smithereens, even if they were fascists, but strange things happen in a war. To us it was a job, a technical challenge and we wanted to see it succeed. So what happened? I'm trying to get back to that moment, so I can tell you exactly how it felt at the time.

Around 9.30 we saw lights coming up the unmade road from the town to the old church. It was a dark night but very still. Then we heard the sound of singing. Someone, I think it might have been Maddocks, said, 'Christ, the bloody fascists are singing hymns!' I believe we laughed; as I say, we were exhausted and not quite sane. Then we saw white figures – boys in surplices or something like it, some were carrying candles; there was a tall banner with the Saint's picture on it and the priest giving out benedictions. We could see all that in the candlelight when they passed immediately below us. Then came the fascists, the thugs in bits and pieces of uniform, all armed as they always were when they met at the church. And then – and that was the sight that gave me a dry mouth and a rising panic – a long procession, it seemed never-ending, of men, women, children, young girls and grandmothers, old men walking with sticks and boys not yet out of school. A lot of them had candles, most of them were singing. They were on their way to church, to meet their death on a saint's day no one had told us about.

'What the hell do we do?' I was Captain Cris, and meant to be in command. But there I was asking my sergeant for orders. He said, 'Bastards! They all gave our boys to the fascists. Got them shot, didn't they? Don't lift a finger for them.' That's exactly what he said, so far as I can remember. You see, Philip, I'm not trying to excuse anything, but at least I can tell you the truth now. Blaker's dead, so he hasn't got anything to worry about – and he always did worry.

I don't know what you'd have done, and I hope you never have to make a decision like that. I don't know what Dunster would have done, would he have rushed down that mountain to tell the people, and been shot by the fascists? Perhaps we could have shouted something from where we were. Perhaps we could have fired warning shots, but that would have given away our position. I knew what the others wanted to do, and I suppose I felt a rising anger at that pious procession, people who could betray our men and see them executed and then go off to pray. What we did, I suppose, was the worst thing we could have done. We did nothing. We turned our backs and climbed away up and across the mountain towards our camp. We were too far away to see what we had done but, of course, we heard the explosion.

Jaunty Blair got to know about it. He got to know about everything. We talked about it that night and I told him we must say the Germans did it. Well, I couldn't have the people in the village against us. Anyway, we weren't meant to be fighting that kind of war. It was only later that Jaunty began to suggest that the whole incident would look pretty bad if it got known. He told me he was afraid the men might start talking. He also hinted, when he was searching for war criminals in Austria, that he wouldn't like to have to add my name to the list. Money solves a good many problems and I had it. I always met Jaunty's demands; he was sensible enough not to make them excessive. I helped Maddocks start up various businesses and, even though he'd deserted, I bought Natty Suiting a bar in Maltraverso. Sergeant Blaker was beyond help.

Of course I thought about it a lot after the war. I used all the arguments. I told myself that bomber pilots over Dresden and Hamburg killed men, women and children in their thousands. Civilians had been blown up nightly in London and Coventry and Berlin. My first duty, after all, was to my men and I couldn't risk their lives. I used all those arguments, but I couldn't help but find myself guilty.

I suppose that's why I wanted to do the *War Crimes* series. I didn't have any desperate urge to expose myself; I didn't want to make a public confession. But I wanted to say that ordinary people, quite decent people as a matter of fact, could do extraordinarily brutal and merciless things if a war gave them permission. I wanted that to be understood. So I started something that our friend Dunster finished. Does that serve me right? Perhaps you'll think so.

Why didn't I admit the truth of his attacks and explain it all, as I have tried to explain it to you? To start with I had Angie to consider. She could only be protected, I thought, she could only be kept safe and happy if I won the case. Imagine the headlines if I had admitted blowing up a church full of worshippers. After that, Dunster would have been at my throat forever. He might have gone on to find out more about the money I'd paid, settling blackmail he'd call it, and I could never stop him. So I had to win, and to do that I had to lie.

Winning has been the hardest part to bear. Now it's over, I think I might have been able to cope with losing. You see, I've twice run away from the truth. Once in the night in Pomeriggio and once in broad daylight in that dreary law court. It's time I stopped running away.

Luckily my father had an old hammer shotgun. When I was a boy we had a neighbour who had to get through a hedge to collect a pheasant he'd shot. He went down on his knees to crawl through and pulled the gun after him. By the barrel. The hammer caught on a low branch and the gun went off and shot him through the head. It's an accident that can happen with that type of weapon.

You don't have to feel sorry for me. Apart from this one thing, so unexpected and so long ago, I've had a very happy life. Angie's been marvellous, and I think you and I have always hit it off, haven't we? I've always felt we understood each other in those terrible board meetings, and I was pleased to make friends with someone too young to give a damn about the war. I would like you to be happy and have no regrets on my account. You were always on my side and supported me, even when I shouldn't have been supported.

I'm sorry to burden you with this knowledge, but there is no one else in the world I can tell. Forget it all now and burn this letter. The past is over and done with.

Hope Sid Vicious doesn't bore you to extinction when he's chairman. Tell him not to make a speech at my memorial service. If he does I won't listen.

Ever,
Cris

That was the last time I read the letter. I got a baking-tin and

Chapter Thirty

I grieved for Cris but grief is never a full-time occupation. Three weeks later I was back in the Malibu Club with a distinct stirring of excitement at the prospect before me. Things were already changing at Megapolis. Sydney Pollitter had been appointed chairman more or less automatically. He was an unknown figure to most of the staff because he never appeared in the canteen – with or without his jacket. I had been told by Gary Penrose that he 'didn't feel the need to work closely with any particular member of the staff' and I no longer visited the chairman's office. All in all, it seemed a good time to think of ways of escape from Megapolis.

Mr Zellenek arrived exactly a quarter of an hour late, accompanied by an unnaturally tall woman whom he introduced as his 'Girl Friday, Posie Mendelssohn. When they entered together, she looked like a tall grass, waving over some small and hairy insect. Like Peregrine Gryce, Maurice Zellenek seemed to favour the larger personal assistant.

'I told Posie here all about you, Mr Progmire. She's been longing to meet you, sir.'

'Zelly's never been so enthusiastic about a project.' Posie's big, dark eyes were full of adoration. I was flattered by this until I discovered that she bestowed the same melting glances at the waiter who took our order, and even at complete strangers at adjoining tables.

'To play roles as far apart as Trigorin and the Scarlet Pimpernel. What range, Mr Progmire! Larry might have done it. Say what you like about Larry Olivier, he sure had range.'

'Range,' Posie told me, 'is what Zelly admires most of all.'

'Range,' Zelly repeated, 'is the name of the game. Have you ever considered taking a crack at *Hamlet*?'

'I did it once. It was a long time ago.'

'You did it once! What a track record, and you're so cool about it. You're still a young man, Mr Progmire. You have all sorts of career opportunities opening before you. You know how old I am? I want you to guess.'

He offered me his small, smiling face to examine, unnervingly bald above and fringed with hair below.

'Zelly is sixty-nine,' Posie let me into the secret. 'But he keeps in shape.'

'I work out, Mr Progmire. With the stationary bicycle. Five miles every morning and I never leave my bathroom. You know who the archetypal figure of today is, naturally?'

'I'm not sure.'

'Tell him, Posie.'

The Girl Friday looked at me adoringly and whispered sexily, 'The chartered accountant!'

'You see,' – Mr Zellenek looked at his assistant with enormous pride, as though she had just revealed the secret of the universe – 'Posie's got the message. Who is the guru of our days, the power behind the throne, the priest in the confessional? Nobody but you, Mr Progmire.'

'Me?' I had never thought of myself as a priest before.

'Forget doctors. Doctors went out with Dr Kildare. Forget lawyers. Perry Mason put paid to lawyers. Social workers? Out of date, with all due respect to your great company. No, Mr Progmire. We are planning a new series. Open-ended and with international appeal. And you know what we shall call it?'

'I couldn't guess.'

'We shall call it *Accountants*.'

'As simple as that,' Posie whispered.

'Posie's right. That says it all. One principal character is a guy about your age, I'd say. Overworked, marriage breaking up, schemed against by the younger accountants from the floor below. Involved with some girl accountant, most probably. And he's the one who gets to know the client's secrets. You would have a natural understanding of such a character, Mr Progmire.'

'Oh yes,' I said, 'I believe I would.'

'Then will you come on board?'

'Zelly hopes tremendously that it will be a yes.'

'It's very tempting, of course.'

'Tempting,' Mr Zellenek admitted, 'is exactly what it is.'

'The trouble is' – I didn't want to make difficulties – 'I haven't got an Equity card.'

'Quite unnecessary.'

'What?'

'Zelly's right.' Posie confirmed it. 'Absolutely no Equity card required. Not for a technical adviser.'

I suppose I must have looked crestfallen, as the door slammed on my entry into show business.

'We want you to technically advise, Mr Progmire. We're going to rely on your experience and expertise to get every detail of an accountant's life true and convincing.'

'He wanted you for *that*!'

I had got home, tired and a little dispirited after my meeting with Mr Zellenek and Posie Mendelssohn. A hard day at the office, I had discovered, isn't nearly so exhausting as lunch at the Malibu Club. 'That was all he wanted.'

'He didn't want you to act at all?'

'Not in the least.'

'Not even an extra in board meetings?'

'Not even that.'

We were in the kitchen. Lucy was pouring tea. Her hand was unsteady so she missed the mug and splashed the table. Her sudden affliction was uncontrollable laughter.

'So you're not going to become a star!' She only just managed to get it out.

'Not this week, anyway.'

'Did you really think you might be?'

'Everything's possible.'

'Of course. Everything.'

It was a sound I hadn't heard much lately, the sound of laughter. I could do nothing but join in. I don't know if that was the moment when I fell in love, or if I suddenly recognized what I should have known for a long time.

It was in that dead week between Boxing Day and New Year's Eve when hardly anyone goes to work and a curiously eerie silence, as well as a powdering of snow, had fallen on Muswell Hill. An elderly Volkswagen car drew up in front of our house at midday and out got Natasha and a tall, dark young man with a plum-coloured velvet waistcoat and a black cap. She introduced him as Jasper Wren. Once again she brought me presents, including a bunch of flowers, only a little wilted, for Lucy. All that had happened at our last meeting seemed to have been forgotten. She thanked me for the money I had sent her and gave me some green candles, an Edwardian biscuit tin and an interesting shoehorn she had picked up in the Portobello Road. Throughout the presentation Jasper Wren preserved a discreet silence and sat staring out of the window. When I went to get them drinks Tash followed me out into the kitchen.

'What happened to George?' I asked her.

'I gave him the boot.'

'But he seemed so fond of you.'

'I know. That was his trouble. Too horribly devoted. George didn't represent any sort of a challenge at all.'

'Is Jasper a challenge then?'

'I'll say.'

'He doesn't talk much.'

'No. He's impenetrable.' She said it with considerable pride.

'One of the silent sort?'

'I've got absolutely no idea what's going on *inside* him.'

'That's what you like?'

'Well, it is interesting. Dad, I wanted to tell you about Dunster.'

'What about him?'

'Well, it's very odd. He's sort of changed.'

'Has he?' I uncorked a bottle and tried one of Jasper Wren's looks of detachment.

'He seems to have rather lost his pip.'

'Tash, what on earth do you mean?'

'Well, he hangs around the house, worrying if he was right about that case. It's not like him at all. He seems full of doubts.'

'I'm not surprised. He made a lot of mistakes.'

'But it is not like him to worry about mistakes. To be honest, I think Mum's getting just a bit fed up with him. More than a bit, actually.'

'Perhaps he's not a challenge any more.'

'No.'

I found a tray and put the glasses and the bottle on it. I put out cheese biscuits which Tash began to eat thoughtfully. 'Whatever's happened,' I said, 'it's bloody marvellous to see you here again.'

'Oh, do shut up, Dad. You're beginning to sound like George!'

When we got back into the sitting-room Jasper Wren had taken off his cap. A black lock of hair had fallen across his pale forehead, and he never said a word.

Lucy and I were married in the Muswell Hill register office. Natasha came and the ever-silent Jasper Wren. Nothing could keep the Mummers away and a reception was held in the Mummery bar. At one happy moment I saw Lucy and Tash talking together in a corner and I realized that something new and entirely different was beginning. Cris had gone, with a wave of his hand and without turning round as he left us on the steps of the Law Courts. The truth had been told and the dead at Pomeriggio had been avenged at last. But above all, Dunster had gone; my Dunster, the great challenge, the perpetual opponent, had vanished as completely as those dead spirits, to be replaced by a new and doubting stranger with whom even Beth was apparently dissatisfied.

Life was going to seem very odd without Dunster.